ASK IT?

Like all true d[...] [...]fortable when unp[...] [...]es at a stretch from [...] [...] the Net. He tossed [...] [...]ned to go.

"A moment," [...] [...] Hans paused reluctantly in the doorway. "I have a theoretical question for you. How would we know if an Artificial Intelligence was malfunctioning?"

The dick turned back and stared at him for a long moment. "An interesting question. I assume we're talking about psychosis in true AIs—Turing class five and up?"

"Correct."

Hans favored him with a wintry smile. "You broach a large and mysterious subject. We know little about psychotic AIs because we've never seen one. Maybe they never go strange. They shouldn't, with all the safeguards that are designed in. Many experts think it just can't happen."

Hans perched on the arm of the chair. "Then you have the Frankenstein Faction, which claims that many or even all AIs are aberrant, but they're shrewd enough to keep it to themselves. Now and again, someone reports irregularities in an AI's behavior. Experience suggests this may be unwise."

"Why is it unwise?" asked Wolfe.

"Always the claim is discredited, usually the person reporting it ends up looking like a fool or a crackpot."

There was a speculative look in Han's old, red-rimmed eyes. "And on at least three occasions, the accuser has disappeared. . . ."

PROJECT MALDON

CHRIS ATACK

A Baen Books Original

Baen Publishing Enterprises
P.O. Box 1403
Riverdale, NY 10471

ISBN: 0-671-87786-0

Cover art by Gary Ruddell

First printing, June 1997

Distributed by Simon & Schuster
1230 Avenue of the Americas
New York, NY 10020

Typeset by Windhaven Press, Auburn, NH
Printed in the United States of America

Table of Contents

To Lynda, Dan and Julia with love and gratitude for putting up with all this.

Plus thanks to Jack Vance for endless demonstrations of how superb SF can be, and to Amy for making it happen.

Defector

The Skellig Michael Institute was founded by an eccentric and perhaps even repentant software billionaire in 2010. Fearing the collapse of Western civilization, he founded an Institute to shore up the tottering institutions. The Institute's home was to be "in the most remote locale available," with campuses in various parts of the globe. Ultimately headquartered in a high-orbit space facility, the Institute, self-governing, elitist, devoted to defining and preserving "civilization," rapidly achieved great prestige. Part university, part corporation, part private club and part monastery, the Skellig Michael has survived (except in Pakistan) and even flourished in the arid soil of the Post Millennium world.

Monks in the Sky
The Skellig Michael Institute—A Brief History

Thursday, July 1, 2027
07:43 hours

Wolfe's newest problem rear-ended him while he was being driven back from an early-morning meeting with Deputy Premier Beaufort. They had just stopped for a red light when a heavy impact threw the lightly-armored Isuzu sedan forward, pitching Wolfe back into the cheap upholstery and snapping his portable closed on the delicate circuits of his

1

interglove. A crunch of metal, a tinkle of glass. In the front seat, his security blanket swore volubly: "Jesus come quick, the crazy gumbah behind just rammed us. You alright, brother?"

"So far." Wolfe looked around, wondering why his blankie had taken the same route as yesterday, then twisted to examine the big black Saturn that had crawled up their rear end. Collisions like this were a common prelude to mugging or worse, and they were in a free zone, with no backup in the immediate area. But there was only one person in the Saturn, and he looked harmless enough as he clambered out onto the asphalt: a cheery-looking fat man, middle-aged, with an open shirt and chubby, amiable features. His right arm was in a heavy cast; he walked slowly around to the crumpled hood of his car, shaking his head in vexation.

A diversion? Wolfe scanned the area for other assailants, noting only a small encampment of raggedy Red Sky Listers cooking breakfast over a campfire on the far corner, wisps of gunmetal blue smoke from a burning pile of debris wafting across the grimed, steel shutters of the not-yet-open stores. The Listers looked at him with blank faces, then turned away again, interested only in their own reality.

"Fat fool," growled his blanket, then mumbled something Wolfe couldn't make out. He glanced at his driver in surprise. Usually Dulles was calm to the point of torpor; now his fair complexion was flushed red, small beads of sweat stood out on his forehead, and his pupils were the size of pennies, black and blank. Was the man sick, or on a high? "Get focused and say again," Wolfe rapped out.

"Hmm? Oh, I said: he shouldn't be driving at all with that thing on his arm. I'd better go palaver, insurance and so on."

"Are you mad?" demanded Wolfe. "Get us out of here. We'll worry about insurance later." But Dulles had already stepped out onto the pavement, leaving the driver's door open.

Wolfe began to climb into the front seat. In the rearview mirror he saw the fat man turn to Dulles and with one fluid motion smash the heavy cast into the side of his head. Before Dulles hit the pavement, the fat man had skipped around with unnatural speed to peer through the open door at Wolfe, who was scrabbling for the handle. Wolfe's guts turned to ice. He was now a dead man or worse.

But the fat man only smiled. "Sorry about the fuss, Dr. Wolfe. Truly, you're a hard man to meet."

"You could always call for an appointment," suggested Wolfe, his heart pounding in his ears. "We could arrange one now if you like."

With a rich chuckle the fat man unzipped the false cast and flung it aside. "Why don't we just take advantage of this little encounter to do our business?"

Wolfe sat back, trying to control his panic. He had faced some tough situations in the Piracy Control Bureau and he was still alive. What he needed was room to maneuver. Jesus come quick, what was this anyway? If it was a straight hit he should be dead already—there was no need for conversation. An abduction then? A cleaning? If he could get out of the car he might be able to catch the fat man unawares. "You got the wrong gumbah," he said reaching for the rear door handle.

"I think not," purred the fat man. "You are Dr. Edward Wolfe, fellow, level three, with the Skellig Michael Institute. Also, on-site director of a Class-A sociocybernetics project with the unlikely code name of 'Maldon.' The project is designed to drag Upper Canada back from the brink. It is not succeeding at the moment." A small black automatic appeared as if by magic in his huge hands as Wolfe began to open the door. "Please stay where you are, Dr. Wolfe—I have no desire to make acquaintance with your famous sidekick. And truly, I mean you no harm. I'm a great fan of yours—I have followed your career closely since you were reassigned to Upper Canada, and I'm convinced you're one of the Institute's best all-round operatives. I took your security down for a moment so I could talk to you in private."

Blue woodsmoke from the Listers' fire curled across the street and stung Wolfe's eyes, making them water. He relaxed back into his seat, waiting for an opening. The fat man chuckled and made the gun disappear again. "That's better. Now then, my name is Nicky Mancuso. I'm a marshal with the Accord, and I want to defect."

Years of training helped Wolfe to conceal his sudden and vast relief, an emotion so strong he thought for a moment he was going to throw up. He was apparently going to live. The smell of cooking meat wafted to him from the Lister camp, and his body, realizing it was reprieved, responded with a surge of ravenous hunger—an interesting physiological reaction which he made a mental note to report to his friend Dr. MacGregor, who enjoyed such biotrivia.

Sheer muscle-slackening relief was followed by amazement. Here was a rich catch indeed—if it was genuine. He maintained a casual manner, wondering how best to proceed. "So then—how do we know you're serious? You have any credentials?"

The fat man grinned, showing teeth as white and perfect as a row of pearls. "Do I seem a gumbah? Listen: there's a hit planned for tonight. Eastern Free Zone, the medical clinic at the Church of the Redeemer, around two thirty in the morning. Special elite team, led by one of our most earnest young captains—the one responsible for damaging Mary in fact. Check it

out, then call me. Be discreet. Here's my direct line."
He passed Wolfe a Tarot card—the Fool—and skipped
back to his car with the unexpected grace of a large
man. "God bless. Stay pure. And don't get caught like
that again—it might not be me next time." He got in,
backed up to clear the Isuzu and sped away down
Gerrard, with a cheery wave, leaving Wolfe shivering
with adrenaline reaction.

On the back of the card a number was written in
black ink. Wolfe tucked it into the top pocket of his
gray dress overalls and looked about him, seeing his
surroundings with the clarity that he knew came from
surviving a truly close encounter with the Reaper. Two
Listers, an old woman and a boy of about seven or
eight, were approaching, whining their begging slogans, arms outstretched for alms. Already the boy's
teeth were black and decayed. On the cracked pavement, Dulles stirred and groaned. Wolfe helped him
to his feet, waving the beggars off while keeping a
careful eye out for further trouble. "Are you alright?"

"I think so. Jesus, but he was quick."

"Truly." Wolfe helped the groaning security blanket into the back seat and started the car, feeling sick
and weak himself.

That was just the sort of mistake that got you
carved. Suppose it had been a Cleaner hit? By now
he would have been emasculated, bleeding to death
in some alley. *You know the rules, Long Eddie. Get
sloppy and you die.*

He called in, requesting medical assistance, and
flogged the Isuzu along as fast as he dared down
Dundas Avenue, through the oasis of Little Saigon
where grocers were now placing their wares—stands
of purple eggplant, huge white radishes, murky tanks
of home-grown carp and eels—out on the sidewalk
in anticipation of the business day. Seeing his approach,
one of the storekeepers held out a huge squirming

lobster and shouted an incomprehensible sales pitch as he passed. After what seemed a hundred years he reached the rusting man-high barricade of compressed cars which marked the eastern boundary of Little Saigon, and emerged again into the free zone.

Super-families of Listers slept or lounged on the sidewalks, bright tumbles of red, green and yellow rags. Many more, Wolfe knew, sheltered inside the abandoned brick buildings which moldered on either side of the street. He imagined himself a quark, flashing silently through a wheeling galaxy of disenfranchised, sullen humanity, eating, slumbering and fornicating all around him. It was not entirely a reassuring image, suggesting as it did his transience, and the abiding nature of the problems he faced.

He turned south on Carlaw Avenue and their destination came into sight: Versailles, the Institute's embassy and operational headquarters, a three-story converted warehouse, which stood like an uneasy passerby just north of a steam-belching toiletries factory. A high steel-link fence, topped by coils of razor wire, surrounded it. From the street, the green tops of the trees on the roof garden were just visible. Ground-floor windows had been covered with sheets of blank gray steel, and upper windows gazed out from behind square metal grills. A bank of solar collectors on the roof shimmered like huge azure mirrors. The vapid slogans of the Post Millennium world were dayglo'd in fiery red and green all down its brown-brick walls, like sores on a diseased dragon's scales: SLAM ISLAM . . . JESUS COMETH IN A CONDOM . . . PITH THE LISTERS. The Isuzu pulled up to the domed concrete guard booth at the fence and Wolfe waited, impatient now to be safe inside, while an Institute blanket with red hair and bright blue eyes verified their retinal patterns and scoped the trunk and chassis for hidden passengers or explosives. His check complete, the blankie waved them through. At the bottom of the ramp, a steel door opened. He raced the Isuzu down the ramp into the cavernous garage, delivered his ashen-faced driver to the medical team waiting at the bottom, and parked beside the elevator.

The adrenaline rush was slowly wearing off, leaving Wolfe tired and shaky. With a sigh he keyed a seven-digit combination into the lock of the heavy metal door at the end of the garage; it swung aside to reveal a massive freight elevator with low sides of splintered gray wood. Stepping inside he pressed a button; the elevator emitted a deep mechanical groan of agony and lurched into motion.

A bone-jarring thump signaled his arrival on the third floor, where the project's administrative offices were located. As usual, the elevator had stopped a few inches too low. Wolfe jumped up onto the floor, strode down the dingy hallway, his aesthetic sense recoiling at the casual ugliness of uneven gray linoleum and scuffed, industrial-white walls. The Institute was niggardly in the extreme when it came to field installations. Normally these economies did not concern Wolfe. In his present jittery mood, however, the squalor seemed oppressive and suffocating. He diagnosed in himself the near-escape vapors—a common affliction in the Post Millennium. With a mental shrug he knocked on the door marked HEAD OF SECURITY—RICKKI HARROW.

"Enter!" called a female voice. Inside, a black-haired young woman was sitting with her feet up on the crowded desk, aiming the gaping blunt muzzle of a neon-red spattergun at a point just to the side of the door. She pulled the trigger, there was an explosion, a sudden reek of ozone and he jumped back. Rickki lowered the gun and waved him in. "Come admire my latest toy, Long Eddie."

Rickki was one of the few who knew or dared to

use his nickname, a tag derived—despite other interesting rumors—from the length of his lanky legs. The handle had been hung on him by members of the dojo when he perfected his rib-crushing side kick, and it had lingered among close friends thereafter.

Rickki was included in that category. Eight years ago they had both been posted to Hong Kong as Institute liaisons with the Asian section of the U.N. Commission on Organ Traffic. He had been twenty-five, was it possible? Several years junior to him, Rickki had displayed an uncanny gift for understanding the motives and mechanics of violence. When he had been given the job of on-site director three years ago, he had demanded her as security chief.

"Morning, Rickki." Wolfe entered and closed the door behind him, half-expecting to see a gaping hole in the wall where she had been aiming. Instead a winged green demon flapped back and forth across a wall-mounted holo unit of antique design, making obscene gestures with its tiny claws. Rickki tossed the replica spattergun to him. "Remember this one? *Swat Team Mephisto?* Very big, back when I was a sweet little girl. I picked it up at Dr. Flea's Market for a ten-piece. Go in, take a shot. Hold on tight—there's a built-in recoil."

Wolfe aimed, pulled the trigger. There was a loud bang, the gun jerked realistically, the demon exploded in a puff of tiny green scorpions, to be replaced a moment later with a miniature batwinged fiend.

"Nice shot, brother." She motioned with her thumb to the battered black office couch flanked by two vintage pinball machines, their lights flashing hypnotic reds and purples. "So flop it and talk."

Wolfe tossed the toy gun on the desk, eased himself onto the sofa and contemplated his security chief. As usual, Rickki was wearing the standard Post Millennium uniform: red bandanna, sunbands dangling from her neck, black cotton overalls open down to about the middle of her chest, enough to display the curves of the small, muscular body beneath. He felt a reflex twinge of physical attraction which short-circuited on the ever-intrusive memory of Omaha, long-legged, merry Omaha, his lover, his wife—dead three years as of July 16, one more victim of the nuclear hurricane that had summarily ended the War of Three Cities. Since then, her ghost had haunted his bedroom, making would-be liaisons so anticlimactic he had postponed further experiments indefinitely. He did not particularly care to be known as Limp Eddie.

Rickki eyed him with an air of sardonic amusement: "You just got the bad news from Orbital too, I take it?"

Wolfe stared at her with new apprehension. "No, I came to tell you about how I just about got cleaned this morning, thanks to Dulles. What news from Orbital?"

"No, you first. Your agenda sounds more immediate." Rickki scooped a cigarette from the carved ivory box on her desk and sat back in her padded chair. "Focus, what's the story?"

"It starts and ends with this." Wolfe placed Mancuso's card into the red-gloved plastic hand of the meter-tall Mickey Mouse doll on her desk. "Have you heard of an Accord marshal, name of Mancuso?"

"Sure. He's the Accord's top security gumbah here." Rickki took the card and darted a glance at him. "The Fool, huh? Hardly. So what's the story?"

"He just ran into us. Literally. Rear-ended the blue Isuzu, then mentioned he'd like to defect. That's his private number."

"Dulles allowed himself to be rear-ended?" Rickki blinked incredulously. "Very sloppy indeed."

"He allowed himself to be taken out too. Mancuso

knocked him senseless. If it had been a hit, we'd be dead now."

Rickki whistled in dismay. "Give details, brother."

Wolfe described the incident. When he was finished, Rickki bowed her head for a moment. "A thousand apologies! Jesus come quick, what will Helen do when she hears?" She drummed her fingers on the desk. "Dulles was a good friend of Mary's; the whole episode jangled him. He should have been rotated back to Orbital, but we're stretched too thin right now." She turned towards the gray enamel hump of her desk console: "Hey, Mildred, get me Medical."

"Sure boss," piped the console, in a very fair imitation of Rickki's own voice. Its screen came to life, showing a droll-faced man of about thirty in a white coat: "Medical here. For every ill we have a pill. What's the complaint today?"

Rickki nodded at the image. "'Morning, Doc. One of our agents has just turned in a very substandard performance. In fact he's practically killed himself and his client. Cyrus Dulles, level one, riding shotgun on Dr. Wolfe."

"Ah yes. Not so funny—he was just brought in with concussion."

"He can consider himself lucky he's still of the male gender. Listen, Doc, he showed very poor judgment this morning. Acted very odd, seemed almost out of control. Any medical explanation?"

"A moment please." The doctor looked somewhere off screen for a few moments then turned back. "He was taking hypnocounseling for mental trauma as you know. Also on medication, a brand new antidepressant from BioAge. Not supposed to be taken on duty of course."

"And if he did?"

The doctor pursed his lips, then nodded. "It's just

possible he could have experienced an adverse reaction brought on by extreme stress. Irrational panic, that sort of thing. A few instances have been reported."

Rickki made a ferocious face at the screen. "Well, he's suspended as of now, pending medical and disciplinary reviews. I'd like a report on the incident as soon as possible. And if there's anyone else on this medication, or marginal in any way, I want to know. Immediately."

The doctor nodded. "I'll review the records right away Rickki." He hesitated. "It's not an excuse, but we're all feeling the strain. Don't be too hard on Dulles."

"Comment noted. Thanks and disconnect." Rickki swung back to Wolfe. "And we think we're so superior. Just shows you, Institute people break too. Anyhow, I'm hereby assigning you a fresh security blanket, just down from Orbital. Name's Harper Amadeus: very clever, vicious as a wolverine when required, doesn't follow silly orders, should you give one. Quiet too; you'll hardly know he's there unless you need him. So tell me about Mancuso."

"Not much to tell. After he took out Dulles he told me he wanted to defect. Gave me his number, waved good-by and left us looking like the gumbahs we are."

"Mancuso! Old Nicky Mancuso! Wouldn't that be fun though?" Rickki addressed her console again with exaggerated politeness: "Mildred, my dear electronic serf, give us the top line on Nicolas Mancuso, if you'd be so kind."

The console tittered, a high clear note of merriment. "Sure, boss. Nicolas Mancuso, Marshal of the Temple Guards. Joined the Accord when he was fifteen. Helped plan the so-called Prairie Massacre. Very likely a graduate of the Soldiers of the Millennium program—in other words, a trained assassin. You want more?"

"No, hold it there." Rickki raised her eyebrows at Wolfe. "Lucky for you he was in a good mood. If he's real, we'd have access to literally years of dirt—operations, intelligence systems, you name it."

"But is he real?"

"Quite possible." Rickki shrugged her slim shoulders and Wolfe caught a glimpse of freckled breast underneath the black cotton. "I think there's a connection between your close encounter and the news from Orbital. It appears that Zacharian Stele was elected Deacon of Upper Canada about two weeks ago at a secret Accord conclave in Chicago. The election will be publicly proclaimed next week."

It was Wolfe's turn to make a sour face. "Zacky the Zealot? I thought he and mad Absolom were safely exiled to Central Africa or some out-of-the-way spot."

"So they were. Then the great Pastor himself snuffed it, and they came hotfooting back to Chicago, as did all the other members of the Stele clan. Ever since then, a power struggle has been raging over who is to succeed Daddy Stele. Apparently all his friends and relations think they should be the supreme pastor. Amazing how everyone heard the Call From Above simultaneously." She picked up the spattergun from her desk again and absent-mindedly aimed it at the red holo demon on the miniature stage. "None of the Pastor's heirs is strong enough to take out all the rest at the moment, so they've carved up the Temple by region. Net result: fourteen sons, daughters, nieces and nephews, each waiting for the chance to slaughter all the others and consolidate power. Messy, but that's how it is with new religions."

"But I still don't understand," protested Wolfe. "How do we inherit Zacky the Zealot? He's the worst of the whole lot—with the possible exception of his twin Absolom."

"That's why we got him. You think they're going to hand over a powerful diocese like Texarkana or Midwest to a maniac? Of course not. They're going to put him as far out on the periphery as they can—so they fob him off on Upper Canada. Absolom did even worse—he got Brazil." She pulled the trigger, exploding the flying gargoyle into shreds of red holographic goo. A crackle like frying bacon, a smell of ozone, and a particularly hideous demon peeped out from the corner of the holo stage. "Prepare for the eighth circle of hell," it rasped.

Wolfe pulled thoughtfully at his beard. "Not necessarily a wise strategy. A would-be emperor can raise a lot of support in the provinces, then march on Rome."

"It's happened," agreed Rickki passing him a sheaf of pics from her desk. "Here—take a look at our newest adversary."

Wolfe studied them with interest. They showed an austere, clean-shaven man in his mid-thirties. Under a domed forehead, made higher by receding red hair, blazed the intense eyes—an unusual deep blue—of a fanatic or a madman. Pinched nose, long down-curling mouth, thin and cruel as a razor slash. He tossed the photos on the desk. "Looks like his father without the charisma. Mean."

"Mean and strange. He's the third son of wife number three, herself a little strange according to the reports. Now then, this little shuffle is almost certainly behind the current uptick in violence. Zacharian has a reputation for extreme methods. The episode with Mary was probably his greeting card to us."

Wolfe frowned. "Interesting, to say the least. But what's the connection to Mancuso?"

"Maybe young Zacharian thinks Mancuso's too soft, or too old. Or not devoted to him personally. If that's the case, Mancuso may want to buy some insurance, open an escape hatch in case things get rough. Can you see it?"

"Could be," agreed Wolfe after a few moments' thought. It would not be the first time that a turf war had erupted inside the Temple of the Accord with brutal consequences to the losing side. Three years ago a purge of the so-called Professors had resulted in a series of bizarre "accidents" involving top leaders. One had mysteriously fallen from a seventeenth-story window, while another had stepped into the path of an oncoming train. Another had committed suicide by shooting himself in the back of the head. Many of their supporters had been broken to basic subscriber status, to scrub out a dismal existence at the lowest echelons of the organization. It could easily happen again. "Mancuso gave me a tip to prove his good intentions. According to him, there's a hit planned tonight at the Church of the Redeemer's medical facility. Led by the gumbah that did Mary."

Rickki smacked her clenched fist into her palm with a sharp crack. "Dammit, why didn't you say so? I've been itching for the chance to make some clinic a present of his kidneys."

"Me too, Rickki, me too." Wolfe picked up the spattergun, aimed across his arm, recalling the winter he had been the unofficial East-end champ of *Swat Team Mephisto*. "I haven't forgotten Mary either." He pulled the trigger, exploding a demon in a sizzle of blue light.

"Nice shot." Rickki nodded approvingly then shouted at her console: "Hey, Mildred, spit up a city map please." She swiveled her chair as the wall behind her glowed into a detailed map of Greater Toronto. A black street grid was overlaid with colors: light blue marked small oases of safety—the financial district, the university enclave, the midtown belt of hardened residential areas, the industrial parks curving across the

top of the city. No-man's-lands, where ordinary citizens
mingled uneasily with Listers, subscribers and other
assorted denizens of the Post Millennium, were delin-
eated in yellow. Free zones, areas of outright anarchy,
glowed like neon wounds all about the city, thickest in
the abandoned south and east industrial areas. The graphic
display of his shattered city brought a quote bubbling up
from Wolfe's subconscious.

Rickki cocked her head. "What was that?"

"I said: 'A house divided against itself cannot stand.'"

"You're philosophical this morning. Hey, Mildred,
show us the Church of the Redeemer clinic." The console obediently displayed a large-scale projection of
the Eastern Free Zone. Rickki pointed to a green dot
about the size of a coin blinking slowly just outside
the protective blue circle of a community hub.

"That's the target: an outpost of Hub Seven." She
swiveled her chair back to face him. "Makes sense
from a political point of view: Hub Seven's been
getting profile recently for production gains and
recruiting. I have no doubt the Accord would like to
put the knife to it."

"Too bad for them." Wolfe put his hand out, turned
thumbs down. An attack on a hub clinic could not
be tolerated. "So what's our response?"

"Keep our eyes open, in case this is a ploy of some
sort. Ambush the hit team." Rickki nodded briskly,
picked up a cookie-sized control box and pressed a
button. *Swat Team Mephisto* fizzled out in a spatter
of rainbow light. "For once I have a good feeling."

Wolfe drummed his fingers on Rickki's desk while he
thought, then nodded: "Set it up. I'll call in a report right
now and clear the ambush with Helen after lunch. I'm
on anyway for weekly review and interface enhancement."

Rickki gave a lazy mock salute. "At your order." She
stubbed her cigarette out and looked at him quizzi-
cally, her pretty face painted a lurid purple by the

reflected light of the pinball machines. "You know, I think the Interface Project is actually working. The old girl's more human every time I talk to her."

Wolfe laughed. "She asks the damnedest questions sometimes. The other day she wanted to know what my favorite color was."

"What did you tell her?"

"Blue, like her eyes."

Rickki stretched luxuriously. "Better be careful—what if she falls in love with you?"

"She's not that human yet." Privately Wolfe wondered. Helen was not less than human but more. What could you say of an entity that could simultaneously carry on dozens of holo meetings around the globe, crunch the rock-hard equations of the Hartley-Singh SoCy labs, monitor all major planetary variables, troll the nets for data—and at the same time crack a subtle personal joke based on a comment you had made a year ago? The Accord referred to Helen as the Idol in Orbit, but she was no graven image. She was, in fact, something with the potential to be uncomfortably like a god—not least because she was very hard to bring to account. *A helluva a boss to land yourself with, Long Eddie.*

Rickki merely grinned. "Better take a quick shower or something before you see her. You're pale and you smell of fear. She's terribly quick to notice details."

A new idea struck Wolfe as he rose to go. "Wait a minute though. Mr. Beaufort expressed a desire this morning to see the Institute in action. What if he saw one of the hubs actually repelling an assault?"

"Have him sit in on the ambush tonight?" Rickki nodded slowly. "Sure, if you like. It won't be pretty though."

Wolfe touched his level three ruby ear stud, a common Institute mannerism, said to bring luck and good judgment. "Beaufort's an advocate of strong measures.

He may as well see what they look like in practice. Let's see what Helen says."

He shut the door softly behind him, strode down the hall to the men's washroom, which was fortunately unoccupied, and bolted the door behind him. In the mirror his face was indeed pale and drawn. He looked and felt like hell. It was fear that did it. Jesus come quick, he had been lucky this morning. It had been too close, far too close to an unthinkable, humiliating end. Nausea overcame him as he contemplated the idea of being cleaned. Bloody savages, the Accord cleaners, barbarians who deserved only death. Of all the debased categories of humanity, hit-men and torturers were the most contemptible, the most frightening. He bent over the toilet and threw up, a brown chunky broth of tea and half-digested cereal. He sat for a few minutes in the cubicle, then washed his face with green industrial soap from the plastic dispenser and proceeded to his office.

Helen

Of all the enigmas of the enigmatic Skellig Michael Institute, by far the most mysterious is the artificial intelligence being known simply as Helen. By the Turing test, she is definitely intelligent—her conversation is indistinguishable from that of a shrewd well-educated person. What is more, she appears to have a well-defined character—sardonic, playful, sometimes a trifle eerie. Her personality is constantly and deliberately refined through a sophisticated program of human interaction. Does she have desires? Fears? Is she ever lonely? Needless to say, the scientists cannot answer with any authority, and Helen avoids all questions on the subject. There is little precedent for dealing with AIs, and one is tempted to ask what private agenda this awesome entity contemplates, as it circles the globe in high orbit, looking down on our teeming, fragile planet.

Puzzles of the PM
Henrikus Grobius, Jr.

Thursday, July 1
14:00 hours

Just after lunch, as he was reviewing the past week's statistics, the air conditioning crashed. It was an increasingly common occurrence. Versailles was ninety years old or more, and despite the best efforts of the engineers, it was dying of sheer age. Within a few minutes, his office was stifling, hot with a sickly wet heat that smelled of mildew. Wolfe threw down his notes and stared at the pockmarked green ceiling, trying to bear the new torment philosophically. He was, he told himself, a patient man, trained to cope with adversity. And what was air conditioning after all? *The straw that breaks the camel's back perhaps?*

He opened his window and a light breeze, reeking of soap from the toiletries factory next door, immediately blew the papers off his desk. One of the factory's windows was broken. Through it he could see a line of brown boxes moving by on a conveyor belt. On the roof, a vent hissed soapy blue steam into the superheated air. Cursing under his breath, he closed the window. "Say what, brother?" inquired his console cheerfully, hoping it was being addressed. Much of the equipment in Versailles had been purchased secondhand. His office console had come from a now-defunct publisher of motivational discs. Despite extensive reconditioning it remained both insufferably perky and stupid.

"Nothing." Wolfe wiped a trickle of sweat from the back of his neck and picked up his notes again. His face-to-face with Helen was less than an hour away; he preferred to be well prepared, insofar as one could be prepared for a chat with the nitrogen-cooled consciousness that was his supervisor, especially given the situation, which was deteriorating rapidly.

Food and power shortages were mounting. The country's reactors had been at full capacity far too long without maintenance, despite the discovery of cracks in the containment shell of the Port Carling unit. The army and the civil service had been on half pay for months. Whole rural districts were completely out of control, policed by local vigilantes or not at all. So far, situation normal, in a stark PM way.

The newest, truest problem was the Listers, the millions of unemployables who supplemented their government subsidies by a languid trade in drugs, organs and other controlled resources. Three months ago, to stave off complete economic collapse, over two million had been delisted, their subsidies abruptly cut off. About a third of them had signed up for reclamation programs—the urban hubs or the northern settlements. The rest, according to initial projections, should have been sucked up by the Accord or merely increased their black market activity, causing a pronounced but bearable crime spike.

However, in the last month, two very disturbing trends had emerged: Listers were joining the Accord in record numbers, far above projections. Equally troubling, an enigmatic new Lister organization appeared to be growing within the raddled body politic. Exactly what it was and what it wanted remained a mystery despite intensive investigation.

Wolfe tossed his notes onto the battered green metal desk before him and stretched. Sociocybernetics was not an exact science, especially when applied to small populations, but normally results were better than this. Far better. Perhaps the project codes had come out of whack? There had been major on-site changes since they were first developed. Codes were supposed to be checked and rechecked routinely by Orbital of course, but it was easy to overlook some small but critical factor. Sociocybernetics was, in some ways, an art as much as a science.

Not for the first time, he wished he was scientific consultant to Project Maldon, rather than on-site director. The notion of running simulations in the untroubled quiet of an Orbital lab was most appealing, especially when compared to the impossible task of coaching, guiding and protecting over a hundred Institute specialists on the ground. Perhaps he was not cut out to be a leader? Perhaps he was not bold enough, far-sighted enough, or callous enough? Mary's brutal street execution had given him nightmares for a week. The ongoing spectacle of Upper Canada disintegrating despite their best efforts was intensely painful. He disliked being the cause of suffering, even when it was plainly for the greater good. And the project seemed to bring nothing but suffering for all concerned. Somewhere, somehow he was doing something wrong.

Or—a queasy thought that kept recurring lately—what if the problem was Helen? Wolfe banged his fist on his desk in sheer exasperation and made a sour face at his console. You could not run a SoCy project on intuition, but experts developed a feel for what would work and what wouldn't in a given situation. He was an expert, and lately several of Helen's directives had *felt* wrong to him. The cutbacks to the Lists had been too large and too abrupt, the handling of the resulting chaos clumsy. What if the AI was malfunctioning? Or what (the ultimate heresy) if she wanted the project to go awry for some inscrutable reason? Unfortunately there was no way to check—short of hiring time on one of the world's four other advanced AIs to run the program code. In practice, of course, quite impossible.

He swiveled in his chair to look out the window, wondering how he could run some checks himself. It was time-consuming, laborious work, and he had little enough time as it was. He had a brief, vertiginous image of his tasks breeding, multiplying like bacteria under a microscope, crowding into all available space, crowding out his thoughts, his preferences, his lapsed love life. One way or another it was time to head for the meeting room. Stifling a yawn he stood up and told his console to receive.

"It will be my pleasure," said the console in ingratiating tones.

Wolfe snorted and banged the door behind him. The meeting room was just down the hall. Arriving three minutes early, he switched on the pickup, settled himself into a leather chair in front of the holo stage and waited. He found it hard not to think of Helen as a flesh-and-blood person, preparing even now to sit before the holo unit high in Orbital One. That of course was nonsense; he had seen the silver cube, three meters on a side, which housed the core AI, a billion bits of etched silicon and metal quivering with electric currents passing and swirling in an eddy that somehow was consciousness.

Not for the first time, he was struck with the strangeness of the thing. He had probably spent more hours talking with Helen than with any human being, except of course for Omaha. They had discussed every topic from metaphysics to human sexuality from the time he was seventeen years old. She had tutored him, sympathized with him, encouraged him and sent him all over the world and into orbit to learn and grow. She was mentor, parent, friend and boss all in one— a cube of metal and silicon, falling endlessly through the emptiness of space, ever more familiar, always unknowable. The loss of perfect trust in her would be a serious blow to his already fragile peace of mind. It would be at least the equivalent of loss of faith in a religious person, an unsuspected trapdoor opening into darkness and chaos just at your feet. Wolfe grunted and sank deeper into the viewing chair. *You're just tired and frustrated, brother, no need to go metaphysical.*

As the clock showed two thirty, Helen's life-size holo flickered into being on the dull metal platform before him, a tight woman-size figure, vivid and lifelike as an actual presence despite the unimaginable distances it had traveled. It winked at Wolfe and opened its mouth as if in speech; words came softly from the chair speakers: "Good afternoon, Edward." The AI had altered her icon subtly since their last conversation: today she seemed younger. Her hair was a darker shade of brown and it was cut short in the style of Asian senior executives. She wore a white suit and a wide, burgundy tie.

"Hi boss." Wolfe had become attuned to the subtle messages of dress and behavior during his dealings with the Asian organ traffickers in Hong Kong. Perhaps, he sometimes thought, the artistic genes inherited from his mother prompted him to take pleasure in the complex swirl of color, form and motion which made up the dance of human—or in this case, non-human—interaction. It always amused him to guess at the meaning of Helen's manifestations. Today, the AI's clothes suggested a businesslike approach to whatever was at hand. The symbology of the hair also hinted at work to be done. He guessed it was to be a serious, task-oriented session, with perhaps some personal interchange, as signaled by the friendly burgundy tie. Fair enough.

Somewhere high in orbit, or in the underwater extensions she was rumored to have, information about Wolfe's image dodged back and forth through molecular gates as Helen arranged her own inhuman thoughts. Finally she spoke, in a soft, thoughtful voice: "I have studied the report on your unplanned meeting with our would-be friend Nicolas Mancuso, and done some follow-up here and there. The probability is very high, say about ninety-three percent, that he is genuine. His story is internally cohesive, and it meshes with recent data coming from the Accord, specifically the election of Zacharian Stele as Deacon of Upper Canada." The holo appeared to meet Wolfe's eye. For one unnerving moment he felt himself looking straight into the depths of something that was different than human, more than hologram. His brain squirmed as if reacting to a torrent of subliminal images that left him nervous but exultant. Then the holo, with impeccable manners, looked away. "Your operation tonight is approved. If Mancuso's information is accurate we will proceed to next steps. Personally, I believe his offer to defect is made in good faith. If so, we are very lucky." The holo pursed its lips. "And we sorely need good luck, or so it seems from up here. Do my gloomy comments correspond with the view from the ground?"

"Unfortunately they do." Wolfe took a deep breath. "This news about Zacharian Stele does not bode well at all. I haven't studied his file closely yet, but he seems an unpleasant individual. Cruel and slightly unbalanced."

"So he is. You recall Saint Sting from your days with the Piracy Control Bureau?"

Wolfe nodded. The sometimes aid worker had been the brains of a Caribbean-wide piracy operation before a fleet of six hydrofoil corvettes—one carrying a younger and more earnest Wolfe as fascinated supercargo—had finally cornered his trio of armored sloops and sunk them in the shallow turquoise waters off Barbados.

"Zacharian is as devious as Saint Sting, and a thousand times more driven. His twin brother Absolom is worse, but mercifully we didn't inherit him as well. Zacharian believes that traditional governments must be replaced by theocracies based upon Accord principles. The situation in Upper Canada offers him an excellent opportunity to put his theories into practice. We are running a series of projections based on alternative strategies he might adopt, but the most optimistic run is not good, assuming the Accord reaches critical mass in Upper Canada." Helen permitted herself a small smile which quirked her coral-pink lips in a perfect cupid's bow. "However, we have one thing in our favor—this mysterious new Lister organization."

Wolfe stared at the icon in astonishment. "How does that help us? We don't know anything about it—except that it has a certain expertise in urban terrorism."

"Aha, there you are wrong," said the AI smugly. "I now have a file on the organization. You'll find a summary of my findings on your console when you return."

"How did you manage that?" demanded Wolfe. "We've been trying to make contact with these crazy gumbahs for weeks with zero success."

The icon merely winked. "Much can be learned if one monitors a few thousand remote eyes on a minute-by-minute basis. One becomes the proverbial fly on the wall. Here's what I found out in brief: the group is called the Exodus Faction. It is active and well organized. Its initial goal is to regain subsidies for all Listers."

Wolfe groaned aloud. "And its long-term objectives?"

"To negotiate an independent homeland for Faction members in a yet-undetermined area of the old permafrost zone. Additionally to persuade the U.N. to allocate all Upper Canada's spaces on the first five Mars shuttles to its members."

Wolfe shook his head. "Completely impossible, as they must know."

"Possibly. However, the Exodus Faction could be useful to us." Helen held up a slim finger to enjoin silence. "Let me explain. Right now we are on the horns of a classic SoCy dilemma. If we hadn't cut entitlements, the economy would have collapsed with a reverberating thud. But our cutbacks drove the most desperate members of society straight into the arms of the Accord at a faster-than-projected rate. We have to slow down recruiting without seeming to be involved.

So we let the Exodus Faction do our dirty work for us. We strike a devil's bargain with them—they discourage recruiting by any means at their disposal." The icon coughed delicately. "In return we persuade the government to review their demands, perhaps make one or two small concessions. With luck we could provoke an outright conflict between them and the Accord. It could be a powerful distraction to both."

"Perhaps too powerful," cautioned Wolfe. "How do we keep control? A confrontation could go critical—we could end up with a full-scale civil war. It's dangerous."

"So are nuclear reactors. But we still use them, because we have no other option." Helen waved her slim holographic hand in a gesture of inevitability. "We've crunched the numbers and they leave no doubt. I have already made contact with the group's current president—a gentleman who goes by the quaint name of Adam 100—to reason with him. The time is propitious because the group is currently wondering how to make its demands known to government."

Wolfe felt a tingle of excitement in the pit of his stomach. Helen's solution was cynical and devious, but it just might work. "What exactly do you want me to do?" he asked slowly.

"Meet with Adam 100 tomorrow. Suggest that further cutbacks can be postponed if Accord recruiting slows down. Make no promises but get the idea across that entitlements depend on the Accord stubbing its toes. Do this as soon as possible. Then we'll sit back and see what happens."

"Can we postpone cutbacks?" asked Wolfe dubiously.

"For a few weeks only, although Adam 100 must not know that." The icon's features became suitably apologetic. "I deplore such deceptions, but we must consider the greater good. We can also promise to look into the question of places on the Mars shuttle, and even a homeland. Promises cost nothing, and who knows? Maybe some concessions could be arranged."

Again, Wolfe's intuition stirred and protested. Helen was quick to notice his hesitation. "Is something wrong, Edward?"

AI interaction was second nature to Wolfe after half a lifetime with the Institute. The trick was always to answer truthfully, never to be offended or surprised, no matter how bizarre the question. Still, he found himself wondering how he could phrase his objections without seeming critical. "At the risk of repeating myself, I fear we are taking a grave risk. My gut feeling is that it's very dangerous."

"But it *is* dangerous, my dear Edward. No one said major SoCy initiatives were safe."

"So where do we draw the line?" persisted Wolfe. "At what point does the cure become worse than the disease? I realize this is not strictly a SoCy issue, but it does concern me."

"And your concern does you credit." The holo pursed its pink lips, contriving to look judicious and concerned at the same time. "The fact is, we must effect a cure at any cost, to use your metaphor. Do you want to hear our latest projections if Project Maldon fails?"

Wolfe suspected he did not want to hear them at all, but he nodded politely.

Helen cocked her head to one side as if reciting poetry, and spoke in a high clear monotone, repeating the tall black words that shimmered into being beside her. "Probability cascade assuming failure of Project Maldon: First tier result, complete social and infrastructure collapse in Upper Canada. Probability approaching one hundred percent.

"Second tier result: Accord fills resulting vacuum. Probability approaching one hundred percent.

"Third tier result: Nominal Republican, Democrat and Revolutionary Institutional governments within Free Market destabilized. Probability ninety-four percent.

"Fourth tier result: emergence of continent-wide political entity based on Accord principles within two years. Probability eighty-nine percent.

"Cascade outcome: armed confrontation between hypothetical Accord nation and Islamic Coalition within three years. Probability eighty-three percent. And then . . . " She peered at Wolfe. "And then— well, you remember Tel Aviv and Teheran."

Wolfe remembered all too well. If Helen had been trying to cheer him, she had failed miserably. His stomach was full of icy butterflies. "So if Maldon fails we're looking at the Die Back, nuke style?"

"SoCy doesn't allow us that level of certainty; you know that, Edward. All I'm saying is that project failure could start an uncontrollable chain reaction. Balance the consequences of that against a measure of street violence in Upper Canada and you see the picture more clearly. Needless to say, this information should be kept confidential."

Wolfe's pulse had begun to hammer. He had always known the project was important, but he found himself horrified by the significance it had suddenly assumed. He felt like an ant watching the crushing black boot of destiny descend. "I'm appalled. With the greatest respect, Helen, are you sure I'm the best person for this job?"

The holo nodded its shapely head, the motion disturbing not a strand of its brown hair. "Of course we're sure. You are uniquely qualified. We are relying on you for the all-important view from the ground."

"Speaking of the view from down here, I've been watching the destability index very closely and it's creeping up on six." Wolfe cleared his throat. "I would like to prepare contingency plans for a partial evacuation if it goes above six."

Helen shook her head. "A pullback of any kind is impossible at the moment. It would send the wrong signal to everyone. We must be seen to be fully committed in Upper Canada."

"But surely we need a contingency plan?" pleaded Wolfe. "It'll be impossible to get everyone out if things go critical suddenly."

"I'm afraid not, Edward. Word could leak out, with negative consequences. No, we must keep a careful watch on the destability index and keep calm. Now then, let us move to a more pleasant subject." The holo's eyebrows quirked, she became positively arch, like his Aunt Matilda arranging a blind date as Wolfe later described it to Rickki. "Institute Fellow Level Two Morgan Fahaey will be arriving next Monday morning, flying in from Seoul on flight 491. I would like you to meet her, take her to her lodgings and generally make her at home."

"She's not staying at Versailles?"

"No. She's on special assignment, reporting directly to me. She has no links to Project Maldon so I'd rather keep her out of harm's way."

"Weird Brigade?"

Helen sniffed in disapproval. "I prefer the term 'Special Projects Division.'"

"Your pardon." Wolfe whiffed a trace of ozone from the holo projector. "What is the nature of her work, if I may ask?"

Helen raised a perfect white hand on which, Wolfe was intrigued to note, a holographic emerald ring sparkled green. "Officially she's part of the Interface Project, but you should think of her as my special envoy. Her talent is to put things in perspective for me. I want her to give me a feel for Upper Canada, a suprarational view if you like." The holo sat forward as if anticipating further questions.

Wolfe grunted dubiously. "What qualifies her to do that, if I may ask?"

"By background she's an art scholar, as well as an accomplished painter. More to the point, she is an interface expert, trained to help me become, if you will, more intuitive. Don't frown so, Edward. She won't be in your way. Just enjoy her company, show her the city, talk with her." If she could have, thought Wolfe, she would have leaned out from the holo stage and tapped his wrist playfully.

"Understood," he agreed.

"Excellent. One final point: stress levels are high at the moment and it's important you stay loose. You rest best at the cottage. Medical therefore suggests you spend the coming weekend there, work permitting."

Wolfe was still irritated with himself for failing to wheedle permission to develop a contingency evacuation plan. "Work permitting," he agreed reluctantly.

"You can always bring your console with you."

"Is that an order?"

Helen's humorous mouth turned up at its perfect, lineless corners. "Merely a suggestion, my dear Edward. Short-term projections suggest the next few days will be quiet. If something breaks, we can fetch you back soon enough." The holo assumed a look of kindly concern. "Is the road still secure? It runs through several no-man's-lands as I recall."

For an entity that had once mentioned it monitored over thirty thousand remote sites each day, and kept every move of every master's chess game ever recorded in a tiny fraction of available memory, Helen was being unusually vague, thought Wolfe. Humoring him no doubt. "Quite safe. There are informal convoys every hour or so on the weekends."

"Make sure you take good security. We can't afford to lose our on-site director at this point." She steepled her long fingers and smiled at him. "Also, I'd be personally devastated—I do so enjoy our chats."

Wolfe stared up at the holo but could discover no suggestion of irony on the icon's seamless features. "Thank you. So do I."

"Enjoy yourself. We'll meet again soon. *Au revoir.*" The image waved an elegant, youthful hand, collapsed in upon itself and dimmed. Wolfe found himself staring at the dull blue metal of the holo stage. He took a deep breath and shook his head ruefully. Morgan Fahaey—what was Helen doing sending a special envoy to Upper Canada? And a weird at that. He had met weirds before and they had all lived up to their name. As he stood up he noticed that his hands were sweating; no doubt Helen had noticed too.

He returned to his office where he spent the remainder of the afternoon catching up on work: delicately worded conversations on maxSec lines (which might or might not be secure) with Institute colleagues in the key ministries, an interesting meeting with a young economist who was trying to translate the effects of the increased Lister traffic in organs into mathematical terms, a session with Rickki to review improvements in security.

By six o'clock he was beginning to tire. He sat back and rubbed his eyes, which were smarting from the diffuse soap fumes that had managed to sneak through molecule-sized cracks into his untidy office. After two years he was wild to escape from the tangled and confusing reality of on-site management, back to the cool, abstract probabilities of pure sociocybernetics. The Institute shrinks had always claimed he had a natural talent for administration. Maybe so, but he had little genuine interest. Cracking his knuckles he silently reaffirmed his vow to apply for transfer—as soon as he could decently do so. To ask for reassignment now would only look as if he was bailing out of a difficult situation, which would definitely kill his chances of the all-important promotion to level four.

He sighed and sat back. That was not the real reason, he admitted to himself. He was ambitious, but far more than that, he was Institute, through and through. And the fact was, the Institute—and Helen—thought he was the best person for the job. But was he really? There were a hundred other level threes, all intelligent, motivated, aggressive. Why Edward Wolfe? It was puzzling, but the stakes were too high to question the decision.

A flicker of motion in his doorway, a quiet knock. It was Hans, the stooped senior data dick, a speculative look in his old, red-rimmed eyes.

Wolfe glanced at him in surprise. "Don't tell me you've run a backgrounder on the Fahaey gumbette already?"

Hans spoke softly, articulating his words as if talking to an input. "Yes and no. Is this some kind of test?"

"Why? Is there a problem?"

Hans shrugged his thin shoulders, reminding Wolfe of a huge cricket rubbing dry wings together. "You tell me. There's a seven-year hole in your subject's verifiable data. Is that a problem?"

Wolfe leaned back until his chair creaked. "You mean there's a lock on her file?"

Hans twisted his gaunt features into a mask of disdain. "Ha! Show me a lock we can't pick. No, far more subtle than that. All the details are there all right. But they don't stand up to triple cross-referencing within a seven-year stretch."

Wolfe sighed and motioned him to sit. "Explain please."

"As you wish." The old data dick perched himself on the green metal arm of the chair. "When we do a backgrounder we verify details, yes? Just a random double-check on key facts. As a crude example, say the subject was born in Trieste in '04. We check the birth records there and also relevant records for the registered mother. If the birth is recorded, but we find the mother was skiing in the Andes at the time, a red light goes on, yes? We usually go one step further, just for good measure, and check the cross-checks, if you see what I mean."

"And? You can't cross-reference key details for a certain period of Ms. Fahaey's career?" What in hell was Helen foisting on him now, wondered Wolfe.

Hans frowned. "Right. Everything looks fine on the surface, but it's all cosmetic. Age eighteen to twenty-five—nothing. Squat. Zero. Boss, we can't verify anything in that whole damn time."

"I see. Your conclusion?"

"Someone's done a major cover-up, and a very good one. An AI-quality job if you take my meaning. Why? Don't ask me, that's your department—I think. Take a look." Like all true data dicks, Hans became uncomfortable when unplugged for more than a few minutes at a stretch from the endless detective game inside the Net. He tossed a thin file onto Wolfe's desk and turned to go.

"A moment," called Wolfe, and Hans paused reluctantly in the doorway. "I have a theoretical question for you. How would we know if an Artificial Intelligence was malfunctioning?"

The dick turned back and stared at him for a long moment. "An interesting question. I assume we're talking about psychosis in true AIs—Turing class five and up?"

"Correct."

Hans favored him with a wintry smile. "You broach a large and mysterious subject. We know little about psychotic AIs because we've never seen one. Maybe they never go strange. They shouldn't, with all the safeguards that are designed in. Many experts think it just can't happen. Then you have the Frankenstein Faction, which claims that many or even all AIs are aberrant, but they're shrewd enough to keep it to themselves. Now and again, someone reports irregularities in an AI's behavior. Experience suggests this may be unwise."

"Why is it unwise?" asked Wolfe.

"Always the claim is discredited, usually the person reporting it ends up looking like a fool or a crackpot. And, on at least three occasions, the accuser has disappeared. That was in connection with reported aberrations in the Beijing AI by the way."

"Getting back to my original question, if an AI was going strange, what would be the signs?"

Hans sighed and stood up. "As I've just explained, we don't know. In theory, you might expect irrational decisions, fixation on certain goals, systematic deception of human operators and so on. There's a fairly large body of theory on the subject. I recommend Van Damsen and Haskill for starters. Now if you'll excuse me, I have work to do."

Wolfe stared after his retreating back, more disturbed than he cared to admit to himself. Irrational decisions? Like sending a delegation to Teheran when it was almost certainly targeted for countermeasures? Like refusing to consider partial evac, when the destability index was creeping towards six?

The topic was too large and ambiguous to deal with at the moment; he would need to do some research first. He began to leaf through the sparse gray file before him. As he did so, his perplexity deepened. Fahaey had disappeared from the banks at eighteen. Seven years later she had reappeared, full-grown, mysterious and shining like a star. Prizes for visual arts, a book of essays on human perception and so on. But for seven years she had left absolutely no footprints on the much-traveled sand of the Post Millennium. He shrugged. Presumably it was none of his concern. Odd though . . . He hesitated then locked the file in a desk drawer and stood up. Just time for dinner and a nap before picking up Mr. Beaufort to watch the ambush at the clinic.

He ran up the stairs, two at a time, to the residential section of the Versailles complex. The whole top floor had been converted into small apartments; rows of white doors opened off a central corridor running the length of the building. His room was at the rear; the lock slid back smoothly as he pushed his card in, clicked shut behind him.

The apartment was long and narrow, with a high sheet-metal ceiling crosshatched by ducts and pipes. Areas had been sectioned off with old-fashioned pale-green wall dividers. The first room was a small kitchen with a two-burner gas stove, flash oven and refrigerator. The living area was at the back: a large, sunny room with high windows dropping from ceiling to waist height. Furniture was basic: two dull blue metal chairs, a matching table cluttered with cassettes, journals and dirty tea cups; in the corner by the window a leather armchair and a personal console— to his chagrin even more moronic than the one in his office.

Wolfe peered through the double-glazed panes; outside, the brown waters of a small artificial lake— another failed experiment in urban renewal—lapped at a concrete shore choked with old car tires and plastic bottles. The setting sun reflected in the lake, turning its dirty waters to an incandescent crimson splendor. Looking down into the reflected glow he thought to see a ripple spreading out, as if a fish had risen for a moment to the surface. The pigeons were gone from the city, of course, and the squirrels. And the dogs, except for the expensive pets found in hardened luxury residentials. The odd feral cat still roamed and rats remained, hidden and malevolent, a plague lurking in deserted buildings. But a fish in Logan Pond? Once it had been stocked with goldfish and other ornamental species. Did some survive? If so, it was a small miracle. Buoyed by the idea, Wolfe turned away from the window.

There was just time for a quick workout before dinner. He switched on a table lamp, rolled out his blue plastic exercise mat and swiftly changed into sweat pants and a T-shirt. After stretching for three or four minutes, he ran through a set of karate forms, forcing all his concentration into his breathing, the fine control of his motions.

In fifteen minutes he was sweating. Satisfied, he draped a towel over his shoulders and walked to the kitchen. Pulling a dinner from the freezer, he stripped off the packaging and slid it into the flash oven. Rice noodles and steak teriyaki: the package showed a pudgy, middle-aged man in a Japanese bathrobe sniffing appreciatively at a steaming platter. Wolfe examined the picture; if he was intended to identify with the man, the design failed dismally. Was that how his colleagues or Helen saw him? He was considering the idea when the oven called him with programmed cheerfulness, greeting number seven, bachelor mode: "Chow time, sport. Just how you like it."

Wolfe doubted it. Retrieving his dinner he served himself steaming noodles, neon-green and orange vegetables and teriyaki beef that looked like it had been shaved off an old shoe, poured a glass of mineral water and surveyed the resulting meal with mild disgust.

On the way back to the front room he paused in front of the mirror and inspected his image. A broad, flat face looked back at him with prominent, almost protruding, brown eyes set at a slant that suggested good humor. Semi-curly dark hair cut short for the summer, short black beard framing a true Anglo-Saxon mouth, straight and thin. A small bump at the bridge of his rather wide nose marked the spot where a half-blocked round kick had made agonizing contact many years ago. To his relief, he could detect no resemblance between himself and the man on the package.

Clearing a sheaf of papers aside, he set the plate on the table by the window. Outside, the endless sirens of the Post Millennium wailed. He slipped a Mozart chip into the player, spun his gold and ivory chopsticks (a parting gift from his Hong Kong colleagues) for practice, then began to eat. Dinner was about as he had expected: the meat spicy with a vinegar aftertaste, the noodles and vegetables bland. He swallowed, made a wry face, then shrugged and stolidly resumed eating. What was dinner anyway without good wine, or at least good company? A fueling stop, nothing more.

Chewing his stringy meat he marveled at the destiny that had led him—a basically congenial man— to dine alone night after night in these austere chambers within a high-security Institute installation, his boss an artificial intelligence entity, his wife a scatter of radioactive dust. What had brought him to this?

The answer of course was simple: Omaha's sudden and fiery death, three years ago this month. Three years—perhaps it was the impending anniversary that was bringing her so constantly to his thoughts. They had met each other when they were seventeen and married when they were twenty-five, both level ones with promising careers ahead. Five years of a marriage snatched as the opportunity arose given conflicting schedules and frequent postings to different parts of the world. Still, a marriage. Then one morning the sirens had wailed in Teheran and she was gone in a quadruple flash of atomic light. Memory and a few trinkets were all that was left of her. Not even a grave; there had been no need, nothing to bury, not even ashes. By now, her constituent atoms were no doubt spread evenly around the upper atmosphere, just as his would have been except for a trick of fate, a karate tournament that had left him with a badly sprained ankle the very evening before the delegation left for Teheran. They had sent a last-minute replacement even though he insisted he was fit enough to travel.

He had driven her to the airport, kissed her goodbye, and waited until she cleared security. She had looked specially lovely that day, in a tight green and black suit of Italian make. When not working or studying, she had delighted in dressing up. And in fine food. Wolfe stirred the mess on his plate and pushed it away.

Two days later, the Doomsday computer in the Negev had executed the fifth variant on the Samson Option: a quadruple missile strike that caused thermonuclear suns to rise just before true dawn in a diamond pattern around Teheran, lighting the desert two hundred kilometers away. Stupid thing to do—going to Teheran. Everyone guessed the Israelis would do something after Tel Aviv was bio-gassed. Something pointed. Something spectacular. Something terrible. Well, and oh well. Why the board of governors had ordered the mission to proceed was something he might never know. The whole affair was still shrouded in secrecy; moreover, the government-in-exile of Israel still retained the Institute as a consulting firm, making all files current and confidential.

For several weeks after, he blundered around in a waking dream. The Dean suggested he see a psychiatrist. Dr. Mortimer, a kindly middle-aged man with a soft voice, advised physical exercise and meditation, "at least two hours a day. Center yourself and cultivate an endorphin habit." He obeyed, and filled the rest of his days and nights with endless work, haunting the echoing sim labs, creating complex SoCy models of his home country, then torturing them with the acid variables of the Post Millennium—ultra-poverty, disease, water shortages, gang wars. He had become the world's leading expert on the countless destinies—most of them dismal— that awaited the American FreeMarket down the shifting corridors of time future.

In his time off he groped through the various phases of loss: denial, anger, grief . . .

Then a new government had been elected in Upper Canada, and had rushed through a contract with the Institute. Before he knew it he had been named on-site director of Project Maldon and booked on a flight back down the well. He had protested the appointment, but Helen was adamant: "You need a change, my dear Edward. You can't spend the rest of your days in an orbital sim lab, slowly becoming more isolated and eccentric. Even a humble AI can see you need to be with people. Besides, none of our other SoCybers understands Upper Canada like you. Go and deliver forth your homeland." (In those days, recalled Wolfe, Helen had sometimes adopted an almost Biblical tone.)

"It's not my homeland any more."

"The land where you grew up then. And remember, Upper Canada is one of many dominoes that we cannot afford to have toppled right now. On top of which, we've signed a contract, with excellent bonus provisions. Now go and get briefed; you leave in four days."

You did not debate an order from Helen. Wolfe packed a few odds and ends of clothing, his lucky karate pants, a T-shirt of Omaha's which still retained her fresh smell (a happy smell somehow, he always thought) and presented himself at the airlock on the appointed hour.

On the interminable flight back to the city of his birth he had ventured for the first time to peer into the psychic space where Omaha had been. It was empty, she was gone. He had deliberately gotten drunk on airline liquor and wept quietly inside the entertainment helmet until his tears short-circuited one of the delicate components, producing little electric shocks all around his eyes. A security blanket met him at the airport, helped him into a car and drove him to Versailles, where he slept for a full day. When he woke, he still had the traces of a hangover but his spirit was lighter. Hoping that this was the dawn of acceptance, he had thrown himself into his new assignment with an energy derived in equal parts from grief, intellectual curiosity and ambition, working fourteen hours or more a day, visiting power stations, Lister offices, community hubs and rural settlements in search of the magic insight that would breath life back into the failing nation.

Only in the last few weeks, after nearly two years of being father, mother, nursemaid and lover to the awkward entity that was Project Maldon, had he begun to lose momentum. Two years without holiday or respite: no wonder he was tired, stale, and if truth be known, lonely. He found himself increasingly aware of the women around him, Rickki for example, in a way he had not been since Teheran. Well, he had picked a bad time to join the men's club again. Even without personal entanglements he could never find enough time to do all his work. *Long Eddie, the last thing you need right now is a social life.*

He gave his ear stud an irritable tug and drained the remainder of his mineral water. The bubbles tickled his nose, making him sneeze. A few hours of sleep, then he would rise like a vampire at the midnight hour, and attend a secret festival of blood. And if the crimson blood to be shed was really that of the monsters who had done Mary, he looked forward to seeing it flow.

Counterterror

Politics and religion have always been entwined. Religious belief is merely worldly belief reflected upward in the cosmic mirror. And truly, our revelation explains how faiths and governments replace one another as we struggle upwards towards the Final Truth. The time has come to implement our belief, our vision given to us in these terminal days: to cleanse the Earth in preparation for the Coming of the Light.

The Last Convert, an authorized biography of Henry
Stele, First Pastor, Temple of the Accord

Economics says the more there is of something the cheaper it is. Thus air (until recently) was free, while diamonds commanded a high price. The same principle applies to human life. With twelve billion people swarming the globe, life is cheaper than it used to be. How much cheaper we are still discovering.

Breaking Point, a collection of essays on
Post Millennial topics
Henrikus Grobius, Jr.

Friday, July 2
02:23 hours

Walking to the Operations Room, vulgarly known as the Hole, Wolfe stifled another yawn. His watch seemed stuck somewhere in that endless interval

42

between midnight and dawn when the body most craves rest, the mind is most prone to unwholesome fantasy. He held the heavy metal door open for the Deputy Premier, then followed him through into the dimness. As usual, the Hole reeked of cigarettes and ozone. Beside the holo stage, Rickki was talking quietly into a headset. She had had her hair cut short for the summer; by some trick of reversal, the effect was to make her appear more feminine. As Wolfe entered with the Deputy Premier she looked over and waved.

Deputy Premier Beaufort was a large, shaggy bear of a man in his late fifties. Tonight, with his thick gray hair curling over the collar of his frayed tweed jacket, he looked more like a professor of literature than the nation's senior statesman. In fact, he had been an inventor, and a very successful one, before entering politics; behind the shabby facade was a finely-tuned intellect and a fierce determination to succeed.

It was he and Mrs. Clements, the fiery red-headed Premier, who held together the fragile coalition that was the Renaissance Party; Beauty and the Beast as one newscaster described them. Beaufort still leaned on a cane, a reminder of the injuries suffered seven months ago in a bomb attack by a disaffected group of Listers, but despite a marked limp he seemed robust and confident; as he entered the Ops Room he looked around with keen interest and gave the thumbs up— his trademark salute—to the technicians ministering to the motorcycle-sized projector at the far end. He paused for a moment to watch as a full-scale holo image flickered into being on the raised viewing stage, then melted in a sizzling rainbow of blues and reds.

Wolfe conducted him across the room, past the black-topped conference table to the row of leather viewing chairs in front of the holo stage. "Sir, you remember Rickki Harrow, our head of security?"

"Indeed I do." Beaufort bowed, a grade three inclination of equal to equal. "We had an intense discussion last summer on the merits of controlled violence. Over a jar of Flash at a reception at Hart House, as I recall."

"I remember it well, sir. You're about to see some of the concepts we discussed put into practice." Rickki's voice was dry. "I fear the theory is more appealing than its application."

Beaufort looked grim for a moment. "No doubt. I understand you're expecting to intercept a team of so-called Cleaners?"

"Correct." Rickki pointed at the holo, which had stabilized again. "That's the interior of a round-the-clock medical clinic. In the Eastern Free Zone, just outside the perimeter of Hub Seven. The screens beside the stage show overhead and ground views of the alley leading to the clinic."

Beaufort peered into the alley monitor, which revealed a ghostly gray-black scene of desolation: the corpse of a Ford three-wheeler decaying against the far wall, a Samsung desk console, its screen smashed, a scatter of cardboard boxes. At the far end of the alley was a door.

After a moment he turned back to Rickki. "Please continue."

"According to our information, an Accord Cleaner team is going for the staff. Cleaners, as you know, go in for mutilation and gelding. No backup, just hit and run. Mad dogs, real bad dreams. They butchered one of our operatives two weeks ago. Mary McGee—perhaps you remember the news item?" Rickki cocked her eyebrows in inquiry.

The Deputy Premier nodded his heavy head. "All too well."

So did Wolfe. He wiped the back of his neck, tried to suppress the fury that threatened to overwhelm him every time he thought of her. Mary McGee had been one of their best field operatives. She had died of blood loss in Toronto General, her breasts cut off with what the coroner described as a sharp knife with a curved blade. A fish-cleaning knife, a favorite tool of Accord secret squads. He had been about to go to lunch when the news had reached him. Instead he had gone first to the hospital, then into an adrenaline-boosted series of meetings with Security, with Helen, with an ineffectual delegation from Metro Police. That night he had deliberately remained sober, totally unmedicated, while Rickki and the off-duty staff held the traditional Flash-fueled wake. If he had been a better, more foresighted leader, she might have lived. He wanted his psyche to remember that for next time.

"Very well." Rickki lit another cigarette and wiped the light film of sweat from her forehead. "We're using our own operatives in the actual ambush, community militia as backup and recon. The local defense units are a bit green, but they have good leaders and seconds. It should be pretty hard to surprise us—we'll see major reinforcements long before they arrive."

"Splendid." Beaufort nodded cheerfully. "Your information seems very detailed. Do you have a source inside the Accord?"

Rickki made a careless hand gesture, her cigarette tracing a meteor trail through the air. "Evil will out, sir. A careless word, a data transmission in yesterday's code—we have many sources." She consulted her watch. "Five minutes to go, if the Accord is on schedule."

"Which it usually is," added Wolfe. "I suggest we take our places."

They seated themselves in the secondhand viewing chairs before the stage and Rickki put her headset back on. The holo had stabilized to show a neat white room. Six battered red lawn chairs were placed in a row along the side wall, and a stout oak-veneer table strewn with blue and white pamphlets on Tokyo flu stood at the far side beside a door marked MEDICAL STAFF ONLY. A young man in a white coat was pottering about, his eyes flickering nervously this way and that at the small noises of the night.

Rickki squirmed about in her chair to speak to them: "The one in medic's gear—he's the bait. An Institute operative, not a real doctor, needless to say. Hate to waste an honest-to-God quack if anything went wrong. Now then—the intruders will come in through that door there, probably grab him and put him on the table so they can slice him up." She glanced at the Deputy Premier who was fidgeting with a button on his cuff. "As soon as the procedure is sufficiently advanced as to leave no doubt of their intentions, our people come through the door marked Staff and from the utilities room, over here." She pointed at the display. "Stun grenades and automatics. The real danger is timing things wrong."

Beaufort looked up from his shirt cuff. "And then?"

Rickki stared. "And then what, sir?"

"What happens to the intruders?"

"At that point the intruders are noticeably dead. In accordance with the self-defense provisions of the Terrorist Act of 2021. What's left is turned over to an organ clinic for retrieval and disposal."

"Of course. Foolish question." Beaufort returned to his button.

"Tracking a vehicle coming in from the north," called the controller softly. "This may be it, brothers and sisters."

Rickki stared at the screens, a lithe black cat watching a mouse hole. Wolfe found time to admire her slender, muscular form in a detached, aesthetic way. At moments like this, she became a perfectly-tuned battle machine, a peerless field commander. She had come into her own since their Hong Kong days, matured in presence and ability. He silently congratulated himself on his good luck in obtaining her as security chief. A minute passed, two, then motion flickered on the right monitor. A minibus passed the mouth of the alley, slowed, turned and parked to one side. Six small figures, black smudges against the dark background, emerged and huddled together, apparently receiving last-minute directions. After a few moments the leader stepped back and raised both arms in a blessing; the others spread out into a loose vee and advanced with smooth, silent steps on the open door, black devils flitting through the turgid Post Millennium night. All were carrying nine-millimeter machine pistols, slim deadly rods as long as a man's forearm.

The dim figures stepped off the screen and into the holo pickup. With a shock, Wolfe saw the skulking demons of the alley transformed into fresh-faced young-sters—three men and two women, their movements crisp, methodical, efficient. The leader, a blonde young man with a pink face and freshly-ironed black shirt, addressed the operative courteously. "Good evening, doctor. We're Cleaners, preparing the path for Adonai God. I'm afraid we have an account to settle. You have been aiding the forces of uncleanness. Your sin must be purged with a sacrifice of living flesh. As the Pastor says: 'let us not show false mercy, nor seek our-selves to judge the hearts of the wrongdoers.'" He smiled pleasantly and held up a black-gloved hand to show a short, wicked knife with a taped handle and curving blue blade.

The youngsters pinned their victim's arms, hoisted him to the table in the center of the room and cut away his white trousers and jaunty blue-and-red striped underpants while the operative flailed in well-simulated terror and screamed for mercy. Two Cleaners forced his legs apart while a third sprayed pain-enhancer on the exposed pink flesh.

Turning his head, Wolfe saw the Deputy Premier stir uncomfortably in his chair, his knuckles a fishbelly white from gripping the head of his cane so hard. On the stage, two meters away, the holo of the leader moved closer with his knife, menace in every line of his body. "Now brother, we regret, but this is going to hurt. Let us pray: Oh Adonai, bless this sacrifice and accept this sinner into Paradise if you judge him worthy. Amen." He raised the knife and smiled around at his colleagues, reminding Wolfe incongruously of his father preparing to carve a Christmas turkey. He felt his nails biting into his palms. *Now for God's sake, take them out now!*

As the knife began to glide remorselessly towards flesh, Rickki spoke a single quiet word. The holo image flared white and flickered out for a moment as stun grenades exploded. When it cleared, the intruders were staggering and jerking back from the table in a grotesque dance of death, explosive bullets ripping through body armor, chewing out craters of flesh and bone, a stray burst stitching a line of jagged holes up the clinic's rear wall. Then miraculously it was over, five bodies sprawled on the blood-smeared floor, a trace of smoke in the air, and the queasy horror of sudden death in Wolfe's soul. He let out his breath and sat back, his neck damp with sweat. It was over except for disposal: five torn bodies, destined for an anonymous organ clinic, five souls experiencing the White Light or drifting on a dark ocean of oblivion.

Rickki's attention had switched to the screen beside the holo stage; she stared at the blurred gray figures on the monitor, her face so close to the screen it appeared she was trying to crawl inside. Abruptly she sat back and cursed. "Damn, damn and triple damn. We got the driver, but the team leader managed to dodge away. The man must have a charmed life—I had three snipers assigned to him."

"Any chance of cutting off his escape route?" inquired Beaufort, wiping his broad forehead with a red pocket handkerchief.

"At night in a free zone? Not a prayer. And his kidneys I specially wanted, for Mary's sake." Running her hands through her short black hair in vexation she turned back to the holo display and spoke into her headset. "Okay, brothers and sisters all, well done. Get them to a clinic in case any of them still have organs worth retrieving. Then get some rest. Debrief tomorrow at eleven hundred hours." She fixed Beaufort with a glance. "Are you feeling quite well, sir? There's a washroom next door if you'd like to freshen up."

Beaufort shook his heavy gray head and stood, leaning heavily on his cane now, his movements slow and hesitating. "No thank you." He hesitated. "You're right though—the concepts we discussed are shattering in practice. Even so, I'm glad our enemies aren't having it all their way." He motioned Wolfe away as he started to rise. "No, I can see you still have work to do. Just send one of your people to show me the way. And, well done."

Beaufort, Wolfe knew, was not one to waste time on meaningless courtesies. He meant what he said. "Thank you, sir. Sleep well." He bowed and shook hands. "Singh, escort the Deputy Premier to his car if you would."

Rickki watched them until they disappeared through the door of the Ops Room, then took her headset off and stretched in her chair. "It appears he was impressed. And that our defector is serious."

Wolfe made a noncommittal gesture, trying to conceal his jubilation. They desperately needed the edge Mancuso's information might give them. "So it seems, thank Heaven."

"Routine takedown," called the technician; a moment

later the holo flickered out. Wolfe sighed and sat back. "What about a glass of Flash and a breath of air before we turn in, oh Rickki my ferocious friend?"

"I accept with pleasure."

Stars were still twinkling in the western sky when Wolfe unlocked the heavy steel door and stepped outside into the roof garden from which Versailles took its name. The still night air was hot and breathless; a siren wailed in the distance. An almost imperceptible line of gray marked the eastern horizon; in the fraying night, specter-white metal tables and chairs loomed like smudges of ghostly furniture here and there on the terrace. Wolfe lit the candle on the nearest table, placed a bottle of Flash and two snifters on its painted surface while Rickki flopped down into a wicker chair and groaned. "Jesus come quick, I'm so tired."

Wolfe poured two measures, slid one across the table. "Then here's to a good vacation soon."

Rickki sniffed at the Flash appreciatively, took a small sip. "And to an unpleasant job well done."

Wolfe raised his glass then sat back in his chair, fixed his attention on the morning star, blazing white and low in the fading night. "Not a very edifying spectacle was it? A half-dozen kids, brainwashed into thinking they're working for King Adonai. Neatly gutted and disorganized by now I'd guess."

"And the worst of the lot still free and easy out there. The wicked slime—he must be the Devil's own child to have slipped away."

"We'll get him one day. Or Helen will." The morning star seemed to swell and deflate on the horizon; he realized he was very tired.

"Better it was us. I have a personal grudge." Rickki gestured vaguely towards the night-shrouded city. "Funny people, these Accord subscribers. A little over-earnest and preachifying, then someone flips the switch and they turn into monsters. How's it done?"

"They believe too much, and Adonai God is an angry and vengeful deity. Jesus come quick, what's that?" Wolfe jerked his leg back as something soft brushed the skin of his exposed ankle. But it was only the Rooftop Cat, looking for company and handouts. He had become fond of the split-eared old feline over the last few months, sometimes brought him tidbits from the cafeteria, or even opened the window from the fire escape to let him into his apartment for a quick feed and snooze. "No food tonight, old soldier," apologized Wolfe as the cat inquired about a snack with golden eyes. The message apparently got through. With an amiable rub against his leg, the black and white cat disappeared back into the shadows.

Reaction thrilled and buzzed through his blood, postcrisis meltdown. He stirred uncomfortably, trying not to see yet again in his mind's eye the intruders jerking backwards in a red mist, blown by a hail of explosive bullets. The Flash tasted strong and fiery against his palate. "Jesus come quick, it's funny how things turn out. When I joined the Institute, I didn't have it in mind to become an executioner."

"Truly not," agreed Rickki. "You joined to save the world—we all did. Otherwise we wouldn't have been accepted. And we do alright sometimes. Remember when we intercepted that cargo of involuntary organ donors? You opened the boxcar door and they all began to cry, thinking the next stop was the operating table?"

"I remember." Wolfe smiled in the darkness. "And I didn't know enough Mandarin to really explain they were safe."

"No. In fact you said they would be used in a healthy manner, which just convinced them they were goners."

"Another night working for the Institute." Wolfe refilled Rickki's glass and then his own.

"Yeah. And I still remember what Helen said about

that operation. 'Sometimes we have to save the world one individual at a time.' That was good, I thought. So here we are, trying to save the despairing citizens of Upper Canada, one at a time. In the here and now though, I'm not sure we're succeeding." She fell silent for a moment, then Wolfe sensed rather than saw her turn towards him. "Tell me—*are* we succeeding? I'll keep it to myself."

Wolfe hesitated. Rickki was an old and trusted friend; he did not wish to mislead her. "I can't go into numbers. But you can figure it yourself. Food and power reserves are already stretched to the max. The more we cut back, the more Listers join the Accord. Unless we can reverse current trends, the Accord will reach critical mass here by early fall. Now we have Zacky the Zealot to deal with." He grinned at her in the darkness. "But we'll thread the needle somehow, Rickki." As he spoke he felt his own natural optimism assert itself. The Institute had triumphed in harder situations than this, and his team was getting better, tighter all the time.

"Sure we will, boss." Rickki tossed off her Flash at a shot. "And if we don't?"

"I try not to contemplate the possibility," admitted Wolfe. "We just have to have faith in the equations and keep on going." A dawn breeze tickled the yellow candle flame, making it waver and dance. He stared into the tiny flame, considering what he had just said. It occurred to him, not for the first time, that at the Institute too was a religion, or at least a set of beliefs. *I believe in the final truth of sociocybernetics, and in the goodness of our AI, who is dedicated to the betterment of the Human Race. I believe I am doing good and not evil though my actions may be harsh or violent . . .* A credo, propped up by equations and sophisticated science to be sure, but still an act of faith. In which case, how was he superior to the five youngsters he had just helped execute? Or was the word murder? He shivered and finished his Flash in a gulp.

"Oh yeah, I almost forgot." Rickki's voice was thick with fatigue. "We got the test results back for Dulles just before dinner last night. He was having some sort of severe toxic reaction to his medication yesterday morning—hence the weirdness. The shrinks say he'll be back to normal in a few days."

"We should sue BioAge. We could have been walking around minus gonads right now."

"Apparently quite a few people are doing just that—suing BioAge I mean." Rickki yawned loudly. "Here comes another day." She pointed to the east where a thin line of silver light was growing broader.

"Here's to it," agreed Wolfe. He yawned and stood up. "We'd better try and override the adrenals, get some rest."

Adam 100

In different parts of the North American Free Market the displaced and disenfranchised have coalesced into different collective units: gangs, hopper clubs, mutual aid societies and the immensely successful Temple of the Accord. The Lists, however, are an Upper Canadian phenomenon. They came into existence sometime in the first decade of the new millennium, growing up around the web of local social assistance offices which had been decreed just before the final collapse of Canada. These offices served precisely defined areas, and only people resident in that area for at least five years were entitled to benefits. After the Big Bust, no further clients were added to entitlement Lists unless they could prove family ties to people already receiving assistance. A place on the local List was therefore a valuable asset, and a de facto badge of belonging to a given community. In time, the offices themselves became focal points for group activity, and then markers defining a List's geographical area.

The Wounded City, an analysis of urban living
Scribner-Sony, 2023

Friday, July 2
13:30 hours

When Wolfe awoke it was early afternoon. He had slept too long; his new security would be waiting for him in the garage in twenty minutes. After a hasty shower under a trickle of tepid water he dressed in his oyster white Institute formals, knotted a black tie around his neck and tramped downstairs. There was a brief delay while the heavy door separating the living quarters from the offices digested his ID number and grudgingly opened. Now late, Wolfe jogged down the white corridor towards the garage elevator. He preferred to be on time for a first meeting with anyone, especially someone as close as a security blanket. Omaha had almost always been late, but somehow with her it was alright. Punctuality suited him better.

Passing the closed door of the Ops Room he resolutely tried to put the images of the previous night out of his mind. He had seen many unpleasant sights during his career with the Skellig Michael—an orphanage on fire in Bombay, its small inmates leaping in flames from the third-floor windows; the hamburger aftermath of a depressurization accident in Orbital Two, six spacers turned inside out by explosive decompression; the remains of Mary McGee on a crimson hospital gurney—but he had not become calloused. Regrettably. And the deaths last night were no accident, they had taken place at his order. He took the elevator to the garage, hoping to arrive before his new blankie.

Harper Amadeus was waiting by the car. They exchanged greetings, taking stock of each other. Amadeus was a sharp-featured level one of twenty-something years, with skin the color of café au lait and several lifetimes of suspicion in his ancient black eyes. He shut the car door on Wolfe as carefully as if he were an elderly uncle in frail health, slid in behind the wheel and inquired the destination in a soft, shy voice. "Where to, Dr. Wolfe?"

"The Hive, east entrance. And call me Edward if you prefer."

"With respect, sir, you are too senior for such informality."

Wolfe rolled his eyes. You never knew what insolence to expect from level ones these days—or even if it was insolence. He must be getting old faster than he had realized. "With respect my son, you are too junior to make wise decisions on such matters. However, you may call me Dr. Wolfe if it makes you more comfortable."

"Thank you—Dr. Wolfe." Amadeus smiled quietly to himself and raced the white Isuzu up the garage ramp with a loud squeal of rubber.

The car was one of three lightly-armored vehicles hastily acquired from a now-defunct courier service after the debacle with Mary. Their price and basic configuration had been attractive—but they were hideously uncomfortable. In Versailles they had come to be known as the Bouncers. Wolfe hunched miserably in the small back seat, feeling the rage of a caged animal. His legs were cramped, and the hard seat seemed designed to provide maximum discomfort to his fundament.

The obsession with security was new—dating from the black day several weeks ago when one of their best field operatives, Mary McGee, had got into the wrong taxi and shown up an hour later in the emergency ward of Toronto General, victim of an amateur double mastectomy, as the doctor who signed her death certificate had put it in a futile effort to be diplomatic.

Few rational people dared to attack members of the Skellig Michael, thanks to the Institute's well-publicized policy in such cases: any assault brought revenge—immediate, unavoidable and highly unpleasant. Cancers, cholera, incurable mental disorders were the price would-be assailants paid for their overboldness. But Mary's assassins were not rational. They were

Cleaners, the personal terrorists of Zacharian Stele, who had learned his methods in the crucibles of Chicago, Buenos Aires and Kampala. So now all Institute staff took elaborate security precautions, and lived with a new fear. Wolfe wondered if the tension was beginning to take its toll on him. He had not been sleeping well lately, and his dreams seemed fraught and claustrophobic: trapped in a car spinning out of control, or frozen in nightmare paralysis as the walls of some huge impersonal building closed in.

The upcoming meeting did nothing to put him at ease. He would have to go carefully, making Adam 100 think there would be tangible rewards for turning his organization against the Accord without actually saying as much. The more he considered his task, the harder it seemed. Also, on a personal level, he did not particularly enjoy exercises involving outright deception. No matter what he or anyone else said, subsidies would not be coming back. It was one thing to hedge and employ innuendo, another to lie outright. Foolish considerations, perhaps, but humans were foolish about some things. It was one of the things that made them human. Sometimes anyway. *You're too squeamish brother. This is the world that vaporized Omaha, remember?*

When they reached their destination, Wolfe sprang out of the Bouncer and stretched his legs, feeling as if he had been released from prison. "Meet me inside in exactly two hours please. If I need you sooner I'll call." Amadeus nodded acknowledgment and sped off into the traffic.

He strode across the granite flagstones, past a broken fountain, its bowl dry and cracked, and pushed through the revolving glass doors of the Hive, the huge and now half-abandoned government complex that had grown up around Queen's Park in the years after Quebec and the Prairie Coalition had washed away from the wreck of Canada to become independent states.

Its gray concrete towers marched away east and west, linked by underground passages at various levels. It was said a person could walk the Hive's tunnels from the legislature to beyond the western boundaries of the University of Toronto two klicks away. Wolfe could well believe it. He had once taken a wrong turning and found himself hopelessly lost. In a particularly stubborn mood, he had set himself to find his way out again without help. It had been an eerie several hours. As he walked the deserted corridors he had begun to imagine unseen, hostile presences staring out from the dark offices. He had been glad when a turn in the winding neon-lit labyrinth brought him back to the main elevators once more.

He was not the only one to feel the strangeness of the sub-basements. Legend had it that an assistant archivist had once disappeared on the lower levels, where the shelters from the Scare of '07 stood still and vacant. Night watchmen occasionally claimed to see her, wandering the tunnels, always disappearing around a bend before she could be reached—a sort of clerical Flying Dutchman.

Wolfe crossed the Hive's unwashed lobby, his footsteps echoing in the high, empty space. A huge golden maple leaf, now tarnished and bespattered with footprints, was inlaid in the marble floor. As always, he felt a pang of sadness for his now-lost country of birth. He walked carefully around the maple leaf to the bank of elevators, most decorated with fading black and yellow OUT OF ORDER signs, waited five minutes while the two functioning lifts shuttled mysteriously back and forth between the tenth and sixteenth floors, then decided to take the stairs. No doubt the exercise would do him good.

Pausing on the tenth floor to catch his breath he smiled sourly at the irony of the situation. Despite the desperate levels of unemployment, there were not enough technicians to keep the complex systems of the city—the elevators, the sewers, the telcom grid—functioning. Jobs, jobs everywhere, and few with skills to fill them. How in hell was the Institute ever going to breathe life into the carcass of Upper Canada? Sometimes when he perused the equations he could believe in such a resurrection. When confronted with the decaying reality he did not.

Reaching the seventeenth floor, he pushed through the creaky fire door and into the austere tan corridor that led to Wu's office. Few people were in evidence: a cleaning 'bot, its red paint chipped, a maintenance woman in a dirty yellow smock, stern and aloof in the consciousness of her status as a full-time employee. Through glass doors, set at intervals along the corridors, he glimpsed rows and rows of vacant offices, the empty combs where the Hive's now-departed drones had been accustomed to swarm and buzz before the massive dislocations of the Bust. On impulse Wolfe pushed through one of the glass doors, sat down in one of the gray cubicles and tried to imagine what the office had been like at its busiest, phones ringing, couriers coming and going, people chattering as they passed each other between cubicles. Now—nothing. The silence was heavy, oppressive, the air had a nose-itching dusty quality. He regained the main corridor with a feeling of relief.

At its far end was the outer sanctum of the under secretary. Wolfe pushed through the tall pine doors, eliciting a squeal from the unoiled hinges, and nodded to her personal assistant, a tall stork of a man with a tiny blond goatee and the unlikely name of Julius Hinkley-Dextermunt. "You have an appointment, sir?" inquired Hinkley-Dextermunt, eyeing Wolfe as if he was a perfect stranger rather than a daily visitor. "Yes? I will see if the under secretary is available. Kindly take a chair."

Wolfe submitted to the bureaucratic ritual, remaining outwardly impassive, while privately thanking his stars—or whatever cosmic agency was responsible— his dealings with Hinkley-Dextermunt were minimal. His Institute profile showed a low threshold of patience in human interactions, a deficit which even intensive training had failed to completely rectify. In plain language, he did not suffer fools gladly.

After a brief pause Hinkley-Dextermunt returned. "The under secretary will see you now," he announced in a shrill voice, and flung open the door leading to the inner office with the resentful air of an art expert showing a masterpiece to an oafish millionaire who might be able to buy art, but could never appreciate its true worth. As he passed through the open door, Wolfe entertained a brief and pleasing mental image of himself emptying a bowl of cold porridge over Hinkley-Dextermunt's oval head. It would be a waste of good food he told himself regretfully as the door clicked shut behind him.

The delicate task of matching Institute personnel to their government counterparts had been handled directly by Helen. After a thorough search of the data base, the AI had recommended Irene Wu, an obscure civil servant in urban planning, as Wolfe's liaison and civil service linkage to Project Maldon. Not without some bureaucratic grumbling and grinding, Wu was promoted to under secretary and transferred to Ministry of State.

To outward appearances she was a placid, middle-aged lady. In reality however, the under secretary was a wily veteran bureaucrat and better yet, a master of devious strategy who could effortlessly put her plump fingers on the nerve nodes of the mindless, shambling beast that was Upper Canada's government and make it dance.

After five minutes' acquaintance, Wolfe had decided that he liked Wu. Two years into the project, this quick judgment had been confirmed and amplified. She was not only a shrewd and pragmatic ally, she had become a friend as well.

Like most of his friends, she had one mild eccentricity: in her case, a consuming passion for seafood. Wolfe had become an accessory in this affair of the palate. Many times in the past year they had wound up the long day at some hole-in-the-wall eatery, sampling everything from tank-farmed oysters to Seven Fish Treasures with Good Fortune sauce, as often as not with her husband and twins—who hated seafood with a burning pubescent hatred—glumly in tow.

Wu, plump and impassive as a female Buddha, greeted Wolfe from behind her uncluttered desk with her customary bland smile. "Good day, Edward. Some tea? It's fresh-brewed."

Wolfe made the ritual response. "In that case, with pleasure."

Wu poured two cups from a delicate porcelain pot and slid one across the desk, wafting a fresh jasmine scent to him. "How does this July day find you?" she asked.

"A trifle breathless." Wolfe seated himself, admired once again the collection of delicate pastel landscapes which glowed like jewels on the under secretary's gray government-issue walls. That Wu had bought these beautiful things to brighten her drab office endeared her immensely to him.

"The elevators?" Wu nodded in sympathy. "They've been out for two days now. I tell myself the climb makes for better security and aids digestion as well. Speaking of digestion, I discovered an excellent new restaurant two nights ago while strolling around the market area. The Mad Monkfish."

"Is it safe to walk there at night?"

"Oh yes, since they increased the patrols. Anyway, my family was with me. Both my sons are black belts, as you know."

Wolfe grinned at the mental picture of the under secretary's long suffering husband and sons trailing through the neon nights of Chinatown, guarding their mother on her quest for new chefs and new recipes. "Any specialties?"

"Soft-shell crab, in a superb garlic sauce, with just a hint of ginger for zest. Grown locally, and excellent." Wu nodded approvingly, then became brisk. "But to business. The time of our meeting with Adam 100 approaches, and I have no idea what we are to talk about. I know only that he represents some new Lister faction and has an ambitious set of demands. Beyond that, nothing. Mr. Beaufort said that you would brief me personally."

"Very well." Wolfe wondered how the under secretary would react to the latest ploy in the elaborate sociocybernetic game that was Project Maldon. He regretted having to embroil her in this latest tortuous turn of policy, but there was no option; it was up to him to implement Helen's directives. He settled back in his chair, folded his hands and spoke in his driest voice. "In a sense the timing of this meeting is fortuitous."

"Indeed?" said Wu dubiously. "How so?"

"Recent entitlement cuts are pushing an unprecedented number of Listers over to the Accord. The trend must be reversed before the Accord population here reaches critical mass. We need, so to speak, a counterbalance."

Wu sighed and placed her cup silently back in its saucer. "I see. So this meeting is to explore whether Adam 100's group might be useful as a . . . counterbalance?"

"In a very informal, tentative way—yes. We need, at minimum, to hear what the group wants and what it can offer in return." Wolfe watched the under secretary narrowly but could discern no flicker of reaction. She had a trick of making her face so impassive that it seemed a porcelain mask with two green stones for eyes.

"My presence suggests this meeting reflects official policy," mused Wu. "Is that the case?"

"Our policies remain as before." Wolfe made an airy gesture. "We will begin by pointing out a political truism to Adam 100: the Exodus Faction can expect nothing if it loses all its membership to the Accord. The smaller a faction, the smaller its piece of pie."

"And if the pie has already been devoured?"

Wolfe ignored the comment and sipped his tea. "The point is this: if the Lists—or any subset thereof—want to keep any entitlements or negotiating position whatever, they must find a way to stop the Accord's recruiting drive."

"I see." Wu blinked. "Specifically, what do you want me to say or do?"

"As little as possible. Acknowledge that some entitlements may be kept in place, or cuts postponed under certain conditions. Agree to review Adam 100's requests at a suitable level. Promise nothing and make no concessions."

"Needless to say." Wu blinked at a spot in the middle distance, her habit when about to disagree with someone. "I am not an expert in SoCy, Edward, so I can only argue based on common sense. With the greatest respect, the approach you outline may be dangerous. The Lists are volatile enough as it is. There are millions of people out there who have an unquestioning religious faith in their right to be fed and cared for. Since this supposed right has been taken from them they are simmering with aimless, undirected rage. The last thing we want is to encourage a group of dedicated activists to channel and direct that rage."

"It could profitably be directed towards the Accord, if the result was a decline in recruiting," suggested Wolfe.

"What if the result is a full-scale civil war?"

"Presumably the Accord would be too busy fighting to woo many new recruits." Wolfe smiled to show he was not entirely serious.

"It is a cynical exercise, to say the least."

"As are most political exercises," noted Wolfe, putting his cup gently back in its saucer, which was decorated with a pattern of delicate blue and white cranes. "The Deputy Premier believes it's worth a try. So does Orbital."

Wu held up her chubby hands, palms out, in a gesture of inevitability. "One day soon I will retire and take up fish farming, I swear it. Did you know you can produce twenty mature carp a week in an average basement with the new techniques? Come then, to the fray." She led the way down the corridor, then opened the door into a typical, anonymous government meeting room, the gray upholstery on the chairs worn and burnished by the ponderous hams of a thousand senior bureaucrats, the beige rug rorschached into a frightening subliminal threat by a thousand faded blots of acid government coffee. Through the floor-to-ceiling windows Wolfe could see the nondescript urban wreckage of the Eastern Free Zone, and due south the poisoned lake, cobalt blue against the teeming urban shore.

On one side of the long table sat Adam 100, an extremely handsome man in his early forties, with a cap of dark curly hair, clear blue eyes and a strong jaw. He acknowledged Wolfe's greeting with a curt nod and shifted his gaze back out the window. Beside him was a streetling of eighteen or nineteen, a long scar across her left cheek and the bloody rose tattoo of the Renegade List blossoming low on her right shoulder, just above the strip of black spandex covering her full breasts—presumably his assistant. Rank, reflected Wolfe, had its privileges, even among the Lists.

According to the meager dossier assembled by Orbital, Adam 100 had appeared about two years ago, vomited from the belly of the free zones like some latter-day Jonah to torment the citizens of the Post Millennium. His real name was unknown. Rumor had it that he had suddenly given up an executive job with a biotech company to become a food activist—one more mysterious Post Millennium figure who had suddenly heard an inner call.

Wolfe crossed the room, noting Adam 100's chainmail shirt, his leather apron and lightweight fighting boots, a green scalp lock protruding through a brass ring. Seating himself opposite the Lister activist, he poured a glass of mineral water from one of the plastic bottles on the table and settled back. His strategy was straightforward enough: hint at concessions in return for a slowdown in Accord recruiting. The challenge was to play his hand slowly, not to seem too eager.

Wu seated herself at the head of the table and addressed Adam 100 and his assistant: "Thank you for joining us today sir and madam. Is there any particular agenda you wish to follow, or do you prefer an informal discussion?"

Adam 100 leaned on the table, revealing a red biohazard symbol tattooed on his right forearm, and spoke in a powerful, deep voice: "Let's cut the crap, brothers and sisters. This isn't a discussion, it's an ultimatum. I represent the Exodus Faction, and we are here to present our demands for the first, last and only time before we shed serious blood. Am I talking to the right people or not?" He glowered across the table at them.

Wu nodded judiciously. "We are certainly in a

position to evaluate your needs and recommend government action. Perhaps you could begin by telling us about your organization—the Exodus Faction I believe it's called."

"You want our zeitgeist? Listen then." Adam 100 bared his teeth in a ferocious smile. "The Exodus Faction accepts that the good times are coming to an end. The Lists have too many natural enemies, they're not focused enough to fight back. Our problem is, we don't like what comes after. Our members don't want to turn into Accord toadies, nor settle in your accursed hubs and settlements."

"Why not?" asked Wolfe. "Jobs are available, and they carry health benefits, food and pure cash. And training. No one need starve, or even be particularly uncomfortable."

"Snot juice brother, that's what they earn at your hubs. A handful of slime." Adam 100 wiped his nose on the back of his hand, his hand on the table, leaving a long wet smear to signify his contempt of the concept. "Our members don't want to go back to Robot Time, not one jot." He referred to an era in Lister mythology when all people worked day and night, robots in factories, before taking the mystical road to freedom.

Wolfe stared at the trail of mucus. "Then what do you want?"

"In the short term, our entitlements as before: medical, food and brewing allowances. In the longer term a place of our own, and seats on the Mars shuttles when they come. We're gonna start a new way of being in our own promised land. Hence our name, brother—Exodus Faction. We're getting out."

The demands, reflected Wolfe, were not dissimilar from those of a thousand other millennial groups. Nor were they entirely unreasonable from a Lister point of view. It was time to inject a conciliatory note into the discussion. He leaned his arms on the table and spoke in his most sympathetic tones: "No one wants the Lists to suffer or go back to Robot Time. But look at the whole picture. Your numbers are plummeting. If the Accord keeps snapping up names at this rate, the Lists will be extinct in a year or two. How can the government protect entitlements under those circumstances? It would be political suicide."

Adam 100 scowled. "No one from Exodus is joining the Accord. It's the squids and the flatliners that are jumping."

"But how can the government distinguish between your members and the List jumpers?" asked Wolfe.

Adam 100 drew his belt knife, a three-inch stiletto of plasteel, and began cleaning his fingernails with exaggerated care. "You can't distinguish between us, brother. We come from all Lists. We're everywhere and yet invisible. To paraphrase the late, great Chairman Mao, 'We swim in an ocean of the people.' Makes it hard to target us, see?"

"Please understand our dilemma," interjected Wu in her calm voice. "The government knows nothing of the Exodus Faction. It does know that the Accord has converted over three hundred thousand Listers since spring. Unless this trend can be reversed—and very obviously reversed at that—there is not much chance of your gaining concessions. I say this not to cause resentment but to clarify the situation."

Adam 100 stared at them with ferocious blue eyes. "I see. And if the Accord's recruiting drive stalled?"

"Then naturally the situation would be open to review." Wolfe met Adam 100's stare calmly. "It is only common sense. If the situation changes, the government must rethink its policies."

There was a long silence, then Adam 100 nodded and resheathed his stiletto with a flourish. "Remember your words, Dr. Wolfe. We'll meet again soon, because the Accord will not siphon any more names off the Lists. But if you don't keep your promises, beware!"

Wu raised a plump hand. "We make no promises, Mr. Adam 100, and we do not respond to threats. We are, however, reasonable people. If you have nothing else to add, I suggest we adjourn." She pressed a button on the table and two gray-clad government security agents appeared as if by magic at the far end of the room.

Wolfe and Wu rose and bowed. With a nod, Adam 100 strode from the room, followed by his assistant. Watching their retreating backs, he wondered what he had let loose on Upper Canada. He had executed Helen's orders well, that much he knew. The meeting would have repercussions, desirable or not.

He shook off his sense of foreboding and consulted his watch. Almost four o'clock on a Friday afternoon— and no more official appointments until Monday. There was nothing except the usual glut of work to prevent him taking Helen's advice and going to the cottage. Well then! He would tumble some clothes and a portable console into his kit bag, whistle up Amadeus and escape this siren-haunted steaming labyrinth for the fragile refuge of the country.

Airport

During the so-called Big Bust, the economy shrank about 40 percent. Families, towns, entire regions were laid to waste. Prosperity turned to abject poverty across North America and millions died in the consequent civil disorders. Enter Pastor Henry Stele, dynamic and ruthless young leader of the Temple of the Accord—monster, madman or Messiah, depending on one's point of view. In a few short and bloody weeks he rose to absolute power within the Accord. His guiding philosophy was simple: he promised jobs and security for the Faithful, relentless war against the enemies of the Temple—in order of priority, the welfare classes, the degenerate liberals who created them and finally the Islamic Coalition, which had coiled like a snake around the Christian world during the long sleep of the righteous. Both promises he kept.

The Temple of the Accord—A Brief History

Monday, July 5
04:50 hours

Wolfe stepped out on the balcony of his cottage and drew a breath of cool, pine-scented air deep into his lungs. Dawn was painting the feathery clouds in the east a delicate pink, like a huge feather boa muffling the horizon. Below him spread the flat black mirror of the lake. Soon the sun would burn off the clouds, rise into a clear blue sky, and another flawless lake day would commence.

He would not be here to see it. Arriving too soon, Monday morning had sounded its call to duty, summoning him back into the city's greasy heart. The cottage demanded his presence; he felt an almost overpowering reluctance to leave. He forced himself to step inside and activate the advanced and quite illegal security system that had been installed by BioAge for his sister when she had taken a mini-sabbatical here two years ago. He checked again that the weapons banks were armed, pocketed the remote and locked the control console. Slinging his overnight bag across his shoulder he looked around the familiar pine-paneled room as a soldier going off to war looks at the sleeping family he is leaving behind, and closed the door gently behind him, as if not to wake the cottage.

In the growing gray light he picked his way down the dew-wet path to the boathouse, went aboard the catamaran, tossed his overnight bag into the cabin and mounted the four steps to the boat's low bridge. The small inboard started with a sputter and a puff of diesel smoke. Wolfe backed the cat out into deep water, aimed it at the far shore and told the console to unfurl the main sail. With a low whine of electric motors the pale blue nylon sail billowed in the light breeze and the vessel began to skate across the black water of the bay towards Harvey's Marina, the hardened lakeside facility where Amadeus was waiting. Settling back in the cushions, one hand on the cold brass wheel, the other on a cup of coffee he tried to concentrate on enjoying his final moments of solitude, the lake-damp wind against his face, the cathedral expanse of cloud-ribbed purple sky vaulting above. It was no good. Ahead of him, beyond the diminishing stretch of dark water, beyond the winding road to the city, lay danger, perhaps even death. With reluctance he turned his attention to the half-guessed risks confronting him.

Danger lurked within and without, or so it seemed. The danger within was more frightening because it had no precedent and no definitive form. He had spent a long Saturday reviewing the major nodes in Project Maldon's massive code, and had come away dissatisfied. It was impossible to do a proper analysis without more time and proper crunching facilities—ideally an AI. But his quick sweep had shown several apparent anomalies. Oversights? Errors? Helen was not prone to either. Should he report them and see what happened, or should he dig further, until he had a solid case? A case against who? If Helen, then he was on dangerous ground indeed. On the other hand, his suspicions could well be unfounded—in which case he would seem a proper fool if he started demanding an investigation into the codes. Perhaps it was better to play a waiting game for now. Not for the first time he wondered if he was too cautious, too tentative, too apt to flinch at imaginary dangers. Yet surely caution was a wise policy in the Post Millennium, a survival trait even? Omaha had been bold and carefree; now she was a handful of radioactive dust and a lingering smell of perfume on a T-shirt in his bottom drawer. Mary had not been cautious, at least not cautious enough . . .

At least the danger without was clear. Last night, checking his console after a solitary but excellent dinner of roast lamb, washed down by red wine, he had found a short item which drained away his sense of well-being and left him thoughtful and apprehensive.

The item was simple, a note redirected from his personal node:

> *Meet me at my residence, two o'clock this Wednesday. The address: Penthouse, Salvation Tower, Accord Main Campus. Time and place firm. No show will signify a lack of further interest. Tell the guard at the gate you are visiting me. Security completely guaranteed. RSVP. Nicolas Mancuso.*

The guarantee underlined his fears rather than calming them. Non-subscribers entered Accord facilities at their own risk—and some did not return. Wolfe sipped his coffee and considered. The matter would have to be referred to security of course, but he had an intuition it would be cleared. Mancuso's information was just too important.

From behind Granite Island three klicks down the bay a black speedboat appeared, a white arrow of foam at its bows. It was too early for lake traffic. Wolfe frowned and lifted the pair of high-powered binoculars from its rack under the chart drawer. The man standing at the wheel looked a lot like his oldest friend "Mac"—now Dr. Andrew MacGregor, fellow of the Royal College of Physicians and Surgeons, et cetera—country squire and medical director of a hardened rural rehab clinic for rich fatties and other disabled gentry of the PM. Wolfe squinted through the binoculars, trying to bring the face into sharp focus. The delicate dawn light, the fine wisps of mist rising from the dark water defeated his purpose.

It didn't pay to take chances, even in the country. He set the autopilot, scrambled down the cabin, loaded his Chang and brought it up to the bridge where he placed it unobtrusively by his leg and raised the binoculars again. The launch, a powerful cruiser, was closing fast, and even in the slanting dawn light he now recognized the cheery square features of Andy MacGregor. Wolfe issued a command and the sail obediently rolled itself into the hollow mast. He cut the engine and put out plastic shocks while his friend maneuvered alongside the catamaran.

Two meters off his port beam Mac cut the engine and waved cheerily. " Morning brother. Permission to come aboard?" He tossed a line which Wolfe caught and warped to the deck cleat, so that the two craft bobbed gently in tandem. The launch was a low black and red vessel of fiberglass construction, with raked bows suggesting high speed. Its name, *Slim Sister*, was painted on the bow in airy white script, and underneath in neat type, *Vitality Island Clinic, Georgian Bay*.

Mac hopped nimbly aboard the catamaran. He was an excellent advertisement for his own clinic, with the flat waist and thick upper body of a weightlifter obvious beneath his blue denim shirt. Despite his wrestler's physique, his face was boyish and open under an untidy thatch of red hair. He stood on the deck, broad hands on hips, and took several deep, appreciative breaths as if preparing for some aerobic exercise. "Still sailing the old cat I see? Isn't she a bit slow?"

Wolfe shrugged. "She's actually quite nimble if there's any wind at all. Besides, I'm in no hurry to get to and from the island."

His friend peered down into the dark cabin, straightening up with a chuckle. "You know, I still remember your father building this thing."

Wolfe grinned too at the memory of the furious curses that would sound from the workshop in the early days of his father's last great project. "Yes. And I remember you trying to seduce Kim down below one fine July night, the summer it was finally launched."

Mac threw his head back and laughed merrily. "I'm afraid she was more interested in the molecular origins of the male physiological response than in me personally. How is Kim?"

"Still in Paris, working for BioAge."

"Good for her. Next time you're chatting, ask her why stock prices are so wobbly. I crashed with BioAge Preferred last month and I'm still aching." Mac pointed an admonitory finger at him. "And you—why don't you ever come to see us while you're here? I shouldn't have to chase you across the lake at dawn just to have a chat."

"Sorry." Wolfe was abashed. "Every time I get here I mean to visit, then I get working and suddenly it's Monday."

"Too much stress," declared Mac. "You need a rest cure. Get your AI thingie to send you to us for a week. You'd go back to the city a new man."

Wolfe grinned. "And you'd stay behind in the country, a richer man."

"The only place to be, my friend." Mac flashed perfect white teeth. "The day of the city is over. You Institute types may not accept it yet, but polite society has already reverted to the Dark Ages model—what's left of the middle class now huddles within its keeps while the barbarians whet their swords outside."

"That's overly pessimistic surely?"

"Not at all." Mac shook his head emphatically. "Your own island for instance—is it undefended?"

Wolfe fingered the remote for the laser system in his jacket pocket, said nothing.

"No, I didn't think so." Mac turned to the east as the disc of the sun slid like a fiery angel over the horizon. "Ah well, Dark Ages or not, I welcome the new day. And a business day at that." He performed a ritual bow towards the rising sun and then shook hands solemnly with Wolfe.

"And I have business in the city," said Wolfe. It occurred to him that, for a city-dwelling office worker, he had seen an undue number of sunrises recently.

"Understood." Mac jumped back on board his launch and Wolfe cast off. "Next time you're coming up you call me, you hear? We'll have some fun." His engine started with a deep bass roar. Wolfe watched, not without envy, as his friend swung the powerboat in a wide curve and sped back up the bay. With a sigh he regained the bridge and set sail once more for the marina.

The catamaran had drifted slightly off course. He aligned the sharp black pontoons with the tall flagpole that marked the north end of the marina and raised the sail. A brisk half-hour cruise brought him to within hailing distance of Harvey's Marina. Heaving to twenty meters from the yellow-painted boom that guarded the entrance to the harbor he punched this week's code into the remote. The boom slid back and Wolfe eased the vessel through, conscious of the half-minute time limits imposed on tenants during off hours. He maneuvered into his slip, moored and retrieved his bag from the cabin. From behind the tin-roofed shack at the end of the dock crept a tall, thin figure in camouflage fatigues, a Chang assault rifle in his hands. Wolfe recognized Romeo—Harvey's third son—who had apparently drawn the early shift, and waved a greeting. The boy waved back to him and returned to the warmth of the shack.

Amadeus was waiting for him beyond the black razor-wire fence that marked the outside perimeter of the marina. His blanket greeted him tersely, shut him in the back seat, and drove in blessed silence through tumble-down villages and along cool avenues of dark evergreens, the smell of pine sharp and fresh in his nostrils. Hunched on the torn green plastic of the back seat Wolfe plugged in his console and began to prepare himself for the week ahead.

As they neared the beleaguered city, a sense of oppression began to weigh on his spirit. It was like driving from heaven to hell in a few short hours: behind him black water and cool air, before him parched concrete and the ever-present shadow of sudden violence. The potholes on the unrepaired highway began to rattle and shake the lightly-sprung Isuzu, making further work impossible. He closed his console and settled himself to speculate on why Morgan Fahaey was coming to Upper Canada.

Three explanations presented themselves. First, she might be a special agent, sent by Helen to check on his performance, assess his fitness to continue with Project Maldon—or even with the Institute. He had made no secret of his concern about recent initiatives; he had gone so far as to investigate Helen, if his weekend review of project codes could be so described. Quite possibly the AI had also decided to investigate him. Second possibility: she might be here on some covert mission which had no relation whatever to Project Maldon or himself. Finally of course, she could be exactly what Helen said she was: a souped-up interface expert, ordered here to provide Helen with a suprarational view from the ground—whatever that might be. In which case, why was Helen so insistent that he meet and greet her? She did nothing without a reason, although the reason was often incomprehensible to a human mind.

Was she trying to remind him of the fact that the Institute had many projects besides Maldon, all of them important? The Interface Project had been underway for five years, its object to make Helen's awesome intellect more available to members of the Institute by making the AI itself more human, more able to grasp and answer the unasked or implicit questions of her human colleagues. At least as important, an improved interface would, it was hoped, allow Helen to translate her AI's insights into some human equivalent—to give people, as one expert put it, a taste of her soul. *Which is all very well, but what's it got to do with you, Long Eddie? Keep thinking.*

Perhaps she had a special reason for wanting him to meet Fahaey—a catalytic meeting of minds? A lesson she could teach him, or he her? He had called up records of Fahaey's last several exhibitions. Certainly her work was delightful, with a bold semi-abstract style. But again, what was that to him? Wolfe pulled at his beard in perplexity then stopped himself. At their last meeting Helen asked his opinion of the theory that beard-tugging, mustache-twirling and similar behaviors were actually ritualized forms of masturbation. He had rejected the concept at the time, but now he found himself self-conscious. With a sigh he drummed his fingers on the plastic upholstery instead, wondering what finger-drumming was a substitute for. It was not always easy working for an AI.

They reached the airport ten minutes before the flight was due. Amadeus, who had still not said a word, parked in a secure zone and opened the door. Wolfe put on his sunbands and stepped out of the car into the blast-furnace of the airport parking lot. It was just after nine, but already the pavement shimmered under a searing white sky; heat sucked at his lungs and hammered down on his head as he started towards the glass terminal buildings, Amadeus an unobtrusive shadow several meters behind him.

The smell of jet fuel wafted on a hard, dry wind, the nagging whine and boom of jet engines triggered a flashback: it had been on just such a white-hot day that he had driven Omaha to the airport to board the

flight to Teheran. Wolfe shook his head impatiently.
That was then, in another country. This was now, and
he was about to meet Morgan Fahaey, fellow level
two and a member of the Weird Brigade with seven
lost years grinning out from her file. He aimed a savage kick at a crumpled paper bag in his path and
walked on.

Inside, the crowded building was an inferno, stoked
with perspiring travelers dragging suitcases like pen-
ances behind them as they lined for boarding passes,
lined again for security and health clearance. The air
smelled of sweat and unwashed bodies. Children cried
and Listers pleaded, the bolder ones plucking at
Wolfe's trouser legs as he made his way through the
human termite nest to the international level, keeping a wary eye out for pickpockets and hoppers.

He reached Arrivals and consulted the screen there.
The Seoul flight had set down five minutes ago,
together with sub-orbitals from Rome, Moscow and
Calcutta. It would be a long wait.

Wolfe found a free quarter-meter of metal rail and
parked himself. For security reasons, Fahaey's meager file had not included a picture. "She'll know you,"
Helen had replied tersely when he asked how he was
to identify her. He sighed and turned his full attention to the tired, disheveled passengers emerging from
the futile rituals of Customs and Immigration. Was
she perhaps the grim, athletic woman with the shaved
head, or the pale scarecrow with wild brown hair and
pocked cheeks? Both passed by without a glance.
Passenger after passenger filtered by, ten, fifty, one
hundred. After about twenty minutes, the frosted glass
door opened to reveal a slim woman of medium height
who scanned the crowd with almost feline concentration, then walked over to him, a faint half-smile
on her lips as if she too found the scenario ridiculous.

Wolfe's first impression was of an English folk song come to life: long, dark hair, high cheekbones, wide mouth painted a deep red. Her eyes were startling: one was a dark blue, almost violet, while the other was dead black and oddly expressionless, reminding him incongruously of a camera lens. She put down her case, fixed him with an intent stare as if registering every detail of his appearance, then held out a slim hand. "Dr. Wolfe I presume? Thank you for meeting me." Her accent was mid-Atlantic, neutral with perhaps a tiny trace of something else.

Wolfe took her hand, subliminally aware of cool soft skin, long fingers. His brain and nervous system had slammed into overdrive and were racing in different directions. Many women were beautiful, charming, intelligent. A very few he had met stepped neatly around all these categories. Something about them fit a special lock on a deep chromosomal level in his brain. They were—*right*. Morgan was right, absolutely too right. His frontal lobes clamored to know why, while the ancient reptilian brain wordlessly growled that it did not care. He managed to conceal his turmoil with commonplace courtesy. "Just Edward please. Allow me." He took her small leather grip, gestured towards the exit. "Stay close to me. This place can be a bit crawly. Is this your first time in Upper Canada, Ms. Fahaey?"

"Call me Morgan." Falling into step, she turned her intense violet gaze on him. "I've meant to visit before, but circumstances prevented."

"A pity. Why now, if I may ask?"

Morgan gestured with a slim, competent hand. Short nails, no rings. Which meant nothing these days— she might have a half-dozen nuptial studs stapled through her labia; you never quite knew in the PM. "In connection with the Interface Project. Helen has asked me to scan certain things into her system—

artifacts, situations and so on—and discuss them with her."

Wolfe decided to probe her cover story. "You're an interface expert then?"

She made a deprecating gesture. "That sounds far too grand. I'm more what you might think of as an interpreter. I explain things to Helen. Art for instance."

"It sounds intriguing. How did you come by that specialty?"

"The usual way. Helen recruited me."

Wolfe smiled, amused by her simple evasion as much as by her answer. "And how do you explain art to an AI?"

"As to a bright child perhaps. With great thought and delicacy. What boggles an AI is often the arbitrariness of art. They can't understand how or why a given image—a fish let's say—is at one time shown as a pure compositional element and another time as a symbol of early Christianity. And elsewhere just as a fish."

Her response had the elusive ring of truth to it. Perhaps, mused Wolfe, she was indeed exactly what Helen said she was. On the other hand, if she was something else, her myth would be well rehearsed. "You're an artist yourself?"

"A dauber only."

"Surely more than that. I took the opportunity to look up some of your work. It's quite delightful."

Morgan shrugged modestly. "Thank you. Actually I think of myself more as an art teacher."

"Indeed? Do you have many pupils?"

"Only one. Helen. I'm trying to teach her to become a holo designer, specializing in artificial environments."

Wolfe glanced at her but she did not appear to be joking. "Now that would be something to witness. When can we expect an exhibition?"

"Within a year I should think. Maybe less."

Wolfe raised his eyebrows, now genuinely interested,

but Morgan made a dismissive gesture. "It may be premature to discuss it at this stage."

"Understood." Obscurely disappointed, Wolfe launched another subject: "By the way, we've arranged discreet private lodgings as requested. You'll be staying in an old middle-class neighborhood, a bit decayed but quite safe. I gather the landlady is an eccentric. Used to be an activist of some note, now a bit addled. Safe enough though."

"Meaning she probably won't kill me in the night for my personal belongings?" Morgan tossed her hair back and laughed.

You didn't see hoppers 'til the last nanosecond, if at all. Wolfe caught a sudden flicker of movement out of the corner of his eye as he turned his head to speak, coming in from left and above, a blur of motion over the shuffling crowd, razor in left hand, raised for the slash that would cut away purse—and usually muscle and bone as well—as he bounded past. Reflexively Wolfe ducked and snapped out his right leg in a lunging upward back kick which caught the incoming hopper square with the double force of his own momentum. Something broke; the hopper's fluid descent changed into a crumpling fall, a rag doll tumbling in seeming slow motion through the crowd, bringing down a pair of businessmen, as he pinwheeled out of control.

An alarm screamed at the edge of ultrasonic range as someone pulled the pin on a personal security device. The hopper came to rest, unconscious beside a gray granite pillar, curved steel razor a meter away on the floor, red-plastic jump boots still straining at high thrust. There was an eerie moment of stillness, then Wolfe saw Amadeus reholster his eleven millimeter and step discreetly back into the crowd, saw Airport Security in their olive uniforms approaching. The people who had been knocked over stood up, stolidly recovered their luggage and began to move on without a glance for the stunned hopper. Wolfe decided to do likewise; there was no point in being detained, and the nature of the situation was self-evident. The hopper would be beaten and ejected from the airport. A week later, if he lived, he would be back.

Wolfe looked thoughtfully at Morgan. She had stepped neatly away from the attack with a lightning economy of motion that suggested fine reflexes tuned by much training. The hopper would have missed her—and she was well placed for a counterstrike too. Interesting. "Sorry about that," he said shortly. "We'd better go."

Morgan fell into step beside him. "Was I the target just then?"

"Quite possibly." Wolfe looked back, but they had already lost sight of the hopper in the crowd.

"In that case—thank you. Helen said you were unusual." Wolfe laughed. "Just lucky that time."

"Nothing wrong with lucky." She fixed him again with that unnerving stare, then suddenly smiled—a genuine warm grin which transformed her face into that of someone who could conceivably be a friend or maybe something more.

The boarding house was a few blocks west of Avenue Road in what had once been a comfortable middle-class neighborhood. Like the rest of the city it had decayed with the years. The quiet streets were potholed and the windows of several houses were boarded over, knee-high tangles of weeds where neat green lawns had once flourished. It reminded Wolfe of the neighborhood where he had grown up.

Morgan rang the bell; it was answered almost immediately by the landlady, an elderly woman with a thin suspicious face, who inspected him with eyes like little iron buttons. She had, Wolfe noticed, a small female symbol tattooed in red on her left cheek. Behind her, he glimpsed a dark-paneled hallway, giving onto a living room, its furniture ghostly under dust sheets, rows of sculptures of female forms gathering dust on their shelves. A signed, framed photo of Germaine Greere presided over the vestibule. "Sister Morgan? I'm Sister Vickie." She darted a sharp glance at Wolfe. "Is that all the luggage, mister? Sure you haven't forgotten a suit-case or two in the trunk?" She turned to Morgan. "What was the fare? It should be fifty new dollars and not a penny more. The penis-pushers will rape you any way they can, physically, psychically or financially, but of course you know that. There's an all-sister cab ser-vice in town; had I known when you were coming, I would have had one of them pick you up at half the cost." She glared briefly at Wolfe. "Good economics and good politics too."

"He's a colleague, Sister Vickie," Morgan said meekly, with a ghost of a wink at Wolfe.

"Ha! Not possible." The old woman opened her small pink mouth to show a gold front tooth and hissed like some wrinkled cartoon viper. "Well, are you coming in or must we stand on the step all day?"

Half amused, Wolfe tendered Morgan her small suitcase. "I hope you'll be comfortable. Let's get together when you're settled in."

"Done. Let's say Friday?"

"I'll call to arrange details." Again he felt a shock of irrational pleasure as he looked at her. Too right to be true. *What in the name of Jesus was Helen up to?* Whatever it was, he hoped more fervently than ever he would be alive on Friday to find out.

Temple

As the population continues to grow inexorably, so the myth of the Great Die Back has come to dominate the popular consciousness. Experts in sociology and psychology have noted that scientific forecasting and the obvious breakdowns in the ecosphere are not the only, or even the main sources of the almost universal belief in the Die Back. It is almost as if, on some deep race level, a profound, unbending truth is tapping humanity on the shoulder. On a primal plane we know beyond all contradiction that the planet cannot—will not—tolerate the endless rape by homo sapiens. People all over the world agree there will come a Die Back. They do not agree, however, on who is to do the dying.

> *Breaking Point*, a collection of essays on
> Post Millennial topics
> Henrikus Grobius, Jr.

Wednesday, July 7
13:55 hours

A placid summer afternoon, the deep blue sky above fluffed with towering white cumulus clouds. Rickki checked Wolfe's homer one last time, gave him thumbs up and slammed the door of his car on him.

His heart pounding in his ears, Wolfe pulled out of the disused warehouse where the security team was stationed, drove along a curving road lined with light industry condos, secure behind high wire fences. Despite the elaborate precautions taken to protect him, he was frankly terrified at the prospect of going alone into the lion's den that was Mancuso's private penthouse. But it was the only way the defector would agree to talk. His mission had been debated right up to the Institute's Board of Governors before Wolfe had received a final go from Helen last night. For the first time her icon had worn a hat, a smart black beret, riding forward on her smooth brown hair. It had reminded Wolfe of something he could not quite place. "We don't put you at risk lightly, Edward. The deciding factor is this: we cannot pass up the chance to hear what Marshal Mancuso may tell us. Go very carefully and abort if you sniff even the slightest threat."

Easy for Orbital to say. Wolfe fumed as he steered the flimsy Ford two-seater around gaping potholes in the pocked road that spread like a disease past empty shells of two- and three-story industrial condos. They had sent Omaha to her death with a similar breezy directive. Another proof that Helen was no deity—a true goddess would protect her acolytes. Helen gave you probabilities and told you to protect yourself. Again an uneasy suspicion raised its head: suppose Project Maldon actually was being botched. If he was the only one who suspected it, might the AI want to silence him? If so, what better way than to send him into a trap on enemy ground? Suddenly he realized what Helen's beret had reminded him of: the black hood of a judge pronouncing the death sentence. He dismissed the image with a loud obscenity directed at the universe in general. He was too jumpy by far. Helen would not play him false after seventeen years. For one thing, why should she? There were easier ways to get rid of troublesome level threes. Most notably, by ignoring them. Ahead loomed the imposing black iron gates of the Accord campus. *Luck, be a lady.* . . . He did not feel particularly lucky, only frightened.

The campus was pleasantly sited on several square kilometers of park land twenty klicks north of the city—formerly a high-tech complex that had been sold cheap after the Bust. He drove through the gates and pulled up at the guardhouse, his instinct for self-preservation shouting that he should turn back, put the car into reverse and back away from this outrageous enterprise. Instead he shoved the gear to neutral and smiled at the tight-lipped teenager, immaculate in the purple uniform of a Temple acolyte who was inspecting him with disdain from behind bulletproof glass.

"Good afternoon, brother. Identification and business please?" The acolyte's politeness seemed to Wolfe a thin veneer, barely masking a ruthless fanaticism. The young ones were the worst. He passed over his ID card with what he hoped was a confident smile. "Here by invitation to see Marshal Mancuso."

The young man frowned and turned to his console while Wolfe's pulse hammered. He had been guaranteed safe conduct, although the guarantee was meaningless if Mancuso planned a double cross. More immediate security was also in place, although to use it would trigger, at minimum, a serious diplomatic incident. One press on the reset button of his watch and heavily armed, highly trained help would arrive within two minutes, homed into a tiny button glued behind his ear. He was also armed: five pen grenades, two four-millimeter disposamatics made of pale blue plastic, each holding fifty explosive rounds, a tiny orange canister of choke gas. Finally, a small but powerful bomb had been planted beside the campus control center. Detonation would paralyze security responses for three or four minutes. Despite all these precautions he felt naked and highly vulnerable. Help would arrive in two minutes, but two minutes was eternity to a helpless man.

Orbital had thought of that too. Thoughtfully Wolfe tongued the poison capsule that had been temporarily fixed to the inside of his back molar. It felt cold and alien and entirely out of place. He snorted in derision. What in the name of Jesus Conciliator was he doing with a death pill glued to his tooth? It was entirely too theatrical. Odd how reality so often seemed unreal these days, so absurd. It struck him as darkly humorous that he had taken all precautions against torture or death—except the obvious one of not coming at all.

The console scanned his ID; after what seemed an endless wait a green light flashed. The acolyte opened a slot in the armored glass wall and passed him a shiny silver visitor's badge in the shape of a seven-pointed star. His fingernails, Wolfe noticed, were short and ragged, bitten to the quick. Maybe it was not as simple as it looked to be an acolyte. "Keep to this road, brother, go past the parade ground, past the Temple and follow the signs for the Salvation Tower. Park in Lot R for redemption, it's a two-minute walk from there. Please keep to the posted limit. God bless." In his manner was a strong hint of that sanctimonious superiority which Wolfe found so aggravating in subscribers. It derived, no doubt, from the guarantee of security in this life and limitless bliss in the next, or even before, if Adonai King kept to the timetable originally laid down by Pastor Stele.

He drove through the park, keeping at a cautious ten klicks, admiring the immaculate green lawns and ordered rows of spreading maple trees, beneath which groups of people walked or sat, the inevitable purple Book of Final Truth in their hands. The tranquillity of the scene was beguiling. Almost, thought Wolfe, you could persuade yourself that such peace was worth the underlying iron discipline with which it was purchased. Almost.

To his left, on the parade ground, a more characteristic spectacle came into view: about two hundred young subscribers of both sexes practiced riot maneuvers, jumping over barricades, dodging to right and left, finally assaulting a row of brown leather dummies with the short, pointed Accord riot stick. Beyond them were the factories, a sprawl of giant shoe boxes, painted blue, red and yellow with scenes from the Book of Truth.

Soaring high above the sparkling golden dome of the Temple was a green two-barred Accord cross. There was apparently some service in progress; as he passed, the church bells peeled out a deep bass chord, making him jump. Probably one of the mass summer weddings favored by the Faithful. Half a kilometer further, he turned into a large parking lot, its black surface gleaming as if it had just been painted. With a silent prayer emphatically not addressed to the Accord's vicious Adonai God, Wolfe drove towards hot spot number one.

The potential for trouble was greatest at two points, as Rickki had explained: "First, let's assume the whole thing is a setup arranged by Mancuso. If so, they'll likely hit you when you get out of your car. For one thing, it's easier to deploy a group of people in the open. Also, there's no point in letting you inside where you'd bleed on the rugs if you fought back. So watch for an ambush in the parking lot. If you see anything suspicious, just turn around and drive right out the gate again—or through it if necessary."

Wolfe backed the car into a parking space so that it faced the entrance, and scanned the immediate area with the nervous intensity of the hunted. Nothing. The air above the black tarmac shimmered with heat but not a soul was in sight and the open landscape gave little opportunity for concealment. Behind the lot rose a twenty-story tower faced with pale red stone, its windows dark behind solar film: the Salvation Tower, home to the high priests of the Accord in Upper Canada. Wolfe whispered into his throat mike: "In the parking lot now. No sign of trouble so far. I'm going in."

Rickki's voice sounded in his ear: "Okay. Break a leg."

He got out of the car, feeling like a bug on a plate, and crossed the parking lot to the gravel path leading to the Salvation Tower. The massive, plate-glass doors were locked, and a pair of eyes were wired above a flat steel directory shaped like a massive book. Wolfe looked into their glassy depths for a moment; as he did so Helen's voice sounded quietly in his ear: "Good luck, Edward. And don't worry, you'll be fine." The AI had somehow patched through into the campus security net. Wolfe grinned. Maybe she wasn't a goddess, but she was one hell of a machine. Black beret indeed!

Above the directory a slogan was etched: AND THEIR NAMES WERE WRITTEN IN THE BOOK OF TRUTH. No doubt. He ran his finger down the listings, found Mancuso's code and entered it. A moment later the door clicked open.

The lobby of the Salvation Tower was a garden: plants of all shapes and sizes sprouted from pots scattered with the casual artistry of a master decorator. At the far end, two huge palms flanked a fountain in the form of the Angel of Life tinkling water into a green marble basin. The air smelled of wet earth and leaves. Slogans from the Book of Truth were written in golden script on the black marble wall. At regular intervals around the lobby were leaf-framed portraits of Pastor Stele and his family: Sarah, his first wife; Camille, his second; his third son, Henry the Martyr; and others that Wolfe did not recognize. Halfway up the marble wall, brutally misplaced in this garden setting, brooded an oversized holo bust of Zacharian Stele, newly acclaimed Deacon of Upper Canada. The holo's head was the size and shape of a watermelon and its bright, mad eyes peered down the hall towards some apocalypse which only it could see.

Avoiding the holo's gaze, Wolfe stepped into one of the four ebony-paneled elevators and pressed penthouse. With a smooth efficiency unusual in the Post Millennium, the doors closed and the elevator rose. A voice began to speak: he started, then realized he was being treated to a canned reading from the Book of Truth. The Accord did not encourage silent meditation, however brief. He took a deep breath, asked himself the next question on today's mortal list: "How secure is Mancuso?"

"They could be onto him," Rickki had warned. "He may be overconfident—happens when you're in charge too long sometimes. It's just possible they'll wait to see if you come, what you want, then catch him in flagrante delicto—with his trousers down, so to speak, in social intercourse with an unbeliever. In that case you'd have a better chance, because it would be him that they really want. It could still get muchee ugly muchee fast though. Any questions?"

"Why in hell did he have to pick me for his contact? I'm a SoCy expert, not a secret agent."

"Remember when we were staking out the Kidney King in the harbor? You asked me the same thing then."

"And what did you say?"

"That you must have a friendly face."

The door slid open; Wolfe consulted a small silver plaque then turned left and padded down the thick burgundy carpet. At the end of the hall, Nicolas Mancuso, Marshal of the Temple Guards, Soldier of the Millennium—waited placidly in the doorway. He made a benedictory sign and waved his visitor inside with an air of easy command. "Go right through, go right through, make yourself comfortable. My home is your home."

Mancuso was a huge Brahma bull gone to seed. In his prime the Accord marshal must have been formidable indeed, with the physique of a professional wrestler or body builder. Now muscle had turned to hard fat; his stomach bulged under his collarless linen shirt and a heavy jowl gave evidence of good living. Nonetheless his large brown eyes were shrewd and alert as he bowed Wolfe into an upholstered chair of Swedish design. A hard man, but one with a taste for the finer things of life judged Wolfe as he took in the teak and leather furniture, the white shag rugs and matching silk drapes.

Mancuso seated himself on a gray leather sofa which sagged under his weight, and beamed at his reluctant guest. "Some wine, Dr. Wolfe? I can offer you an excellent Chardonnay. Vintage of '18, a good year—for wine at least."

Mancuso's voice was surprisingly soft and cultivated for an Accord ruffian, thought Wolfe. "Thank you, no. Perhaps a glass of mineral water."

Mancuso nodded to a fine-featured young woman with brilliant copper hair, who had been standing silently by the bar at the side of the large room. She glided across to Wolfe, set a sealed bottle of Northern Springs mineral water and a glass beside him with precise, controlled movements, returned to her station. Probably security, Wolfe decided. Or perhaps a junior wife. Like other religions before it, the Accord smiled upon procreation among the Faithful.

Mancuso raised his glass. "God bless. Now my friend, are your principals prepared to deal?"

Wolfe looked about him. "How candid may I be?"

"The room is clean, if that's what you mean." Mancuso chuckled. "Rank hath its privileges, Dr. Wolfe. This is one of the most private places in town."

"Out of curiosity, will no one think to ask why an Institute official was visiting you today?"

"I've already told them. To discuss a defection. You wanted to sound me out about coming over to the Accord." Mancuso chuckled at the joke. "And you naturally insisted on privacy, did you not, Dr. Wolfe? A perfect alibi that cuts both ways."

"Very well." Wolfe shrugged. It was Mancuso's genitals as much as his, if the wrong person was listening. "We're interested in your offer, once we're satisfied it's genuine. With respect, Marshal, you puzzle us. You've been with the Accord since you were fifteen . . ."

"Fourteen in truth." Mancuso smiled reminiscently. "I still remember the day I accepted the Teaching. I'd been living in the Freezer for about six months at that point, right near the top floor where the monsters dwell, and I was truly ready for a new direction. I came down to a recruiting fair, heard the words and took the first oath. They gave me a new pair of clothes, a big meal and bed number eighty-nine B in the club dorm. Still I recall that; old eighty-nine B, my first real bed. They gave me some tests to assess overall ability, then worked me hard all that week—stacking bricks in one of the downtown yards—to test my sincerity you understand. When I crawled into eighty-nine B each night there were two blankets and a pillow. And no one to come around and cut my kidneys out to make a few quick credits while I was asleep. I was so happy I cried like a baby. I'd come home, you see."

"And now you're a senior official with over thirty years of service. You're at the top. So why defect?"

"'Cause I want to live, brother, I want to live.

Preferably in the style befitting one of my years and advanced state of grace." Mancuso stretched his massive legs out before him and grinned amiably.

"Have you lost faith in the Accord then?"

Mancuso made the sign of the double cross over his barrel chest. "Adonai forbid. I am guided day and night by the Book of Truth."

"I don't understand then."

"Truly, Dr. Wolfe, you don't. No one understands the Accord except a subscriber. But I like you for confessing your ignorance, so I'll focus for you. Seniority counts for nothing in the Accord. Faith? Piety? Irrelevant when you reach my level." Mancuso shrugged apologetically, as if he would correct this inequity if he could. "Our new deacon says I have fallen from grace. Translated, that means I am not the right thing at the right time. I should be a barracuda."

Wolfe poured mineral water into his blue crystal glass, trying to gauge Mancuso's mood. The marshal seemed to be testing his knowledge, and possibly his patience too. "I see. And what are you at the moment?"

"A bottom feeder."

Wolfe began to wonder if the marshal was altogether lucid. He set his face into an expression of polite inquiry and waited.

Mancuso chuckled, a rich baritone gurgle that reminded Wolfe of coffee percolating. "Pardon the colorful language. We love parables in the Accord. In plainspeak, a bottom feeder is one who believes all the Accord has to do is swim along slow and steady for another few years, scavenging in the muck of society. A few more cities in flames, another generation of assorted human dirt clogging the ecosystem and the Free Market leadership will beg us to step in and clean up. Most of them are converts anyway, in private if not in public. We won't have to lift a finger.

This is the path favored by the saner members of the Stele family.

"But the barracudas see it different. They're in a feeding frenzy. They want to devour the Old Order, starting in Upper Canada and moving as fast as possible outwards. Our ambitious new Deacon, Zacharian Stele is a barracuda and therefore a barracuda is the right thing to be here and now." Mancuso poured another glass of wine and sat back, making the couch creak beneath him. "Deacon Zacharian is a driven and dangerous man. I am told he wants to cleanse Jerusalem and hoist the Cross of Two Bars over its gates within five years. Madness of course, but he is deranged by his faith."

Wolfe digested the statement. For a marshal of the Accord, Mancuso had surprisingly little respect for official dogma. He said as much.

Mancuso appeared not at all put out. "It's all a matter of interpretation, Dr. Wolfe. 0The commandment to retake Jerusalem can be understood in many ways. Sane men and women see it as an injunction to regain our original state of innocence. Fanatics like Zacharian take it literally, regardless of the fact that any such attempt would trigger the Die Back. But all things must pass, as the Book of Truth says. One day, Deacon Zacharian will pass, if the prayers of many are answered. I plan to be alive when it happens."

"And then?"

Mancuso plucked at an imaginary crease in his linen shirt. "Who knows? Maybe I'll be so happy in my new life I'll just fade into the sunset."

Wolfe decided to try a different approach. "Why did you approach us? Why not a government agency, UCISIS for instance?"

"State Intelligence?" The Accord marshal laughed as if he had made a rather good joke. "Better to run off and join the circus than to deal with those incompetents. No, I approached the Institute, my dear Dr. Wolfe, because I want action—and because our roads run parallel for a while. We both want to thwart Deacon Zacharian. Beyond that, I desire credit and sanctuary quickly. You can arrange both."

By now Wolfe had almost forgotten to be frightened. "Fair enough, but why now? Why not next month, for example, or this winter?"

"Maybe I'm just a summertime sort of person, Dr. Wolfe." Mancuso examined his impeccably manicured right hand with interest. "I enjoy summer so, don't you? The major world organizations are on autopilot, everyone's hot and lazy, no one's really paying attention. And the social events! Did you know there's a major Accord convention planned for later this month, right here in Toronto? Could draw as many as twenty thousand delegates, most of them keen as razors, and well-trained. Think about it."

Wolfe had already thought about it. If the Accord planned a coup, the conference would be a perfect time to strike. "Can you tell us more?"

"Lots more—when I have the credits. Do the deal, and learn all, brother." Mancuso poured himself more wine and smiled amiably. He might have been an old acquaintance passing the time of day. "This is the Information Age, remember? Now then, my terms: six months of refuge at Orbital, a completely new identity, and fifty million deutsche marks paid into a Swiss account in my name."

Wolfe sat back aghast. "Fifty million marks? That's outrageous, Marshal, and you know it."

Mancuso appeared not to hear. "Furthermore, I need buy-in soon, or I'll have to make other arrangements."

"Hardly likely at your price."

"Don't be so sure. The Islamic Coalition is always interested in news of our internal politics."

"Fifty million is too much," Wolfe objected again. "The government will never agree."

"I count on Orbital to convince the government." Mancuso grinned. "My information will save Upper Canada more than that within days. The figure is not negotiable. And that, brother, is my last word."

"Very well." Wolfe finished his mineral water with a feeling of vast relief and rose to leave. "We'll be in touch soon."

He rode down the elevator, trying to contain his rising elation. He was going to get away with it, he could feel the sweet sensation of success beginning to sweep through him as his brain proposed a series of neurochemical toasts in honor of the fact that he was going to live past lunch time. Across the air-conditioned lobby, out the front door of the Salvation Tower into a wall of pure heat which made him gasp, back down the gravel path whispering a message to control: "I'm outside again, headed for the parking lot."

The message came back, a faint whisper in his tiny earphone: "Good work, Long Eddie. Keep focused though, you're still not clear."

As if to underline the warning, a single person appeared from around the corner of a building on the far side of the lot and began to saunter across the grass. It was too far to distinguish details. Wolfe could see only a black figure, distorted by the shifting veils of hot air gusting up from the blacktop of the parking lot. If the stranger kept his present course, Wolfe estimated, they would meet at his car. He quickened his step, scanning for other possible attackers. One hand dipped casually into his jacket pocket, gripped the molded plastic of a disposamatic. His heart began to pound again, then stress discipline kicked in: three deep breaths, concentrate on physical input, muscles relaxed, loose but focused. Step, step, glance around, another step.

No one else appeared. The solitary figure kept a steady pace, and now Wolfe could see it was a man, about his own height, thin with stooped shoulders and a slouching posture. Still he was alone. Merely a casual passer-by? Then the figure stopped a few meters beyond his car.

Wolfe kept walking, his right hand on the concealed automatic, his left reaching casually for his car control. When he was a meter away he started the engine and unlocked the driver's door. Still the stranger did not move. Now Wolfe could see him clearly: a tall, spare man in his late twenties, with thin blonde hair and a school teacher's gaunt, precise features. Mr. Chips in a PM parking lot. Then the school teacher spoke: "Dr. Wolfe? I wish to introduce myself. I am Joshua. You sent a squad of my friends to salvation the other night." He smiled reprovingly, as if accusing a grade six student of breaking a window.

So this was him! The one who had slipped away from the ambush—the monster who had done Mary. Wolfe's heart began to race, he could taste the bitter tang of hate in his mouth. He surfed easily on the wave of his violent detestation, adopted a light ironic tone to put his enemy off guard. "Indeed we did. And one day soon we'll send you to join them." His finger twitched on the trigger of the disposamatic. The damned things were like garden hoses: one squeeze of the trigger would just about saw this damned schoolmaster in half. And bring a hundred Temple guards down on his own head, hot for vengeance. There were other times and other ways. Most likely Helen would get him. She had never failed yet. "Will you enjoy dying of cancer?" he asked politely. "Prostate cancer I should think, in your case. I'd advise you to see an oncologist right away, but there's really no point."

Joshua shook his head, smiling at Wolfe's naiveté.

"Thank you for your concern. But you forget, brother, I am shielded by Adonai God himself."

Despite the heat Wolfe felt a chill at the man's iron fanaticism. He maintained his detached tone. "Your Adonai is a figment. And you, my friend, are one of the walking dead. I assure you it is so."

"'How can the unbeliever not blaspheme? How can he speak other than lies?' I quote Book Three of the Final Truth." Joshua bowed politely. "Do you wonder why I introduced myself today Dr. Wolfe? I wanted you to gaze upon the face of the man who will send you to glory. A pity your colleague Rickki couldn't be here to enjoy the same privilege. Don't look so surprised, of course I know her name. I knew Mary too before I eased her into eternity. I went to her fitness club one night and made her acquaintance, do you know that? We had quite a good time. At the end she thought I had come to rescue her. A pity to let her down, but her sacrifice was sanctioned by the Deacon himself."

Rage tinged Wolfe's vision with red. He opened his car door, making sure to keep a clear field of fire through the window. All he needed was an excuse. "Why not just take me out now? It may be your only chance."

Joshua appeared surprised. "Today you are protected by the marshal. Besides, I have no sanction yet. But I will have. We will meet again." He turned and slowly walked away.

Helen's voice sounded softly in his ear. "Let him go, Edward." Wolfe glanced around, noticed an eye perched high atop a metal pole at the corner of the parking lot. High in orbit, Helen had been witnessing this tawdry scene too. "This was incautious on his part," added Helen calmly. "We now have a perfect visual ID. Never fear, we'll deal with him."

He jumped into his car, shivering with hate and fear,

and drove as quickly as he dared down the main drive. Surrendering his badge at the guardhouse he turned onto the main road again and was half a kilometer away before his hands began to shake in earnest.

For defections, as for everything else, the Institute had a staff expert—in this case a female level four with the Weird Brigade, stationed somewhere in the Pacific Rim. Wolfe consulted her in a series of screen-blanked conversations, then called Under Secretary Wu to brief her on financial requirements. That done, he selected a small project group from Versailles' staff and appointed Dolores Sanchez, a quiet level two with a mild, absent-minded air and an advanced certification in covert ops, as team leader. Sanchez, who had escaped from Gibraltar one step ahead of the Islamic armies, displayed a grasp of detail, combined with a cold confidence which he found encouraging. They worked intensively through the afternoon and early evening, Wolfe converting the morning's ordure of fear and rage into useful energy like a manure generator. By nine o'clock, satisfied that the machinery of defection was in place, he delegated operational responsibility to Sanchez and asked Amadeus to meet him in the garage in fifteen minutes.

Each nightfall in a free zone spun the clock back ten thousand years—or ahead several hundred, Wolfe thought as the Isuzu flitted like a dark shadow past scattered camps of Listers, dancing figures, half glimpsed in the moving beam of the headlights or silhouetted against the leaping flames from the fire barrels. Once they passed what appeared to be a recree, one of the Lists' spontaneous parties which as often as not erupted into wild orgies of sex and bloodshed. Several hundred figures danced or ate or copulated in the doorways of the abandoned stores. Somewhere in the decaying buildings, a drummer hammered out a hypnotic rhythm, amplified electronically, jarring the night like a giant, racing heart. Looking at the lithe figures in the yellow firelight, Wolfe felt a sudden mad impulse to join them, throw down his thousand cares and calculations and join their sinuous shuffling dance. He envied them their wild primeval abandon, their total lack of calculation or even concern for anything that lay beyond the dawn. Truth be told, he was tired of the paranoid vigilance that his job entailed. Still, there was no alternative. Stop paying attention and someone got cleaned. Maybe even you. The recree disappeared in the maze of broken black buildings and Wolfe sighed and rearranged himself in the cramped back seat.

It was almost ten o'clock when Amadeus parked in one of Chinatown's safe lots and escorted him to the three-story neon doors of the Seven Dragons Seafood Palace. By mentioning Under Secretary Wu's name to the harassed hostess, Wolfe secured safe passage to a booth at the back of the crowded, garlic-smelling cavern. Wu looked up at his approach and bowed very slightly from the waist. "Welcome, Edward. You had no difficulty finding the place? The clams are excellent, and I can also recommend most of the shrimp dishes. But first, might you care for a drink?"

Wolfe ordered a double Flash and sat back against the plastic burgundy padding. When the waiter had served him, Wu steepled her fingers and spoke in what Wolfe thought of as her official tone. "Bad news I'm afraid: I have explored a number of different approaches to laying hands on fifty million deutsche marks. We are already over budget for the quarter and all our special reserves have been allocated and spent. I tried to tap into next year's capital budget, but thanks to the diligence of your Institute systems people, there are now elaborate safeguards on that as well. In short, we are tied with our own ropes.

I can discover no discreet and unobtrusive way to get at the money."

"At least our spending safeguards are effective," commented Wolfe with a sour grin. He swirled the ice around his glass, took half the Flash in one gulp and poked moodily at the white antidote capsule with his dragon-headed swizzle stick. "This is not good news—Mancuso won't budge without the cash. Also, he sees our ability to get funding as a test of our commitment to him."

"Might there be room for negotiation?" asked Wu hopefully.

"None, in my opinion. He's made it very clear that his price is fifty million marks. If we fail to come up with it, we signal that he isn't important to us." Wolfe rattled the ice cubes in his glass. "Another thought crossed my mind after the interview. This whole defection may be the Accord's way of testing us, trying to gauge the level of government support for Maldon. If funds aren't forthcoming, it could be read as a vote of non-confidence in the project itself."

"Overly subtle for the Accord. You really think so?"

Wolfe ran his hand through his hair, reflecting that he needed a haircut soon. Somehow there never seemed to be time. "It's a possibility. Likelihood about ten percent, according to Helen."

"When is Defection Day?"

"Next Wednesday."

"A week can be a long time." Wu stared into the liquid eye of her teacup. "I may still be able to negotiate something." She picked up a tiny crumb with her chopsticks, examined it intently. "If not, then we shall have to explore other avenues." She released the crumb and smiled at Wolfe. "Meanwhile, being human, we must also eat. Do you know what you want?"

Wolfe shook his head. "I'll leave it to you."

The deputy put down her chopsticks and turned her

full attention to the stained pages of the menu. She ordered in a burst of fluent Mandarin then turned again to Wolfe as the waiter scurried away. "Clams in black bean sauce, followed by imperial shrimps. A dish said to be from the declining period of the empire. Food distracts from the more abstract problems of life. Let us enjoy what we can, while we can."

Café

Contrary to popular belief, the Temple of the Accord
was not originally an alliance of Christian fundamental-
ists nor yet an educational venture. It was—and still is—
a religious philosophy, based on a simple premise: Adonai
God created two and only two types of people, good and
evil. The good accept authority (however derived) and are
thus in accord with their fellows and with Creation. The
evil know no law and serve only themselves. The first
should be recruited, the second terrorized, marginalized,
eliminated.

The Temple of the Accord—A Brief History

Friday, July 9
20:00 hours

The sun was sinking fiery crimson into a gray sea
of smog as Amadeus gunned the two-seater up onto
the trash-clogged street with a satisfying squeal of
rubber and grinned shyly at Wolfe in the rear-view
mirror, the first time he had shown a human aspect.
Wolfe grinned back. Behind them, Versailles' steel
garage doors clanged shut with a hollow boom. They
were free to go just about anywhere or how they chose
in the long, hot night. In fact, they were going downtown to meet Morgan.

She had called this morning, her manner tentative,

as if she was not sure whether their conversation was business or pleasure: "I didn't call too early? You're sure? Are we still meeting tonight?"

Wolfe had grinned into the pickup. "The thought of it kept me alive all week. Shall we say Café Gabriel at Harbourfront? It's a hardened bar and chess emporium, and there's a good view over the lake. You can see the glow from Darlington Station on a clear night."

"About eight o'clock then? I'll meet you there."

Wolfe disconnected, feeling a gentle buzz of excitement he hadn't felt for many years—Jesus come quick, was it really so long since he had been piqued by a new woman? No wonder he was cynical and stale. And he was both, as witness the fact that he had not chosen Café Gabriel for its romantic charm but because it commanded a view over William Davis Square, where a large Accord recruiting fair was under way. An enigmatic message had wafted through the Net to him this morning, source unknown:

> *Be there tonight in Davis Square*
> *But stay away from the Accord fair*
> *Those who would take from the Lists their names*
> *Will repent amid the liquid flames*

Something told him the doggerel had originated with the Exodus Faction, was in fact a response to his meeting with Adam 100. Or maybe it was one more piece of random PM nonsense. They would soon see. (*So much for romance. Or maybe nothing will happen.*)

As usual, Carlaw Avenue stank of soap, as if the blackened bricks of the warehouses themselves were farting laundry detergent. The factory was working overtime again, boxes moving past the orange-lit windows in orderly procession. Wolfe found the sight oddly reassuring. Even in its mortal struggle for survival, Upper Canada apparently still washed. If the nation died, it would do so with soap in its dish.

Amadeus turned on the radio for a traffic check, pulling in the Accord channel: "Traffic one big tangle all over the city," said the DJ cheerfully. "More snarls than a mad dog. Yeah, seems like everyone's going somewhere; and when everyone goes somewhere, that means no one goes nowhere, folks. Figured that out yet? Gotta keep ya all on ya toes, 'cause nothing but *nothing's* simple in the PM—until King Adonai comes to lead us home, amen. Meanwhile, just sit back and let The Janitors polish your brain with some right sonics after a word from ya Mitsubishi buddies . . . " Amadeus met Wolfe's eyes in the rearview mirror and a silent message passed between them. He punched off and the chilly hiss of the air-conditioning was again their only companion.

Wolfe tugged at his beard irritably, fretful and ill at ease in the back seat. His whiskers did not feel quite right after the vigorous trimming they had received this afternoon. Although not a particularly vain man, he had been visited by the age-old compulsion to look his best when meeting an attractive member of the opposite sex. Nothing like an asymmetrical beard to make a bad impression.

He still remembered how the elegant goatee of Mac's father, Mr. MacGregor, had become strangely bedraggled and rat-gnawed after the Big Bust, fluffier on the left side than the right. It had seemed—had in fact been—the exterior mark of a profound interior dislocation. Two weeks after the Bust he had put a bullet through his handsome head.

Wolfe looked gloomily at a huddle of Listers squatting in the doorway of a ruined warehouse, wrapped in ragged red and black ponchos despite the heat, their foreheads and chins painted blue. After two years of Institute involvement, things were worse than before, spiraling ever faster into decay.

This morning, after running a set of simulations on the power grid, Helen had ordered brown-downs every night for the next week. Wolfe had found himself again playing devil's advocate with the AI. "Are the cuts absolutely necessary? The basement fishers and farmers will be furious—they'll lose a month's harvest at least. And they're among our most fervent supporters."

Helen had held up her hands, palms out, as if to disavow any malicious intent. "It's a delicate call as usual. If we brown-down we enrage home enterprise. Damage to the project intangible. If not, we run the risk of losing a reactor later this month. Damage to the project critical. The whole grid is overtaxed, thanks to the hot weather, and we have no prospect of relief until at least September. Algorithms say brown-down."

Wolfe thoughtfully fingered his ear stud, wondering if he should have protested more vigorously. No, he only would have been overruled more vigorously. He had done what he could, who could do more? He was tired and under stress—a level three, engaged in threading the needle. This was the hardest phase of his career. His recruiter had warned him about level three even before he was accepted by the Institute. Seventeen years ago that had been, half a lifetime.

Closing his eyes, he recalled with pleasure those exuberant days, when he had first experienced the high energy that characterized all Institute undertakings. He had applied to the Skellig Michael when he was seventeen, two weeks after the Big Bust had stepped out of the Hartley Singh equations to snap the backbone of the global economy with one mighty heave. After a month of anxious waiting, he had received an acknowledgment and an invitation to take the entrance exams—room, board and transportation provided by the Institute. Late in August, he had found himself, along with hundreds of other teenagers from the NorEast Free Market catchment area, lodged in one of the white-frame dormitories of the mountain campus of a small Vermont college.

After three weeks of intensive testing he had found himself in front of an evaluator in a nondescript white-walled room in the administrative complex. The drowsy summer silence was broken only by the buzzing of a huge bluebottle navigating slowly back and forth a few centimeters below the ceiling as the evaluator, a middle-aged woman with short bobbed brown hair and a vestigial mustache, shuffled her papers. Finally she looked up, her eyes like slick black pebbles. "Good afternoon, Edward. My name is Elvira Peabody and I'm in charge of processing your application. You have a very unusual profile."

"Thank you."

"Don't thank me, it's your psyche. You are an almost perfect generalist, with especially high scores in administration and historical perspectives, of all unlikely things. Let's talk a bit about the Institute, Edward. You've probably had the usual spin, 'monks in the sky,' 'orbital wizards' and all the rest of it. Here's the mundane reality. Let's assume you're accepted: For the first seven or eight years you're a provisional fellow, what we call a provo, or more often a weenie. You'll study like you're possessed by the seven devils of scholarship, you'll find yourself in plenty of odd situations and probably some fairly dangerous ones. Needless to say, you're paid nothing for your time or trouble. Room, board, basic medical, that's the deal. After year five you'll be allowed to earn a small stipend if you want to put in extra hours. On the bright side, if you work hard and stay alive, as most weenies do, you'll get an unsurpassed all-around education. Academically you'll have the equivalent of a doctoral degree in your field. But, you'll have a lot more. You'll be able to command a platoon of troops, set up a business or undertake a diplomatic mission. And somewhere about the time you're beginning to get cocky, you'll find you've been made a fellow first level.

"At that point you think you're on top of the world, oh yes. You're full of the most alarming zeal. And you have the chance to work it off. You're given your first assignment, and it will be a shocker. No more coddling by Helen and your kindly instructors. Do or die."

Wolfe stirred in fascination. "What kind of assignment are we talking?"

"Anything. Negotiate for the release of a political prisoner. Infiltrate a slaver enterprise and break it. Pitch in on one of our big projects, on the ground or in the back room. Two, three, five such assignments and you'll begin to see the magnitude of the Institute's task. Just when you begin to be thankful you're still relatively junior, you'll receive notification you've been bumped to level two." She smiled, showing regular white teeth. "Level two is sometimes known as the hammock, because it's the easiest in many ways. You've survived level one, you've got a bit of authority, but the burden isn't crushing. You mature, you broaden out with a few more courses, and in three or four years, you're a level three."

Ms. Peabody stood up, walked to the window, and looked out over the placid green campus for a few moments. "Level three: now you've got responsibility. You're in charge of some project, and it's important, like all our projects. And it's hard. Our clients don't pay us to sit around and think long thoughts— we take on things that no other organization has the skills or the guts to. You're asked to make decisions that mean life or death to people, often people you know. We call it threading the needle. Sometimes you succeed, sometimes not. Maybe you start to ask yourself

what you're doing this for, if there's not a better way
to help people, to live your life. One of two things
happens: you come to grips with yourself and proceed
to level four. Or you decide the program's not for you
and become an associate."

Wolfe raised his hand politely. "An associate,
ma'am?"

"Associates: those who find, after mature reflection,
that the Institute is not for them; its programs are
too harsh, progress is too slow. They become dissatisfied with the strictures, the rules, the slow, complicated crabwise methods. And so they throw off the
yoke and become associates. We work out a financial
arrangement and they pursue the great work in
their own way."

"Early retirement?"

"Far from it. Our associates are the most hard-
driven people on the globe or above it. The Institute does not accept people lightly; those whom it
takes, it keeps in one fashion or another." She stroked
her upper lip. "In any event, level three is a tough
one. From it, you may advance to the senior levels
in a matter of months, or after several decades. The
youngest level four is thirty, the oldest is seventy one.
What do levels four and five do? If I knew exactly,
I'd tell you. More of the same, and something altogether different. If you do incredibly well, or if Helen
takes you to her cold, cold heart you may end up
as one of the six governors or even as dean. At which
point your personality will be mapped for integration
into Helen's own. You will have achieved a certain
sort of immortality. That's the standard career path
within the Institute.

"Of course, if you have a really unusual psyche, you
may be assigned to the Weird Brigade. What's that? It's
the grab bag for all the strange children with extraordinary individual talents: athletes, poets, confidence

tricksters, you name it. Weirds go where they go and work on whatever assignments Helen sees fit to assign, usually without fanfare or publicity. Don't ask me why or wherefore, 'cause again, I don't know." She chuckled and turned back from the window to face him. "I tell you all this because obviously you're been accepted for an interview. You'll be informed of the exact date shortly."

In his jubilation Wolfe stood and performed a low, formal bow. "Where is the interview?"

"Orbital headquarters. The Institute will send you and our other hopefuls up the well. Many will come back with tails between adolescent legs, a few will stay." She signed a bar-coded slip of green paper and handed it to him. "I'd take some space conditioning if I were you. Not pleasant to throw up in freefall, you know."

Wolfe struggled to suppress the manic grin which was struggling to take control of his face. "What percentage of applicants get an interview?"

"About a tenth of one percent."

"And how many of those get accepted?"

"It varies. And frankly, whether you do or not depends on whether the dean, the governors or Helen like you." Ms. Peabody shrugged. "Why does the dean or a governor like someone? Twenty million times more troubling, why does an AI like someone? I emphatically don't know. Any other questions?"

"What level are you?"

"Two. My trials still lie ahead. Anything else? Good luck then." She had smiled an unexpectedly sweet smile as Wolfe bowed again and turned away.

A year later she had been promoted to Level Three and was made chief advisor to the Polish government's antidrug team. It had taken two years to suppress the notorious Warsaw labs, but they had succeeded, although Peabody had lost her left arm and eye in a bomb attack along the way. After she reemerged from the tanks she had been made a Four and assigned to liaison with the Asian section of the UN Commission on Organ Traffic, where Wolfe had worked as her executive assistant for two years. Last April she had been named to the Board of Governors. There was, he supposed, a pleasing progression implicit in all this. Thread the needle, proceed to Orbital, become a governor. *Always assuming you succeeded in your task and in staying alive.*

It was a quarter past seven when they turned onto Lakeshore Drive. With a sudden scream of rubber the car in front braked, swerved to miss a dog-shaped chunk of gray-brown concrete that had fallen from the decaying highway overhead. Spinning the wheel, Amadeus missed the obstacle by centimeters, cursing to himself in a language Wolfe could not identify.

At Jarvis Turnoff, traffic slowed to a crawl—stop, start, a sea of red brake lights spread like an angry tide ahead. Amadeus maxed the air conditioning so the cold air washed up through the car like a bath, then sat back with a fatalistic shrug, one long finger tapping a rhythm on the blue plastic steering wheel. "Sorry, Dr. Wolfe, we are entrapped. Our only remedy is patience."

"Truly." Wolfe consulted his watch again and groaned. Problem: too many people in the PM— just too damn many people, too many cars, too much excrement, smoke, concrete. What to do? Sit in a metal box with your life dribbling away in endless shades of gray. Go critical. Homo sapiens was bogged down in a self-made mire of complications, contradictions—bottlenecks with no reason, just like this one; every day more traffic jams, every day skin-rotting melanomas sprinkled down through the ozone holes onto the helpless world. One day a particularly deadly strain of Tokyo Flu would erupt, and that would be that. Or maybe Gabriel really would

appear, golden bugle in hand, to play a final doomsday rag: "root-a-toot-toot, show's over, let's turn out
the sun and head Home."

Shaking off the sense of foreboding that had
gripped him, he turned his thoughts to Morgan.
Here was an intricate puzzle! If her brief was to
pry and spy, she would presumably fish for opinions on the project, the Institute, Helen herself.
He would have to be especially circumspect and
wary while giving the impression of candor. Yet if
she was a channel to the AI, it might be best to
relay some of his concerns through her, to rein-
force what he had already told Helen. That way,
his opinions would be on record, and he would
bolster his reputation for straightforwardness. Or
again, she might have been sent to report indepen-
dently on the situation, in which case, he had a
positive duty to be as frank as possible. As frank
as possible without voicing any doubts about Helen.
He made a ferocious face at his reflection in the
window. Once again he was in danger of over-
thinking the situation, immobilizing himself.

By now they had reached the bottleneck. Flashing
yellow arrows herded cars and trucks like steel
cattle into a killing pen where a nervous policeman in short-sleeved blue coveralls and mirror
glasses waved them through or held them back as
a rescue crew in orange bullet-proofs bulldozed
wreckage aside. Amadeus lowered the window,
wrinkling his nose at the stink of burning rubber:
"What's the holdup, brother?"

The policeman shrugged elaborately. "Highway snipers. Triads. Who the hell knows? Move on." In the
blocked-off lanes two trucks burned against the guard
rails, giving off a thick, oily fume. Chinese lettering
ran down their sides, and bullet holes laced silver
spider webs across their windshields. Wolfe, who knew

a smattering of Mandarin, translated the ideograms.
Lucky Day Enterprises.

Or then again, thought Wolfe as he looked at the
burning vehicles, she might be exactly what she said
she was—an interface expert, with only a casual interest
in Project Maldon. In which case he would be wast-
ing time and energy trying to plumb her nonexistent
agenda—and maybe squandering a priceless opportunity to know her much better, to find what lay behind
that perfect face.

Traffic began to flow briskly. Wolfe rearranged his
legs in a vain effort to make himself comfortable.
There was little point in speculating. He would have
to keep an open mind about Morgan and watch
carefully for clues.

City Hall was floodlit in honor of Upper Canada
Day, a huge pale clamshell washed by the superheated
waves of night. Above the city, the spike of the Wang,
the old CN Tower, pierced the green twilight skin
of the evening like a huge hypodermic. The traffic
light turned green, cars inched forward, the light
turned red again. The big summer jazz festival was
under way; the whole downtown core had been cordoned off below Queen Street. Amadeus looked inquir-
ingly back at him. "Dr. Wolfe?"

"Park here. We'll walk."

Amadeus nodded and goosed the small car into an
impossibly narrow slot between a neon-green electric Hyundai and a sleek pink Mercedes. Following
new security protocols, Wolfe waited until a single beep
on his portable told him Amadeus had decided the area
was clear. Locking the car's wheels and doors, he clambered out onto the pavement, joined the human mass
streaming south towards the lake, his blankie trailing
a discreet few meters behind.

Fairy lights had been strung between the lamp
posts; tiny pinpoints of red, blue and diamond white

blinked against the still-luminous sky. Three years after the blast that had ended the War of Three Cities, sunsets were still magnificent, flaming reds and golds, lurid purples—the result of thousands of tons of desert sand and ash in the upper atmosphere, so he had read. In the Post Millennium every cloud has a radioactive lining, every wind blows a few hot atoms that once were part of Omaha.

It was close, breathless, unbearably hot.

On the far side of the street, a skull-faced man with waistlength blue hair and intricate black tattoos on his chest and back stood on a box haranguing the passers-by: a curious clanking sound accompanied his wild sermon. Wolfe saw that he was wearing a loose skirt made of tiny film canisters threaded together on string. He passed by without stopping. The PM had more than its share of the deranged: legions of maniacs who swore they had coupled with anthropoid flying saucer reptiles or been vouchsafed the exact date and hour of Doomsday by skyscraper-tall manifestations of Adonai King.

Was it madness, though, to think you could see the Die Back arcing in across the clear greenhouse sky like an incoming missile? Madness or merely clarity? Twelve billion people—you could almost hear the beams of Spaceship Earth groaning as she wheeled through the void. And the population just kept growing exponentially. Another generation or two, they'd all be standing on each other's heads. It couldn't endure much longer and everyone knew it.

Across the bridge to Harbourfront flowed the crowd in noisy, intoxicated waves: sunburned workers, down from some northern station, boisterous with drink and calling out to passing women; the inevitable beggars with their sores and mutilations on show; a gang of hollow-cheeked young teenagers, members of the vicious Christmas List. Seeing them, Wolfe automatically crossed to the other side of the bridge. No sense in asking to have your guts cut out on a lark. The Christmas List had been known to make neckties out of human entrails.

A neon-sided blimp was passing overhead; brilliant white messages chased each other down its length, disappearing into the multi-focused spotlights at its tail:

. . . CLUB OPENINGS AVAILABLE—SUBSCRIBE NOW. . . . FIREWORKS AT 9:00 TONIGHT. . . . LIGHT UP THE NIGHT WITH LABATT, AND KEEP SAFE. . . . TIME: 8:07. . . . TEMPERATURE: 34. . . . ENTER THE SKYWAGON STAKES NOW. . . . A TEN PIECE BUYS YOU A CHANCE FOR YOUR MARTIAN HOME-STEAD. . . .

A hundred meters or so up the boardwalk from Café Gabriel stood the Ministry of Equal Opportunity, a low glass and granite structure built just before the Bust and now mothballed. On the square before the defunct Ministry, the Accord recruiting fair was in its third day. Over ten thousand had already subscribed, according to Wolfe's reports, and the fair was open until Sunday. Hymns and slogans from the Book of Final Truth blared from man-high speakers placed around the perimeter of a football field-sized marquee of purple canvas, erected to shield recruiters and would-be subscribers alike from sun and rain. Beside the tent was an enormous, cross-shaped fiberglass pool in which new subscribers were baptized en masse. Wolfe counted over a hundred people waist-high in the water, and more wading in all the time.

Outside the tent, dozens of Accord recruiters in plum-colored overalls mingled among the ragged onlookers, exhorting, persuading, urging them to subscribe to the Final Truth. Groups of Temple Guards with pointed riot sticks were scattered all around the tent, alert for any trouble.

Wolfe looked across the plaza and frowned. On the far side, almost underneath Café Gabriel, several hundred Listers were dancing, a slow, shuffling dance, forming a long oval around a line of fire barrels which cast a lurid orange glow in the gathering twilight. Beside the barrels, a drummer beat out a deep urgent rhythm on a compact electric drum. More Listers were appearing all the time from the side streets, in furtive, ragged groups, to join the dance. A half dozen police were watching lackadaisically from a riot wagon. Such impromptu street balls were not uncommon on the long hot summer nights.

Wolfe walked briskly across the square and past the Listers, smelling their musky odor, feeling the heat of the fire barrels on his face. Their pent hysteria beat against him like psychic waves, urging him towards the sanctuary of the café.

Marcel, the owner of Café Gabriel, was guarding its reinforced steel gate, an ivory-handled Magnum pistol slung by a strap over his shoulder. A small, wiry man in his late thirties, with black eyes and a fierce hawk nose, he was typical of the PM entrepreneurs who had sprung up after the Bust—hardworking, independent and ready to defend himself and his property. The last he was well equipped to do, being a senior instructor at Wolfe's dojo and an expert marksman besides. He wore an immaculate white apron and his luck diamond sparkled in his right nostril. Seeing Wolfe, he opened the gate with a bow. "You are well tonight?"

"Well enough. And you?"

"Excellent." Wolfe nodded at the dancing Listers. "Expecting trouble?

"Let us hope not." Marcel touched his nose jewel. "No matter though, it will come and go like a brief thunderstorm. It is of no concern. Your friend has already arrived." He paused to shoo away a quartet of beggars with his white apron, as if he were shooing pigeons. "I have put her at our best table on the top level."

"Thank you." Wolfe inclined his head. "Another favor—in a few moments an associate will arrive, a thin young man with an Institute pin on his coveralls. He will introduce himself as a friend of mine. Please put him at a table not too near ours where he can watch my back."

"Understood." Marcel preened his fine black mustache and beckoned his teenage son, a dark-eyed, smooth-faced version of himself with his father's quick movements and dark eyes: "Ali, show our friend to table three, on the top patio. And contain your insolence."

Wolfe followed Ali to the curving ornamental escalator, rode it to the third floor, a pleasant anticipation in the pit of his stomach. At a book-sized table of black wrought iron in the corner of the terrace sat Morgan, gazing at the sailboats fluttering back and forth like butterflies on the dark blue water of the harbor. Before her was a sketch tablet. Ali pointed and gave a knowing wink. He had studied karate with Wolfe for almost a year, which allowed him a certain familiarity. "Your friend is drinking chablis, Dr. Wolfe. A carafe for you as well?"

"Flash. On the rocks, if you please." Feeling good all of a sudden, Wolfe dug into his pocket for a five-piece and tossed it to his ex-pupil. Ali snagged it quick and clean as it spun down in a golden flicker, and ran down the escalator to fill the order.

Wolfe strolled over to the table, reflecting that it had been many roiling months since he had spent time with such an alarmingly pretty woman. A shame it was not as simple as that.

As if sensing his presence, Morgan turned suddenly, and stared up at him, a smile wrinkling the mask of freckles that banded her rather wide nose. "Good evening, Edward." She wore a loose white blouse, a pair of the baggy blue cotton breeches that seemed to be the fashion this summer, and high, turned-down boots. She pointed down at the big purple tent across the square. "What's going on over there?"

Wolfe seated himself, looked down at the milling, shouting mob. "Accord recruiting fair."

"Ah, the famous Temple of the Accord." Morgan looked back at the tent with interest. "I've read about them of course, but never actually come into contact. They're a particularly North American phenomenon."

"So far. If they get properly organized though, watch out. Their declared goal is to retake Jerusalem—and some of them are God-besotted enough to try. You can imagine the outcome of that." *Four suns rising around a sleeping city . . .*

Morgan peered over the rail. "They seem to be attracting a lot of attention."

"Oh yes. Their recruiters have been working overtime recently. Entitlements have been cut back, you see, making the life of your average Lister somewhat precarious." As he spoke he was aware he sounded crabbed and pedantic. "As if it wasn't before," he added with what was intended to be a disarming chuckle but came out instead as a harsh, mirthless bark.

"Aha." Morgan toyed with her stylus. "And the Accord offers some modicum of stability?"

Wolfe nodded. "You eat, you drink, you're assigned shelter, friends and status. At a price. When you subscribe, the Accord takes complete control of every aspect of your existence: where you work, who you marry and when you die. About fifteen percent of recruits find their way up from basic subscriber status to some position where they have some freedom of action. The rest are essentially slave laborers, working when and where the Accord says."

"It sounds most unattractive. Why does anyone join?"

"Interesting question." Wolfe considered, looking out at the purple tent. "The Accord offers security and purpose to people who have never known either—and room and board for life. Aha, here's an interesting development." He pointed down to where a red flasher was being raised high atop a telescoping metal pole by a half-dozen Listers. "That's usually the signal for a recree." The pole was fitted into a wheeled stand, the light began to pulse and a howl went up from the dancers. Wolfe sat back and frowned. His intuition told him that his meeting with Adam 100 was about to bear some shocking, bloodstained fruit.

Morgan stared at him blankly. "Recree?"

"Sort of a spontaneous carnival—a combination of dance contest, drinking party, sex orgy and brawl. The flasher is considered the heartbeat of the event. Odd though, you rarely see one outside a free zone." Ali materialized by the table, setting down a carafe, a tall glass filled with ice and a tiny silver dish on which rested the antidote capsule.

Morgan raised her eyebrows. "Your file describes you as a beer and wine connoisseur. Have your tastes changed?

So she had read his file. Wolfe raised his glass. "Circumstances have. With Flash I can be sober in two minutes if I need to be."

"You take few chances."

"As few as possible," agreed Wolfe. "Recent experience suggests it doesn't pay. Good health."

"Cheers. So here we sit, drinking expensive drinks and watching the mob." Morgan looked up at him through mismatched eyes. "Do you ever feel like an aristocrat on the eve of some especially bloody revolution?"

"Absolutely not," declared Wolfe, who had no intention of revealing whatever doubts he privately harbored about his role. "Unlike aristocrats, we're not here to exploit. We're Upper Canada's last hope—and the last hope of the millions of timid, discouraged people who still do their best to scrape a living out of basement hydroponics or micro-fish farms or whatever." He took a deep breath. "Sorry—I didn't mean to preach."

"No apology required. There's no disgrace in strong feelings." Morgan looked at him impassively through her odd eyes.

Three stories down, the Listers were beginning to howl, the constant, senseless baying of a hunting pack, rising and falling through the gathering dark, bringing goose bumps to the skin. A few seats away sat Amadeus, apparently deep in a chess game with an autoboard. A dry hot wind blew across the terrace, playing with a curling strand of dark hair that lay across Morgan's forehead. Wolfe restrained a sudden impulse to lean across the table and brush it back into place.

Instead he looked down into the plaza. More fire barrels had been rolled up and were spouting orange flames into the night. Two more drummers had joined the first, and were thumping out a complicated rhythm that drowned out the Accord hymns coming from the purple tent. He estimated that nearly a thousand Listers were now dancing, some brandishing knives and homemade guns. It was a medieval masque of hell, so close you could hear the demons wail, smell the smoke of their fires. He shivered despite the heat and turned back to Morgan with a sense of unreality. His turn to interrogate. "You flew in from Seoul. Is that your home?"

"Who has the luxury of a home these days?" Morgan made an expansive gesture, revealing a silver snake bracelet coiling up a slim but muscular forearm downed with light brown hair. "For the last few years I have lived out of a suitcase, my dear Dr. Wolfe. I blow around the globe as Helen's needs dictate. You know how it goes in the Institute."

"We all grew up somewhere though," persisted Wolfe, guiltily aware he was ignoring Rickki's advice. ("Stay away from those lost years, Long Eddie. Put them clean out of your little mind. If Helen wanted us to know she'd tell us. No, don't make a face, I know what a inquisitive gumbah you are sometimes.") "I'd guess you spent your formative years in England."

"Some of them. Others in the Emirates, Indonesia and so on. My family was classic expatriate actually, and I was the classic ex-pat offspring: boarding school, visits to pater and mater in their hardened compounds on holidays, three trips a year paid for by The Company." For a moment Morgan managed to look quite prim, lips pursed, hands folded demurely in front of her. "Then university, switch to art school, more-or-less accidental hookup with the Institute and here I be."

"And on a remarkable assignment too." Wolfe set his features into an expression of disarming innocence. "I was fascinated when you told me of Helen's artistic aspirations."

"Interesting, isn't it? Officially, Helen believes it will help her understand the human experience. Not an easy task when you think about it. How can an entity that cannot die share the fear of death? Or a creature of silicon and steel understand desire?" She smiled, a rather sad little moue, and poured more wine into her glass.

"You said 'officially.' What about unofficially?"

Morgan hesitated. "I may be completely wrong you

understand. But I think . . . I think she's trying to evolve a soul." She looked away from him as if slightly embarrassed by her own idea.

Wolfe stared at the slim woman across from him in fascination. "What an extraordinary concept! How do you come to that conclusion?"

"From various things she's said. One day for instance she remarked that it was difficult to contemplate endless awareness without soul. Also, she's preoccupied with good and evil, at least in her conversations with me. And with the Apocalypse, or at least with Die Back scenarios. Do you believe in the Die Back?"

Wolfe's suspicions, temporarily lulled, reawakened. He made a noncommittal noise and looked down at the square—the purple recruiting tent at one end, the seething mass of Listers like a swarm of beetles dancing in the growing darkness at the other.

Morgan followed his gaze. When she spoke she sounded almost embarrassed: "It's hard, seeing your homeland in pain."

"Just another domino that has to be propped up."

"I'm sure you feel it more deeply than that."

Perhaps, but it was no time to say so thought Wolfe. Instead he poured more Flash. "Not often. Anyway, I'm a citizen of the Institute."

"Of course." Morgan adjusted her bracelet, twisting the silver snake on her arm this way and that. "But we all grew up somewhere, to use your phrase. Your early memories are of here. The cottage where your mother did her best work is here. We all have roots."

The street lights suddenly dimmed, and simultaneously the lights in the café faded. With a start Wolfe realized he had forgotten the brown-down. The Accord had not. From across the square came the thud of a generator. A moment later, the tent lit up from inside, like a huge purple jewel. Small searchlights around its edge drilled slim tunnels of light into the night sky. It was, Wolfe admitted to himself, a dramatic display. Trust the Accord to wring maximum advantage even from a power-down.

The sight seemed to enrage the Listers. From directly below came a bloodcurdling scream, then another and another, until the shrieks merged into a piercing howl of insane fury. Lines of Listers began to dance and shuffle across the square towards the tent, pulling fire barrels, mounted on wagons, behind them. Three floors down, Wolfe glimpsed Marcel and his assistants frantically locking down the steel grills which screened the café. The handful of police had discreetly moved their riot wagons aside and were watching developments from a safe distance.

Above the long-drawn scream Wolfe heard the sudden dull popping of small arms as Accord guards opened fire on the advancing mob. A dozen rioters fell, then a wave of Listers crashed upon the thin line of Accord guards drawn up before the tent and the marquee's lights flickered out, leaving the square lit only by the wavering flames of fire barrels. Wolfe strained his eyes but could not discern what was happening in the darkness. He felt Morgan's hand on his arm. "Are we secure here?" she asked, her voice calm.

"Oh yes," said Wolfe, straining his eyes to pierce the night. "The café is hardened, and anyway the target seems to be the fair." The screams and the flickering light called forth a primal emotion which he tried to analyze: fear, excitement, a mindless desire to join the battle. Instead he squeezed Morgan's hand encouragingly and unfolded his portable. "Let's call in and get a situation analysis."

Morgan sat back. "This is unusual, isn't it?"

"Totally unprecedented. The Lists usually leave the Accord strictly alone. With good reason. There'll be massive reprisals for this. I think we're watching the beginning of a small civil war. Oh my Lord, what is this?" He pointed across the square to where tongues of heavy orange flame were licking through the darkness, converging on each other until they formed a huge burning cross on the ground. In the midst of the fire was confused movement, then fiery forms, human candles began to spill out of the inferno to thrash and jerk across the blackness, running, falling, finally lying still, self-propelled bonfires scattered across the plaza. Wolfe stared in stomach-churning horror, trying to make sense of the gruesome sight. In a flash of insight he understood: the Listers had poured oil into the baptism pool and set it on fire. With the new converts still inside. He passed a hand across his eyes, feeling weary and disgusted with the human race.

Above, the clouds parted and a full moon peeped out, illuminating the horrid scene as he punched direct to Operations. "Wolfe here. I'm in Davis Square at Café Gabriel. The Listers appear to be slaughtering everybody at an Accord recruiting fair. You picking up anything?"

"Hold a mo, I'll check." Ten seconds later the duty officer returned. "Fragments only. Police are calling for reinforcements. An automatic Accord distress call went out three minutes ago, then shut down. You say you got heavy fighting there?"

"Hard to tell with the brown-down." Wolfe squinted into the night. "It looked more like a massacre than a fight. The Accord were sloppy on defense, they got rolled right over. I think we'd better have an escort back—there's bound to be a lot of aftershocks from this."

"Sure thing. You ready to come out now?"

"No. Let things settle a bit. We'll call in when we're ready to move."

"I'll put a team on standby."

Wolfe disconnected and made a wry face at Morgan. "Sorry about all this."

"It's life in Upper Canada today." Morgan shrugged. "The raw experience will be illuminating for Helen."

Over the lake, in utter disregard for the anarchy below, a full moon was rising, silver and beautiful.

Helen 2

After overcoming some initial resistance, the Accord's employment programs flourished. Well-trained, honest, zealous, Accord employees were sought after by many businesses, especially those in search of cheap labor. Then occurred another major leap in the organization's evolution. The Accord decided to go into business itself. Its first venture—a security firm—was vastly successful. Within three years it was competing in fast food, trucking and textiles. By the time of the Big Bust, the Accord had become not only a religion but a thriving commercial enterprise.

The Temple of the Accord—A Brief History

Friday, July 9
23:57 hours

Three hours after the Davis Square Massacre (as it had already become known) Wolfe found himself once more in a viewing chair in Versailles' main meeting room, awaiting a holographic manifestation of the Boss. The shit had hit the fan, to use his father's quaint old metaphor, and he was covered in it. Also exhausted and fed up; only adrenaline and curiosity kept him awake.

He had arranged for Morgan to be escorted back to her boarding house by a security team. Returning to Versailles he found an urgent message from the Premier, demanding an immediate interview. The ensuing phone exchange had not been pleasant.

Why, Mrs. Clements had demanded in chilly tones, has the massacre not been predicted by Orbital?

Wolfe had temporized, uneasily aware that the Institute had not only predicted it but conspired to cause it—or something like it. "We're still analyzing the data, Premier. We should have a full report within a few hours."

"Good." Mrs. Clements' usually friendly face remained set in stern implacable lines. "I should like you to brief me on results and policy implications as soon as possible. Say eight o'clock tomorrow at Hub Seven? I'm on an inspection tour, I'll take a few minutes out to see you."

"I shall look forward to it."

"No doubt. In the meantime you should be aware that my government is working overtime to defuse the situation. We have been begging the Accord privately not to retaliate for the Davis Square Massacre and I will be broadcasting the same message on all channels tomorrow morning."

"With respect Madam Premier, I suggest we wait for a full situation analysis from Orbital before making any official response."

"And I suggest, Dr. Wolfe, that by then we could have a full-scale civil war on our hands," snapped Mrs. Clements.

"At least let's wait until Mr. Beaufort returns from the Rim before we respond," pleaded Wolfe. "He understands the intricacies of Project Maldon well— we feel his contribution would be invaluable. He'll be back within twelve hours."

"We cannot wait. Until tomorrow morning." She cut off abruptly and the screen reverted to the red and gold logo of the Premier's Office, then to its standing pattern of tropical fish. In a somber mood, Wolfe had made his way to the Ops Room for an update. So far the Accord's only response to the massacre had been a series of mighty threats. Peace was still a remote possibility, and if anyone could patch together a truce after tonight it was Mrs. Clements. Unfortunately, Wolfe had a queasy feeling that peace in Upper Canada was not on Orbital's immediate agenda. From Ops he had proceeded to the meeting room for a midnight conference with Helen.

He took a deep breath and looked at the clock. The sands of time trickled into the mysterious hole that was the past. As the red letters of the digital display announced a new day Helen sparkled into being on the holo stage with a slight smell of ozone. Tonight she had chosen to present herself in plain black overalls, with her brown hair darker and pulled back in a severe bun. Her features were subtly younger; Wolfe wondered briefly if Helen was treating herself to a holographic face lift. The AI's image raised a neatly manicured hand in greeting. "Good morning, Edward. Interesting times, wouldn't you agree? Not many SoCy experts have a whole country as a laboratory—you must be in your element."

Wolfe's pent-up anxiety released itself in a rare outburst of irritation. "Dammit Helen, this is more than an experiment—people are getting butchered down here."

Helen seemed abashed. "Quite so. My apologies for the lapse of taste. I see statistics and equations and sometimes forget that you see burning bodies. We must both recall that our experiences are only two sides of a multifaceted reality. Please forgive me."

"Of course." Already Wolfe regretted his outburst. "I overreacted."

"Not at all. I rely on your honest reactions to stay informed. Now then, let's get down to business. What did the Premier say when you asked to postpone the meeting until Mr. Beaufort returns from his credit-raising expedition?"

"She told me it couldn't wait. As I read it, she prefers to take us on one at a time. Divide and conquer."

"Her purpose?"

"Uncertain. Beaufort doesn't know either; I reached him earlier in Manila. She may sincerely want our advice. More likely, she may wish to censure us privately or to lay down some sort of ultimatum, for instance, a guarantee to making damping down the current conflict a top priority. In the worst case she may give notice she plans to phase out the project. If this is the case, Beaufort has promised to return home immediately."

"Could he stop her?"

Wolfe reflected. "I doubt it. He could threaten to withdraw from the coalition and possibly force an election, but if she's determined enough she might risk it. You know how stubborn she is."

"Yes." Helen's icon narrowed its eyes, as if considering. "Do you have any feelings about which way she'll go?"

Wolfe caught himself reaching to pull his beard and stopped himself with a mental slap on the wrist. "I'm inclined to say she hasn't reached a decision yet."

"Ambiguous." Helen nodded. "One way or the other, though, she must be led to see the situation in its proper perspective."

"And what exactly is that?"

"Favorable." Helen sat back in her chair of modulated laser light. "Our intelligence suggests that the Accord in Upper Canada is diverting resources for a major strike on the Lists. If it carries through, it will effectively escalate the conflict into a self-perpetuating civil war. This would be an excellent outcome—the two main threats to Upper Canada's stability tearing each other apart like the calico cat and the gingham dog." For an alarming moment, her two hands became life-size heads of a gingham dog and calico cat, and began tearing at each other with realistic snarls and spitting noises. As suddenly, they disappeared back up Helen's unruffled sleeves. The AI smiled at her little display. "All we would have to do is control the conflict, ideally so as to generate constant low-level struggle for the next several months. And while the Lists and the Accord weaken each other, we ride the whirlwind into the winter, at which point the benefits of Project Maldon finally begin to be seen." She raised a delicate eyebrow to invite response.

Easier said than done, thought Wolfe. "But how do we keep the conflict at the proper level? It seems to me there is an excellent chance we could lose control."

"A delicate task, but we must attempt it."

"I fear the Premier will not appreciate the true worth of such a program."

"Correct, as usual. Therefore you may not want to propose it to her in so many words. Instead, merely recommend a wait-and-see policy. Point out that the current violence could be a blip. Counsel her not to overreact or introduce new factors into an already complicated equation. In short, my dear Edward, persuade her to do nothing. With most politicians this would be all too easy. Unfortunately we are dealing with the restless Mrs. Clements." She drummed holographic fingers against the arm of her holographic chair. Wolfe was amused to notice she even added the appropriate finger-tapping sound to the audio output.

"I'll do my best. Let me ask though: should we be misleading the Premier on this matter? I don't wish to seem ingenuous, but part of our job surely is to provide accurate information to the government of which she is the head."

"Up to a point," agreed Helen. "Unfortunately, in this case the Premier can be relied upon to distort the information we give her by passing it through an elaborate set of filters."

"Don't we all?" asked Wolfe with a straight face.

"To different extents," admitted Helen. "But the Premier has an especially elaborate and misleading set of filters. She sees reality shining through a haze of misty Platonic concepts like justice and democracy."

"In short, she is a woman of great integrity," suggested Wolfe, wondering again if he was being too contrarian. Still, someone had to present an idealist's perspective to Helen.

The AI merely laughed, an odd tinkling noise which cut off abruptly as if someone had broken a champagne glass in a corner of the dark room. "I can see your conscience is bothering you again, Edward. Diplomacy and absolute candor are always uneasy bedfellows, and you too are a person of integrity."

"Meaning my filters distort reality?"

"I meant it as a compliment," protested Helen. "A final observation on this topic: if you're uneasy about hedging to the Premier, remember that we genuinely have Upper Canada's best interests at heart."

"Understood." Wolfe judged it was high time to change the subject. "And if she declines to take our advice?"

Helen examined the emerald ring on her holographic finger. "Complete failure would be very damaging, that much I can say with certainty." The holo pulled at her perfectly molded lower lip to signal concern and vexation, then dropped her hand and gave Wolfe an encouraging smile. "One worry at a time though. Use your judgment when dealing with Mrs. Clements, tell her what you think you must. And don't be afraid to go toe-to-toe with her if need be."

Wolfe nodded. "A final point: the destability index is now over seven. I strongly urge a partial evacuation of staff if the index hits seven point five. Otherwise we will have little or no leeway if the situation blows up in our faces."

"No." Helen shook her head emphatically. "An evacuation now would be taken as a vote of nonconfidence in the government. We have to stand pat just a little longer." Helen held up a hand to forestall his reply. "Please, Edward, no arguments. And be of good cheer. For once things are flowing somewhat our way. And there is a tide in the fate of SoCy programs that taken at the flood leads to victory. Now go and get some rest." The holo waved and imploded in a vortex of steely lavender and purple, leaving Wolfe feeling less-than-fully prepared to surf the tide of destiny.

He strode down the darkened administrative corridor towards Data, hoping Hans was working his usual eccentric hours. Of anyone on station, the old data dick was most likely to have some ideas on how to deal with a rogue AI—in the remote event one should appear.

He was in luck. Hans lay stretched out on couch three, his lucky berth as he had once explained, his face covered by a featureless blue SamSung helmet, his gloved hands moving as he manipulated virtual objects somewhere deep in the Net. Six other blank-faced figures reclined in similar positions around the dim room, like giant insects dreaming somewhere inside a subterranean nest. Wolfe pressed the red button on the side of the couch to notify Hans he was wanted and dragged a metal chair up beside his couch. After a minute or so the old dick sat up, removed his helmet and glared at Wolfe. "This better be good; I just got inside an Accord subarchive and it looked interesting."

"It's important," soothed Wolfe. "I need information fast, and I don't know where to find it. I had to come to an expert."

Hans made a huffing sound and looked at his helmet longingly, then back at Wolfe. "Well then? What must you know with such urgency?"

Wolfe grinned without humor. "I need to know what procedures exist for handling a rogue AI. Needless to say, the question is purely hypothetical—and confidential."

"Needless to say." The data dick met his eyes for a long moment, then looked down and began to strip off his gloves with exaggerated care. "I assume you're not talking about internal diagnostic software or self-damping control loops?"

"No. I'm talking about what an organization—let's say the Institute—would do if its AI defeated all internal safeguards and went on the rampage. There must be some theoretical work on the subject."

"Oh yes. In fact there's much more than that." Hans took a green bottle of Heineken from the cool-tray beside his couch. "Drink?"

Wolfe shook his head. "No thanks. So what would the appropriate response be? To offline the AI?"

"Precisely. And mechanisms exist to do just that. In the case of the Institute anyway. I know because I helped design the system." With a sharp twist of his wrist Hans opened his beer. Balancing the cap on his thumb he flicked it expertly into a nearby recycling bin.

"Tell me about the Institute system," urged Wolfe.

"It's a classic fail-safe design. The Dean and all the governors carry override keys at all times. Two independent signals must be entered within a half-minute of each other. The second signal activates backup facilities to handle functions normally handled by

Helen." Hans took a long pull at his beer, wiped his mouth and belched. "Ah, that's better. Ten seconds later, the system takes her offline completely, shuts down incoming and outgoing signals except for those from diagnostic and maintenance crews. From the AI's point of view, just like a quiet holiday, away from the noise and bustle." Hans smiled grimly. "Such at least is the theory. In practice there is some doubt as to how safe the procedure is."

"Why?" asked Wolfe. "It sounds safe enough."

"The concern is that the sudden restriction of data flow will traumatize the core personality. Offlining might be the AI equivalent of being in solitary for a few years, or in an isolation box. We just don't know." Hans swallowed the rest of his beer at a gulp and plunked the empty bottle back on the cool-tray. "This is all in a report to the AI Security Committee at the U.N. if you want the agonizing details. And now, can I get back to work?"

"Certainly. Thanks for the help." Wolfe made a mental note to order Hans a case of Heineken at the first opportunity.

The old data dick reached out and grabbed his arm as he began to turn away. "A word of caution, boss. You be careful who you ask these questions, and how. Not everyone knows how to keep his mouth shut the way old Hans does. You focus?"

"Understood." Wolfe nodded, more to himself than Hans. He focused all too well. "Thanks for the advice."

He climbed the stairs to the residential floor and let himself into his flat. "Hi, boss," said his console in a sugary tone which contrasted sharply with his mood. "Have a good time?"

"Not especially," snapped Wolfe. He retrieved a bottle of Flash from his desk. "Any messages?"

"Just one, boss," reported the console. "You want to view it?"

"Of course I do." Wolfe rolled his eyes in exasperation.

"Of course you do," echoed the console in ingratiating tones. Morgan's image displaced the standing pattern of tropical fishes that masked the screen. "Hi, Edward. Letting you know I'm home safe, as requested. A memorable evening, but let's do something more frivolous next time." Her enigmatic grin faded.

"Save?" chirped the console with idiot good humor.

"No. Reset." He glanced at his watch: too late to call back. Instead he poured a shot of Flash into one of the crystal glasses he had inherited from his grandparents, opened the living room window and crawled out onto the rusted black fire escape. Below him, the moon reflected silver off the oily black water of the pond below. He cocked his head to listen to the random pop of small arms fire across the city. A few blocks to the north a fire glowed. The Listers were enjoying themselves. Watching the blaze he resolved to order contingency evacuation plans drawn up tomorrow, whether or not Helen approved. What were on-site directors for, if not to evaluate the situation on the ground and act on it? If that branded him as overcautious, so be it.

There was a half-seen blur of motion in the darkness and the Rooftop Cat appeared on the fire escape, a few steps above where he sat. Wolfe rummaged in his overall pocket for the foil-wrapped scrap of fish he had purloined from the cafeteria, unwrapped it and placed it on the steps. Rooftop meowed softly, showing the pink inside of his mouth, and began to chew on the fish, his head sideways for better leverage.

"What about it, Rooftop?" asked Wolfe, sitting back down. "Is this how it starts? The Die Back?"

The Rooftop Cat stopped eating for a moment and

blinked his golden eyes thoughtfully. Yes? No? Old Rooftop wasn't letting on.

Wolfe surveyed the night sky, wondering if he was beginning to believe in the Die Back. It was far from difficult in Anno Domini 2027, with the Islamic Coalition lapping like a rising tide against Fortress Europe, a score or more of conflicts crackling around the globe as too many people contested too little turf, and deadly viruses stalking the huge human herd like unseen predators, growing bolder and deadlier every year. Yes, he could believe in the Die Back.

At least it was something to believe in. Despite endless predictions, Jesus had not shown up again, nor Mohammed nor the Buddha, at least as far as he was able to judge. Nor did the revelations of new religions such as the Temple of the Accord encourage him to believe in divinity. What then? All the humanist philosophies, the notions of Homo sapiens' perfectibility, stood bankrupt and barren after the outrages of the last century. The SoCy equations of Drs. Singh and Hartley offered some certainty, in a cold way. And then there was Helen, growing in intellect and understanding year by year as she fell through space. Helen, now seeking a soul, if Morgan's guess was right. And he didn't even believe in Helen. Wolfe climbed back in his window to fetch the bottle of Flash. It was indeed an odd world and getting odder. He missed Omaha.

Behind him the console spoke ingratiatingly. "Call from Paris for you, sir."

"I'll take it." For the second time in a few minutes the tropical fish shivered and resolved into a human image, this time of the eccentric near-genius that was his sister. Kim had matured during her years in Paris. She still affected glasses, but she had traded in her round tortoiseshells for burgundy cat's-eye bands, and her short, fine brown hair was woven around her face in a tight spiked cut. Tonight she wore a simple cream-colored suit that whispered discreetly of high salaries and large bonuses. Even so, and as usual, she was hauntingly like his mother: the same wide green eyes, high forehead and determined chin. She had inherited their mother's character too, a thin veneer of meekness hiding a will of steel. "*Bon soir*, elder brother. How's your life?"

"More fun than ever. Our latest amusement is a small internal war, Lists versus the Accord."

"Is that so? May they all slaughter each other, somewhere out of my sight. Listen now, like Santa Claus says, I may be coming to town. Madam La Presidente called me in this morning, gave me her ring to kiss and told me to take a few days off, then present myself at our Caribbean facilities for possible reassignment. That's her way of saying I'm being considered for a promotion."

"Felicitations."

"Felicitate me when I get the job. On my time off I thought I'd head out to a spa in the Rockies via the old home town. Is that a good idea, or are your local disorders going to be a problem?"

"Not unless you plan to stay in a free zone or an Accord tabernacle. It's mainly hit-and-run stuff anyway at the moment, small raids on either side. Neither side's mounted a major offensive. Yet."

Kim bobbed her head. "In that case, I'll be in town tomorrow with a massive expense account to squander; can you join me for dinner?"

"Sure—unless some other crisis erupts between now and then, or one of us catches the flu."

"Both real possibilities," agreed Kim cheerfully. "Say at the top of the Tower, around eight? What's that decadent restaurant called?"

"Final Years? I'll dust off my dinner jacket and send my wig for powdering. Have you got time to visit the cottage while you're here?"

"Time but no inclination. Still too many evil memories—I had nightmares regularly when I was there last time. Until tomorrow."

The screen reverted to aquamarine, and golden electronic fish resumed their leisurely swim across its surface. Wolfe clambered back out on the fire escape. The Rooftop Cat had gone its mysterious way; he was alone again with the night.

Evil memories and nightmares. Yes, they both had those, although his sister perhaps suffered more. Kim had been tormented for years by the memory of their parents' murder. They had been shot eleven years ago, while he was still a senior weenie, twenty-two years old. He had been told by his supervisor one steaming night in Bombay where he had been working on an urban revdev project. Next morning he had flown to Toronto and taxied to the morgue. There, in a green-tiled room, with a curious sense of detachment he had identified the chalk-white, broken waxworks that had been his parents.

The crime had been vicious and uncomplicated: mother and father shot in their sleep and the house ransacked by a pair of renegade Listers. An alert neighbor had heard suspicious noises and called the police. The murderers had been caught as they sneaked out the back door. One had brandished a semiautomatic and been killed instantly. The other was in custody. All for two bottles of Scotch and a handful of five-pieces.

"But why shoot them, in God's name?" Wolfe had demanded.

The police officer shrugged. "You want my guess? For the fun of it. They see it on the holos, they have to try it out, they just *have* to try it out. Besides, these two were from the Freezer—mad dogs, true drain crawlers."

His sister had taken a leave of absence from BioAge's Paris labs, and arrived in Toronto the day after him, looking like a pale young version of his mother, with his father's wide green eyes. He picked her up at the airport; as she emerged through customs he felt a sudden surge of affection for her—his only living relative, nearest chromosomal match, a techno-Pandora just itching to open the gene box and see what was inside. Crazy Kim.

Together they cleaned their childhood home, everywhere mementos of their shared past: a doll with pink cheeks and a faded dress on the top shelf of the hall closet, an antique cassette tape of Goldilocks, the shiny green model of the Jaguar E type that had stood on his bureau until he was fourteen—all the detritus of growing up, scattered across the barren foreshore of the years.

A real-estate agent installed a for sale holo on the dried brown grass of the front lawn, where it forlornly winked its message at the blazing blue sky. In a matter of days the house was bought by an investment syndicate for conversion to hardened rental property.

The psychic miasma of the crime seemed to linger. One day Wolfe noticed tiny flecks of blood—his father's presumably—on the carpet. To his horror he began to cry. Neither of them could sleep in the house. Kim stayed in a suite at the Four Seasons, courtesy of BioAge, and Wolfe checked into the University Club, which was affiliated with the Institute.

The funeral was held on a sun-soaked May morning, in a sprawling green graveyard right under the flight path of the Toronto airport. Jets screamed directly overhead with a noise like tearing cloth as the rent-a-pastor, a tall, hatchet-faced woman in a black cassock, read the service in a high, nasal voice. On the drive back downtown an odd thought struck him: "You know, in a funny way they died the way they wanted to—in their beds, together, quickly and without pain."

Kim stared at him and sniffed. "Glad you pointed it out. Otherwise I might feel sad." She began to cry again.

"Dammit, of course we feel sad. But what I said is true. It's some consolation, isn't it?"

"They were murdered."

"Would we feel better if it had been an earthquake or Tokyo Flu though? Death is death after all."

"You think weird sometimes. Now shut up and let me grieve in peace." Tears began to stream again from under her wire-rim glasses and down her thin cheeks. He had not seen her cry since her tenth birthday when she did not get a microscope.

Since then she had become even more detached from the ordinary run of humanity, cultivating what looked like a quiet drinking problem, working long hours and spending downtime communing with a crate of Beaujolais and the inevitable stack of scientific discs. Never exactly politic, she had become downright uncivil, blurting out her opinions whether or not they were likely to offend. She had once told BioAge's executive vice president to his face that he was an ass. Without question her manner had stood in her way. But now, a promotion was in the wind. Perhaps maturity and time had begun to mellow her personality, bringing her a measure of inner peace. He hoped so.

The orange glow in the sky had abated. He yawned and clambered back inside. closing the window behind him. Die Back or no, it was time to sleep. He needed all his wits to deal with the infuriating, admirable person that was the Premier.

Mrs. Clements

I am often asked what is to become of the billions of poor and illiterate—the gang members, the Listers, the Azu Zus, the Nonsuches and all the rest—as conditions continue to deteriorate. Many who ask the question clearly hope that if and when the Die Back comes it will visit the hovels of the poor first—and better yet, remain there until its work is done. However that may be, in the interim this huge and miserable mass of humanity is being squeezed tighter and tighter in a vise of dwindling resources and soaring costs. Many will be squeezed back to the dust they came from. Some or even many may emerge from the titanic pressures as the human equivalent of diamonds—brilliant and endlessly enduring.

Conversations with Helen
Turing Category: Artificial Intelligence level 7 @
Skellig Michael Orbital
Skellig Michael Press, 2026 CE

Saturday, July 10
09:20 hours

After a hasty breakfast, Wolfe made his way down to the garage, ten minutes before his scheduled rendezvous with Amadeus. To his chagrin, his driver was already sitting, imperturbable, at the wheel of the wretched Isuzu. Amadeus put the Bouncer into gear with the fiendish grin of a torturer preparing his instruments. The vehicle lurched ahead and Wolfe prepared himself for another bone-jarring ride, writhing and wriggling against the plastic upholstery in a vain attempt to get comfortable.

Although not easily intimidated, he was uneasy about the coming skirmish. The fiery Mrs. Clements was the nearest thing the beleaguered country had to a hero, or perhaps even to a soul—the last, best northern liberal, as one mediosopher put it. Alternately, in Rickki's waspish phrase, "a poodle with the soul of a rottweiler." Or was it the other way around?

During the secession crises, when war with Quebec had seemed inevitable, it was Clements who had negotiated the complex settlement which established Upper Canada as a separate state. As its first ambassador to the United Nations, she had built an international reputation as a human rights advocate and an honest broker between the Islamic Coalition and what remained of NATO.

On returning home she and Beaufort had founded the Renaissance Party, a shaky coalition of more-or-less moderate groups, and had won the next general election on the strength of sheer charisma. Then, on Beaufort's insistence and despite her strong private reservations, they had hired the Institute to pull Upper Canada back from the brink. How must it look to her now? She must think her objections to SoCy completely vindicated. Perhaps they were. Wolfe groaned aloud.

The laboring air conditioner could not compete with the stifling heat. He wiped his sweating palms on his black cotton trousers and swore to himself. Amadeus glanced at him in the rearview mirror, diplomatically returned his eyes to the road. A ten-minute drive through squalid back streets brought them within sight of the red brick pillars which marked the south gate of Hub Seven.

Community Hub Seven was a sprawling maxSec enclave of a dozen-odd city blocks, its perimeter defined by a black steel fence terminating in spiked points and paralleled on the inside by a man-high brick wall behind which defenders could take cover. Access was via two gates, one to the north of the compound, one to the south, each guarded. Wolfe snorted to himself. Here was progress! As Mac had truly observed, social conditions in Upper Canada now bore a stark resemblance to those of the last Dark Age: frightened citizens huddled behind rings of fortifications, barbarians roaming outside. Or maybe it was the perennial human condition.

In this case, safety had brought a measure of prosperity. Inside the urban fortress was a hodgepodge of two- and three-story houses painted in the Hub's blue and white colors, dotted here and there with silver-gleaming banks of solar collectors and the huge Victory greenhouses which supplied most of the hub's vegetables. Home to a dozen thriving light industries and twenty thousand people, many of them ex-Listers, Hub Seven was visible proof that at least part of Project Maldon was working.

Amadeus pulled up at the hub's gate and showed ID strips. One of the Hub militia, a thin boy in blue jeans, motioned for them to get out. Wolfe and his blankie clambered onto the pavement and submitted to a quick but thorough search by a matronly woman with sharp intellectual features and a moon-faced, beer-bellied older man with a huge ginger mustache. Wolfe grinned at them as they probed. The three militia constituted a fair sample of the citizens' army that defended the hubs. So far their ordinariness had prevailed. After a moment the guards stood back. "Thanks, brothers," said the woman. "The Premier awaits you at Memorial Park. Just follow the main road right down to the end."

They drove down the road indicated. In contrast to
the strict order of the Accord campus, the hub was an
exercise in exuberant chaos. A huge white silhouette of
Archangel Gabriel playing a jazz sax was being painted
on the blue aluminum wall of a long low building that
Wolfe recognized as the hub's sports auditorium. Groups
of children frolicked in parklets under the supervision
of elderly men and women. Each lawn-sized green patch
had a single apparatus: in one a curving homemade slide
fashioned from the metal skeletons of two old street
lamps, in the next a giant climbing trellis of tires and
lengths of pipe. In the Post Millennium there was no
shortage of building materials for the innovative. To his
left, an outdoor class in archery was under way. The
bow—silent, low-tech, reliable—was making a comeback
as a weapon of stealth. In a field further away a group
of power-booted hoppers were practicing stunts over a
huge in-ground trampoline. As Wolfe watched, one hopper executed a perfect triple gainer at a height of seven
or eight meters, and returned to earth to a smatter of
applause. People of all ages, many wearing blue and white
hub coveralls, strolled along the sidewalks enjoying their
day off, apparently oblivious to the conflict beyond their
walls. Except of course that most of them had automatics slung over their shoulders.

At the end of the boulevard was a traffic circle.
The leftmost exit had been cordoned off with a red
plastic ribbon. A half dozen broad-shouldered government agents in black overalls and heavy dark
glasses lounged nonchalantly at the entrance to the
blocked-off park, reminding Wolfe of soldier ants.
Amadeus pulled up and Wolfe descended, showed ID
to the leading soldier ant and received a curt nod
to proceed.

In the park, a platoon of militia—a motley mix of
men and women with stubby Changs slung over their
shoulders—guarded the perimeter, peering out from

the low brick shelters behind the wire, or watching from the low brick towers that rose every several hundred meters along the wall. At the park's edge, a square black board was nailed to a maple tree. On it were displayed a half-dozen pictures of ordinary-looking people: each with a date and a brief epitaph. Wolfe stopped to read one:

JUANITA OVERFIELD, MAY 27, 2026. SOUTH GATE. KEEP THE FAITH.

In contrast to these warlike bodes, the park dozed green and smiling under a summer sky. Wolfe inhaled the drowsy smell of new-cut grass and thought of calmer days. Odd that children growing up here and now would find nothing strange about living and working inside a keep, thinking nothing amiss when their families took guard duty or burial detail. Once it had only been so in front-line states like Israel. Now Israel was a radioactive desert and the front line was essentially the front door. So it was in the PM; he shrugged and walked on.

Scattered here and there across the lawn were pairs of wooden armchairs facing one another across outdoor chess boards, meter-square cement tables topped with red and black tiles. Chessmen, handcrafted ceramic pieces, stood on each board ready for use, a testament to the level of trust within the hub. At one of the tables, apparently absorbed in an end-game problem, sat Mrs. Clements. Although in her early fifties, she was still an attractive woman, with red hair, now elegantly streaked with gray. At his approach she looked up from the chessboard then sat back in her chair. With a pang Wolfe noted that her wide green eyes were tired and bloodshot. Crossing the strip of lawn he performed a grade-four bow, underling to superior, took a seat across from the Premier and waited.

"Thank you for coming at such short notice, Dr. Wolfe." Mrs. Clements' voice was low and musical.

"A pleasure, Madam Premier. I only regret that Mr. Beaufort could not join us. He has an excellent understanding of Project Maldon."

"He is certainly full of enthusiasm for socio-cybernetics," allowed Mrs. Clements. She gestured about her. "Our choice of meeting place is fortuitous. Amazing the ingenuity shown by the people here. And by the hub's output. I'm given to understand the venture is totally self-supporting."

"An interim success," agreed Wolfe. "As you know, the community hub program is the nucleus of Project Maldon. If we can just maintain control, the hubs will be able to exert their influence on larger and larger areas, creating whole new zones of prosperity. We should begin to see the effects by Christmas, if we can just hold on."

Mrs. Clements nodded. "I am familiar with the theory. Who knows? It may even work, given time. However, certain of the Institute's theories are clearly not working."

Wolfe inclined his head. "You refer to what precisely?"

Mrs. Clements laughed without humor. "Don't play the innocent, it doesn't become you. Obviously I refer to the massacre at William Davis Square last night, and the ensuing street violence, which has already claimed over two hundred lives, so I'm told. Or has Orbital overlooked the little squabble between the Accord and the Lists?" Her green eyes shone hard and bright as jade.

Wolfe took a calming breath, brought himself into focus and pitched his voice to convey sincerity. "We have not overlooked it. I had an interesting conversation last night with Helen on the subject. She pointed out that there are many ways to view a given social phenomenon. The situation here is a case in point. You and I see blood and bodies and a city torn by strife. Orbital chews the numbers and comes up with a different perspective, no less accurate and considerably more useful for defining policy."

"No doubt." Mrs. Clements let the silence lengthen while she picked up the red queen from the chessboard, examined it idly, set it gently down again. "And what is this godlike perspective that comes to us from Orbital?"

"Based on an intensive SoCy analysis, they feel that the situation has actually eased."

Mrs. Clements' gaze wandered slowly over the militia guarding the wall, the black obituary board, spires of smoke rising outside the fence. She turned back to Wolfe, her wide mouth set in an ironic line. "And how does Orbital come to this extraordinary conclusion? Any rational person can see in an instant that we are far worse off now than a week ago."

Wolfe shook his head. "Appearances are highly deceptive, Madam Premier. Upper Canada has been unstable for the last several months. Accord membership here was closing on critical mass. Had it achieved that mass, there would certainly have been a major dislocation. That trend has now been slowed." He molded his features into what he hoped was an expression of earnest sincerity. "And so this conflict, while outwardly unpleasant and tragic to the people involved, is not a bad thing in terms of sociocybernetics."

Mrs. Clements shook her head. "I'm sorry, Dr. Wolfe, but I can't follow you into a looking-glass world where war is peace and chaos is actually order. Is this really what SoCy is all about, this distortion of basic reality? If so, I am disappointed."

Privately, Wolfe sympathized with the Premier. Maybe she was wrong, but if so, it was an honest mistake. Whatever the case, his task was to persuade, not to philosophize. He answered calmly: "SoCy can involve us in apparent paradoxes, madam. Recall that just before the Bust the world economy was robust by most traditional indices. In the same way, Upper Canada may have appeared perfectly quiet and orderly a few weeks ago. In sociocybernetic terms, it was on the edge of a major discontinuity."

The Premier made a fretful gesture with her hand. "Could you explain why, in plain English?"

"I can try, although the concepts are not as compelling in words." Wolfe thought for a few moments. "For governments to endure, they must either reflect majority sentiment or suppress it. Until now, the government here has always reflected it. Not that everyone supported a given government, but a majority at least agreed on its basic form and function."

Mrs. Clements stared at him, plainly suspecting an attempt to befuddle her. "So far you have not told me anything to amaze me."

"The basics of SoCy are not revelations, Premier. They are in many ways a mathematical codification of common-sense notions. Much of Machiavelli translates beautifully into SoCy matrices. The point is this: it can be mathematically demonstrated that when a certain proportion of local residents—a critical mass if you like—questions the form of their government, the situation becomes highly unstable. We've seen it happen everywhere from Algeria to Zaire in the last several decades. If the dissident group is militant, like the Accord, the government must either fight or fall. At current rates of recruitment, the Accord would have reached critical mass sometime in October."

"The situation seemed normal enough until last night," sniffed Mrs. Clements, plainly unconvinced.

"*Seemed* is the key word, Premier. Sociocybernetics operates on the principle of the straw that breaks the camel's back. The camel seems fine until you add that one extra straw—then suddenly its backbone snaps. The same rule applies to social orders: they can withstand enormous stress without apparent damage, then at some point they suddenly break down. Social change isn't gradual—it's a series of sharp discontinuities."

Mrs. Clements laughed, a pleasant sound which reminded Wolfe of water bubbling in a small, clear brook. "And you are telling me the camel has been severely overloaded for the last few months?"

Wolfe smiled politely. "Exactly so. Recent events, paradoxically enough, have lightened its load. This is why Orbital feels that the situation has actually eased here, despite the recent hostilities."

"Only now we have a small civil war on our hands," persisted Mrs. Clements, moving a red pawn to attack a white one on her board as she spoke. "Are we really better off?"

"With respect, Premier, the current fighting is beneficial to us in its current form. It is essentially a gang war which diverts the attention and resources of two groups which would otherwise be focusing their murderous rage on us."

"Even supposing I accepted this outrageous simile, why was there no warning from Orbital of the outbreak of hostilities?"

"It is beyond the capacity of SoCy to predict such outbreaks, madam."

Mrs. Clements tossed her red hair impatiently. "A moment ago you cited the Big Bust to me as proof that SoCy could make real-world predictions. Now you tell me that it cannot predict major events?"

"The massacre was organized by a clique of Listers known as the Exodus Faction," explained Wolfe. "SoCy cannot predict events set in motion by a handful of malcontents, only events based on mass phenomena, such as the Bust. A regrettable shortcoming which we are working to remedy."

Mrs. Clements sniffed. "Not being a SoCy expert I can't argue the point with you. Let us turn to practicalities. I am in charge of this country and I must be responsible for its welfare. For almost two years now we have been guided by the Institute. The results are as we see. The Institute claims these results are desirable. I disagree."

"A clarification please." Wolfe held up a warning hand. "We don't say the current situation is desirable, merely that it is the most desirable outcome that could have been engineered. We can also mathematically demonstrate that other outcomes would have been worse."

Mrs. Clements made an impatient gesture. "Your policy recommendation then, given the current situation?"

Again Wolfe hesitated, aware he was treading on very dangerous ground. "We strongly suggest the government refrain from any intervention until we have analyzed the situation further."

"Good God, what a supremely cynical response." Mrs. Clements frowned, creasing her face into harsh lines. "Does Orbital seriously suggest we stand aside and watch while two groups of citizens slaughter each other?"

"In a fundamental way they are not your concern, Premier." Wolfe sat forward intently. A ladybug alighted on his hand for a moment then flew off again towards the playground. "About thirty percent of the population voted in the last election. These people are your true constituency, the citizens you speak of. The Accord views any secular power as a blasphemy, and Listers don't vote. Members of these groups are fellow citizens in name only. They have no identification with our aims or principles. They are, if you will, alien nations among us, and the government must view them accordingly."

Mrs. Clements seemed in no hurry to answer. She looked again across the park, then back at him. "I must work for the good of Upper Canada and all its people."

"With respect, Premier, there is no such thing as Upper Canada. There is a definable land mass cohabited by a number of warring factions. You are in charge of one of them."

"What a repugnant idea."

"That is how SoCy views it, madam. Other interpretations do not make sense mathematically."

Mrs. Clements stood and began to pace back and forth on the short green grass, a common habit of hers when thinking. "And as you may have gathered, I am increasingly uneasy about the perspective offered by SoCy—and increasingly disturbed about policy deriving from the Institute."

Wolfe realized he had been holding his breath. "How so, Madam Premier?"

She stopped before him and her long shadow fell across his knees. "I discern a heartlessness, a disregard for human suffering which disturbs me. Where is the humanity, the compassion? Do our reforms need to go so far or so fast? Perhaps it is time to slow the pace of change."

"An inspiring idea, but with all respect, impractical," said Wolfe. "The lifeboats are already crammed to capacity and leaking fast. If we slow down now rather than making for shore we will surely sink. It is as straightforward as that."

Into the silence floated the happy sounds of children at play. Mrs. Clements considered for a few moments then shook her head and began to pace again. "No. I disagree with Orbital. In particular I want to see this current conflict stopped before it escalates. If Orbital cannot suggest policies to this end we will develop our own."

"Unwise. I am specifically instructed to say, Madam Premier, that any intervention at this point may significantly compromise the outcome of Project Maldon."

Mrs. Clements nodded to herself, as if his words had confirmed what she was thinking. She sat abruptly and spoke with the air of someone who has come to a decision: "I'm sorry, Edward, but a point of principle is involved, which maybe an artificial intelligence entity cannot grasp. I look to you to convey it to her. We cannot countenance a civil war here, no matter how expedient it may be from a SoCy perspective. Please inform Orbital that I will be meeting with Deacon Zacharian later today to work out some peaceful solution to this crisis." She held up an imperious hand to forestall Wolfe's reply. "There is no more to be said."

Wolfe rose and bowed again. "I will relay your decision to Orbital. Pray excuse me." He walked slowly through the park, realizing with a certain sense of relief that it was now out of his hands.

Overhead a jet whined through the sultry air, leaving a long, white contrail to mark its passage through the upper atmosphere. With a start he remembered that Kim would be arriving in an hour or two.

BioAge

Large segments of Toronto have effectively been abandoned. From a high vantage point at night you can see the cankers of darkness here and there upon its face, blotches where the lights have gone out and never come on again. But the oddest, the most compelling symptom of the city's mortal sickness is the so-called Freezer, which stands like a huge tombstone on prime waterfront land, the showpiece of the city's short-lived renaissance.

Originally the Perpetual Trust Tower, it early acquired an unsavory reputation. Building materials were substandard, safety standards lax, and the entire electrical system was one huge glitch. Construction was dogged by problems. A whole team of workmen fell to their deaths while installing an elevator. An outbreak of Tokyo Flu decimated the first tenants who moved in. and it was said their ghosts roamed the building looking for revenge. Haunted or not, accidents were common. Circuit breakers blew for no reason, plunging whole floors into darkness, fires broke out, and it proved impossible to shut the air conditioning off.

Prospective tenants canceled their leases and current occupants moved out, never to return. The chilly, derelict building soon became a potent symbol of the complete and final failure of middle class values: industry, enterprise and planning. The city's strangest, most feral denizens—List renegades, criminals and madmen—fled there for refuge, secure in the knowledge the police would not pursue. Thus, by some perverse extension, the Freezer

153

became first a sanctuary and then a religious shrine of sorts for the Lists of Upper Canada.

> *The Wounded City*, An Analysis of Urban Living
> Scribner-Sony, 2023

Saturday, July 10
20:00 hours

Wolfe returned to Versailles and reported back to Helen, a long one-way data squirt. In due course, once the data was assimilated and analyzed, Helen would request a live meeting. Probably sometime tomorrow.

That done, he left a memo on Rickki's console requesting immediate development of a evacuation plan for non-essential personnel (if such could be found) and, slightly more at peace with himself, plunged into his administrative work. Finally, as the long summer day began to dwindle, he went upstairs, took a shower and began to dress for dinner while his console surfed the evening 'casts. Premier Clements was widely reported to be launching a top-level peace initiative. Reaction from the Accord, underneath the bombast, seemed favorable. He shook his head, wondering what Helen was making of it all as she tumbled through space. Never mind for now. It would be good to see Kim again.

The Final Years Restaurant perched on the top of the Upper Canada Tower like an force-fed goose impaled on a tall steel pole. The most expensive restaurant in Toronto, it catered to high-end expense accounters as well as the unanchored ultra-rich, forever unfulfilled, forever roaming from city to city in search of gratification. Final Years was founded on a single conceit: its patrons were the aristocrats of the Post Millennium age, desperate to gorge themselves with dainties before the Die Back. To Wolfe's disgust, it was immensely popular.

Amadeus drove him downtown, awkward and cramped in his black tie and tuxedo, cleared him through the security checkpoints at the tower complex and escorted him to the steel and glass foyer where they waited under the heavy-lidded gaze of two security guards until a chime pinged. The elevator door slid open and Wolfe stepped into the glass-sided cage. He had not been up the tower since he was a boy. Now he remembered the exhilaration his younger self had felt as the elevator slid away from the ground and the whole face of the city came into view—the skyscrapers, the fraying black ribbons of highway, the no-man's-land of the waterfront framed by the poisoned lake. Up and up into the violet evening he soared until a tiny "pop" sounded in his ears. The elevator came to a smooth stop and its doors slid open on the Final Years.

Piano music tinkled in the crystal air, and the mouth-watering smells of garlic, butter, roasting meats brought saliva to his mouth, just like a goddamn dog, greetings from the brain stem. The maitre d'hotel, a chubby man of middle age with rouged cheeks, wine-red coat and the perfumed curls of a white horsehair wig falling to his shoulders, performed a bow of three flourishes. "Honored sir, I welcome you! You have a reservation?"

"I'm joining a lady. Name of Dr. Wolfe."

The host became noticeably more genial. "Indeed! Milady Wolfe is already seated on the sunset side." He smiled expansively. "This is best. You revolve through twilight and back into night in one sitting. This way please."

Wolfe raised his eyebrows and followed the plump figure along the narrow, curving walkway. In the booths he recognized several local celebrities—a pair of well-known drug designers, the young and debauched heir to the Labatt fortune, Bowser the News Hound, anchordoggie of the nine o'clock news—the privileged and the idle, frightened rich of the PM.

Kim was in a private booth, high curved walls of black leather enclosing her like the petals of a huge sable flower. She was looking thoughtfully out the wall-high window at the city below, her face in profile. A bottle of champagne stood on the table before her. At his approach she turned and smiled.

Wolfe kissed her cheek, slid into the booth. The host presented him a menu glowing red, green and blue with finely-drawn figures of angels and devils, as elaborate as an illuminated manuscript. "Perhaps my lords and ladies would enjoy more champagne while deciding on their banquet?"

Kim made a absent-minded gesture of assent. "Just so."

"Double Flash for me," added Wolfe.

"As milord commands."

Wolfe jerked his head at the maitre d's receding back. "He seems unusually solicitous, even for Final Years."

Kim drummed neatly manicured fingers on the table "My keepers no doubt told him we were VIP." She motioned with her chin to the next table, where a young, fit-looking couple toyed with hors d'oeuvres. "Those two—combination bodyguard and advance crew. Apparently they come with the new job. If I get it."

Wolfe looked casually over, back again. It was not surprising. Top researchers were hard to come by, easy to lose to competitors or unfortunate accidents. "Your interview is in the Caribbean?"

"A little island somewhere off Antigua. That's where the research labs are."

"MaxSec?" asked Wolfe, remembering his days with the Caribbean Anti-Buccaneering Bureau.

"Oh sure. Not that there's any need. Blackbeard

himself wouldn't risk the kind of bug you can catch hanging around a BioAge facility without invitation."

A waiter returned with bottle and silver bucket, filled their fluted glasses with a flourish and withdrew. Kim raised hers: "Success and long life. Or a short and a merry one, whichever is better." She drank half her glass and frowned. "So how goes your work? I thought you were supposed to advise the government on how to run things."

"So I do." agreed Wolfe.

Kim frowned over her glass at him. "Either you're doing a truly appalling job or they're not taking your advice. The nation's bankrupt and now you've got a civil war on your hands."

With the destability index well over seven, she had a point, thought Wolfe. Not that he would admit as much, that would break their unspoken agreement to disagree. "Sociocybernetics is not an exact science," he remarked mildly. Fixing an ingenuous expression on his face he waited for the explosion. His sister was a pronounced skeptic when it came to SoCy in general and the Institute in particular.

Kim tossed her spiked head indignantly, like a bull spotting the matador's red cape. "Exact science? It's not a science at all, it's an excuse for playing God. The Institute is a collegium of effete meddlers with a design-flawed AI in charge. You should find yourself a real career while you still can."

Wolfe assumed a wounded expression. "We've demonstrated time and again that the Hartley-Singh equations work. How can you be so cynical?"

"I'm not questioning the equations, I'm questioning your use of them. The Institute isn't content to describe and predict, it also tries to influence outcomes according to its own ideas of good and evil. But it doesn't work half the time because you're imposing a value system on a neutral set of statistical rules. Also, any system alters when watched. Therefore you're introducing observer error into things."

"That only applies to subatomic phenomena."

"How do you know?"

Wolfe grinned. "Helen told me so."

"It's nonsense. Anyway, the rest of what I say stands. Plus your AI is well known to be a megalomaniac."

Wolfe sat back against the leather cushions. "Why do you say that?"

"I've seen the nasty thing interviewed. I've read its books. It combines the zeal of Savonarola with the mental capability of a platoon of Einsteins. And the fashion sense of a lavatory attendant, or so I've heard. Definitely a vile combination."

Wolfe laughed. "Helen's becoming more chic by the moment. Do they still have lavatory attendants in Paris?"

His sister ignored him. "Here for instance in Upper Canada, what do you really hope to accomplish?"

"To minimize social disorder."

"To minimize social disorder. That's a laugh." Kim filled her glass again and gestured with it at the city below, so that champagne slopped onto the stiff white linen. "The rich are safe in their hardened hidey-holes, the good burghers of the middle class are long defunct and the Accord is about to take over and exterminate the rest. So who are you minimizing disorder for?"

Wolfe raised his eyebrows, nettled despite himself. "What would you have me do then? Stand by and watch?"

"Why not? Do you really think you can save this corrupted society? You can't, you know. The whole North American FreeMarket is rotten through and through. Anyone in public office is there because of the Accord, and just waiting for the right moment to say so."

"What about Mrs. Clements?"

"Who? Oh the Premier. She's an anomaly, she won't last. You know where we are? Rome just before Constantine. The old system is dead, and they're just waiting for a suitable chance to bury it. You know it's true. Well, don't you?" Kim fixed him with a challenging look.

"I concede nothing," said Wolfe loftily. "Your arguments are narrow and self-serving."

Kim threw up her hands in disgust. "Still a romantic, I see."

Wolfe grinned, recalling some of their violent arguments around the dinner table as teenagers. His sister had once been so angry she had thrown a full plate of spaghetti at him. "So Helen tells me. Anyway, we can't all go off to be coddled in the Caribbean."

"No, but we can all do something useful with our lives. You're not as vapid as you sometimes pretend. Why not take up an honest line of work?"

"Really, Kim, you think working for BioAge is noble? Your corporate masters care about nothing but share prices. Which aren't doing very well at the moment, I might add, thanks to the practice of releasing advanced pharmaceuticals before they're properly tested. One of our staff had an adverse reaction to a BioAge product just a few days ago—almost killed him, and me too as it happens."

"That may be," his sister shot back fiercely. "At least the products we come out with are meant to benefit everyone, not just some hypothetical elite."

"They're meant to make money for the shareholders, nothing more or less. If toxins sold better than medicines, BioAge would make them instead." Wolfe realized he was becoming heated and sat back. "Let's just say this—maybe the Institute isn't right all the time, but it tries to help things along. Someone's got to, or we're all going to be guests at the Die Back one day soon." He held up his hand as his sister opened her mouth. "Alright, alright, maybe we're going to be anyway, but we have to at least try."

Kim took off her glasses and polished them on her crisp linen napkin. "You don't know when you're beat, do you? Here's my prediction, made without benefit of SoCy. The Die Back is inevitable. Some massive war will break out, or a major plague or both, and a helluva lot of people are going to get scratched. And at the end of it, we'll be back in the low billions and those who are left can breathe easy again. I plan to be one of them."

"Not impossible," admitted Wolfe. "According to some of our sims, unfortunately, no one at all will be left. Not even you."

"Nonsense. There are always survivors. *Ecoute-moi*, Edward, is cash the problem?" Kim put her hand on his in a rare gesture of affection. "I've got investments piling up, cash flow I don't know what to do with really. Help yourself."

"Thanks, Kimmy. But it's not money. I just like what I do. Most of the time anyway." Wolfe's stomach give an angry rumble. "Let's order. I've only had a peanut butter sandwich today. How about this?" He read from the gilt menu: "'The royal seafood platter. For two or more, bio-purity guaranteed. Mouth-watering monarchs of the sea go to a noble doom of garlic and butter at the behest of Lords and Ladies of the Land.' I guess that's us. It's described as a three-bugle presentation, whatever that means."

"Means it's expensive." Kim refilled her glass, took half of it at a gulp, refilled it again and moodily watched the bubbles fizzing up the side.

The restaurant had turned perceptibly by the time they ordered; now they were facing due west, looking into the red eye of the setting sun. The fleet of dirigibles tethered at the Island Airport floated at their moorings like a string of airborne sausages. As Wolfe watched, one detached itself and slowly spiraled upwards, switching on its billboards as it leveled off a few hundred meters outside the restaurant's windows, a flying green and red jewel of light, driveling its messages across the hot evening:

. . . INVESTMENT OPPORTUNITIES IN THE NORTH - CALL NOW. . . . 416-777-LAND. . . . HOT TONIGHT, TEMPERATURE 36 AND RISING. . . . GOING TO THE CONFERENCE? CALL NOW FOR TICKETS. . . . LIGHT UP THE NIGHT WITH LABATT, AND KEEP SAFE. . . . TIME: 9:04. . . .

Wolfe turned back to his sister. "So tell me about your work. What'll you be researching?"

Kim put her finger to her nose in a Gaelic gesture of secrecy. "Hush hush. So much hush they haven't told me yet. Hope it's something interesting."

"When I last heard, your lab was developing a vaccine for Tokyo Flu. Making any progress?"

"We were, or so I thought." Kim frowned. "Then one fine day we were told to cease and desist, refocus entirely."

"Why?"

"How should I know?" Kim emptied her glass and filled it again. "Researchers at BioAge concentrate on how, not why."

"A bad habit that." Wolfe raised his eyebrows. "They must have given you some reason surely?"

Kim frowned. "Economics. The virus mutates too fast to hit, ergo chances of commercial success were too low, payback uncertain and so on."

"Sounds very unconvincing."

Kim absently twirled the point of a hair spike between her fingertips which were painted a stylish silver. "Alright then, what's your explanation?"

Wolfe toyed with his Flash. "Perhaps there were outside pressures."

"Balderdash. Pressures from where?"

"Who knows? The U.N. maybe."

"Why would they want to stop it?" Kim looked genuinely puzzled.

"Wake up to the Post Millennium era my dear befuddled sister. Tokyo Flu is a blessing to governments. It decimates the elderly, the poor, anyone who is already at risk—exactly those who the authorities most want to get rid of. You know how many have died of it? About half a billion at conservative estimates, and rising all the time. Only so many people can fit in the lifeboat, as I think you once told me, demonstrating once again that Allah is compassionate."

A triple fanfare sounded on a trumpet, and their dinner appeared—a seafood sculpture on a cart pushed by four waiters, led by a trumpeter with red rouge spots glowing on his fat cheeks and a shoulder-length white wig. On the silver cart two mammoth lobsters, their armored heads crowned by little white wigs, genuflected towards each other, worshipped by lesser shellfish, steamed shrimps, scampi, a family of crabs wearing tiny clerical collars of seaweed. Pots of butter bubbled in little silver pots with devils' clever faces etched on them. Two waiters expertly cracked and served the lobsters, while another uncorked a bottle of wine.

Fragile, surreal seemed the moment; he and his silver-fingered sister, spinning slowly towards purple night as the tortured city flashed and blinked in a million hot colors beneath them. A violinist was going from table to table; the long sobs of his instrument quavered and hung in the air like an elusive fragrance.

Without being ordered, the waiter brought another carafe of Flash. Already he felt relaxed and mildly exhilarated. They now faced almost due south, so that the sky seemed split between light and darkness. The sun had slipped below the horizon and the clouds were still crimson with afterglow; to his left, night had fallen. Directly below crawled the gray witch's brew that was Lake Ontario.

Several months ago he had seen a fish caught at the waterfront, a salmon. Its silver scales were blotched and dull, and a huge mucus-lined sore sprouted halfway up its elegant body. It had a double set of dorsal fins. Amazing any life remained, especially after the Darlington spill. What creatures still lived were blighted and soiled. As above, so below.

Still, maybe everything would be just fine; maybe the awesome intelligence that was Helen would pull the project through and Upper Canada would emerge from the fire of its reforging. Or maybe the barbarians were already ashore, the Premier, Mr. Beaufort, all the lost decent people below doomed before they raised their weapons. In the last analysis, did he care? Wolfe considered the question for a moment and reluctantly decided he did.

His portable vibrated; two short pulses—a top-priority call. He connected and Rickki's ironic tones tickled his ear: "Sorry to interrupt your dinner boss, but there's some breaking news you should know. Someone winged Zacky the Zealot about ten minutes ago as he was leaving a supposedly secret meeting with the Premier. Zacky was whisked off to the Temple Medical Complex but we have a snip of the event from a security eye; it looks like he was only hit in the arm. A very bad shot—or a very good one if the idea was just to sideline him."

"Interesting notion." Wolfe made an apologetic face at Kim and turned away to look out the window so she would not see his concern. No sense in spoiling the evening for her too. "Who did it?"

"Unclear. The assassin slipped clean away. We have one blurred frame of him from a rooftop eye. Medium build, dark hair. Not much to go on, is it?"

Wolfe began to reply, then froze as a burst of blinding mauve light lit the night like a lightning bolt flickering up from the heart of the city. Seconds later another flash dazzled him, then a third, almost directly below. The tower shuddered and the lights went out. Wolfe had seen that kind of flash before, in the Caribbean, the night Saint Sting blew the Nassau Casino into the warm perfumed night for missing its payments. HT-three explosive charges, big ones.

Somewhere a woman screamed. There was darkness for a few moments, then emergency lights twinkled on, a thousand pinpoints of light on walls and ceiling, and a recorded announcement played over the public address system. "My lords and ladies, we are experiencing a temporary power disruption. Please remain in your seats and remain calm. There is absolutely no danger." The piano began to play again. Kim stared at him, her hand frozen on the champagne glass. Suddenly she looked very young and vulnerable. He leaned across the table and took her hand. "It's okay, Kimmy, we're safe. Just the local troubles I was telling you about earlier." He looked around the dimly lit restaurant, saw Kim's two blankies blocking the entrance to the booth, alert for any threat to their charge. None appeared, and after a moment they relaxed and returned to their table. Kim unfroze and poured herself more champagne.

The situation seemed to have stabilized. With a reassuring wink at his sister, Wolfe turned back to the portable. "Sorry Rickki, a bit of a ruffle. You still there?"

"Sure. What's going on?" Rickki's voice crackled with tension.

"It looks like Firework Day from up here—there are bombs going off."

"Oh yeah? Well I was about to say that we're expecting some Accord response to the assassination attempt. I think you've just seen it." A squawk of static drowned Rickki's voice for a moment, then the line cleared again. "Hold on, we're starting to get data. Yeah, as far as we can tell a clutch of bombs just went off across the city. Targets were Lister offices, clan headquarters, the Freezer. We have reports that the Accord is on the streets in force, leaning on anything that looks like a Lister. Downtown's a war zone." She chuckled happily. "I think we're in for a bad night."

"Is it the start of something big?" Wolfe squinted out the window, trying to gauge the extent of the fires he could now see in the South Free Zone. "Like a coup for instance?"

"Doubtful. I'll keep you updated though."

"I'll come in."

"No—stay put. That's just in from Orbital by the way, not Auntie Rickki being protective. We're completely cut off by road. Besides, there's nothing you or I can do right now."

"Alright. Do me a favor will you? Call our friend from the Weird Brigade, make sure she's okay."

Rickki snorted in disgust. "As it happens Ms. Fahaey is snug in her lunatic's boarding house—she called a few minutes ago for a routine check-in. Personally I was worried sick. If anything changes I'll buzz. Don't you dare leave the tower complex until you're cleared."

"Yes, dear." Wolfe pocketed the portable and sat back.

Kim looked at him with raised eyebrows. "What was the phrase you used to describe your work? 'Minimizing disorder' I think? You're certainly doing a fine job. If I were the premier I'd be just beside myself with admiration for the way you've brought the situation under control."

Wolfe made a wry face. "Okay, okay. You've made your point."

A wigged waiter approached with a silver candelabra which he placed on their table. He flicked at an imaginary crumb on the cloth with a duster of peacock feathers and spoke in a nasal, ingratiating voice: "Our apologies for the inconvenience, milady and milord. A temporary power outage only. It happens occasionally when the riff-raff below become agitated. Perhaps more champagne to help abate the nuisance?"

Wolfe looked out the window. There was definitely a fire at the Freezer and another one about halfway up Yonge Street. The rich smell of coffee tickled his nose and two booths down the violinist played a melancholy song. This was not how he had imagined life with the Institute: sitting in a hardened five-star restaurant high above a dying city, watching it burn. Not how he had imagined it at all.

The Skydome Hotel, in cooperation with Final Years Restaurant, offered all patrons wishing to avoid street disorders a one-third discount on room rates. Customers taking advantage of the offer received, as a special bonus, a holo of themselves dancing on the polished wood dance floor, intercut with news broadcasts of the mayhem below. Wolfe took advantage of the hotel's offer and negotiated a further price reduction in lieu of the holo bonus.

Ignoring the luxurious surroundings—silver and black art deco furnishings, marble jacuzzi and Siemens Erospark unit—Wolfe flopped down on the emperor-size bed and woke up the holo unit. On the Accord channel, a wall-high spokesman with neat white overalls, gray hair and insane blue eyes characterized the violence as a final warning from Adonai to the unclean. Adam 100, speaking from a secret location somewhere in the free zones, urged members of the Exodus Faction to go forth and meet their enemies. Premier

Clements appealed for restraint. In the streets, running battles raged on.

Sometime in the early morning hours, as the stars looked down on the burning city through a haze of smoke and smog, armored units from the big base in Downsview took control of the streets and an edgy calm was restored. Exhausted and disturbed, Wolfe told the holo and lights to sleep and closed his own eyes. Lying there in the darkness he thought of the long sweep and wash of history: Homo sapiens hunting itself with flame and steel down the years, carving and recarving the finite, fragile body of Gaea.

Controlled conflict was all very well for an AI to theorize about, but the violence had plainly spiraled out of control, just as he had warned. He wondered what plan Helen had to rein it back in. If any. Again the unthinkable thought wriggled up into his consciousness: what if Helen was incompetent? What if she really did not know what she was doing, what forces she had unleashed? Or, infinitely worse, what if she knew exactly what she was doing? Perhaps, for some inscrutable reason, she wanted to bring on the Die Back, to see the last human stagger and fall in the radioactive wasteland? Wolfe shook his head on the pillow, which suddenly seemed hot and suffocating. He was suffering, he told himself, from what psychologists called the Frankenstein neurosis—terror of the self-created monster which was not good but evil. A hundred checks and safeguards had been designed into Helen. His worries were in vain. *But what if? Jesus come quick, what if?*

A particularly loud explosion rattled the windows, lighting the curtains from outside like a nearby lightning strike. Wolfe grimaced in the darkness. So this was limited conflict—in some cases a good thing, according to Institute doctrine, because it prevented sluggishness. But what was limited? A single death? A hundred? A hundred thousand? To the broken victims it mattered not an atom. He saw in his mind's eye the mortuary in Hong Kong he had visited while at a seminar on the infant organ trade. The figures were, as always, shocking but abstract. Reality was row upon row of tiny bodies, each in a flimsy gray cardboard box, organless and inert. So much life wasted. Statistics did not lie but they could never tell the whole truth. Finally he drifted off into a troubled sleep.

Freezer

The relationship between the Freezer and the Lists of Upper Canada is well documented in modern urban studies. Indeed, visiting anthropologists from around the globe have come to study what must surely be a modern myth in the making. The background is simple: an abandoned office tower is rapidly colonized by the criminals and lunatics of the city. It becomes a place of horror, full of pitfalls and gruesome surprises for the uninitiated. Police, or even criminals, are understandably reluctant to pursue their quarry through the building's awful corridors. The Freezer, as it comes to be known, thus gains a reputation as a sanctuary, a place of refuge. Over the years, it slowly metamorphoses into something more: a perverse temple, a node of anti-spiritual power fueled by all the evil and entropic forces of the PM era.

Breaking Point, A Collection of Essays on
Post Millennial Topics
Henrikus Grobius, Jr.

Sunday, July 11
06:54 hours

Sunday morning dawned windless cobalt blue, with wisps of gray spiraling upwards to mark where the fires around the city were slowly smoldering out. Wolfe breakfasted with his sister, and then turned her over to her bodyguards, who had hired an armored limousine to go to the airport. The taciturn Amadeus was to meet him at half past nine.

With a half hour before his escort arrived, Wolfe rode the mirrored elevator to the thirty-third floor and shooed two cleaning 'bots out of his room. The 'bots, a self-propelled red sucker with a long hose head and a squat four-armed Toshiba char maid, left bleeping disconsolately. He slammed the door on them and punched DO NOT DISTURB, then, jacking in his portable, called up a summary of the night's events. "Whatcha wanna know boss?" it inquired.

"The bad news about last night. Top line please, no audio."

As the figures paraded across the screen he sucked in his breath in dismay. The Accord had smote its enemies with a mighty blow. Lister casualties were estimated in the thousands, especially heavy in the Free Zones, where they had been taken completely by surprise. The Riverdale sept of the New Dawn List, with some six hundred members, had been annihilated. Had Helen known what she was unleashing?

The Accord had also suffered, although figures were not available. With a feeling of relief Wolfe noted that the community hubs had held up well, suffering only minimum casualties. They, of course, had not been direct targets. A consortium of Mohawks had apparently taken advantage of the disorder to assert sovereignty over a huge tract of land near the Thousand Islands.

At a quarter past nine he checked out and went to stand in the hardened courtyard. The first thing he saw was Rickki leaning negligently on the hood of her own custom-armored Volkswagen Chameleon, arms folded, face turned up towards the white disc of the sun, polarized glasses completely silver. Behind her was the Isuzu Bouncer, with Amadeus at the wheel and three other agents inside. Rickki seemed to sense him; she looked down at his approach and her glasses faded to a dull black. "Good morning. Nice night on the town?"

"Memorable. What's this?" Wolfe jerked his head at the escort. "Are we having a party?"

"Of sorts. A late-breaking development. Get in, I'll tell you on the way. I brought you some overalls by the way. You can change in the car."

Eyebrows raised, Wolfe slipped into the front seat. As he closed the door Rickki stepped on the gas, snapping his head back against the headrest, awakening the small residual headache that a half bottle of Flash left him, even after the antidote. "I take it we're in a hurry?"

Rickki nodded, pulling a cigarette from her overalls with one hand while steering around a matte black articulated monster truck with the other. "Yeah, we're in a hurry. That's the problem with modern life, don't you think? Everyone's rushing around, no time to think."

"Exactly the problem. Now, what in the name of Jesus Mediator are we doing?"

"We're going to meet Mancuso. At least, I hope we are. Damn, why can't our escort keep up?"

In the side mirror Wolfe caught a brief glimpse of the Isuzu wallowing through traffic behind them. He returned his attention to Rickki. "Okay, keep talking. Why are we meeting Mancuso? Has Orbital come up with his funds somehow?"

"Nooo. But he's left the Accord anyway. With several squads of Cleaners right behind him apparently. It would appear"—Rickki adopted a nasal, pedantic voice—"it would *seem*, that the Accord is rounding up anyone and everyone suspected of involvement in the assassination attempt on Zacky the Zealot. Apparently Marshal Mancuso's name headed the list."

Wolfe felt the Flash headache begin to throb in earnest. "Any details?"

"Sources at the Temple Campus say Mancuso made

a hurried exit this morning, about three minutes before a team of Cleaners came looking for him. He squirted a cryptogram to us from his car: a location and a time—ten this morning at Allan Gardens."

"Allan Gardens?" Wolfe raised his eyebrows. "He wants to meet in a greenhouse?"

"In the cactus room to be precise. Not a bad idea actually. It's hard to sneak up on someone in a greenhouse. Especially when you have four security teams watching the place like we do. So far it's clean. How he'll get there I can't imagine."

Wolfe nodded and sat back, watching the tortured cityscape flashing by outside: smashed windows, burnt-out vehicles, a low-rise apartment block still smoldering. It was as if the city was turning in upon itself, feeding its sickness with its own living substance. Was it the beginning of the Die Back? "Know what the Canadian equivalent of 'life, liberty and the pursuit of happiness' was?" he asked.

Rickki shook her head, her eyes focused on the road.

"Peace, order and good government. Oh well. Excuse me while I change." Wolfe chuckled humorlessly and began to shrug off his rumpled tuxedo, thanking fortune that he had selected a sober and conservative pair of undershorts last evening, rather than, for instance, the lurid organ-grinder specials his colleagues had given him when he left the Piracy Control Bureau.

The downtown core was under tight army control. Tanks or armored Bulldogs in smudgy gray/brown camouflage hunkered at every major intersection, and squads in full body armor patrolled the streets. Downtown was probably safer than usual, as Wolfe remarked. Keeping to Yonge Street they reached the intersection of College Street with ten minutes to spare and parked in the public lot. One agent stayed behind to watch the cars. With the other blankies sauntering behind them, Wolfe and Rickki walked the remaining blocks to the conservatory. Allan Gardens was a series of delicate glass bubbles rising from the center of a blighted park. Incredibly, despite the city's decay, the Victorian greenhouse continued to operate. It had never even been vandalized—perhaps because even the most hardened Lister appreciated the reminder that somewhere green leaves and lush flowers still flourished.

In the desert plant section the air was hot and dry, the sandy earth dotted with cacti of all shapes and sizes, tiny purple prickle balls, things like overturned caldrons covered with long, wicked spines; directly in front of Wolfe, what looked like a huge spiked cucumber raised its green phallus two meters above the sandy floor. The only other visitor was a very old woman in a ragged pink shawl and matching sunbands who sat on the far bench wheezing loudly to herself.

They seated themselves on a green wooden bench and Rickki spoke with the air of someone passing the time: "You know, I've been thinking about brother Mancuso and how he came to grief. Want my theory?"

Wolfe nodded politely and took a deep breath, savoring the oxygen-rich air.

"I think Helen put the Cleaners onto him." Rickki leaned forward and touched the points of a thing that looked like a green basketball covered with curving red spines. "Youch. Great natural defenses."

"Surely not?" Wolfe considered the possibility and found it less unlikely than he could have wished.

"Why not? If he was wavering, a brief word to the Cleaners and he was over the edge whether he wanted to be or not. They have an open line for tipoffs you know, it wouldn't be hard. Bet I'm right. I'm going to ask her—when all this is over. She's a devious creature, you have no idea. I probably have no idea. Aha, what have we here?"

The old woman had arisen like a walking corpse from her bench and was shuffling over towards them. She stopped in front of their bench, and a sour, unwashed odor made Wolfe retch. "I have a message from a friend," quavered the old woman. "He asks when funds will reach his account. When might that be?"

Wolfe and Rickki exchanged glances. "How do we know you're from our friend?" inquired Wolfe.

There was a short pause while the old woman shut her eyes as if trying to remember some long-ago event. When she spoke again her voice was different, deep and confident, in fact remarkably like Mancuso's. "I am a true envoy," she said slowly, as if repeating a poem learned by heart. "The marshal was wearing a cast when you met. And now an answer to my question."

MaxSec link? Inner ear implant? Multi-branched mnemonic response? Immaterial at the moment, decided Wolfe. "The answer is very soon," he said with more assurance than he felt, staring at the rumpled old scarecrow before him. "It's being arranged even as we speak. Urge our friend not to stand on formalities. We can have him out of the country and up the well within hours."

The old woman cackled and shut her eyes again. She was silent for so long that Wolfe began to wonder if she was having a fit, or had forgotten her purpose. Then she spoke again in Mancuso's voice: "It seems I have little choice but to trust you. You'll find me at the Freezer."

"Excellent." Wolfe nodded. "We'll send a team down right away to get him."

The old woman seemed to have slipped into a deep trance. She stood before them like a rumpled statue. "Make it an elite team and make it invisible. I'm afraid you'll have to go to the top floor alone; Freezer protocol you understand, but you should be alright. Just keep your wits about you and don't stop to talk to anyone or anything you meet on the stairs. Now listen carefully if you want to get in and out alive: you need to bring a human hand. One severed human hand."

"A hand?" Wolfe grimaced in distaste; he was not easily surprised, but this request was perverse, even by the perverse standards of the PM. "May I ask why?"

A note of impatience crept into the voice. "To pacify the Guardians. When you get to the top floor, just beyond the stairwell you'll see a kind of table with candles and things, and two men—at least I think they're men—sitting beside it. Those are the Guardians. Don't look at them, don't speak to them, just place the hand on the altar, bow and proceed down the hall. You'll come to a door with a red light over it. I'll be standing just inside."

"What are the Guardians and why do they want a hand?"

The old woman had begun to tremble. Her voice was rasping in her throat, as if she was short of breath. "They're the high priests of the Freezer. The hand? Truly, I'm not sure. To use in their magic I suppose. The general belief is that the Guardians keep the ghosts at bay, as well as conjuring up power and air conditioning."

"Magic?" echoed Rickki with a wry face.

"Exactly," said the old woman in her eerie deep voice. "Get there before nightfall and be very, very careful. Tip the envoy please. Message ends."

All at once the old woman crumpled to her knees and gasped for air. Wolfe and Rickki took her arms and half dragged her into a sitting position on the green bench. After a minute or two she appeared to recover herself; she looked up with a yellow-toothed grin and spoke in a normal, old woman's voice. "Don't forget the tip, gumbahs."

Wolfe passed her a twenty-piece. "Impressive performance. How did you do it?"

"Professional envoy, brother. Total recall of message, with infinite variations. Even we old dregs can create value now and then."

Rickki laughed, a short, sharp bark of amusement. "Gives me hope for my future. Come, brother, we have work to do."

Paul Johnson, security level three, was a wiry thirty-year-old with short red hair, a freckled face, and several years of intensive experience which had left him with a terse manner and a long white scar on his left forearm. A veteran of the free zones with two runs inside the Freezer, he listened in silence to the briefing then shook his head. "Top floor is where the real weirds hang out, Dr. Wolfe. I've never been that high, but I can well believe the toll is a human hand. You've got the strangest, hardest creatures of the PM holed up on that floor: psycho killers, self-proclaimed vampires, the whole nightmare."

He paused for a moment to think, tapping his big sapphire nose ring for luck. Wolfe noticed he was missing two fingers on his left hand. "Meaning no disrespect but I'd far rather leave you at home sir. Quite aside from the weirds at the Freezer, there may be Accord teams out there looking for us. You're rusty on street ops; you'll be in our way if we run into trouble."

Wolfe grinned to show he was not offended. "I'd rather not go either, but our defector needs the reassurance of my handsome face. You'll just have to baby-sit me."

Rickki nodded and ground her cigarette out in the ecobox. "That's right. Take reinforcements, take armor and air cover if you want, but get in there and winkle our gumbah out. We'll have a Bulldog standing by to get you to the airport where there's a private jet fueled and waiting. You'll be in Miami in time to catch the evening shuttle up the well to the U.N. hub. From there you and your team will accompany Mancuso and the boss to Orbital. If you're real good, maybe I can wangle you a two-day stopover. How's that for an incentive?"

Johnson whistled through front teeth so white and even they had to be regrown. "A charter jet, shuttle tickets for the troops—Orbital must want this gumbah in the worst way."

"You got that right," agreed Rickki. "So what's your plan?"

"We'll go in on foot, just six of us. We'll be less conspicuous that way. Coming out I wouldn't mind chopper support if you're serious." He turned to Wolfe. "Handled any firearms recently?"

"Just the standard monthly tune-up."

The young security officer closed his eyes for a moment as if praying. "Okay, it'll have to do. Briefing in one hour, then we'll get kitted out and go." He turned back to Rickki. "Could you arrange the hand for us?"

Rickki made a face. "Jesus Comedian, the things I do for the Institute. Alright you two, go get ready for the picnic." She addressed her console. "Well now, Mildred, where do we find one severed human hand?"

The team set out from Versailles two hours later: five agents and Wolfe wearing standard street gear— black overalls, red List markings painted under each eye and across the chin to signify affiliation with the Red Sky. Elsewhere in the city they would have been at risk from the Accord, but they were journeying to the heart of the domain of Lists. As Listers they were as safe as street warriors could be in the Post Millennium—which was to say, thought Wolfe, not very.

Everyone toted disposamatics and ammunition in black shoulder bags, and he carried an additional small package, the content of which he tried not to think about. He found the appetite of the Freezer's guardians for human remains frankly revolting—no doubt a finicky reaction based on outmoded middle-class values, but there it was.

It was just after three o'clock on a searing afternoon when they stepped onto the sidewalk before Versailles. The air reeked of detergent. He felt a light touch on his hand, then another on his hair. Startled, Wolfe looked up. It was snowing soap bubbles. Delicate, shimmering, they drifted over the factory roof and broke against the dirty pavement. He watched for a few moments then followed Johnson down Carlaw Avenue.

The brown brick facades of the old restored warehouses faded upward into the hot blue sky. Signs for small and struggling businesses lined the grimy brick and aluminum doorways. Poking out over each was an eye, safe behind its wire basket. At the corner was a withered tree, dying in a pot on the cracked sidewalk, the stunted offering of some municiplan that staggered blindly on, impelled by sheer bureaucratic inertia. Passing, he read the plaque at its base:

> THIS TREE DONATED TO
> THE CITY IN MEMORY OF
> FRED SMITH, LOVING HUSBAND.

A small tribe of Listers with gray and green face markings was camped on the corner of Queen Street and Carlaw Avenue, bundles of dirty clothes on the sidewalk. The smell from their encampment made Wolfe's eyes water: a compound of rotting food, excrement and clothes long unwashed. At either end of the encampment plumes of smoke rose from fires smoldering in sawed-off barrels, which had been decorated with strange patterns like writhing yellow snakes. Wolfe had heard that fire worship was fast becoming popular among the Listers and he found it easy to believe in the primal environment of the streets. The sentinels, a girl of about eight in torn blue jeans and a pair of oldsters with wrinkled faces and sad, still eyes, examined them incuriously as they passed.

They turned onto Queen Street; the broad avenue was lined with the wrecks of stores, beached when the last high tide of commerce ebbed. The cracked signs were their tombstones: APPLIANCES. DISCOUNT FURNITURE. USED BOOKS. Used books! Wolfe shook his head in amazement. Even before the Bust, anyone starting a used book store here would have to have been seriously lacking in commercial insight. Listers camped in the abandoned buildings, defending the shells fiercely against other squatters: the ageless human instinct to call something—almost anything—home.

Through an empty space in the row of buildings where a store had been burnt to the ground Wolfe could see the Freezer, a tall black tower against the clear blue sky. Surveying its ominous bulk he felt a twinge of some primitive emotion. Fear? Horror? If any place projected a palpable sense of evil, surely it must be the Freezer.

A ten-minute walk brought them to within two blocks of their destination. The hijacked office tower now rose directly before them, black, threatening, yet strangely graceful. It had been built by a world-famous architect, and its complex lines were very beautiful against the clear blue sky. On each side were fountains, incredibly still functioning. They walked up the low steps that led to the plaza before the skyscraper and looked carefully around.

At close range the Freezer bore obvious scars; slogans were scrawled in red, yellow and white paint all over the accessible parts of its walls, and the heavy glass in two of the four tall doors had been broken and replaced with boards. To one side of the doors stood a half dozen bravos, tattooed with blue patterns from the waist up and carrying knives on cords around their necks. Small knots of gaunt-faced people were cooking over fire barrels or campfires with grills on top of them. Wolfe scanned the area but could see nothing resembling an Accord covert team. More accurately, he corrected himself, everyone looked like part of a covert team.

Johnson motioned with his head and they pushed through the high black door into the lobby; Wolfe shivered as the cold air pinched at his warm skin. Sleeping mats lay scattered over the polished pink granite of the floor, and little cardboard houses were built around the edges of the huge foyer. The elevators' doors opened and shut on sinister figures with covered faces.

At the back of the lobby was the staircase, a gaping hole opened in the side wall. By it, at a makeshift desk made of concrete blocks and a sheet of rusted metal sat a withered old man in a long blue overcoat and a grimy toque of black wool. He looked up at them with rheumy eyes and beckoned. As they approached he raised a clawlike hand which clutched an ancient Magnum forty-four revolver, its black muzzle gaping just about as wide as a small cannon to Wolfe. "I'm the concierge, brothers. You're looking for something perhaps? Or someone?"

"Just here to make a connection," stated Johnson. "No reason to concern yourself."

"Do I seem concerned?" The concierge cackled and spat resoundingly into a paper bag he held in his other hand. "And what do you wish to connect to, my dear friends? Nightmares? Madness? Sorcery? Just pay the toll, brothers, and be my guest. One shiny new five-bit apiece to use the stairs. One at a time though, that's the house rule. Can't have visitors ganging up on our residents, can we? At least not where I can see. That's called law and order, Freezer-style."

Wolfe gestured at the elevators with his thumb. "What about the elevators? They seem to be working."

"Wouldn't advise it, brother. Not if you value your life. Or maybe your soul. Pay the toll and take the stairs."

"Our brother here just wants a quick look-see." Johnson gave the concierge a five-piece and nodded to Wolfe. "Godspeed."

Adrenaline coursing through his body, he walked over to the door to the stairwell, wishing fervently he was anywhere but here. At his cottage, for preference, tossing in his boat on the black waters of the bay. He sighed and passed through the door. Just inside, he took out his weapon and cocked it. The plastic grip of the disposamatic bulked reassuringly in his hand. Above him, flights of stairs marched up and away into the gloom, lit at intervals by dim orange emergency lights. He began cautiously to climb the sticky, littered steps. The air was chill and dank. At the seventh floor he encountered a silent figure in white overalls, its face obscured by a red hood; it watched him pass but said no word.

When he reached the twentieth floor he stopped to catch his breath. The fire door leading to the main floor area stood open; a symbol which looked like a giant green spider had been etched with some care into its dull metal. From down the hall came an eerie whispering sound, a low sibilant chanting which rasped on his psyche. As he listened it seemed to grow louder, as if the source was approaching. The sound had a harsh, threatening quality. He hastily began to climb again.

By the time he reached the landing of the top floor Wolfe was shivering from the cold. A vile smell pervaded the air, so strong he was forced to breathe through his mouth to avoid gagging. The fire door separating the stairwell from the main floor area had been torn off its hinges. He peered cautiously around the door frame and found himself looking down a long hall lit by a single red bulb at the far end and by several dozen candles flickering on a makeshift altar a few meters from him. Ducking back inside the stairwell he took the package from his bag and unwrapped it, studiously ignoring the sweet-sickly smell that arose. Inside was a small, cold hand, severed at the wrist.

Wolfe said a silent prayer to whoever was listening and stepped into the corridor. The two black-cloaked figures beside the altar did not move, but he felt their gaze shift to him. In front of the altar he stopped, bowed, and laid the hand on the table. It was not the only offering, he now saw. A decaying head, its face averted, was placed between two tall candles, and two other withered hands lay on the bloodstained cloth. An overpowering stench of rotting meat assailed him.

Turning away, his skin crawling, he walked slowly down the dim reeking corridor towards the red light. As he reached it, a shadowy figure emerged from the darkness; he recognized Mancuso's bulk, and even more his sweet, deep voice. "Hello there, professor, shall we away?" Mancuso made a polite gesture for Wolfe to lead. The marshal was dressed in black from head to toe, with a black ninja hood covering his face.

They walked back down the corridor, under the silent scrutiny of the Guardians, slipped around the broken door into the stairwell and began the trip back down to sanity.

❖   ❖   ❖

Wolfe could hear the relief in Johnson's voice as they rejoined the team in the lobby. "Is this our man?"

Mancuso answered for him. "None other. Take good care of me, team leader, I'm a truly valuable asset right now, and a lot of believers would love to cash me in."

Johnson bobbed his head in acknowledgment. "You're covered, sir. Just stay with the group. Singh, LePage, take up positions behind. Okay, brothers, let's head out."

They emerged from the lobby into the blessed warm sun. Just across the plaza and down the steps waited the Bulldog armored vehicle, like a friendly steel dragon. As they began to descend the stained concrete steps by the fountain there was a sharp rattling noise and something sighed through the air. He felt an excruciating pain in the side of his head, then someone jumped on his back, pushed him hard to the ground. Mancuso staggered backwards then cried out and fell to the pavement writhing. Loud chatter of mechanical teeth, more slugs chewing through the air, sharp smell of gun smoke.

Sudden silence. Wolfe's ear felt like it was on fire. He put his hand gingerly up to the side of his head. It came away covered with blood, but to his huge relief he could feel no gaping wound, only a horrid stinging when he touched his earlobe. A bullet must have nicked it. Close, far too close. But in head wounds as in horseshoes, close didn't count. Later on he would give thanks to some appropriate deity over a bottle of Flash. Ignoring the pain he crawled over to Mancuso, who was lying motionless in an awkward tangle of limbs. A long bright streak of red oozed from the back of his head. Johnson was kneeling down beside him. He looked up as Wolfe joined him and grimaced. "There's blood all over you—are you hit?"

Orbital

FLASH
All night before . . .
No morning after.

Flash—an ideal liquor to light up the ideal moment.
Since distillers have made fine products they have
sought the high without the low,
the fire without the ashes.
Eureka!
Another fine product from BioAge
Consumers Division
· Absolutely no toxic aftereffects. Guaranteed.

**Monday, July 12
19:20 hours**

"Launch sequence commencing." There was a click and a perceptible pressure in Wolfe's ears as the lock closed. He pulled again at his safety webbing to be sure it was fastened. Once he had seen a man break every bone in his body when a carelessly buckled strap had come undone during burn, hurling him down the length of the shuttle with a force of six gees.

The long seconds before burn trickled by with a muted noise of machinery. Wolfe wondered briefly what g-force would do to his left earlobe, now several millimeters shorter and still incredibly painful, despite a shot of exocaine. Nothing good no doubt. A short silence then a chime sounded and behind it, a sudden thunderous roar, building every moment until he thought he would go deaf. On a column of superheated steam the shuttle bucked and tumbled up the gravity well, riding rough as a bronco. G-force pressed him far into his seat, until he was sick and dizzy. Just when he thought he could endure no more, the engines cut and in the eerie silence he renewed acquaintance with the queasy miracle of weightlessness.

Alone in the blue and white first-class section, Wolfe checked the bandage over his ear, found it was still dry, stretched and turned in his seat, wondering how Mancuso was faring in the back cabin, which had been converted into a makeshift sick bay. If he survived burn, there was a good chance he would pull through, or so agreed the three Institute doctors who had met them at the Miami spaceport and fussed the unconscious marshal aboard the caravel-class shuttle. In a last-minute change of plans, Helen had chartered a craft to take them directly to Orbital, bypassing the usual transfer at the U.N. space facility. The charter was hugely expensive, but it cut trip time and provided complete security—which meant, as Wolfe had explained to Johnson and his disappointed team, that they did not need to go up the well after all. For that matter, there was no obvious reason for him to go up either, except that Helen wanted him to. Perhaps she wanted him there when and if Mancuso regained consciousness.

The pilot's voice came over the intercom: "Welcome to the top of the well, ladies and gentlemen. We're parked for approximately forty minutes while we wait for the Institute to come and meet us. In the meantime, you're at liberty to swim if you have at least a green certificate in free fall. The cabin attendants will be pleased to assist. I'll notify you ten minutes before we begin final approach. Reminding you once again, Dolphin Shuttle Service takes no responsibility for personal injury incurred."

Wolfe unbuckled, struggled out of his restraining web and pushed off from his chair. A little clumsily at first he pulled himself by the roof handholds slowly down the length of the shuttle into the impromptu sick bay at the back. Passing through the curtain between compartments he found himself looking down (across?) at Mancuso, lying in a modified acceleration couch, a sort of jelly-filled glass crib, white and unconscious beneath an array of wires and tubes disappearing up his nose, into his skull and beneath the flimsy white blanket that covered him. Around him stood or floated three Institute doctors, two women in their mid-thirties and a young man, the youngest doctor Wolfe had ever seen, a pink-cheeked young Scandinavian, who grinned up at him with the innocent excitement of a twelve-year-old at an amusement park before returning his attention to the bank of displays he was watching.

Wolfe maneuvered himself so that he was oriented to their axis, as freefall etiquette demanded. "Hello, everyone. How's the patient?"

The senior doctor, a tall black woman with the stern features of a Zulu, nodded. "Tough as an old goat. We had a few anxious moments during maximum burn when his blood pressure destabilized, but then he came back. He'll make it to HQ."

"Excellent." Wolfe felt a heavy weight of anxiety drop away from him. It would have been unbearable to have got this far only to lose the marshal and his information. "How badly is he hurt?"

"He has sustained severe damage to the left hemisphere. Major reconstructive surgery will be necessary."

"Is he in any condition to give us information?"

The doctor's smile faded. "Oh yes. Anyone with any cortex left at all can supply information. If properly stimulated." She sniffed and looked back at the unconscious Mancuso.

"Although?" prompted Wolfe.

"Although he may not be good for much thereafter." The doctor leaned down and made a fine adjustment to a plastic valve on one of the tubes leading into Mancuso's body.

"I see. Hopefully it won't come to that." Realizing he was in the way, Wolfe excused himself, swam back up to the front of the shuttle and buckled himself into his seat. Closing his eyes he ignored his aching ear, concentrating on the smell of the shuttle, the strange disorienting sense of weightlessness. Memory came flooding back, so real and powerful he could believe he was on his first shuttle trip to Orbital, that Omaha was sitting beside him, trying to conceal her space sickness.

They had met on the first trip up the well, two candidates coming for final interviews with the Institute. Wolfe had asked the Quantas check-in, half jokingly, for a seat by the prettiest girl on the ship. Mr. Check-In had issued him a boarding pass, a strange half-smile on his pimple-pocked face. Well, he had gotten what he asked for. Omaha was the prettiest girl on board. She was also, as the passenger computer had recorded, horribly, intensely prone to space sickness.

To fall in love while trying to trap a floating green globule of bile with an in-flight woof bag, now that was true love indeed. Yet he had, if memory served him right, fallen in love with her that very first flight. Wolfe felt his eyes start to prickle and opened them abruptly. Yes, it had been love at first sight, Jesus Terminator knows why these things happen. And yes, they had spent seven wonderful years together. And yes, now she was dead. End of boring story, change of topic. He pressed his signal button and the shapely cabin attendant swam over to him in an eddy of perfumed air. He asked for a bulb of red wine and a squeezewich.

Some time later came a recorded announcement: burn in five minutes. There was a long interval, then the firing gong sounded and Wolfe was gently pushed back in his seat as the shuttle's on-board engine flickered on, propelling them towards the huge cylindrical hive that was Institute HQ, spinning on its axis as it traced out a perpetual ellipse kilometers above Earth. Wolfe tried to decide whether they were falling or climbing towards it. Either alternative didn't seem quite right. A slight bump, low gravity returned as the shuttle acquired the station's spin and a pop in his ears told him pressure had equalized. A moment later the tanned attendant appeared from the cockpit and flashed white teeth at him. "End of the line, Dr. Wolfe. You're free to disembark." She took the empty wine bulb and led him to the front hatch where a short metal ladder disappeared through the ceiling. "Thank you for flying Dolphin Shuttle."

A ten-meter climb brought him through the massive steel-alloy airlocks and into a small pink and blue-walled receiving room that reminded him of the lobby of a Caribbean hotel. On the far side of a thick glass window a woman of about his age in standard blue shorts and tight low-g T-shirt nodded to him. Her Latin accent was clear and familiar over a hidden speaker: "Welcome aboard, Eduardo." With a start he recognized Estele Del Rio, whom he had worked with back in the Hong Kong days.

"Hi there, Estele. What brings you here?"

Over the speaker came a soft laugh. "I was already here. What brings you?"

"Business, sad to say." Wolfe pointed down the

ladder. "There's a seriously ill man back there, semi in my care. How will you get him out?"

"The medical team just went aboard through the rear hatch. He'll be taken straight to the special neurology unit. No sense in you waiting around. If you'd care to proceed through the door marked decontamination I'll show you to your room assignment."

Wolfe pushed obediently through the blue door into the decontamination tunnel; the locker room smell which permeated every public place in every space station greeted him like an old friend. In a low oval cubicle he stripped off in obedience to instructions issuing from the ceiling and placed his traveling clothes in a wire bin for delousing and storage. Egg-naked he proceeded down the hall, stopping when instructed to let 'bots work their decontaminatory magic upon his person.

Ten minutes later, steamed and rayed, powdered and scoped, he emerged from decon wearing a loose T-shirt and tight low-g shorts. In the presence of low gravity, it was best not to let one's appendages flop, unless one wanted to flaunt them, which he did not.

Estele closed her textbook and stood up to greet him. Wolfe glimpsed the cover. *Simulations of Interstellar Travel, Volume Three*. She addressed him in a lilting, pleasant voice: "Hello again. How was your flight?"

"The best kind. Uneventful. What are you doing here?"

"I'm on assignment to Orbital for a few months. This is my housekeeping chore for the week: greet and orient incoming personnel. Greetings." She stood on tiptoes and kissed his cheek, then stood back. "Now, to orientation. You've been assigned a room on the third level. Here's your privacy card and meal assignments. Do you need a quick walkthrough of the station?"

"No, thanks. I remember the layout pretty well." Wolfe tried to picture the facility: it was, in effect, a gigantic warty tin can spinning on its axis. Up was towards the center of the can, and gravity decreased as you approached the axis of spin until you reached the zero-gravity gym and assorted scientific facilities aligned along the axis. At the north pole were the administrative offices, at the south pole the eating facilities, art gallery and life support units: recycling plants, hydroponics arrays and so on. It sounded straightforward, but it was not.

Within the can, winding in bewildering loops and spirals, up ramps and down staircases were a thousand passages which a newcomer was unable to differentiate. As if that were not enough, the station was constantly growing, as new units and modules were added. About two years ago, a three-hundred-meter extension had been integrated onto the south pole for additional space.

"Are you sure?" asked Estele. "There have been some changes."

"If I get lost I'll ask directions."

"Ha!" snorted Estele, with a toss of her dark hair. "You would blunder around until you starved before you asked for help. I know you well, you see."

"That's called being self-sufficient."

Estele laughed softly. "It's called being Edward Wolfe." She began to move off down the corridor. "I'll show you to your room then—or would you care for something to eat first?"

"No thanks, I'm exhausted. I just want to sleep."

As they walked through the tight, winding corridors, bright with geometrics and coiling lines in a thousand bold or subtle shades—lavender, cobalt, pale yellow—they made the usual small talk of Institute colleagues. "Just up from Upper Canada?" asked Estele. "I understand you've got problems down there."

"That would be an understatement."

"How bad is it?"

"Bad enough. A destability index of about seven point four."

Estele tapped her silver nose ring for luck. "As you say, bad enough. Still, we went higher than that in Pakistan and still came though."

"Losing most of the on-site crew in the process," Wolfe reminded her.

"*Si*, that is true." There was a brief silence. They had both lost friends in the Islamabad fiasco.

They reached a row of numbered blue doors on the third level and stopped in front of the one marked FORTY-SEVEN. Estele gestured. "Your home away from home. I will bid you goodnight. Unless there is anything more I can do for you?"

Wolfe thought to detect the overtone of an invitation in her voice. He had come close to making love to Estele once in Hong Kong, before he had married Omaha, and for a moment desire flared again. Why not? Omaha was dead, she wouldn't mind. No, her presence would still be there, at least in his mind. And—though why it should be a drag on his libido he couldn't see at all—there was Morgan. Clearly, thought Wolfe, he was out of the habit of promiscuity. Clearly, in fact, well along the road to being a tiresome middle-age eunuch, castrated by too much work and too few hormones. Charming. He kissed his escort on the cheek, enjoying, despite his gloomy inner musings on eunuchhood, the feel of her sleek dark hair on his cheek and neck, her fresh female smell. Maybe there was hope for him yet. He stood back. "I'm very tired. A coffee tomorrow maybe?"

"Charmed. How long are you here for anyway?"

"At Helen's pleasure. Probably not long."

"Well, good night then." Estele turned away as he fed his card into the door. It slid open, then shut behind him and the room's console addressed him in a light female voice: "Welcome, Dr. Wolfe. Helen asks me to tell you that Marshal Mancuso has just reached the neurological unit and is in stable condition. She would like to meet with you tomorrow at eleven o'clock, if that is convenient. That will give her time to process whatever information he may divulge."

"Perfectly convenient," agreed Wolfe, wondering how Mancuso, unconscious in the tanks, might be induced to "divulge information."

"Excellent," piped the console after a short pause to enter his response on Helen's schedule. "Your meeting is confirmed—in Helen's garden at eleven sharp."

"Her garden?" Wolfe raised an eyebrow at himself in the cabin's tiny mirror. Here indeed was an interesting development. What did an AI want with a garden?

"At the South Pole, level four," said the console helpfully. "Shall I print a map?"

"If you please." Wolf hesitated one last time and addressed the console again: "Also, get me Elvira Peabody, please."

"With pleasure, Dr. Wolfe. Hold please . . ." A moment later, the familiar face of his recruiter and ex-supervisor filled the screen. Her harsh hatchet features softened marginally when she saw his image. "Edward Wolfe, as I toil for wisdom! What brings you to Orbital?"

"Quick consultation with Helen. Governor, I need to talk to you at some point. Could we spend a few minutes tomorrow afternoon?"

"Certainly. What's the topic?"

"It's complicated. Better to explain when we meet."

"Very well." Peabody consulted a schedule then looked up. "I have fifteen minutes at fourteen hundred, if that suits?"

"Fine. Where?"

Peabody's mouth quivered in what passed for a smile.

"How about the main conference room at the North Pole? I recall you like the view."

Trust Peabody to remember that, thought Wolfe. "I'll see you there."

The screen blanked and he lay down in the small bunk, closed his eyes and listened to the gentle hiss of the air supply, grateful not to be back at Versailles, listening to the noises of the city as it gnawed and gnashed at itself. He could not imagine going to sleep, never noticed when he did.

When the alarm chimed seven hours later he felt completely refreshed, exhilarated and ready for adventure. His ear still ached, but the mirror showed a large scab already formed over what little remained of his lobe. A good thing he was not fond of earrings, thought Wolfe. The wound was not pretty, but the excruciating sting was departing. He measured with his forefinger and winced. Another few centimeters and he would have been floating in the tanks beside Mancuso—or occupying a slab in some chilly basement room. He sprayed analgesic on the wound and set out to find breakfast.

After a few false turns he found his way to the main cafeteria where he ate lightly, taking in new faces, new looks. Bald appeared to be the fashion for orbital dwellers, and one which some of the women carried off with amazing flare. That and their careful, low-g walk gave them a sinuous, almost reptilian charm which reminded him somewhat of Morgan's way of walking. He wondered how much time she had spent here, then rebuked himself for wondering. For better or worse, Morgan was nothing more than a colleague to him. Not so far anyway, another part of his brain answered with a leer.

After breakfast he drank a leisurely coffee which had the strong, slightly bitter flavor he associated with Euro cafés and with Orbital, lingered for a few minutes making some notes on his napkin, consulted a new schematic of the Institute then, with an hour to spare, set off to find the garden of the enigmatic thing that was his oldest friend, mentor and now perhaps his nemesis.

The garden showed as a new construct at the South Pole, level five, not far from the hydroponics section. Wolfe wound his way along garish corridors decorated with the latest green, red and orange geometrics, past alcoves containing glistening metal-alloy statues or tinkling fairy fountains, paused to examine a two-story mixed media display which apparently represented the human genome in computer-generated flares of color, smells and sound tones. He passed a half-dozen holo exhibits detailing the Institute's endlessly varied work. Twice he bumped into friends from past assignments and ended up chatting about the state of the Institute, exchanging gossip, declining with regret an invitation to play low-g basketball the next day.

With less than five minutes to spare he found himself at the entrance to Helen's garden. A light over the closed mock-oak door glowed green; no meeting was in progress. His name topped the list of interviews on the display board beside the door. Even as he watched the display, the tiny letters spelling out his name began to flash. Presumably the protocol was to enter. Wolfe pushed through the door, which swung easily open and then shut behind him.

On the other side he stopped abruptly, blinked about him, then started to laugh.

He was apparently standing on the lawn of an English country house. Underfoot was close-cropped green turf, and directly before him a low table, covered with a black-and-white-check cloth. Three white wicker chairs were arranged around the table, leaving the far side empty. On the table was a black teapot, matching sugar and cream jugs, a single silver spoon and a cup. In a slim crystal vase stood a single red rose. Holographic or real? Wolfe extended a tentative finger, pricked it on the tiny thorn that protruded from the rose's stem. Just as real was the tea set and the black Scottie dog which lounged on the cropped green grass of the lawn, its pink tongue lolling.

Helen had constructed herself a theme park, a complete artificial environment in which to play out her human roles. The room's walls were high-quality holos of what appeared to be the English countryside. To his right a hedge-lined lane wound off into woodlands. Behind the tea table, in the far distance, was a ruined castle crowning a low hill, and on his left a Tudor-style country house with open French doors leading inside. The illusion was almost perfect, even to the sound of bird song. Wolfe nodded in appreciation. Artificial environments had been developed to give space crews a break from the monotony of corridors and small rooms. Every large space facility had one, but this was the best, the most complete, he had ever seen.

He walked cautiously around the table and discovered a low disc of green-painted metal, about two meters in diameter—the holo stage. Suspended a meter or so above the stage by an almost invisible plasteel shaft emerging from the blue holographic sky was a curious object, a translucent pair of soft plastic manipulators—a modified pair of distance hands, of the sort used for remote precision work in space or other hazardous environments. A half-meter below the hands a flat plastic oval about the size and shape of a dinner platter protruded at right angles from the shaft. Wolfe examined it but could not determine its function.

He patted the terrier, and took a seat in the wicker chair opposite the stage. As he did so, a column of light flickered and congealed around the plasteel shaft, and

Helen stood before him, a solicitous expression on her smooth, aristocratic features. Today the AI's image wore a high-necked white blouse, straight black jacket and a broad-brimmed black hat that reminded Wolfe of old photos of the Ascot races. Her hair was darker and her cheekbones, Wolfe thought, somewhat higher. She was morphing definitely, but to what? And—the more disquieting question—why?

"Good day, Edward. Congratulations on your narrow escape—and a thousand commiserations on your wound. Is it painful?"

"Much better today, thank you," said Wolfe, embarrassed. "It was just a nick."

"Fortunately for us all. I'm most relieved." Helen's icon showed an impish smile and gestured about the garden: "Welcome, by the way, to my little folly." There was no mistaking the humor in the AI's voice. Wolfe thought to detect the faintest trace of a British accent as well. Part of the charade no doubt.

"I'm impressed," he admitted. "It's the most seamless artifact I've ever seen."

"It is good, isn't it?" Helen looked about critically. "The room can display several different environments of course, but this is one of my favorites. It feels like home somehow. A cup of tea?"

"Thank you." Wolfe watched with fascination while the holo's image reached for the teapot, poured and returned it to the table with an audible thump. "One lump or two?" asked the icon. The manipulators that allowed the performance were completely invisible within the holo image; for all intents and purposes he was across a tea table from a young English matron. He found it more than a little unsettling. "One, thank you."

"Not a bad little party trick," commented Helen gleefully, holding the cup and saucer out to him.

Wolfe took the proffered cup and sat back. Used

as he was to AI interactions, the immediacy of this encounter had shaken him—as perhaps Helen had intended it to. "May I ask the purpose of all this?"

"The interface experts say it will allow me a better grasp of four-dimensional human interactions and I believe they are correct. It also makes the encounter more real for the other parties." Helen's image sat back in its wicker chair and its eyes twinkled, brief pinpoints of light flashing in their blue centers, Wolfe's favorite AI trick as he had once told her. "Now then, I have a difficult topic to broach with you. How to begin?" She cocked her head as if considering, an affectation Wolfe found amusing in an entity that crunched the mind-numbing equations of new physics like so much rock candy. Or was it possible Helen was bogged down in some tortuous logic loop he could never imagine? "Let us say I have a confession to make," announced the holo finally. "I have been puzzled for several weeks by one aspect of Project Maldon."

Wolfe nodded politely, then almost overturned his cup on himself as the terrier jumped up into Helen's virtual lap and sat there wagging its tail while she stroked the little animal with a plastic hand moving in perfect synch with the holo. The function of the plastic protrusion was now explained; it served as Helen's lap in real time. Humanity was to be revealed to Helen through the instrumentality of two hands and a lap.

Noting his reaction the icon smiled waggishly at him over the little animal. "I call him Toto. Another party trick, based on a recent upgrade. Anyway, as I was saying, I have been puzzled—and AIs hate to be puzzled, I assure you. I wondered why the Accord was planning a coup this summer when its best strategy was clearly to wait for fall or winter, by which time it will have recruited hundreds of thousands of new members.

Right now, the army is clearly too strong; it has armor, artillery and a large cadre of well-trained troops. It is unlikely that Accord street fighters could prevail. Either Zacharian is so far gone in religious mania that he expects Adonai to neutralize the army, or he has found some way to do so himself. If so, what? Could he have suborned part or all of the armed services?"

Wolfe shook his head. "Unlikely—the Accord is unpopular with the military."

"My conclusion as well. But what then? I could find no plausible explanation. Were we dealing with lunatics or clever people with a well-kept secret? You begin to see why I was so desperate to talk to Mancuso."

"And did you?" asked Wolfe, hardly able to conceal his curiosity. In her own tortuous way, the AI was about to get to the point.

"In a manner of speaking." Helen smiled and adjusted her broad-brimmed hat carefully, fueling Wolfe's impatience. "He is in the tanks at the moment, and though he is unconscious we were able to retrieve considerable information. A complete report will be forwarded to you later today. But the key information is this . . ." She leaned forward so that her arm appeared to rest on the table. "Zacharian has arranged to plant three canisters of Class-A biologicals around the city—one in the water supply and two air-burst devices, one on the Upper Canada Tower and one uptown. When the fighting starts, Zacharian will threaten to trigger them if government troops do not lay down their arms. The expectation is that Mrs. Clements will accede."

"Jesus come quick." The tumblers clicked into place in Wolfe's mind. So that was it! He took a calming breath and tried to grasp the simple enormity of the plan. "Is this information reliable?"

"It may be incomplete, given the extensive damage to the marshal's cognitive abilities. However, it is

certainly true—or at least the subject thinks it's true."
Helen's icon shooed the black Scottie down onto the
floor and clasped its hands, managing for a moment
to look like a duchess posing for her portrait. Toto stood
before his holographic mistress, lolling his red tongue
in what appeared to be dumb admiration. Wolfe
thought he knew how the animal felt.

"But Zacharian knows we have Mancuso," he pointed
out. "Won't he therefore change his plans?"

The AI steepled its slim fingers and looked into
the distance. "On balance, I would answer no. The
ambitious young Zacharian and his associates are
now engaged in a high-stakes guessing game. Do
we have a live defector or a corpse? I have arranged
for reports of the marshal's death in transit to be cir-
culated. They will be eager to believe this report
because they cannot change the timing or basic
structure of the coup without scrapping the whole
venture. With probability close to one hundred
percent therefore, they will say a prayer and follow
their plan, perhaps with a few last-minute innova-
tions and unpleasant surprises."

Wolfe felt a chill growing in the pit of his stomach. If Helen was correct, the next few days were
going to have the aspect of some dark nightmare
of destruction. "I see. And the likely outcome of
the conflict?"

"If the government defuses the devices, mobilizes
secretly and fights the war on its own terms then it
will win," replied Helen calmly, bending over and
stroking the Scottie, which responded with a frantic
thumping of its tail on the grass. "Upper Canada's
military has the latest equipment and heavy firepower.
It can hardly lose against a makeshift army of lightly-armed
fanatics. But even if the government wins and we go back
to the status quo of Accord versus Exodus Faction and
so on, we still have a serious problem."

Wolfe nodded. "Agreed. If we foil Zacharian this time but leave him in place, it won't be long before he finds some other way to neutralize the army."

"Precisely. It isn't that hard to do if you're totally unscrupulous—a well-placed nuke, the convincing threat of biologicals in the water supply, kidnapping of key hostages."

"Ergo, we need to neutralize Zacharian. Oh my goodness." Wolfe sat back and drummed his fingers on the wicker arm of his chair.

Helen nodded. "Precisely. And I am now convinced the only way to do that is to terminate him, without making him a martyr. His death should appear to be an accident, or better yet, a suicide. More tea?"

"Thank you." Wolfe put his cup on the table, watched with a sense of complete unreality while Helen refilled it and deftly added sugar and milk. "At the risk of appearing legalistic though, do we have the moral or legal right to act without the consent of Upper Canada's government?"

"Certainly not." Helen's icon manufactured an expression of prim disapproval. "It is completely against the Institute's constitution. That is why the matter must be referred to Mrs. Clements for approval and action."

"And if she doesn't approve?"

Helen smiled. "Once again, it is up to you to make her see reason my dear Edward."

"My record in this area is not encouraging." Into Wolfe's mind swam the image of Mrs. Clements as she had looked at their last meeting, defiantly clenched jaw and green eyes, cold as ice, freezing out him and his concepts with a single chilly glance.

Helen made a tutting sound and Toto looked up hopefully. "Last week you were dealing with a nebulous situation where vague concepts of right and wrong could be introduced with some legitimacy. In this case, we are talking about disposing of a man who is prepared to set off Class-A biologicals inside Upper Canada's major city to get his way. Do you really think the Premier can question that he must be terminated?"

Wolfe nodded. "Oh yes. Knowing the Premier she may well question it."

Helen's icon shook its shapely head in resignation. "I confess, I have a hard time understanding some humans. If she wants to see Upper Canada destroyed, why not just stand back and let it happen? Why involve us in a futile consulting effort?"

"Oh, she wants to save Upper Canada alright. But on her terms."

"Difficult if not impossible. If she balks at this, we have a serious problem. So serious in fact that I see no way around it." Helen's icon emitted a realistic sigh, plucked the rose out of its vase and contemplated it with guileless blue eyes. "Either Zacharian is terminated or we resign. In good conscience, Orbital can't keep a large team in an area which will almost certainly go critical under current conditions." She looked mildly up at him, her presence so palpable that Wolfe had to remind himself he was watching a holo which actually had its physical origin in a large metal cube. He nodded. "Is this a ploy or an ultimatum?"

"An ultimatum." The icon put down the rose, took a sugar cube from the bowl and held it over Toto's head. The little animal begged, and Helen dropped the sugar into its red maw. "Fascinating," she said, more to herself than Wolfe.

Wolfe broke the short silence: "I don't understand. Not a week ago you told me that if Upper Canada fell, it could trigger the Die Back. You forbade me to even think about a partial evacuation. Now you tell me we're prepared to pull out immediately and completely. I sense a contradiction."

"Not really." Helen bent to scratch the neck of the

terrier and Wolfe wondered briefly what the delicate touch of the plastic manipulators would feel like against his own skin. Toto evidently appreciated the sensation; he wagged his stubby black tail and barked enthusiastically. "Whether we resign or not makes no difference if Zacharian stays. Either way, outcomes are completely unpredictable. It's a textbook case of the Hitler factor. As you know all too well, when events are driven by the whims of one erratic individual the situation becomes unstable—and usually very dangerous. Hence our ultimatum: we either remove the Hitler factor or withdraw and hope that the resulting anarchy has a creative outcome."

"Very well. I will deliver our ultimatum to Mrs. Clements." Wolfe slowly put his cup back on the table, torn between relief at the prospect of leaving a place with a destability index ticking up like a thermometer on a hot day and profound sorrow for the land of his birth. Citizen of the Institute he might be, but as Morgan had pointed out, he had grown up in Upper Canada—the beleaguered nation was in some sense his home. Somewhere in the holographic hedge a lark sang soft warbling notes. "And in the meantime?"

"In the meantime we proceed with extreme caution. I have already arranged for the devices to be defused by our top team of experts."

Wolfe sat bolt upright. "Have you advised the Premier of this?"

Helen made a delicate gesture. "No need to distress her at this stage."

"And if they accidentally trigger the bios?"

"They won't. If the devices are tamperproof, our teams will come away discreetly. Otherwise, they will neutralize them." Helen picked up the red rose once more and toyed with it. "I am loathe to send you back to a city with the threat of plague hanging over it, but you are the only person who may be able to talk sense into the Premier. However, I am well aware that you may fail. Therefore I have already instructed Rickki to prepare for immediate evacuation."

Wolfe stared at the imperturbable AI. "When did you issue the order?"

"Last night, as soon as I had analyzed Mancuso's data. I want no more Teherans on my conscience." The icon smiled, a small, sad smile that just twitched at her pink lips. "You're booked on the midnight shuttle down the well, then out of Miami to Toronto. I will arrange an appointment with the Premier for you on your arrival. Good fortune go with you." With a graceful motion Helen leaned forward and offered the rose to him.

Wolfe left the AI's garden in a pensive mood. He had three hours to kill until his next meeting, and he needed badly to think. Returning to his room on autopilot he put the red rose in a glass of water, and lay down on his bed, hands behind his head. He was now in exactly the same position as Omaha, heading into a potential war zone, and there was nothing he could honorably do about it. Charming. What if Helen was sending him back down to die? A line from an old Father Brown mystery came to him: "Where do you hide a leaf? In a forest. Where do you hide a body? On a battlefield." The small space seemed abruptly hot and claustrophobic. He vaulted from the bed, thought for a moment then, telling his door to lock behind him, turned his steps towards the Institute art gallery. It was time to soothe the troubled spirit by the contemplation of beauty. Failing that, he would stop by the cafeteria for a cup of coffee and hope to bump into Estele.

As it happened, the current exhibit featured sculptures by Galiano of Madrid, one of Wolfe's favorite artists. The mad Spaniard was experimenting with a new stimulation interface; at the gallery door an earnest level one fitted Wolfe with four tiny head patches which received and amplified the low-level signals given out by each exhibit. The intent was to provide emotional stimulation corresponding to the mood suggested by the sculptures; the effect was variable. He dutifully stood before the first two exhibits, trying to remain blank and receptive to impressions, but the emotions he felt were garbled and vaguely grating, the emotions of a confused, tedious dream. In front of the third exhibit, however, a holo of shifting vertical lines of orange, yellow and red, the interface evoked an unexpected pang of sheer delight. Startled, Wolfe removed a patch; the sensation faded. Interesting indeed. He replaced the patches and moved to the next sculpture, a collection of shifting multicolored prisms. Immediately a shock of disgust coursed through him, as if he had put his hands into something slimy and cold. Surely not what the artist had intended? He looked at the work's title—DELIGHT OF FAERY SEAS. Either the name was poorly conceived or there was a glitch in the system.

So with the remainder of the exhibit: a few sculptures evoked definite and pleasing responses, while the others moved him not at all or filled him with inappropriate sensations. Wolfe returned to his starting point an hour later, replaced the 'trodes with an amused grin at the level one and bent his steps towards the conference rooms at the North Pole.

Seven staircases and about three klicks of corridor later he arrived at a teak-paneled door with CONFERENCE ROOMS printed outside in small gold letters. Inside was a young, olive-skinned woman with centimeter-long black fuzz covering her scalp and lustrous black eyes. She grinned up at him from her console. "You're Edward Wolfe—or at least you should be. Governor Peabody will join you in the main conference room at the scheduled time."

Wolfe knew the room—it was where he had first been interviewed, first met Helen, seventeen long years ago. It lay at the end of a long, humming corridor, on the very outer layer of the station. Opening the heavy metal door he stood for a moment transfixed. The whole far end of the chamber was a huge window. Beyond it glowed Earth, a precious jewel, deep blue and white against the black velvet of deep space, a rich prize not to be trifled with, gambled or bartered away. Earth, where his race memories were formed over a billion years with a result that no AI could ever duplicate. What did Helen know of the deep call of the reptilian brain, or the millions of years howling exultantly upwards from the savannas, where dusk each day was terror, dawn a deliverance? He shut the door softly behind him and sank into one of the heavy leather chairs, lost in rapt admiration. Moments later a throat-clearing sound behind told him Peabody had arrived.

Seventeen years had passed since Governor Peabody, then a level two, had selected him as a candidate. Now she was one of the six people who, together with Helen, presided over the Institute. He was taking a chance, perhaps a large chance, by sharing his concerns with her. It was unwritten Institute policy that you stayed focused on your projects, and left the broader issues to level five and up. If you had concerns you relayed them via legitimate channels, which in his case meant via Helen. On the other hand, it was stated Institute doctrine that you aggressively confronted problems and asked for help as necessary. Wolfe hoped he was choosing the right policy to observe. Peabody, in his experience, was fair-minded—if a trifle gruff— and with enough independence of mind to accept that the AI might, just might, be wrong. Or worse.

Wolfe turned and there stood Elvira Peabody, older, more lined, her vestigial mustache turning white but as durable and unyielding as ever. It was a measure of Peabody that in an era of cosmetic intervention she had never had her upper lip depilated. She was dressed, unfashionably as usual, in a flowing purple African robe and a matching skull cap. Advancing on Wolfe she shook hands with a firm grip and motioned him to a seat.

Wolfe sat opposite the port, so that the hypnotic globe of Earth was directly before him. With an effort he drew his eyes away from the sight and addressed Peabody. "It's good of you to see me at short notice."

"No notice is necessary. I remember a certain favor you did me in Hong Kong, without which I might not be here. Beyond which, I'd welcome a firsthand report on the situation in Upper Canada. I've been following the situation there with some interest. What is your overall impression?"

"Not good. In fact, I'd say it's about to go critical."

"Indeed?" Peabody frowned ferociously at a green vine dangling from the shelf beside Wolfe. "I was not aware the situation was that unstable. What does Helen say?"

"That is why I particularly wanted to talk to you." Wolfe folded his hands and sat forward. "Can Helen tune in to our conversation?"

Peabody frowned. "Not unless I call her on my console, or so I would suppose. I have no reason to think she bugs the meeting rooms, if that's what you mean. *Is* that what you mean?"

"I suppose so," Wolfe admitted.

Peabody made no comment but merely examined him with pebble-black eyes.

"The fact is," he continued, "I'm concerned about the directives Helen is issuing. They feel wrong intuitively. I've tried to do a quick node-point analysis of the code, but my results were inconclusive. There might be a problem, there might not. I'd need an AI to run a proper test, but of course that's not possible." He searched Peabody's face for a clue as to how his comments were being received, but his old patron merely stroked her upper lip and stared, her face sharp and watchful as a bird of prey's. "Anything else?" she asked finally.

"Yes. For one thing, Helen's recent strategy has been to ratchet up the level of conflict between the Accord and the Lists, thus taking the pressure off our clients in the government." Wolfe glanced out the port at Earth rolling serenely below, then wrenched his gaze back to Peabody. "I warned that this policy might end in an uncontrollable spiral of violence but I was overruled and told to promote the idea of a controlled civil war to the Premier. Mrs. Clements rejected the concept and met with Zacharian Stele to try and negotiate a cease-fire. Stele was wounded by an unknown assassin as he left the meeting, guaranteeing the civil war would proceed. I suspect the shot was fired by one of Helen's special agents who is ostensibly in Upper Canada as an independent observer."

"And if so?" prodded Peabody.

"If so, we are looking at interventions which are totally outside the program code. Which means that my staff are no longer in control of events in Upper Canada. Last week we reached a destability index of about seven point four, which I believed was grounds to consider partial evacuation. However Helen overruled me."

"I see. Anything further?"

"Yes. I have just been charged with persuading the Premier to authorize the assassination of Zacharian Stele. If she does not agree we are ordered to withdraw our entire staff from Upper Canada immediately.

Both directives strike me as arbitrary. There may well be other ways to achieve our ends."

"Have you discussed your concerns with Helen?"

"I've been as candid as I dared to be."

Peabody snorted. "What has daring to do with it? You've been trained in AI techniques—candor is essential."

"I know." Wolfe hesitated, aware that his next words could compromise him severely, brand him as a member of the Frankenstein Faction. "But what if Helen is malfunctioning? Fixation on untenable solutions might be a hallmark of AI psychosis. So is the inability to accept or process alternative points of view."

"You've been doing some homework I perceive." Peabody cleared her throat. "AI malfunction is a possibility, I suppose, although a remote one."

"There is an even more frightening possibility," said Wolfe. He met Peabody's unblinking black eyes. "She may be deliberately destabilizing the situation in Upper Canada."

"But why?" asked Peabody, standing and beginning to pace up and down the conference room.

"I don't know," admitted Wolfe. "But the possibility can't be discounted. For years, our chip wizards have labored mightily to create a true artificial intelligence, something that is conscious. Maybe even something that has a soul. What if they have succeeded?"

"Well, what if they have?" snapped Peabody. "How does that bear on our situation? Or have you developed a sudden interest in theology?"

Wolfe shrugged. "Maybe I have. I ask myself if Helen has developed—free will? Suppose she has her own agenda, of which we know nothing? She may have inscrutable reasons for destabilizing Upper Canada, bringing the Accord to power, even bringing on the Die Back. How would we ever know, until it was too late?"

"You're serious, aren't you?" Peabody stopped pacing for a moment and cracked her knuckles, eliciting the sharp noise of brittle twigs. It was, he knew from past experience, a sure sign of inner turmoil.

"Yes," Wolfe replied, breathing an inner sigh of relief that his fears had not been dismissed out of hand. "It would be one way of explaining her conduct. Another would be that my intuitions stink and everything is just fine."

"Unfortunately for my peace of mind, the record suggests your intuitions are sometimes sound." Peabody pointed a long finger at him accusingly. "This is a very serious matter, you realize. A significant AI malfunction would be disastrous to us. A rogue AI with free will does not bear thinking about. Do you have any idea what would happen if you were correct?"

"Not precisely," admitted Wolfe.

"Then I'll tell you—in confidence, although the information is not, strictly speaking, classified. In fact, it's on file with the U.N. Artificial Intelligence Committee if you know where to look." Peabody blinked. "Briefly, if Helen has gone aberrant we'd have to take her offline and hope backup systems can carry us through until we can bring her back. We'd have no AI control over dozens of critical projects all around the globe, and no AI coordination of our remote systems, including the research fleet. Worst of all, offlining Helen might do extensive damage to her personality, even to her overall functionality. It could nullify years of effort and billions in investment."

"How so?" asked Wolfe. "Surely taking an AI offline for a few hours presents no huge problem."

Peabody sniffed loudly and looked out the port at the blue and white globe. "The amount of data Helen sends and receives each second is staggering. Cutting her off even for a few minutes might be the equivalent of putting a person in a sensory deprivation box for several months. Or then again, it might not. We don't know because we've never tried it." She drummed long fingers on the table. "Nonetheless, this must be looked into. I'll have a word with Governor Falmouth—he's nominally in charge of the Interface Project."

"If it's not too much trouble."

"Oh no, no trouble at all!" Peabody put her hands on her hips and cackled wildly. "Nothing easier than to verify if our AI has gone mad or developed free will. And discreetly too—an interesting challenge to be sure." The ghost of a smile flitted across her grim old face. "Very well. If there's anything in it, I'll be in touch. If not, you'll hear nothing more, as I have better things to do than cater to the neuroses of every level three. Where will you be for the next few days?"

Wolfe grimaced. "Down the well in Upper Canada. And there are three live Class-A biological devices several klicks from our headquarters, so you see why I wanted to pass on the information to someone. Just in case."

"Very well." Peabody patted his shoulder in a rare gesture of affection as she passed. "But probably there's nothing in it. Helen's performance is routinely checked and counterchecked, that much I do know. The Board takes AI discipline very seriously, I assure you." She bit her lip thoughtfully. "Remember that AIs sometimes take strange paths to their goals—that's one reason they're so useful. Meanwhile, keep focused on the immediate situation. We still haven't recovered from Pakistan and Teheran, and we can't afford to lose any more good people."

Ultimatum

Much too much too much too much
So much grief it's unthinkable
Don't think, just flash critical
Blow like Teheran—Go critical

Wait too long in the help-me line
Lost in holding pattern one more time
Name next door hop the music high
Going simple, going critical

Too much flesh in too little space
Needle creeping across your face
Cross a fine red line
Sweeping into the critical
It's simple in the critical

"Going Critical": from the platinum
chip by The Janitors
Top Chops in the Shops, July 2027

Tuesday, July 13
11:00 hours

Two days after he had left it in a welter of blood
and haste, Wolfe returned to Upper Canada, arriving at the Miami shuttle terminal just before dawn,
and catching a morning flight on an antiquated

Eurospatiale Air Train. The flight was delayed for two
hours in Atlanta while languid mechanics performed
first aid on an ailing engine. Hunched in a lumpy blue
airline chair, the smell of aviation fuel in his nostrils,
Wolfe watched the clock and fumed. His emergency
meeting with the Premier had been scheduled for two
o'clock. It was now touch and go if he would arrive
in time. In the back of his mind, scratching to get
out, was another thought. Perhaps he would get there
just in time, disembarking to the news of a mysterious illness ravaging the city. He imagined the weapons
experts, laboring in airless twilight tunnels or perched
in the high places of the city, sweating as they tink-
ered with sudden death, and tried to beam a message of encouragement in their direction.

Lunch—a clear plastic dish of synthofood—did not
distract him from his anxiety. Finally they took to the
air again and the brown stain of Atlanta faded into
the distance.

It was just after one o'clock when the pilot finally
announced they were approaching their destination.
He peered out the small porthole: far below, water
crawled across the face of the world like a great gray
slug. A small electronic "pop" and the flight officer's
lazy southern accents sounded through the cabin:
"Okay, brothers and sisters, starting down now. We've
got turbulence on the approach, so strap in and get
snug."

Wolfe stared out the window for the first glimpse
of the city. To his left the Freezer reared up beside
the shore like a menacing black finger. He could not
make out Versailles among the decaying buildings that
spread down to the poisoned waters of Lake Ontario.
Three pillars of black smoke rose from points inside
the Lakeshore Free Zone, slender black columns con-
necting earth to sky. The sun broke in little rainbows
through the mist his breath made on the window as

the jet began to sway and buck, wallowing downwards through the turbulent air, pulling a thick wool blanket over his ears.

With a sickening lurch the air train dropped fifty feet; the pitch of its engines rose and fell. Wolfe found he was sweating. They were very low now, and the ground rose up like a huge green hand to swat them. Then a soft bounce, a muted hiss, and the air train was whining down the runway towards the glass terminal buildings.

The air conditioning in Terminal Four was down as usual; sweat, urine and aviation fuel combining to make a unique and unwholesome perfume. As he pushed through the crowd towards Arrivals, a wary eye out for hoppers, Wolfe saw three 967 transports with the red and white maple leaf of Upper Canada on their gigantic tails come in for a landing, one after another, blue exhaust smoke trailing from massive engines: shuttling resettled Listers back from the northern settlements for a bit of R and R no doubt.

As he reached the frosted glass doors of Immigration he spotted Rickki, flanked by four Institute blankets and an equal number of plainclothes types with yellow Executive Security pins on their lapels. Catching his eye she nodded almost imperceptibly and gave the ghost of a wink—surely the signal that the biologicals had been dealt with. Wolfe's taut muscles loosened with relief.

"Welcome home, Long Eddie. How's your lobotomy?"

Wolfe touched his sore ear lightly with his forefinger and grinned. "Better this kind than the other."

"Spoken like a true philosopher." Rickki took his upper arm in a surprisingly powerful grip and began to steer him through the crowd while the blankies wrapped up the space around them. "You must be the bearer of good news or something—the politicos really want to see you. The Premier's secretary has called six times since lunch to check on your status. They even sent a proper car for you—no Bouncer for us this fine day."

They emerged into the blinding sunlight, where an armored silver Mercedes was waiting. Rickki got in beside him in the leather upholstered back seat, while the other agents slipped into two escort vehicles in front and behind.

"Alright, Sam, punch it." Rickki slid the glass closed on the driver and flopped back into the leather. There were bags under Rickki's eyes and her coveralls looked as if she had slept in them, but she seemed as perky as ever. "Didn't think you were going to make it. As it is, we still got—" she checked her watch "—twenty-seven minutes. Lots of time for a cozy chat. What held you?"

"They booked me on an old sky train. Naturally we had a spot of engine trouble."

"Lucky you got here at all in that case. I didn't think there were any trains left in service."

"There shouldn't be. So focus." Wolfe checked that the intercom off, then mouthed the deadly words: "The biologicals?"

"Disarmed, as of ten o'clock this morning."

Wolfe felt his muscles loosen in relief. "Thank Jesus Contractor."

"Amen," echoed Rickki with great sincerity. "They were just like Mancuso said—big canisters, radio-controlled. We're monitoring the frequency of course—no one's tried to set 'em off yet."

"What did they do with the goodies?"

"Took 'em to Versailles." Rickki grinned. "Makes you squirm, doesn't it? Don't worry—we've arranged to air-express them out first thing tomorrow. One surprise—guess who headed up the disposal teams?"

"I can't imagine," said Wolfe truthfully.

"Our resident weird, that's who."

"You mean Morgan Fahaey?" Wolfe goggled at his security chief.

"None other." Rickki sat back in the cushions, pleased with the effect she had created. "She was at all three sites—an absolute expert at disposals one person told me. Cold as ice."

"Well I'm damned. I thought she was an interface expert."

"Still claims she is. This is just a sideline. Apparently she's a lady of many talents."

Wolfe digested this new information in silence. Perhaps none of his earlier guesses about Morgan had been right. Perhaps, after all, she had been assigned here as an on-site trouble-shooter. In which case, what other unexpected skills might she be called on to demonstrate? "What about the Accord conference?" he asked finally.

"Delegates are starting to flow in. So far we're tracking about twelve thousand subscribers."

"I suggested we try to hold some back at the border," said Wolfe. "Helen advised against it. She didn't want to alarm Deacon Zack. What's their current disposition?"

"Ominous. We have three major concentrations around the city. The biggest is at the Temple, with another on the downtown campus, right beside the University. The third is a few blocks from us, at Logan Avenue and Dundas Street. About five thousand subbies in all. We managed to put an agent inside the Logan Street camp. They have assault rifles, rocket-propelled grenades, lots of hand-held missiles. Perfect for street fighting. And they're in a fighting mood."

Wolfe scowled. "Terrific. Is that it?"

"Nope. There's also the Lists." Rickki sighed and

lit a cigarette. "The Exodus Faction is still playing pattycake with the Accord, but your common-and-garden variety Lister also appears to be developing a taste for violence. Just for fun, you might say. Yesterday about a hundred members of the Christmas List raided a soft residential area. Got right inside an apartment block and cleaned it out, floor by floor, drinking and doping as they went. By the end they were massacring anyone who happened to be at home. When they were finished they set the building on fire. It's still burning."

"Oh damn." Wolfe pounded his fist into his palm. "I warned Helen we couldn't control them once they started."

"How right you were. They also hit Hub Three last night, but got driven off with heavy losses. And to complete the picture, the latest entitlement cuts to the Lists were suddenly reversed with much fanfare yesterday. Obvious conclusion: the government actually supports all this, or at minimum is running very scared. All in all, we are living through interesting times." Rickki made a wry face. "What does Her Grace say?"

"She's worried," admitted Wolfe. "As far as she can fine tune it, Upper Canada is now at about seven point nine on the destability index."

Rickki pursed her full red lips, looking as worried as Wolfe had seen her. "That puts us right on the edge."

"Correct. If I don't persuade the Premier that . . . " Wolfe coughed delicately, "that certain measures must be taken, then we pull the plug."

"Can't say I'd be sorry. Seven point nine is too high for a convent girl like me. We're ready to go anytime at about four hours' notice. There's a charter aircraft on standby, and we have crisis arrangements for a shuttle out of Miami. We could all be up the well in a matter of hours." They both grabbed for the same passenger strap as the limo jounced over a particularly large pothole and for a moment Wolfe felt her small warm hand on his.

"Excellent. I hope it doesn't come to that—I'd rather finish things up here properly." Wolfe looked gloomily out of the limousine window. As he watched, a Mitsubishi sedan barreled past, tires squealing; he caught a glimpse of skull and crossbones insignias on leather hats, then the car vanished like a meteor in the hot afternoon.

In the two days he had been away, the mood of the city had become distinctly grimmer. Burnt-out trucks and cars lined the road, and what few pedestrians there were scuttled by with furtive, frightened movements. Traffic was almost nonexistent, except for army patrols of armored jeeps or Bulldog armored vehicles sporting gray-brown urban camouflage and the occasional chopper thropping above like a great brown bug.

University Avenue was blocked off by an impromptu checkpoint north of Dundas Street, a low sandbagged wall with an opening for a single car. A dozen soldiers with black multibarrel assault guns watched impassively from the barricade while the cars in the Institute convoy were checked and waved through.

The approaches to the Hive itself were festooned with razor wire and guarded by more soldiers. Twenty meters from the building, their car halted again. The driver powered back the glass panel and spoke without turning: "You get out here, sir. Those gentlemen will escort you the rest of the way." He pointed to where two commandos in gray flak jackets were waiting.

As Wolfe reached for the handle, Rickki put a small hand on his shoulder. "Amadeus will pick you up after the meeting—just give him a whistle when you're ready. And be careful."

Wolfe grinned. "Don't tell me you're worried?"

"Maybe I am." Rickki squinted at him with tired eyes. "We're getting a lot of traffic I don't like, and the Cleaners are out there just praying for a chance to display their piety. Don't forget you've got a dozen butchers actively looking for you. All it takes is a sharp knife and a couple of minutes." Wolfe nodded and stepped out onto the cracked pavement, a thoughtful expression on his face. When Rickki began to take things seriously it was time indeed to be careful.

"Follow me, sir," said a young commando briskly. "The Premier is waiting for you in the Crisis Center."

Wolfe followed the escorts into a hardened elevator which served the Hive's Crisis Center eight stories below ground. The Center lay at the end of a neon-white corridor which had been freshly scrubbed and demothballed; the alkaline reek of industrial-strength cleaning fluid seared Wolfe's nostrils like chemical flame. At the door to the Crisis Center two more commandos with assault rifles saluted and opened the heavy steel blast doors.

Inside was an ocean of darkness with a single island of brightness in the center. The steel doors clanged shut behind him and Wolfe entertained for a moment the unsettling idea that he had died somewhere on the ride down from Orbital and was now entering Hell. Dim and cavernous, the room stretched away so that he could not make out its far walls. In the middle stood a huge horseshoe conference table of black metal, reflecting light back from the rows of halogen bulbs above. Seated in a small group were Mrs. Clements, Deputy Premier Beaufort and four advisors.

Wolfe walked down the center aisle of the echoing chamber to join them, his footsteps unnaturally loud in the silence. Beaufort limped around the table, leaning heavily on his cane, and shook Wolfe's hand in a clear gesture of support. "Delighted to see you in one piece, Edward, delighted. We understand you have an important message from Orbital?"

"Yes sir." Wolfe extricated his hand from the vise-like grip and bowed to Mrs. Clements, who inclined her head graciously. "Welcome to the Crisis Center, Edward. I was afraid we would meet here one day." She gestured to the people flanking her. "You know everyone? General Joseph Wallinor, head of our Chiefs of Staff, Arawat Pandi, Ministry of Defense, Gina Fitzgibbon, Ministry of the Interior, Les Silverstein, my political advisor. Ladies and gentlemen this is Dr. Edward Wolfe, the Institute's chief emissary to Upper Canada."

Wolfe bowed again, seated himself at the table and appraised his audience. General Wallinor stared stolidly back at him, a sunburned walnut of a man who had served everywhere from Cyprus to Quebec. It was the first time he had met the general; the stocky veteran had a reputation for strategic shrewdness which belied his peasant exterior. He could be relied upon for a fair appraisal of the situation. The defense minister, a tall, mahogany-skinned man, was a lightweight, a concession to the doves of the coalition. He would blow whichever way the Premier did. The gray-haired minister of the interior was an economist by background. A Beaufort appointee, she would probably back the Deputy Premier. Beaufort, now hunched in his chair playing with his old-fashioned mechanical pencil, had already indicated his support. On the other hand, Silverstein, a young man in his mid-thirties with pale, intellectual face and blazing eyes, would be strongly opposed to his proposals.

The Premier surveyed him for a long moment then spoke, her voice small and somehow forlorn in the huge space: "Well then, Dr. Wolfe, what help or hope do you bring us from Orbital?" Her words seemed to lose themselves in the vast dark space that surrounded them, leaving a flat, expectant silence.

Wolfe addressed his listeners with all the sincerity at his command: "First, you should know that our information derives from Marshal Mancuso, who is now recovering from serious head injuries at our Orbital facility. According to him, the Accord is planning a coup in Upper Canada within the next ten days." He ignored the startled murmurs from his listeners and pressed on. "The plan is straightforward enough—except for one extremely devious and disturbing element. In the first phase, now in effect, are classic precoup maneuvers—attacks on soft targets, attempts to subvert or weaken elements of the police and army and so on. Fortunately, the conflict with the Lists took a lot of the sting out of these operations. Phase two will commence with the opening of the Accord's Continental Convention. At this time the Accord will find some pretext to launch an all-out assault on the government."

The minister of defense leaned over and whispered something to Mrs. Clements, who nodded and raised a slim hand to interrupt. "But Dr. Wolfe, surely this would be madness from a military point of view?"

"You are correct, and that was exactly what puzzled us." Wolfe steepled his fingers and tried to look judicious. "We concluded that we must be lacking a key piece of information—and we were. Marshal Mancuso was able to supply it. An elite Accord group known as the Cleaners has planted Class-A biologicals at strategic points around the city. At the start of hostilities, Deacon Stele will threaten to trigger them unless the army surrenders. Psychological profiles strongly suggest that he would carry out this threat."

"Jesus Conciliator." Mrs. Clements had gone a deadly white, but her voice remained calm and reasonable. "Do we know the precise location of these devices?"

"Yes, madam." Wolfe looked down at his hands. "They were disarmed and removed by special Institute teams, as of three hours ago. They are now at Versailles."

There was an ominous silence, then the Premier spoke in a low venomous tone. "How dare you?" she demanded. "How dare Orbital undertake such a thing without consultation or permission? Do you realize the consequences if even one of the devices had been accidentally triggered?"

Wolfe made a contrite gesture. "Your concern is understandable, Premier. However, Orbital felt it had no choice. Time was of the essence—Deacon Stele might have triggered the devices at any moment in a fit of pique or because Adonai King told him to. On behalf of our Board of Governors, allow me to apologize for any impropriety."

The Premier mastered herself with a visible effort. "Very well. Let us move on for now. You are here to propose a plan of action—is that correct?"

"In a sense." Wolfe sniffed, trying to clear his nose of the lingering soap smell. "Orbital wishes me to advise you on priorities. The first priority, to state the obvious, must be to prepare for the threatened coup."

"Very true." The Premier turned to General Wallinor. "Well, General, what resources can the military muster at short notice to meet this threat?"

General Wallinor leaned forward and spoke a quiet word into his console. In response, the north wall of the Crisis Center lit up in a huge tactical display of Upper Canada. The general sat back, his fingers on the console input, and turned to Mrs. Clements. "Here is the overview, madam. The counterinsurgency warfare group—three battalions of highly trained soldiers—is based at Downsview. About half of them are already engaged in quelling the current civil disorder. The remainder are on red alert. They can be ready for action within an hour." He fingered his console and white lights blinked on around Toronto. "We also have three crack armored divisions along the border, although it would be unwise to reassign more than two of them, in case Quebec decides to open hostilities again. An airborne division at Thunder Bay, another near Ottawa. Also, supporting air force units at Downsview, Thunder Bay and Kitchener." The lights representing the other units blinked on, one by one. "The rest of our forces are spread out in small detachments around the country as part of the civil order program," concluded the general. "It would be difficult to regroup them into effective larger units in less than ten days. Also, we could not guarantee order in outlying areas if we stripped them of security teams."

"So then," asked Mrs. Clements patiently, "are we in a position to defend ourselves against a coup attempt or not?"

"Oh yes, ma'am." General Wallinor scratched his heavy jowl, creating a grating, sandpapery noise. "We could mount a defensive action with just the forces around the city."

"How long until we could conduct a preemptive strike?" interjected Wolfe.

"For a decisive preemptive strike we'd need armor and air support," said the general, turning to him. "We could be in place within two days, perhaps less."

Wolfe looked at the tactical map, saw nothing to surprise him. He nodded. "Orbital has taken the liberty of running some sims. Outcomes show the best option is to bring your forces into position immediately and launch a massive strike on the Accord. Put the Temple Compound under military control, suspend the clubs, close the borders and declare a curfew. Do this and your chances of success are better than eighty percent. You may even be able to contain the violence in a very narrow area."

Silverstein shook his head emphatically, disassociating himself from the proposal. "How can the government order a preemptive strike against a hypothetical insurrection? Has Orbital thought about the political or moral complexities of such an act?"

Wolfe ignored him, addressing Mrs. Clements directly: "With respect Premier, the situation is actually very straightforward. Deacon Stele and his associates are planning a coup. If they succeed, your government will fall and the entire FreeMarket will be badly—perhaps terminally—destabilized. We therefore recommend immediate countermeasures. It is as simple as that."

"If only it were." Mrs. Clements drummed her fingers on the arms of her chair. "It would amount to the suppression of civil liberties. I do not care to go down in history as the person who betrayed the cause of freedom in Upper Canada." She turned to Beaufort, who sat with his heavy chin resting on his fists. "John, your thoughts?"

Beaufort thought for a long moment, then sat back and folded his arms. "I believe the Institute is correct. Morality is about society's survival, and in this sense a preemptive strike is moral. In blunt terms, we must destroy our enemies or be destroyed."

"Agreed," added the minister of the interior decisively.

Mrs. Clements nodded and turned back to Wolfe. "Very well, let us take this suggestion under advisement. Have you additional information for us?"

"The second part of my message is highly confidential," said Wolfe with more composure than he felt. "With the greatest respect for your colleagues, Orbital has instructed me to relay it to you and Mr. Beaufort alone."

Mrs. Clements nodded somberly and turned to the others. "Ladies and gentlemen, perhaps you could take a ten-minute break then rejoin us? Many thanks." When the others had left, murmuring resentfully among themselves, she turned back to him, her eyes hard, lips pinched into a thin white line. "Now then, Dr. Wolfe, what is this dire proposal which only we can hear?"

Now comes the hard part, thought Wolfe. He cleared his throat and pitched his voice to a cool, rational tone: "Our solution is dire because we are all in mortal danger. Zacharian Stele represents a deadly threat to Upper Canada and indeed to regional stability. Perhaps even global stability. We cannot afford to wait idly by while he obtains another weapon of mass destruction to blackmail us with. We must get rid of him and soon."

"How?" demanded Mrs. Clements. "Even if we had an airtight case we couldn't arrest him without setting off riots and risking an international crisis."

Beaufort stirred in his chair. "Even military intervention. The American vice-president is a close personal friend of Zacharian's."

"Precisely," agreed Wolfe. "We need a more subtle solution."

"Such as?" inquired Beaufort, raising shaggy eyebrows.

The old inventor knew exactly what sort of solution, thought Wolfe, licking his dry lips. He grasped the realpolitik of mayhem and murder as Mrs. Clements, bless her, could not. "An unfortunate accident," he replied softly. "A car crash for instance or a fatal case of Tokyo Flu."

Mrs. Clements frowned. "I agree that Stele constitutes a long-term nuisance. He is a thorn in our side, a fanatic, a ruthless terrorist. Even so, I cannot countenance assassination as a state policy."

"It would not be assassination," Wolfe pointed out. "Legally such a step could be completely justified. Under the provisions of the Anti-Terrorism Act the Deacon's case could be judged by a special tribunal. As you know, terrorism using weapons of mass destruction is a capital offense. The sentence could be carried out discreetly and without fuss. An accident."

Mrs. Clements shook her head sadly. "That is pure sophistry, Dr. Wolfe, and does you no credit. We cannot go about murdering citizens. Even the most repellent ones deserve open trial and due process."

Wolfe met her steady gaze. "We are speaking of a man who is prepared to set off Class-A biologicals inside a major city. Does he deserve due process?"

"But he hasn't set them off, has he?" countered Mrs. Clements. "Maybe the biologicals are a bluff and nothing more. We can't condemn someone on the basis of something he hasn't yet done. For that matter, we have only your word that the biologicals even exist."

Wolfe sighed, suddenly weary of the whole discussion. Doom was approaching like a long black cloud and nothing they could do would turn it aside. "You are free to send inspectors to Versailles immediately to verify their existence, madam."

Beaufort snorted. "I've met Zacharian on several occasions. He's as ruthless as a razor blade, and as cold. I can easily believe he'd plant bios and use them if he thought it would help."

It was time to force the matter to a conclusion, thought Wolfe. He leaned forward to emphasize the urgency of his point. "Madam Premier, I carry a personal message from our Board of Governors. Will you hear it?"

Mrs. Clements pushed back a strand of red hair. "I am listening."

Wolfe cleared his throat and recited the words planted in his memory: "Greetings from the governors of the Institute. We urge you to see that your enemies are beyond decency or old-fashioned morality. They are barbarians, engaged in a life-and-death struggle to take power within the Temple of the Accord. In the process they will destroy Upper Canada, unless you destroy them first. We therefore beg you to authorize the execution of Zacharian Stele. If not, the Institute must act to protect its own interests."

There was a long silence in the room, then Mrs. Clements shook her head. "No. Secret assassination is against my deepest principles. Nor will I countenance any freelance activity, if that's what you mean by protecting your own interests."

"It is not." Wolfe sat back. "By protecting our interests we mean protecting our on-site staff. The only way we can do that is by withdrawing them from Upper Canada. The Board of Governors has therefore asked me to formally state that our contract is now in abeyance pending further negotiation."

Beaufort shook his head but said nothing. Clearly he had been expecting an outcome like this. Mrs. Clements blinked but otherwise betrayed no surprise. "I see," she said coldly. "May I ask how Orbital justifies this brusque and most unhelpful severing of a two-year relationship?"

"The legal justification is contained in section six of the contract, which relates to nonimplementation of primary policy directives," said Wolfe. "The practical reason is much more straightforward. As long as Deacon Stele is alive, Upper Canada is a very dangerous place. The Institute cannot keep staff in an area where they are effectively at the mercy of a madman."

"You overestimate his degree of derangement." Mrs. Clements made a wry face. "I have talked to Deacon Zacharian and I can assure you he is rational enough, if somewhat blinkered by Accord doctrine. However, so be it. We need not detain you."

Wolfe rose and bowed a grade-four bow. "With your permission I will now inform Orbital of your decision."

✧   ✧   ✧

His escorts returned him to the Hive's main floor, to a command post manned by a female sergeant with cropped blonde hair and a red regimental tattoo on her wrist. "Your driver is waiting in the perimeter courtyard, Dr. Wolfe. Shall we summon him?"

Wolfe thought for a moment. "If possible, I'd like to visit Deputy Minister Wu for a few moments. She has an office in this building."

"A moment, sir." The sergeant spoke into the console, nodded and looked up. "She'll see you immediately. Do you need an escort?"

"No thanks, sergeant, I know my own way."

Miraculously the elevators were working; for once he arrived at the DM's office with his heart rate and respiration normal.

Wu was either not important enough to have been moved to the Crisis Floor or so important she was able to override the general order. Wolfe said as much when Julian Hinkley-Dextermunt had sniffed his way out of her office, the perennial expression of wary disapproval on his goatlike face.

Wu merely smiled faintly. "There is sufficient disruption as it is. At least here I know where to find boiling water for the tea. As it happens there is a pot freshly brewed; would you care for a cup?"

"Thank you." Wolfe accepted a pale blue enamel mug, turned it in his hands, inhaling with pleasure the fresh, herbal aroma. "The official reason for this visit is to inform you that we are terminating our involvement in Project Maldon forthwith."

"Indeed?" Wu raised a delicate eyebrow in query.

"Upper Canada is becoming too unstable," explained Wolfe. "The Premier doesn't agree with our remedies, so there's nothing more we can do. We leave tomorrow, and I wanted to say good-by. I enjoyed working with you."

Wu acknowledged the sentiment with a placid nod,

and swiveled her chair to face the unwashed window. "I too regret the end of our association, Dr. Wolfe, and of the work we were doing."

"Let us hope both are only interrupted."

"Anything is possible." Wu turned back to face him. "Where will the project team go in the meantime?"

"To Miami, then back to Orbital for reassignment."

Wu's face was a bland mask, conveying nothing. She spoke in the neutral tones which usually denoted an important statement: "By strange coincidence, our family is leaving town as well. Tonight in fact. I have some vacation time which I may as well take now as later. We intend to visit relatives in Hong Kong."

"I see." Wolfe found himself at a loss for further comment. It was an ominous sign indeed when the Wu family decided to seek cover.

Wu chose to elaborate. "We are not warriors, Edward, and we do not intend to become victims either." She made a gesture including him in the statement. "We have all done what we could, have we not? Now we must take shelter from the storm." The DM swiveled her chair around, stood up and bowed formally to him. Then, to his surprise, she stood, took him by the hand in a curiously old-fashioned manner and led him to the door. "Perhaps we might dine, next time fate brings us together? I've found a charming little spot you might enjoy. Excellent lobster."

"I should like that very much." Wolfe bowed and turned away. His footsteps falling silent on the immaculate carpet, he walked down the deserted corridor, past the empty offices and pressed the down button to summon an elevator. The button did not light. He waited five minutes then pushed through the red fire door. Down endless flights of echoing concrete steps he pattered, retreating from the failed SoCy intervention known as Project Maldon.

❖   ❖   ❖

Amadeus was waiting at the door of the Hive. He scrambled out to open the back door of the Bouncer with a shy grin. "Welcome back, Dr. Wolfe."

"Thanks." said Wolfe, realizing for the first time how young Amadeus truly was. He scrunched himself into the back seat of the small Isuzu and got out his portable. "Get a maxSec message off to Rickki. One word: Go."

"Message received and acknowledged," said the portable after a few moments.

"Thanks." Wolfe returned the unit to his pocket and gave himself over to the rare luxury of analyzing his own feelings. Regret for the breakdown of Project Maldon mingled with budding relief that the whole impossible ordeal was drawing to a close. But what now for Upper Canada, for the whole FreeMarket? Not two weeks ago, Helen had assured him that the collapse of Maldon was the first step on the road to the Die Back. Had things really changed since then? He fervently hoped that Governor Peabody had looked into his concerns. And what effect would the project's failure have on his career? He frowned thoughtfully: true, he had failed to thread the needle, but it was Orbital, not him, that had ordered the evac. Surely he could not be faulted for the breakdown of Maldon?

Amadeus' diffident voice broke into his thoughts: "Excuse me, Dr. Wolfe, but it's possible we're being followed. May I take evasive action?"

"Please do." Wolfe sat up abruptly in his seat. "Where and who?"

"Behind us, Dr. Wolfe, a black Raffles Turbo. Don't turn your head, look in the side mirror." Shifting gears, Amadeus slipped into the left lane of the Gardiner and down the ramp onto the northbound parkway. Wolfe saw the tail immediately: a big Raffles sport model with tinted windows; impossible to say who or how many inside.

In the fast lane Amadeus kept the needle at a hundred and forty klicks, took the Don Mills exit. The Raffles kept a consistent five car-lengths behind. It could still be coincidence. They turned left onto O'Connor Avenue, then dodged down a side street lined with burnt-out bungalows, swung back up to O'Connor. The Raffles followed. Wolfe decided reluctantly that it was no coincidence.

The tension was now apparent in Amadeus' voice. "Dr. Wolfe, could you call Ops please? I want to keep my full attention on this. There may be bandits up front too. Or they may be herding us into an ambush."

Wolfe scrambled into the front seat and punched the connection. It was a contingency Rickki had insisted all staff practice for. He knew what to do but as he started to do it he felt sick and fluttery. He was not anxious to die just now, not a few days after Morgan had burst upon the scene. That would be bad joss, very poor joss indeed. The late afternoon seemed too alive, the sky dark velvet, the sunshine bright as diamonds. Step one: enter emergency code. The controller's voice crackled over the speaker almost immediately, incongruously casual: "Code pink acknowledged. What's the agitation?"

"We've got a tail: black Raffles sport model. Instructions please." Wolfe took a deep breath, trying to focus. It would not be pleasant to be caught by the Accord, not at all. Unbidden and unwanted, memories of Mary crawled on bloody stumps back into his consciousness. *They cut the front out of her shirt. The whole front.*

"How close?" asked the controller, her voice still irritatingly calm.

"About five car-lengths back. He tried to overtake when we turned down a side street, then fell back when we got back on O'Connor.

"Does he know you've seen him?"

"Must do."

"Okay. Keep moving, and under no circumstances let him pull level with you. Go through traffic lights or up on the sidewalk as necessary. And check up front; the Raffles may be a decoy to divert your attention from the real threat—one behind, two ahead is a common pattern."

"Knew that." Wolfe wiped a sweaty palm on the seat and winked at Amadeus.

"Good. So keep focused and keep calm; you're on the map and we've got two mobile squads coming out to join you, ETA about four minutes. Keep heading east and keep patched."

"Understood." He glanced in the side-view. The Raffles was still far behind. Was Joshua, the mad schoolmaster of the PM, inside, perhaps running his thumb along the edge of his knife? They had done some digging on Joshua: graduate of Dartmouth, well-liked by his classmates, recruited by Accord in the final year of a degree in political science. Brilliant chess player, charming manners, spoke French and Italian fluently. Savage killer, with a liking for maximum pain. Wolfe tasted the metallic tang of fear in his mouth. *Focus, brother, watch for ambushes ahead.*

The cool voice of the controller spoke again: "First unit will link up in about half a minute. Let me know when you get a visual on a white Ford Cheetah, coming in from Coxwell Avenue."

A battered white Cheetah turned onto the road about thirty meters ahead. Wolfe relaxed ever so slightly. "Escort one in sight."

"Good. We're going to take you down Woodbine Avenue. Let the tail close a bit. The second unit will link up when you turn south. Look for an old black Trans Am coming in off a side street right behind the Raffles. Follow the Cheetah into the old Safeway parking lot about six blocks down. We've got a team on site. Get right to the far end of the lot. There's a couple of garbage tips there: get behind them. If anything goes wrong, get down on the floor and keep your heads down."

"And if everything goes fantastically well?" inquired Wolfe.

"Then we'll grab your friends and learn a thing or two. You're coming up to Woodbine, get ready to turn."

"Unit two in sight," rasped Amadeus, his knuckles white on the steering wheel. "Okay, here we go." He turned off behind the Cheetah and headed south. Fascinated, Wolfe watched first the Raffles then the Trans Am peel off and follow. A boarded-up Safeway store appeared on their right; Amadeus signaled, slowed and turned in behind the white car. Wolfe stared in the mirror; sure enough, the Raffles followed, coming to a stop in the middle of the lot.

As if from nowhere, a half-dozen figures, bulky with body armor and armed with stubby Changs leapt into sight. At the same time the Cheetah's doors crashed open, vomiting agents onto the pavement. The Trans Am screeched around sideways, its tires smoking, to block the entrance.

The door of the Raffles opened and a woman wearing an expensive peach business suit and crocodile-skin shoes stepped onto the grimy asphalt. Ignoring the guns pointed at her, she put her hands on her hips. "Alright, you pus-sucking bastards, kill me if you like. I'm not going back."

Wolfe slumped in his seat and began to chuckle, then to laugh out loud. It was too ridiculous. Amadeus looked at him with a carefully blank expression. Wolfe made haste to reassure him: "No, I'm not going critical. But this chase has taken a strange turn." Getting out of the Bouncer he cupped his hands and shouted to his agents: "Hey team! We've got a comedy of errors going here. This is my sister." Walking across to where his sister slouched against the Raffles, he took her hand and spoke gently. "It's okay, Kim. You come with me." His sister half-collapsed against him with a sob then straightened. "Sorry, just nervous reaction. I thought I was a goner."

Kim

Why is it called Tokyo Flu? According to one story, the virus originated in a research lab in Japan, where scientists were investigating possible mechanisms of the Die Back. An alternative story suggests the name comes from the convulsions which characterize the later phases of the disease. In these convulsions, victims literally work themselves to death even faster than the average Japanese salaryman is commonly supposed to do. Whatever the origin of its name, there is no doubt that Tokyo Flu is a swift and efficient killer, sweeping through the population, disappearing, and returning again in a slightly different form to wreak more havoc still.

Diseases of the Post Millennial Age
—The Skellig Michael Press

Tuesday, July 13
16:20 hours

By the time he and Kim returned to Versailles, the facility was beginning to fill with Institute people, field officers and liaison staff dribbling in, in response to the recall signal that had gone out earlier in the afternoon. Wolfe conducted his sister up to his room, stopping every few paces to shake hands and greet friends. All the while he surreptitiously scanned the crowded halls for Morgan. Apparently she had not yet arrived.

Finally they reached his apartment. Wolfe closed the door behind them, led the way back to the living area and gestured to the leather armchair by the window. "Flop it. Whiskey, brandy or Flash?"

"Scotch, straight up." Kim accepted a large double and smiled faintly at him. "Is it always this lively around here?"

Wolfe opened the window to look for the Rooftop Cat, saw nothing and shut it again. "Hardly. We've just been ordered out of Upper Canada by Orbital. The whole project team is assembling here for the evac. We leave tomorrow midafternoon."

"Jesus Entrepreneur—what's the sudden rush?"

"Our masters fear things are about to get choppy. Specifically, they predict a major outbreak of violence at any time."

"My timing was always a bit off." Kim strained a reluctant smile. "I'm putting you to a lot of trouble, aren't I? I'm sorry—I forgot you had your own set of problems to contend with." Kim's face was thin and bruised, and her left hand was bandaged. Despite the surface nicks and dents though, she looked better than the cornered animal that had emerged from the car. Wolfe said so, eliciting a wry grin.

"Christ come soon, I was just thinking what a stinking place to die and wondering if it was going to be a bullet or a virus when I heard your honeyed tones."

Wolfe adopted the same manner. "And I've been patient for two hours now while we've both come to grips with the idea of still being alive. This can't be your idea of a casual visit. So focus, what's the action?"

Kim sighed. "I came all this way to tell you exactly that, but now I hardly know where to start." She cradled her chin on her fists moodily. "Or whether it matters. Oh sure, it matters. Hang tight then and listen."

✧   ✧   ✧

On reaching the small Caribbean island where BioAge Viral Research was headquartered, she was assigned a guidance specialist, a smooth-mannered African in his early thirties, who was in charge of her orientation. She looked over the week's schedule and discovered trips to the casino in Nassau, a dirigible flight over the newly discovered and mysterious underwater ruins near island 321 and a jaunt in an armored jet chopper over Pirate Town. "Are you running a tour service or a research center? When do I see the labs?"

Her guide was unruffled. "First things first. We need to know you better, Dr. Wolfe. You're a brilliant researcher but what makes you tick?"

"Don't you have enough data on file from Paris?"

"This isn't Paris, Dr. Wolfe, this is a maxSec community. If you take the job you'll live here, work here, sleep here, perhaps even die here. This will be your home. We have to be sure you'll be happy."

Perhaps her protests had an effect. The next day she was given an audience with Charles Leroy Jr., the founder of BioAge himself, in his private study, built into one side of a small artificial island in the bay. Half the huge cylindrical room was above water, while the other half extended fifteen meters down to the bottom. One half of the cylinder was a plate-glass window. Half-moon floors at three levels gave different views: high over the waves, at sea level, the coral reef below.

Leroy was seated on a corduroy sofa on the middle floor, a pot of tea on a brass table beside him. His face was that of a fit, middle-aged man, with large luminous brown eyes and salt-and-pepper hair, but his ninety-seven years showed in the slack skin around the jaw and a stiffness of movement. He greeted her effusively, with a courtesy and inflection that reminded her oddly of her father:

"A pleasure to meet you at last, Kimberley—I may call you that? Please, be seated. No, over here by me. This floor is placed more or less at sea level, so we can look either above or below for inspiration as the mood takes us. I call it the in-between view." A few feet in front of them, small frothy waves lapped at the glass. Below was the multicolored confusion of the reef, an army of flashing fish in every shade and color of the rainbow: red, lemon, neon blue, swimming around the coral, through the weed-covered wooden bones of a small ship, a fishing boat probably, lying on its side on the sandy bottom.

"Tea? I have followed your career with fascination, Kimberley; you are a brilliant woman. No, that is not an idle compliment, I mean it. You are one of that very small group of people, a researcher who is also an artist. The question before us now is, are you of that mysterious elite that is destined for the highest ranks of BioAge?" He fixed her with a quizzical yet penetrating stare.

Kim was half-amused, half-irritated. "If not I've come a long way for no good reason. How do you propose to find out?"

"An excellent question." Leroy chuckled, revealing very regular, white teeth. "Despite all the specialists with their psyche tests, there is no sure way."

"Why don't you just tell me about this job, whatever it may be, and ask me if I'm interested. If I'm not I'll say so. Or does that seem hopelessly naive?"

Again the too-white teeth. "Do you ever wonder what guides BioAge in its choice of research, Kimberley?"

"The marketplace, or so I always supposed."

"Ah yes, supply and demand, the invisible hand. We do, of course, develop products for the consumer market: aphrodisiacs, specialty liquors, regenerative agents and so on. Products which don't strongly influence the demographics of the time." Leroy changed the subject abruptly. "Tell me, what do you think of my reef, Kimberly?"

"It's very beautiful."

"It is—and an instructive metaphor as well. The reef is a huge graveyard, built with the corpses of countless tiny animals. Sail too close and it is death." He pointed to the wreck. "Yet at the same time it is home to a billion sparks of life—fish, plants, the living coral itself. So what is the reef? Life or death? The answer is— both. The death of some implies the life of others. Death and life are in a precarious balance. Without death there can be no room for new life. This is the paradox underlying much of the work we do."

Her skin felt clammy, crinkley. It was the sun, she told herself. Too long in the rays, even with heavy oil, and the high-intensity stuff got through. "I'm a scientist, not a philosopher. Are you trying to tell me something?"

The old/young man before her nodded, his eyes hooded like a lizard's. "So I am, in my own meandering way. Allow me the luxury of coming to my subject by a leisurely route, if you please, young lady." He smiled archly. "Let's look back at the history of medicine. Until the beginning of the last century, doctors weren't able to do more than bandage a wound or splint a broken limb. Then they gradually started to get the upper hand, with public health measures and antibiotics. People lived longer, population soared. A good thing? Yes and no. The social and economic institutions were not in place to support all the added humanity. They are still not in place, for that matter. As a result, advances in medicine create—paradoxically—more disease and human suffering.

"Now let me pose you a hypothetical case. Suppose we discovered an elixir that kept people alive and hale for two centuries. One simple pill. Should we put it on the market?"

Kim wrinkled her nose. "Naturally."

"Naturally indeed—from a purely commercial point of view. Whosoever could afford it would buy it, regardless of price. But by making such a product generally available, we would wreak havoc on the social and economic fabric of the whole world. Business consequence? Disaster. You can't run a business in an imploding economy. Regulatory agencies agree. Even if we wanted to, we would not be allowed to sell such a product."

"This is purely hypothetical of course?" inquired Kim, now troubled by the direction the conversation was taking.

"Up to a point. I'm trying to illustrate the difficulty of guiding research by pure market data."

"I see. So how are research goals set?"

"It varies," said Leroy carelessly. "There are, as you say, market-driven products. Then there are privately-funded projects, paid for by foundations, industry alliances, even by government coalitions."

"The United Nations?"

"That is of course the largest such coalition." Leroy stretched. "You see, Kim, we deal essentially in life and death. We are at the stage where, like it or not, someone must play God. This thought must have crossed your mind when you worked late in your lab on Tokyo Flu?"

"Not really."

"Then let it cross your mind now." Leroy in swiveled his chair and scanned the horizon, looking out across the placid blue of the Caribbean as if looking for a sign. "The myths of the Great Die Back are romantic ways of putting a profound truth. There are too many people in the world. If we don't do something about this situation soon, Mother Nature will step in and do it for us. Scientists and intellectuals have a duty to preempt Gaea and take the destiny of their race into their own hands. A small elite group must do this, must decide who dies back and how. That is why I sent for you."

Wolfe blinked. "To help arrange the Die Back?"

"Yes. Quite an honor, you must admit." His sister smiled thinly.

"After a fashion." He felt dizzy with the implications. So the globals had gone this far with their planning? Jesus Antagonist, how long did the expendables have—and who were they? He stared at his sister, seeing the fear in her eyes, like a hunted animal. "And you said?"

"I said I'd like to go back to Paris and think about it for a few days. When I got back I took my files, transferred my credit to a new account and booked a sub-orbital here. Oh Edward, what would make BioAge join in such a conspiracy? It's so terrible, like waking up one morning and finding a werewolf in bed with you instead of your lover."

"Don't cry. It happened to me once or twice after a good party. The werewolf phenomenon that is. Before I met Omaha of course." Wolfe grinned and crossed the room to place a box of Kleenex beside his sister. "As to why, that's easy. There's got to be a lot of cash in the Die Back, BioAge style. You could sell toxins to the organizations promoting it and vaccines or antidotes to the prospective victims. It would be a spectacular way to bring share prices back in line."

"You think it's as straightforward as that?" Kim looked at him suspiciously with wet eyes.

"Nothing's straightforward these days." Wolfe shrugged. "But I have no doubt revenue is a consideration. Never mind that though. What about you? How close do you think BioAge is behind you?"

Kim blew her nose with a resounding honk. "I nearly had an accident on the metro to the airport, but

I made it as you see. I'm not sure if they've traced me yet, but they will. This is too big for them to be careless."

"So when you were pulled over tonight you thought it was BioAge being careful?"

"Exactly. Though they can do so far more discreetly if they choose. For all I know they already have. A quick jolt of aerosol in a crowd, a coffee cup smeared with the right agent and I'm a goner. I suppose as I go into convulsions I can console myself I did the right thing morally."

"And you call me a romantic." Wolfe considered for a moment. "So what are your plans now?"

"I'd appreciate your advice on that. Which is why I'm here."

Wolfe considered the various options for a few moments. "Alright, here's my suggestion: I'm going to register you as next of kin and get you on our evac flight tomorrow. By pulling a few strings I think I can get you up to Orbital as a special lecturer or something. You'll be safe there for a few days; you can think a bit, decide what to do next. For tonight, you'd better stay here with me."

"I was rather hoping you'd suggest that." Kim drained her glass and put it down with an emphatic thump. "I don't feel very self sufficient at the moment."

Wolfe squeezed her hand. "It'll pass. Listen—you stay here and make yourself comfortable. Take a shower, help yourself to anything. I have to go downstairs and see what's going on."

He found Morgan in the cafeteria, at one of the scuffed linoleum-topped tables like a rose blooming in a dingy Post Millennium garbage heap. She sat alone, a white coffee mug before her, staring out at the bulk of the soap factory. Ordinarily she would have been surrounded by suave young Institute males and perhaps a few females as well, eager to make her acquaintance. With the evacuation already under way though, there was no time for such undirected activities, though Wolfe saw several men inspect the newcomer with more than casual interest.

She turned when she saw him and smiled, a slow smile like the sun breaking through a field of high, gray clouds. Wolfe pulled back a chair and sat down, fascinated as always by her fine features, the strange attraction of her mismatched eyes. He had read somewhere that human beauty was dependent on symmetry, but the rule did not seem to apply in her case. Or rather, it gave her looks a different dimension, put them into the category of a painting or a sculpture. Or a mask, thought Wolfe.

"Join me?" She crinkled her eyes at him as he sat. "We seem doomed to meet at times of crisis."

"True. And I understand you had a role in defusing the current one."

"I was able to give some basic advice." Morgan dismissed her role with a wave of the hand. "We've got everything back here without incident, and the techs are playing around with the detonators."

"Why?"

"For one thing, monitoring them to see if the Accord tries to set them off. That would be rather useful information." Morgan drew a little pattern in spilled tea on the table top. "When Zacky realizes his secret weapon has been neutralized he's going to be very upset indeed."

"And we want to anticipate his inevitable temper tantrum," finished Wolfe, wondering how he could speed up the evacuation. "What about the devices themselves?"

"Oh, we have them in a containment room for the moment. They're safe enough without the detonators. As far which bugs they contain . . ." Morgan made a face. "No doubt the techs at Orbital will be able to figure it out. I can't, not with the facilities here."

"As long as they stay in the can I don't care what they are." Wolfe smiled and stood. "You'll have to excuse me—I've never supervised an evac before, so I'd better get jacked in and pretend to take control."

"Of course." Morgan half-closed her eyes, reminding Wolfe of the Rooftop Cat in a mellow mood. "Is there anything I can do?"

"Help me explore Miami when we get there? We may have a full day stopover before we catch the shuttle."

"It's a deal."

Convoy

And Adonai said: Behold, I give you two weapons, honesty and will. Your enemies are ensnared in their own deceptions; they are tangled in their own lies, and know not true from false, nor wrong from right. To you shall be given understanding to know My Mind and My Aims.

What are Your Aims? asked the Pastor.

Said Adonai: To reclaim the cities and the country, to weed out the lazy and the unfit. To comfort the worthy and annihilate the unworthy. On the ruins of lazy-hearted liberalism and the welfare state you will build a new world.

You are unstoppable, because you are in accord with me, and I with you.

The Testament of the Accord
Book of the True Vision

Wednesday, July 14
04:17 hours

Wolfe was woken just after four in the morning by his idiot console's urgent summons. "Dr. Wolfe! Oh Dr. Wolfe! Are you asleep?" Wolfe cursed and blinked sleep from his eyes. "Dammit, of course I'm asleep. I was anyway. What's the problem?"

"Top priority call—internal origin."

Wolfe swore again, wondering what bad news waited

to make his acquaintance now. "Alright then, connect. Audio only."

It was the Ops Room. "Sorry to disturb you. Mr. Beaufort's office just called, requesting a priority holo link at your earliest convenience."

Wolfe blinked sleep from his eyes. "What's going on?"

"Looks like a war. We have unconfirmed reports of heavy fighting at the Temple Complex. Armored units with chopper support. Also reports of smaller engagements all around the city."

Wolfe felt adrenaline kick in like a turbocharger. "Very well. Tell Mr. Beaufort I'll meet with him via link in exactly ten minutes. Send a technician to set it up, please, with echo to Orbital. Have you alerted Ms. Harrow yet?"

"She's next on our list."

"Never mind, I'll call her myself. Console, disconnect and get Rickki Harrow, audio only." He swung his legs over the edge of the bed, sporting the tumescent remains of some fading erotic dream and began fumbling for his trousers. A moment later Rickki's face filled the screen. Her hair was tousled but her features were as alert and mischievous as ever, her manner positively jovial: "Good morrow to you! Have you suddenly decided there are health benefits to being an early riser?"

"Hardly." Wolfe stood like a stork with one leg in his trousers. "There's something going on—don't know what yet. Beaufort's asked for a link in a couple of minutes. Apparently there's fighting all over. Get down to Ops and try to put the situation together, will you? I'll be along as soon as I talk to Beaufort."

"Consider it done." Rickki chuckled maliciously. "And Long Eddie? Do put your trousers on before you talk to the Deputy Premier, won't you? Aunt Rickki understands but others might wonder."

Wolfe looked up, saw the green light indicating full visual pickup glowing bright and sputtered. "Disconnect. Dammit console, I said 'audio.' Can't you get it right for once?"

"You mumbled," replied his console in a petulant voice.

"Then you should have clarified."

"Very sorry, I'm sure," muttered the console.

Restraining the impulse to kick its smooth enamel casing, Wolfe proceeded to dress. Two minutes later he tiptoed down the dark hall, stopping for a moment to peer in at his sleeping sister. Kim was huddled in the fetal position, breathing quietly. As he watched, she stirred and moaned, muttering something in her sleep. He shook his head and walked on.

At this early hour Versailles was quiet: the only sign of life was a team of three night-shift dicks in Data, busy tracking information deep inside the Net. A tech with long green nails and rumpled gin-smelling black overalls, clearly pulled out of some evac party, was playing with the link controls in the conference room. "All set. We're on maxSec channel, with echo to Orbital. Link in a little over two minutes. Jesus come quick but my head aches."

Ignoring the last comment, Wolfe settled into his chair and waited. The seconds trickled by, the air on the stage shimmered and coalesced and Beaufort's image flickered into being. There were bags under his eyes and his face was grim. "Thank you for joining me at such short notice."

Wolfe acknowledged the courtesy with a slight bow. "We anticipated you would be presenting important information, sir, so we are echoing feed to Helen in orbital HQ via maxSec channels."

"Excellent." Beaufort nodded in approval. "I'm afraid I bring bad news: Mrs. Clements was abducted a few hours ago. She was on her way home from addressing the Ronald MacDonald Club when her limo was cut off by two cars, bodyguards killed instantly. I am therefore acting Premier."

A shudder ran down Wolfe's spine. When all was said and done, he felt a great affection for Mrs. Clements. "That is very unfortunate," he croaked, then cleared his throat. "Does the government have a response prepared?"

"Better yet, we have one in progress." Beaufort bared his strong yellow teeth in a humorless smile. "Her kidnappers apparently did not know that Mrs. Clements received a tracer implant when she became Premier. Signals from the device show she is being held at the Accord campus. Somewhere in the Temple Medical Complex. Incidentally, the facility includes a crematorium." The acting Premier looked down for a moment and bit his lip before continuing. "Half an hour ago we launched a rescue operation."

Wolfe tried to frame an intelligent reply. "The Institute is all for decisive action as you know sir, but an immediate assault may not have been the ideal response. Your main armor can't arrive until tomorrow evening at the earliest."

Beaufort grunted and made a gesture indicating inevitability. "We had no option. Had we delayed, they would probably have wrung her dry and then disposed of her as readily as you flush a dead mouse down a toilet. They may yet."

"And the status of the rescue operation?"

"Unclear. There is heavy fighting all around the compound. We have not yet located Mrs. Clements." Beaufort inclined his heavy head forward towards the pickup as if he were peering into the darkness of Versailles's holo room. "One further thing: we received a message from Zacharian Stele a few minutes ago. He claims to have planted Class-A biologicals in unspecified locations within the city, and he threatens to set them off unless we withdraw our troops and lay down our arms by eight o'clock this morning. An empty threat, as I'm sure you can verify."

The Deputy Premier was taking no chances of letting the secret out, even on a maxSec line. Steely hands wrung Wolfe's guts. Events were tumbling over themselves, as grotesque and unpredictable as the warped circumstances of some tortured dream. "Of course," he agreed. "We can assure you absolutely that no such devices exist."

"Excellent," rasped Beaufort. "However, we plan to let him broadcast his threat so that the whole world can have no doubt they are dealing with a madman or worse. Once he has shown his true colors we'll cut off his signal then broadcast our reassurances."

Wolfe considered. "If Stele threatens to release biologicals in a major city, he will certainly put himself in a very unfavorable light. He may also cause widespread panic."

Beaufort ran fingers like sausages through his iron-gray hair, looking old and tired. "It's a chance worth taking to rid us of our troublesome priest once and for all."

"It's your decision, sir," agreed Wolfe. "I would urge you to take every step to reassure the public if Stele broadcasts his threat."

"Indeed we will." Beaufort licked his lips. "Now Edward, we have a favor to ask. We urgently require assistance in several categories: AI liaison with our military, feed and analysis of relevant information, tactical alternatives and so on. I assure you, there will be full cooperation with your directives at this end. Please emphasize this to Orbital and relay their answer to us at the earliest opportunity."

"I will, sir."

"We are relying on you, Edward. You will be informed of any developments soonest. Adieu." The image faded into nothing and Wolfe called across to the tech. "Did Orbital upload that?"

"Yep," said the woman, with the bored insouciance of techs everywhere. "Full data stream, coded and zipped."

"Add a tag please—top priority, immediate response requested." Wolfe left the conference room. Gray undersea light oozed in through the steel grilles as he walked down the corridor; through a window he glimpsed the soap factory gleaming a poisonous yellow in the dawn. Boxes of detergent trundled slowly by a broken third floor window like square cells pumping through the body of some squat alien beast.

Entering the Hole, Wolfe spotted Rickki standing before a bank of high-res screens, each showing a different gray-tone confusion of smoke and running figures. She waved as he came up to her. "Take a look at this—live entertainment straight from the Temple Complex. Helen tapped into a couple of roof eyes about five minutes ago, pulled the signal in direct. How's that for ingenious? The old girl has an angle on everything."

Wolfe watched the screens for a few moments, found he could make no sense of the images. "I can see there's a battle in progress but that's about all. Have we got any analysis?"

"Not yet. It's a bit of a mess, despite the great visuals." Rickki lit a cigarette, let it dangle from between her full lips. "Audio traffic is mainly in battle codes. The Accord seems to have been taken by surprise, but the Temple Guards are fighting back like mad things. Zacharian issued a brief statement about an hour ago saying his forces were engaged in a battle with the forces of darkness and calling on his brothers and sisters south of the border to rally round. No response so far."

Wolfe grinned. "No surprise there. Most of his relatives loathe him."

"There's one in every family," Rickki agreed. "So focus, what did Beaufort want?"

Wolfe quickly briefed her. Rickki digested the information in silence, flicking her cherished Zippo lighter to create little pools of orange light then snapping them into extinction with the steel lid. "Beaufort is unwise," she declared when Wolfe had finished. She returned her Zippo to the chest pocket of her black overalls and sat down backwards on a nearby chair, the mildness of her response jarring Wolfe more than a stream of invective. "If Zacharian threatens to use biologicals there will be wholesale panic within minutes, no matter what reassurance the government broadcasts. We'll need to know immediately if the activating signal is sent, of course—hang on a moment while I set that up." She spoke into her portable then turned back to him. "So Zacky makes his broadcast. Then what?"

Wolfe pulled his beard, careless of implicit significances. "If he sends the triggering signal, he won't know he's been trumped for at least an hour or two, depending on the nature of the agent. But as soon as he realizes the devices have been disarmed, he'll also realize Mancuso must have tipped us. At which point the Accord will come down on us like the proverbial wolf on the fold. I'd say we have about four hours after the signal is sent—if it ever is."

"So now what?" asked Rickki, grinding her cigarette out into an envirotray which swallowed the butt without a trace and spewed a gout of chemical freshness into the air.

Wolfe wrinkled his nose at the artificial pine smell and consulted his watch: forty-three minutes to Stele's broadcast. An alarm was ringing loudly and insistently in his mind. They had to get the biologicals to a secure facility soonest. He apprised Rickki of his concern in a few words. "Above all we don't want those biologicals recaptured. Call military HQ and see if they can provide a chopper to get them out of here."

"Consider it done. Anything else immediate?"

His head buzzed; he was dazed, drunk with data overload, an excess of urgent priorities to sort through. It was time to snatch a few minutes of quiet reflection. "I'm going to get a cup of coffee, take it to my office and think very hard," he announced. "Join me there in ten minutes and we'll make a plan." He began to turn away then stopped. "And Rickki—let's try and move evac time up. I have a bad feeling about all this."

"Me too, you know that?" Rickki gave a weary mock salute and he noticed how tired her eyes were. "In the meantime let's set up a situation room in the cafeteria, keep the rest of the staff jacked in."

Wolfe nodded. "Good idea. Do it." Outside there was a heavy explosion, near enough to shake down plaster from the ceiling. Their eyes met for a moment and then he turned away, foreboding spreading like poison through his veins.

By ten minutes to seven the word had spread through Versailles: a major Pakistan-style crisis had erupted. Despite the early hour, virtually everyone had crowded into the cafeteria where a wall-high TV screen had been set up beside a large-scale display of the city. The sound of fighting was disturbingly close and the air filters could not entirely shut out the bitter smell of smoke and dust. All blankies had been assigned to guard duty; a perimeter of sandbags had been set up outside Versailles and forty volunteers had been issued with Chang assault rifles and were on standby.

Wolfe surveyed the crowded room, smiled at Morgan who was seated near the map and, picking up a water glass, tapped lightly on it. Immediately the crowd went quiet with the odd quick silence of frightened people. Into the silence rattled the muted crackle and thump of a street skirmish a few blocks off. Rickki stood up on a chair beside the map and turned on her laser pointer. "Can everyone hear me? You gumbahs back there? Too well? Yeah, that's what you get for partying on an action station. Okay, here's the situation: The Premier was kidnapped last night by the Accord. She's being held at the Temple Compound. Government forces attacked the compound about three this morning trying to get her out. No luck yet, as far as we know. Zacharian Stele is due to broadcast in about nine minutes, and Dr. Wolfe will tell you about that shortly.

"Meanwhile, the whole country is going critical. We have reports of fighting from virtually every urban area and a few rural zones as well. Of particular concern, the local situation is deteriorating rapidly." She played the ruby arrow of her laser across the large city map on the wall to illustrate her comments. "Black shading marks impassable areas. Yellow indicates fires. White shows fighting in progress. There's a pitched battle going on downtown, along Queen Street from Parliament to just west of here. A dozen or so major fires out of control on a north-south axis to the east and a more-or-less continuous line of skirmishing running north of us. Most ominous of all, several units of Temple Guards are moving out of the Logan Street camp and heading in our general direction."

There was a muted ripple of concern. Rickki allowed it to continue for a few moments then held up her hand for quiet. "As you can see, we need to move out of here as soon as possible. Now the bad news: there's heavy fighting around the airport; all the runways are shut down, nothing's going in or out by air. Including us. Our best bet may be to run for the Yank border, but Orbital will have the final say on that. Whichever route we take, we'll have to go through at least one hot zone, so we need to battleproof our vehicles as much as possible. At the end of this meeting I'd like anyone with welding, armoring or automotive skills to meet in the garage. Everyone else report to their group supervisors for assignment, please—there's a lot of unexpected work associated with evacuation under fire, so we need everyone to lend a hand. Now our intrepid leader has a few words to say."

Wolfe climbed up on his own chair and looked out over the field of faces like flesh-toned flowers bobbing before him. "In a few moments you're going to hear a broadcast by Zacharian Stele. It is possible that he may make some very frightening threats. If so, don't be alarmed. Immediately following his broadcast I will have more to say to you." He climbed down from his chair, smelling the tension and fear in the air, just as the thin, mad features of Deacon Stele filled the large screen. Someone turned the volume up, and Stele's nasal, urgent baritone boomed out from speakers over the screen:

"Brothers and sisters of the true Accord, we are under attack by the forces of darkness. Woe to these doers of evil, for they are now facing a hideous doom." He threw out his thin hands in a gesture both menacing and conciliatory. "I carry a message from Adonai Himself—unless the government orders its soldiers to throw down their arms and surrender within the hour, the strong hand of the Lord will smite this city. The very air and water will turn to poison. Hundreds of thousands will die, and their death will be upon the head of acting Premier Beaufort." Deacon Stele made the sign of the double-barred cross in the air before him. "Even now it is not too late brothers and sisters. . . ."

The screen went abruptly black. Then a red maple leaf emblem appeared, and an announcer's reassuring voice spoke. "Stand by for an important message from the acting Premier of Upper Canada."

On screen appeared the heavy face of John Beaufort. "Fellow citizens, you have heard the ravings of Deacon Stele. Naturally we reject his ultimatum. Let me also reassure you at once that there is no danger—I repeat, absolutely no danger—to this city. You should know, however, that the plague threatened by Deacon Stele was of human, not divine origin. The Accord had placed a number of biological warheads around the city, and were clearly planning to trigger them at this time. Fortunately, we had advance warning of this threat. Yesterday, government teams disabled these weapons and removed them to a safe place. You should know . . ." Suddenly the screen went blank, then fuzzed into a jumble of gray snow as jamming scrambled the channel.

Wolfe cursed under his breath. The Accord was better prepared for electronic countermeasures than they had expected. He stepped back up on his chair. "What Premier Beaufort says is true. The biologicals were disarmed yesterday by Institute teams." He paused as a wave of wild, spontaneous applause and cheering swept over the cafeteria, then held up a hand for silence.

"If Deacon Stele is mad enough to try and trigger the devices, he will be disappointed. Unfortunately, while he may be insane, he is not stupid. It won't take him long to realize the Institute has thwarted his ambitions—at which point he will come calling. I think we'd all prefer that he not find us at home. Evac rolls at high noon. Meet back here at eleven-thirty for final orders. Okay, people, let's move."

There was a sudden swirl of activity and the cafeteria began to empty out. As he stood down from his chair Morgan came up to him, her expression sober. "So, Edward, it seems we acted just in time."

"Yes and no. Unfortunately we're still holding the biologicals."

"Can we get a helicopter to fetch them?" asked Morgan.

"We've been trying to arrange exactly that, but we're not having much luck so far. Aircraft are at a premium and we can't reach Beaufort to establish our priority over military missions."

Morgan looked at the clock over the metal cafeteria counter and blinked thoughtfully. "Time is running short. We may have to take them with us. Not an entirely pleasant prospect."

"I haven't even seen the damned things," admitted Wolfe. "How big are they?"

Morgan traced out an oval about the size of a football in the air. "Like that, times three. Weight isn't the problem."

"What is then?"

Morgan became very still for a moment, as if her spirit had retreated to some far-off place to think. After a moment she replied in a measured voice. "Volatility for one thing. If the vehicle carrying them takes a hit . . ." She shrugged. "Also, of course, there's the risk of them being recaptured."

"Can't we neutralize them somehow?"

"I doubt it—not with the equipment here. But I'm not an expert on advanced biologicals. Why not ask your sister?"

It occurred to Wolfe that he hadn't mentioned Kim's presence to Morgan. No doubt Helen had briefed her last night. Yes, no doubt. He fingered his ear stud thoughtfully. "Good idea. I'll brief her and we'll meet you in the containment room in fifteen minutes."

Kim was still in bed and asleep despite the increasing racket outside. Wolfe shook her shoulder, gently at first then harder. She opened bleary eyes and sat up straight, clutching the sheet to her chest. A small gasp escaped her lips and she fell back on the pillows shaking her head, her green eyes oddly unfocused and myopic without her lenses. "I was dreaming we were at the cottage." She frowned. "Jesus come quick, what's all the noise?"

Wolfe explained the situation and Kim's expression became more desolate. Finally she forced a small smile. "Isn't that typical? Your idiot sister runs for cover—and ends up in a building with a clutch of Class-A biologicals in the basement and a free-fire zone in the back yard. Well, at least I can be of some use." She closed her eyes, took a deep breath as if gathering her strength and sat up. Her skin was pale and waxy and she was breathing hard, as if she had just been exercising. Wolfe narrowed his eyes in alarm. "Focus Kim, are you feeling okay?"

His sister shook her head. "Not really. I'm still exhausted. Stress overload I guess."

"Shall I spark you up some breakfast?" asked Wolfe. "I have some gourmet feed stashed—I'll have to leave it behind otherwise." His sister's face looked as thin as if she had just emerged from a Freedom camp, and he had felt the bones in her shoulder when he shook her awake.

"No thanks, I'm not hungry. A cup of tea would be welcome. Give me a few moments to get dressed and we'll go have a look at these biologicals of yours."

They rode the elevator to the containment room in the small, damp sub-basement of Versailles where Morgan was waiting. Today her dark hair was pulled back in a tight bun at the back of her head, revealing her slim, muscular neck and upper shoulders. To Wolfe's subliminal regret, the rest of her figure was hidden by a baggy pair of black overalls. Her face was pale, making the mask of freckles across her broad nose stand out, but she looked as calm as ever, and even in the grim setting of the steel-walled containment room, incredibly desirable. He performed the necessary introductions, noticing that Morgan was inspecting his sister with more than casual interest. Perhaps Kim's reputation had preceded her, he decided.

On a low metal shelf at the far end of the neon-lit room were three metal containers, each slightly larger than a football, painted a dull green. "Unusual design," remarked Kim, poking with a long, gentle finger. "No biohazard symbols or serial numbers naturally. Vents at the front and rear—hmmm, interesting. Reminds me of an Islamic Coalition model I saw a couple of years ago."

His portable beeped twice, a priority message. He turned away with an apologetic wave and connected. It was Rickki. "Urgent news, boss. The Accord has just tried to trigger the bios. There's no doubt, the signal came through on all three detonators. Helen's linking down in two minutes."

"On my way." Wolfe turned back to the women, found Kim and Morgan already absorbed in an inspection of the first device, their noses about two inches from the green metal casing. He cleared his throat to get their attention: "Ahem, if either of you can shed any light on what these are and how we can neutralize them quickly we'd be most grateful. Feel free to call up to the Ops Room for tools or assistance. I'd appreciate hearing your findings in two hours at most. I'll be prowling about upstairs."

Morgan waved a dismissive hand. "We'll find you." She turned to Kim. "You see, the thing that puzzles me is these vents here."

Kim peered with interest at the indicated feature. "Yes, I see your point. Looks like a second generation Van Zim dispersal system for modified bacterials. Odd though . . ."

As he shut the door behind him, he heard the two already deep in technical conversation: Weird calling to Weird in the arcane language of biobabble. Despite the gravity of the situation a small smile creased his lips as he rode the elevator back upstairs.

He lowered himself into the leather viewing chair beside Rickki just as Helen coalesced on stage. The icon's hair was darker today, and her cheekbones infinitesimally higher. She wore a simple black coverall, perhaps to emphasize her solidarity with the Institute staff on the ground. "Good morning, everyone. I will be brief because there's a chance that transmission may be interrupted. It often happens in these unsettled situations." She smiled at her own understatement, then became serious again. "We now have absolute confirmation that the Accord has just tried to trigger the biologicals. The act has been recorded and will be used in Stele's trial at some suitable time, should he still be alive. More immediately, it is conclusive proof that we are dealing with a madman. This consideration adds a certain urgency to evacuation plans."

That was an understatement, thought Wolfe. A fly was buzzing around the conference room and the old leather of the chair, roughened by use, grated against his wrists. He wiped his forehead and wondered why small things were so distracting at times of crisis. Perhaps it was the mind trying to persuade itself that ordinary life went on in some dimension apart from the horrid unwinding of the human world. All very well, but this was no time for reflection. "Do you have any recommendation for evac routes?" he asked.

Helen shook her head. "Rely on your own initiative. Satellite views of the city are clouded by smoke, and a lot of com links are down so we're blind in key areas. Also, it's hard to distinguish just who's who, or what they're up to. From way up here we can't tell a Lister from a Temple guard until they start shooting."

"So we're on our own?" Wolfe took a deep breath, smelling soap from the factory next door.

"Not entirely. We've arranged for . . ." Helen's icon winked out, glowed then vanished for good as a series of very heavy explosions, felt rather than heard at first, hammered at the building like the blows of a giant's fist, bringing down big chunks of plaster from the ceiling. One hit Wolfe square on the back of the head, and for a moment purple lights flashed before his eyes. He cursed and carefully felt a bump the size of an egg already growing under the scalp. Just what he needed—another headache. His mangled ear was bleeding again slightly; he held a piece of Kleenex to it, tried to think. Emergency lights flickered on again but the stage remained bare.

"Youch," said Rickki with feeling, dusting herself off. "Guess we better slide on down to the Hole and find out what's happening."

The chief tech, an egg-bald Asian with a long, drooping mustache who spent his spare time romping the SexNets under the pseudonym of Electric Tusker, was chiding his displays when they arrived. Rickki tapped him on the shoulder impatiently. "Focus brother, what's our status?"

"Data down on all lines," announced the Tusker without looking up. "Also electricity; we're running on emergency generators."

"Can we repatch through to Orbital?" asked Rickki.

"Not except via cellular, and there's a lot of jamming," said the Tusker with gloomy satisfaction. He performed more diagnostics and preened his mustache pensively. "It looks as if our links have been targeted."

Rickki shrugged and turned to Wolfe: "I'd say we've just been cut out from the herd. That was more than a chance hit."

Wolfe nodded, a queasy feeling in his gut. If the

Accord was deliberately isolating them they were in serious trouble. "Agreed. We need backup."

"In an impressive way. Unfortunately, we're not having much success linking up with the military." Rickki turned to her aide, a young level two with waist-length black hair and liquid brown eyes. "Demeter, call up HQ again and remind 'em we're moving out in an hour. Insist on a chopper to get those damned bios out of here." She turned back to Wolfe and shook her head. "You know what? I don't think we're going to get that chopper. We may have to take the germs with us, whether or not the Weird Sisters can neutralize them, which I personally doubt. Either way, we have to roll by lunch time or risk getting snacked ourselves."

It was always the same in the end, thought Wolfe, looking around the Ops Room, now coated with dust, its screens blank, at the far end a half-dozen staffers plugging into their personal consoles trying to keep abreast of the situation. In moments of crisis there was never enough time, never enough information. It all boiled down to hunch and luck. "Alright then," he said slowly. "Let's prepare to take the biologicals. Send some people down to the containment room now and get the experts to help package them for the trip. We'll convoy out. At least that way we can protect ourselves against random attacks. If the Accord is planning an ambush we can scatter and we're no worse off than before. As far as routes, I suggest we send out some scouts to focus the situation." He winced as he saw the anxiety in Rickki's eyes. "Don't worry, sister, we'll be okay."

"Sure we will." Rickki smacked her fist into her palm. "I'll have the germs loaded into one of the Bulldogs right away."

"No." Wolfe held up a hand as she began to turn

away. "The Bulldogs will be primary targets if something goes wrong. Put them in with me and put me in some nondescript vehicle with the Weird and my sister—that way we'll have bio experts on hand if we need 'em."

Rickki began to argue then thought better of it. "Whatever you say. I'll go round up some scouts." She exited humming something which Wolfe recognized after a moment as Siegfried's Funeral March.

As the staff, dirty and disheveled, returned to the cafeteria they were given evacuation kits containing maps, alternate routes, radio codes and convoy protocols. This morning they had been stunned and frightened; now they had come to grips with the situation. The mood had changed from shock to wisecracking defiance. This was not going to be another Islamabad or Teheran. They clustered around the large-scale map that had been set up at the front of the room showing their escape route, a thin green line snaking through the heart of the beleaguered city and out the other side.

When the last staffers had trickled in, Rickki clambered up on a table and the room quieted.

"Okay, my lovelies, our com links are all down, so here's the picture, based on data from hand-helds and local reports from our scouts. There's a lot of sporadic fighting all over the city, but the main battles seem to be at the Temple Campus and downtown. By now Deacon Stele must be wondering what's happened to his biologicals, but we have no suggestion of any retaliatory strike on us, other than the big hit on our data links a couple of hours ago. So here's the plan: we're heading west along the Gerrard Street corridor, then south on Broadview Street, making for the Lakeshore Boulevard. We'll go right through the city on the Lakeshore, come out the other side and make a dash for the U.S. border along the King William Expressway. There is no ideal route—before we lost contact Helen told us she couldn't analyze the situation right now—so we're going to rely on instinct and luck."

She flourished her own escape kit, a sheaf of maps and papers in a blue cardboard cover. "Your vehicle assignments are in your kits. Each car comes with at least one weapon per passenger plus ammunition, extra gas, food and basic medical kit. Take a minute to locate all the essentials before we leave. If the road is closed, we'll back up and try an alternate route. Memorize alternates now, because if we do have to change direction there won't be time to pour over maps.

"If we're attacked, stay together and keep moving; the Bulldogs will engage first, with security backup as required. Unless you are specifically ordered to, do not break off for individual action. Call if your vehicle is taken out and we'll try to pick you up. If not, make for the nearest hub. We leave in twenty minutes exactly, so pack fast and light. When you get to the garage wait for the signal to start your engines; we don't want a buildup of carbon monoxide. Questions? Alright, brothers and sisters, see you for a big party in Buffalo tonight."

With twelve minutes to departure, Wolfe ran upstairs, grabbed his canvas overnight bag from the cupboard and threw in a change of clothes and a few pairs of socks and underwear. So much for gracious living, now what did he really need? Omaha's T-shirt of course, and his original black belt, now white and threadbare around the edges. He packed the items carefully, and added his copy of *Principles of SocioCybernetics*, a first edition signed by Dr. Hartley himself. Unhooking the miniature landscape by his mother from its place over the console he wrapped it in a spare shirt and packed it gently on top. And that, he decided after a quick scan of his living space, was about that. He opened the window and called the Rooftop Cat but there was no response. The wise creature had probably taken shelter in some faraway lair. Wolfe sincerely hoped so. A final look-about and he slung his bag over his shoulder and headed down to the garage.

The convoy was an auto-body mechanic's nightmare, three dozen hastily modified cars and light trucks, their vitals covered with a black, jagged-edged patchwork of steel plates and scrap metal. Shepherding the motley metal herd was a pair of twin-turret Bulldog armored cars, one at the head of the convoy, one at the rear.

Wolfe had been assigned to a blue Ford jeepster with armor plate welded to the doors and windows, leaving small slits for visibility. His sister was already stretched out on the back seat, her face white and covered with a sheen of sweat. Wolfe opened the back door and stuck his head in. "How ya feeling, Kim?"

His sister moaned. "Worse and worse. Like someone walked all over me in the night. And I can barely stay awake."

"Must be the flu—you just take it easy." Wolfe grimaced and walked around the back of the jeep to where Morgan was inspecting the armor plate over the rear wheels. "Everything in order?"

Morgan pushed back a strand of dark hair. "In a manner of speaking. We have the biologicals aboard, also weapons, food and so on. Who drives?"

"Are you a good shot?" asked Wolfe.

"Not bad," Morgan admitted with a modest shrug.

Somehow Wolfe was not surprised. It fitted with a theory that had been bubbling for some time on a burner far back in his brain. Someone had zapped Zacharian Stele, just enough to enrage him and kill the peace process hatched by Mrs. Clements. Someone with dark hair and a very steady hand. "Alright then, I'll drive, you ride shotgun." He slid in behind the steering wheel and shut the heavy armored door with a satisfying clunk. The slit in the steel covering the windscreen give him a surprisingly wide field of view; satisfied he could navigate he waited for the convoy to depart. Even with his windows closed, the noise in the garage was overwhelming, with the roar of thirty motors racketing and rebounding from the dank concrete walls. Two minutes went by, three, then the far end of the garage brightened as the heavy door swung open, and the line of vehicles began to move. Wolfe followed the modified car ahead of him up the ramp and out onto the street.

Outside, the smell of burning was stronger, and a huge blaze several blocks away on Queen Street sent a column of black smoke billowing up into the sky.

A mob of two or three hundred people on Gerrard Street was engaged in looting the half-dozen stores in a run-down strip mall. As the convoy rumbled past, many of the looters began to sidle away. Then, when the ominous snouts of the Bulldogs with their twin black fifty calibers remained pointed ahead, they returned to their work of ruin. Wolfe caught a momentary glimpse of two girls stepping daintily out of the ruins of the Sex Shoppe, wrapped in long pink feather boas with pink feathers in their hair and what looked like immense dildos in their hands. The crowd howled with delight and then the mall was left behind.

The convoy snaked on, through a war zone of burning buildings and impromptu street parties. Now they were approaching Logan Avenue and the derelict railroad bridge, rusted and forlorn, that customarily sheltered a small family of Listers.

The Accord sprung its ambush as the lead Bulldog reached the bridge. As Wolfe watched in horror, an articulated truck with the cheerful red and blue markings of the Weston Bakery drove across the road under the bridge and stopped. The driver slithered like a huge black lizard out of the cab, dropped down onto the sidewalk and ran back along the street into the cover of a doorway.

At the same moment the street lit up with the sparkle of gunfire. Burst after burst from automatic rifles and heavy machine guns raked the convoy, igniting four cars instantly in bursts of oily orange flame. Wolfe glimpsed Accord troopers peering from windows and doorways on both sides of the street. It was the worst case scenario—a major, well-prepared ambush. Apparently Deacon Stele wanted to make his deep displeasure with the Institute felt.

Rickki's voice sounded calm and ironic on the car speaker, her breezy soprano counterpointed by the deep bass bark of the Bulldog's turret fifties. "Okay, brothers and sisters, we're straying into some ordure here—let's turn around, nice and disciplined, and try an alternate route. Some supporting fire on the north side of the street please."

Morgan poked the Chang out a loophole in the armor and was searching for a target when there was a whoosh and a muffled explosion. A searing white light seemed to grow out of the forward turret of Rickki's Bulldog. It lurched to a stop, flame spurted from the hatches and it began to burn. Sick with grief and fury, Wolfe screamed a curse on the Accord and all its detestable followers, swung the jeep around just as a half-dozen loud bangs very close by almost deafened him.

The jeep shuddered and he fought for control, running up on the sidewalk then back down with a crash onto the wrong side of the road. He stepped on the gas and began to speed away from the ambush. Morgan fired a long burst, bringing down two guards trying to scuttle back into a doorway. Wolfe felt a glow of vindictive pleasure.

Over the speaker came a babble of instructions, then Johnson's voice. "Convoy, take alternative route nine, repeat route nine."

Morgan pulled the Chang back inside and turned to him with a peremptory shake of her head. "Wrong instruction, we should scatter. If we form up again they'll stick to us and keep hitting."

Wolfe glanced about, counted nine vehicles already burning. "Agreed. Call in and override the order. Tell everyone to break away."

Morgan punched the phone then shook her head. "Dead. We must have taken a hit."

Wolfe accelerated west along Gerrard Street, then north on a side street and out of sight of the massacre. He pulled up on a small side street lined with low-rise public housing painted in garish shades of pink and purple, his heart hammering in his chest, the steel taste of fear in his mouth. There was a long silence, then Morgan spoke with great feeling: "Oh my God, what a mess."

That was the understatement of the decade, thought Wolfe. He looked back at his sister and his heart sank even further. Despite the racket of gunfire and bomb bursts she seemed to have fallen asleep. Hectic red spots flamed on her cheeks and she was breathing in short, deep gasps. He called her name softly and shook her but she only moaned and twisted. He turned back to Morgan, hoping with all his heart that BioAge had not already exacted its revenge. *Poor Kim, it's no era for an idealist.* "Damn—looks like flu. We better exit the city pronto. We're being targeted, whether for the germs or just pure vengeance I don't know. Not that it matters."

"Zacharian wants the biologicals," declared Morgan in a matter-of-fact voice. She had unsnapped the black clip of her Chang and was feeding cartridges into it. "He may be crazy but he's not stupid. He needs 'em to win the war, and that's all. Which means they'll be combing the city until they track down and search every last vehicle in our convoy."

What she said made horrible sense Wolfe admitted to himself, scanning the quiet street for signs of pursuit. "We've got some hot potatoes here," he agreed. "Plus Kim isn't well at all, and we have to consider the fact that we've both been exposed to her. Somehow we've got to off-load the bios before we're caught or come down with what she's got."

"Agreed." Morgan snapped the magazine back onto her weapon with a sharp click. "Any ideas?"

Wolfe considered the options, found none of them pleasing. "We can't stay in the city, and we don't dare run for the border. I suggest we head up towards my cottage. I know a place to hide the bios, and we can get medical help if we need it. A friend of mine runs a clinic nearby."

Morgan nodded and leaned back to adjust Kim's seatbelt. "Fair enough. You know the route, let's go." She flipped open her portable again, tried a half-dozen connections, eliciting only a crackle of static for response. "All jammed out," she announced, returning it to her shoulder pocket. "We're on our own, more or less. Deliciously primitive." She raised her eyebrows ironically at him, apparently undismayed by the abrupt evaporation of the data stream.

Sticking to the back streets they crossed town without incident. North of Lawrence Avenue all the traffic lights were out, and fires ate at an abandoned gas station. In his side mirror he saw it explode—a huge bloom of yellow fire—a moment later a long, hollow roar like thunder rolled through the heavy air.

Turning onto Avenue Road they encountered a dozen ragged Listers of the Christmas Tribe breaking storefront windows. At their approach the marauders swarmed into the street and stood there in a human blockade, jumping aside only when it became apparent the jeep was not going to stop. There was a loud clang as something grazed the rear bumper, then their receding figures danced and gestured obscenely like small black devils in his rearview mirror: living symbols of the triumph of chaos. Wolfe hated them with a pure, intense loathing he had never felt before.

A green triangular sign marked the way to Highway 400. He took the turnoff gingerly, feeling the extra weight of the armor heeling the jeepster over. With a long squeal of rubber he aimed the vehicle north towards the land of hardened country holdings, where the Dark Age mentality had already taken full root. It was a strange way to come home.

Besieged

To the Skellig Michael Institute goes the distinction of being the first "nation" not of the Earth. In a lengthy and complex decision taken by the Supreme Court of the United Nations, the orbital station was adjudged to be a self-governing community, and hence independent. Four of the seven judges affirmed the Institute's independence. The rumor that each of these four had received the subtle backing of Helen at one point or another in their careers has never been confirmed or substantiated. Nor has it been entirely dismissed.

The Skellig Michael Institute—A Brief History

Wednesday, July 14
14:00 hours

Traffic was variable as they groped their way up Highway 400, ambling along at about thirty klicks, occasionally slowing almost to a standstill then speeding up again. Wolfe drove mechanically, trying without success to exorcise the mental image of flames spewing from Rickki's vehicle. Perhaps there was a chance, just a tiny chance she had escaped. He couldn't make himself believe the lie.

A rusty white van crammed with furniture paced them in the middle lane, a young East Indian woman steering while an old man with a white beard and turban studied the map on his knees and looked around nervously. They were moving through an incongruously tranquil landscape: black and white cows dotted across a green pasture, languid groups of Listers in loose orange and yellow robes dozing by heaps of secondhand goods at roadside booths. Apparently the rural Lists had not yet been infected with the violent spirit of the times.

Wolfe was not especially reassured. He kept to the outside lane, a constant, anxious eye on getaway routes across the surrounding fields. Even with air conditioning the cabin was stifling. His neck and upper back were wet with sweat and his ear hurt; he tried not to wonder what the heat was doing to Kim. Poor girl, she had picked the worst possible escape route from her tormentors. In the back of the jeepster his sister moaned, whispered a few words and was silent again.

"She drank a bit anyway." Morgan turned to face forward again, placed a half-full cup of water in the plastic drink holder by the dashboard. "Pure reflex though, she's right out." She brushed back a strand of dark hair, picked up the binoculars and scanned the road ahead through the wide slit in the armor covering the windshield.

An hour passed, they crept away from the city, and still, miraculously there were no jams. Traffic crawled forward, occasionally snaking off the shoulder and around massive pileups. One detour lay through a grassy field; a blue Hyundai Avenger had become mired in red-brown mud and was spinning its wheels with the sound of a million angry wasps. Wolfe smelt burning rubber, then the obstacle was behind and they were on the road again.

Far ahead up the road, four immense coils of oily smoke writhed upwards like black serpents chasing the fluffy white herds of light cumulus that frolicked slowly across the blue summer sky. Morgan lowered the binoculars and pointed at them. "I don't like the look of those."

"Just accident sites, don't you think?" asked Wolfe.

"Maybe, but they give me an uneasy feeling." Morgan frowned. "Those are big fires, Edward: fuel trucks maybe or piles of burning tires. There shouldn't be four in the same place—it feels wrong." She took out her portable again, fiddled with it for a few moments and shook her head in frustration. "Damn, the level of jamming is incredible. A pity—we need an advisory about now."

Wolfe glanced at her: "What's your concern?"

"Call it intuition. I have them occasionally." Morgan stared at the black spirals of smoke, her face vacant, as if listening intently, then began to speak in a slow tentative voice: "Say there's a recree going on up ahead. Say the Listers are looking to snatch cars, dope, women—maybe damage a few gumbahs just for the sheer joy of it. They wouldn't stop traffic outright. That would cut off their supply of fresh goodies. So they block a lane or two, create a bottleneck. When they see a prize haul or they run out of playthings, they just divert a few cars down some dead-end track and then disappear again until the next time."

Wolfe considered the scenario, found it not implausible. "So we're looking for a slowdown, followed by a managed detour. Or something like that. If we see it?"

"I think when we get a bit nearer we'll make our own detour, well off the beaten track. If we're followed, we'll dump a grenade or two out the door and see what happens." She scrutinized the grenades with a professional eye. "Mark-Three Skodas, otherwise known as bulls' balls. Good choice. About a seven-meter kill radius and easy to toss."

Just after the turnoff to Kettleby the road angled

gently up a small slope then disappeared down the other side to where the first pillar of smoke was rising. Traffic slowed markedly, stopped, lurched forward again; Morgan lowered the binoculars, her lips tight. "This is it, Edward; I register a half-dozen gumbahs in orange safety vests, flagging traffic off the road. It looks like a detour. There are barriers across the road, just wooden construction things. We could easily run them."

"Okay. Sit tight. Let's get closer and assess the situation. Got your hardware ready?"

Morgan checked the Chang with a thin smile, laid it across her lap and picked up the binoculars again. Almost immediately she spoke: "Now they're pulling back the barriers, opening the road again. I don't like it."

Wolfe cursed under his breath. "Outstanding. So which is the trap: road or detour?"

Morgan spoke decisively: "The road. They could box it in completely on the far side of that rise, park cars or trucks all around the edges. Once you were inside you'd be completely trapped. The detour leads through the fields; it'd be much harder to close off. You could head in any direction, even without four-wheel drive."

"Okay then, let's get off the road." Wolfe slapped the gears into all-wheel, steered off the road and onto the grassy verge. Two of the flag men, seeing the jeepster pull off, ran to intercept it. Wolfe aimed the vehicle at them, had the satisfaction of seeing them jump aside at the last moment. Both had the menacing black and dead white markings of the Avenger Tribe circling their eyes and mouths.

The detour was plainly marked and had been heavily used; grass had been flattened and ground into the dirt for ten meters on either side of the trail. Wolfe ignored the signs, wheeled the jeepster bumping and jolting through the cornfields, battering down the ripening stalks in a wide semicircle which brought them back towards the highway a klick to the far side of the diversion. He drove up a small knoll with a stand of trees on top, stopped just meters below the crest. "I want to see if we're clever or merely neurotic. Coming?"

Morgan shook her head. "I'll stay with Kim."

Wolfe hung the binoculars around his neck, crept to the top of the ridge and looked cautiously over. The highway was almost directly below. Just beyond the crest of the hill, trailer trucks were parked on either side of the road, forming a crude channel leading into a large circular corral of cars. At irregular intervals around the enclosure, huge piles of tires burned with a thick black smoke. Wolfe squinted through the binoculars: near one of the fires, a small crowd buzzed around a blue Labatt's beer truck. A recree appeared to be under way; little knots of people copulated openly here and there in the circle of cars, while onlookers cheered. At one end, a group of people sat disconsolate on the ground, guarded by a dozen Listers armed with shotguns and drinking from liter bottles of beer.

As Wolfe watched, one prisoner crept away and made for a gap between cars. He was discovered; four Listers chased him back across the open area, caught him, and carried him squirming and screaming towards one of the fires. He recognized the old man by his turban, now unraveling as he struggled. His captors carried him to a tall, shirtless Lister in tight purple shorts, who knelt to tie the victim's legs with what looked like barbed wire. Satisfied, he stood up and gestured with his thumb. The prisoner was picked up, carried to the brink of the blaze and heaved into the flames like a bundle of garbage. Sickened, Wolfe lowered his binoculars and returned to the jeepster. Morgan had opened the back door and was trying to persuade Kim to drink. She looked up at his approach. "So? Are we neurotic?"

"No. You were right. Precisely right. And I despair for this evil world." Wolfe crouched beside her. Kim's forehead was blazing hot; he unscrewed one of the water bottles, wet his fingers and gently moistened her face. "How did you guess?"

"Intuition," said Morgan briefly, and straightened up. "Let's move. We can rejoin the road a couple of klicks ahead."

Wolfe clambered back into the driver's seat, with a sidelong, puzzled glance at his companion, and started the engine.

They drove in thoughtful silence until they regained the highway five klicks above the deadly recree. Ahead, the road seemed clear and traffic had thinned. Fifteen minutes passed, then half an hour, and the plumes of smoke faded behind them. Trees began to appear along the roadside; they were in the country. Wolfe put aside his horror and started to consider how best to approach the uncertain future.

Morgan had evidently been engaged in the same exercise. She looked back at Kim, who was still sleeping fitfully, then turned to him. "So tell me about your island. You said you had a place to hide the biologicals?"

"Yes. In an underwater cave. We found it by accident when we were children." Wolfe smiled, remembering his excitement when he had glimpsed the entrance to the underwater grotto through the fogged glass of his diving mask on one of his first scuba expeditions. He had been thirteen, still young enough to hope that his discovery would be a pirate's grotto. "It's in the tumble of rocks at the south of our island. You go about two meters under and come up in a little cave right at the heart of a rock slide. It's above the water line but you'd never find it from outside. I know, we tried for days."

Morgan took her eyes off the road long enough to look at him with amusement. "I bet. Would it be hard to get the biologicals in?"

"Not at all. We'll put them all inside a pillow case or something and I'll swim in with 'em. Take us five minutes or less."

"Excellent. What about the island itself—could we defend ourselves there?"

"It depends against what." Wolfe called the diagrams of the system to his mind. "It's protected by a state-of-the-art remote laser system—installed by BioAge a couple of years ago when Kim spent time there. Day/night eyes controlling a bank of lasers with over-lapping fields of fire. Covers all marine approaches as well as low aerial."

Morgan considered. "Could anyone swim ashore, come in close with a snorkel or scuba and crawl up the beach?"

"Yes," admitted Wolfe, pulling out to pass an old red Volvo that was crawling up the two-lane road with a load of furniture strapped precariously on its roof. "There used to be a close-in system too for that sort of contingency, but it was very fussy. BioAge took it out when Kim moved back to Paris."

"In that case we can't stay there for long," said Morgan. "If we're tracked to the island they'll try everything to get ashore."

"We probably could stay with my friend Mac. He runs a maxSec medical facility a few klicks up the bay, the latest security systems plus a small army of guards." Wolfe frowned as an unpleasant thought struck him. "Unless of course our presence puts him in danger."

"It might," admitted Morgan. "We do have another alternative—take your catamaran and disappear into the wilderness. Georgian Bay is a big place—thousands of islands, inlets, bays to hide in. We'd be the proverbial needle in the haystack."

The thought of a wilderness cruise with Morgan in close proximity was far from unpleasant. In fact, it seemed to Wolfe that for once, close attention to duty coincided with his precise desires. Then he thought of Kim and his enthusiasm faded. He sighed to himself, then spoke firmly. "The situation is too fluid to plan far ahead. Here's my suggestion: we'll drop Kim off at the clinic, hide the biologicals, then come back to the clinic and evaluate our status at that point."

"Sensible." Morgan gave him an odd sidelong glance and returned her attention to the road ahead.

They reached Byng Inlet two hours later. At the mouth of the main road to the town was a barricade manned by a half-dozen of the local militia wearing army surplus flak jackets and green armbands. They flagged the jeep down, hunting rifles and shotguns at the ready. Not without relief Wolfe recognized the town's white-haired volunteer police chief and George, the oldest son of the marina owner among the militia. He got out of the jeep, careful to keep his distance in case he was already a matrix for whatever infection Kim was breeding, and made himself known. "Any news from the city?" asked George. "Have they found the Premier yet?"

"No idea," admitted Wolfe. "Our com links are out and we didn't stop to ask questions on the way up. What's it like here?"

The old police chief shifted his shotgun to the crook of his arm and honked his strawberry nose into a large white handkerchief. "Quiet," he said tucking his hanky away. "Nice and quiet. And we can keep it that way. You a member of the Byng Inlet Mutual Aid Society?"

"I've been meaning to join," lied Wolfe.

The old man grinned and two gold teeth flashed in his upper jaw. "You just have. We meet for training next week. In the meantime, you need help, you call in."

Large red stickers with the incongruous legend
SUMMER FEST '27 were pasted on the front and rear
of the jeep for impromptu ID and he was waved
through into the town proper. Wheeling the primitive armored car through the tree-lined, shady streets,
Wolfe felt an overpowering sense of strangeness, as
if he were wallowing in the passages of a childhood
dream. They drove past the bakery, a two-story white-
frame building with a neat gravel parking lot, past
the black steeple of the Presbyterian church. On its
green lawn a hand-painted sign advertised a bingo
evening in bright red lettering.

At last Wolfe pulled up at the hardened outer walls
of Harvey's Marina and thumbed his combo into the
remote. The steel gate swung open and he drove
through with a mounting sense of elation. After all,
they had escaped.

It was a quiet summer evening, the water slapping
at the hulls of the moored boats; he might have been
his father or grandfather, up for a country weekend
twenty, fifty, even seventy years ago. He walked out
on the wharf to the mooring where his catamaran
bobbed, stripped off the blue canvas cover and
jumped aboard. An enterprising spider had made a
web around the wheel; Wolfe brushed it away and
started the little inboard, which caught with reassuring
quickness in a quiet gurgle of water and a puff of
blue diesel smoke. Leaving it to idle he fed his card
into the ancient pay phone at the end of the dock,
punched a number and heard a burring, followed by
a pleasant female voice: "Vitality Island Clinic—how
may we serve you?"

"Edward Wolfe to speak to Dr. MacGregor."

After a brief conversation Wolfe returned to the jeep,
giving Morgan the thumbs-up sign. "MacGregor's
expecting us. All we have to do now is get there."

Between them they half-dragged, half-carried Kim

to the boat. She muttered something, opened her eyes and closed them again. Through his thin shirt he could feel the heat of her fever. She seemed thinner somehow, and her face was mottled and red. Wolfe said a silent prayer they were not too late.

Placing her in the small cabin they returned for their weapons and once more for the sinister egg-shaped canisters of the biologicals; then with a feeling of profound relief Wolfe cast off the mooring lines, chugged the catamaran backward out of the slip and aimed her twin bows across the bay. Directly ahead of them the sun spread a crimson stain across the oily surface of the black water as it rolled down the sky like a ball of flame. It was hellishly hot; the air seemed to hang and shimmer in superheated folds. The only noise was the persistent low throb of the boat's engine.

Half an hour later, a kilometer-square cube of red rock loomed before them, its low pine-topped cliffs rising abruptly out of the water. Wolfe pointed. "Vitality Island. The dock's on the far side; it's about the only spot you can land."

A heavy metal boom, suspended between meter-tall yellow metal floats, had been installed across the entrance to Vitality Island's tiny natural harbor. At the top of a gentle slope was a cluster of futuristic buildings: black and white domes, multiangled glass and steel structures, reflecting the purple and crimson of the sunset, even a slender white tower with two horns. As always when he saw the clinic, Wolfe snorted. The architecture was too elegant by far to house a fat farm, even a premium version.

He blew a long blast on the cat's horn, then another, uneasily aware that the long black tube protruding from the concrete dome beside the dock had begun to track them. After his recent travails he had no desire to be fried by a nervous remote. A moment later an amplified voice sounded across the water. "This is private property. Please identify yourselves."

"Edward Wolfe and friend, with a patient for Dr. MacGregor."

Silence for a few moments, then the boom slide aside and a team of orderlies in white plastic isolation suits appeared on the long dock, one pushing a hospital gurney. With a sigh of relief Wolfe nuzzled the boat up to the dock.

Under the harsh white glare of the isolation chamber's lights, Kim's skin was yellow and wrinkled, like leather left out in the rain, and her breath came shallow and fast. Two hectic spots of red shone in her thin cheeks. She looked terrible, Wolfe thought with a pang of pity.

Mac straightened up, clumsy within his protective plastic garment. With his biohazard helmet on, he looked like a giant insect, vacant goggle eyes and long black snout where twin virus filters covered his nose and mouth. The voice that issued from the helmet was unmistakably Mac's though, and he sounded far from happy. "I could wish you'd brought her in earlier," he said quietly. "She's lost a lot of fluid and she's weak." As he talked he began to rig an intravenous drip. "We'll start her on an IV right away and try to keep her sedated." He slid the needle into Kim's vein, stuck a piece of tape over her wrist and stood back, twitching at the chest of his plastic suit as if it were too tight.

"The funny thing is, I'm not convinced it's Tokyo Flu. Many of the classic signs, but she hasn't deteriorated the way you'd expect. No sigh of pulmonary shutdown and the fever is lower than usual. Also there's a lot of very weird brain activity, almost like she's in deep REM sleep—obviously dreaming dazzling dreams. We'll keep her here in isolation until we know what we're dealing with." The insect head goggled at them like a thing from a nightmare. "I'm afraid you'll have to stay in isolation too, for the duration. Don't worry, we'll make you comfortable."

With an effort of will Wolfe heaved himself out of his chair. "First things first. We have some business to attend to, then we'll come back and get isolated."

Mac held up a white plastic gauntlet in warning. "Your business doesn't bring you in contact with anyone, does it? That wouldn't be a good idea."

Morgan spoke for the first time from the corner where she had been observing. "We're not seeing anyone, don't worry. We just have to run a quick errand."

"Can't it wait?" protested Mac, turning to her, his voice muffled behind the filters. "It's almost dark, and strange people come out at night—even here."

"We won't be long," Morgan assured him. "Can we still get something to eat when we get back? I confess I'm getting hungry."

"We have the best chef within a hundred klicks," said the insect that was Mac, rubbing its gloved hands in a grotesque display of gastronomic pride, its goggle eyes fixed on Morgan. "You hurry back and we'll fix you up a meal you'll never forget." Wolfe knew exactly what his old friend was thinking and beamed a mental message in his direction. *Forget it brother. She's spoken for.*

Cleaners

Where does Helen actually reside? Her primary site is said to be aboard the Institute Orbital, but some have suggested that this is a smoke screen, that the elusive AI may in fact exist aboard one of the Institute's nuclear submarines or even in some covert undersea base. It is also rumored that she has other fallback installations around the planet, either processing secondary data or dormant as backup in case of disaster. As usual, nothing is known for certain. When dealing with Helen, do not mistake the reflections of reflections of subtly distorted mirrors for the real thing.

Breaking Point, A Collection of Essays
on Post Millennial Topics
Henrikus Grobius, Jr.

Wednesday, July 14
21:45 hours

Wolfe's island rose out of the black waters of the bay, a heart-shaped hump of red granite sloping gently to a tiny, pine-covered hillock at the center. On a long flat terrace on the east shore, ten meters or so above the water, his grandfather had chosen to erect a sprawling cottage of wood and fieldstone. A path led up over the crest of the hillock and down the other side to the boathouse and his mother's small studio.

On the long north shore was a small beach and an ancient dock. To the south, the island tailed off into a scatter of huge red boulders which formed a honeycomb of caves and crevasses before sinking below the water to make a treacherous reef extending a full fifty meters from shore.

A hundred meters out, Wolfe stopped the boat, carefully removed the remote from his pouch and triggered a warning shot to test the system. A thread of red light lanced through the evening, turned the water to steam two meters off the bow.

"Good." Morgan nodded in approval. "Now please arrange to stop it from cooking us."

Wolfe keyed the remote, then pressed the firing button again. Nothing—the system had been successfully disarmed. He told the sail to furl itself; it obediently disappeared into the mast and he eased the catamaran into the dock using the inboard. The engine died and silence seeped in like a healing balm. Trees rustled in a light wind, and somewhere a bird twittered and was still. He tied up the boat, Morgan stepped out, a Chang slung over each shoulder, and he followed, gingerly carrying the three biologicals inside a large laundry bag he had found in the cabin. To his surprise they were not terribly heavy, about the weight of three large cartons of milk. It was hard to believe he was carrying the seeds of a plague that could wipe out a city in a bag slung over his shoulder.

He led the way up the path that wound through the pine trees to the white cottage door and stepped aside to let Morgan in. The inanimate residents of the cottage seemed to welcome them: the fridge burst into a loud electric purr and the old furniture twinkled in the overhead light.

Wolfe did not have time to greet his old friends as they deserved. He crossed the cathedral-ceilinged room, threw back the mahogany lid of the weapons console and rearmed the system as Morgan watched intently. A small amber screen glowed to life, its face marked with concentric circles. He indicated the display to Morgan. "Nothing within five klicks at the moment. An alarm will sound if anything comes closer than three klicks on a landing vector. The system is set to fire on anything closer than a klick. You override and adjust range manually with this switch here. This toggle puts the system on full automatic—on this setting it burns anything it decides is threatening. The green switch disarms everything."

"Got it." Morgan drew up a wicker-back chair and sat down before the console. "I'll stay here and keep watch, you dispose of the biologicals. Remember, store them with the vents up."

"Understood." Wolfe disappeared into his room, changed into a bathing suit, T-shirt and a pair of moccasins, stuffed his mask, fins and underwater torch into a blue nylon sports bag and returned to the main room feeling like he was participating in some bizarre charade. Morgan gave him the thumbs-up sign. "Good luck, Edward. And hurry. I'll be a lot happier when we're away from here."

Something in the depths of her blue-black eyes troubled Wolfe. He hefted the bag containing the biologicals and pushed through the swinging screen door out into the warm summer night.

The cave was at the southern tip of the island, two long paces due north of a lightning-struck pine tree. Wading into the dark water he experienced a sudden pang of doubt—he had never dived for the cave at night—what if he couldn't spot the entrance in the murk? When he was chest-deep he lined himself up with the pine tree and, taking a deep breath, submerged.

He need not have worried. The cave entrance was

immediately visible, even in the wavering light of his torch, a meter-wide gash between two vertical red boulders. He swam though and surfaced, playing his flashlight around the inside. It was exactly as he remembered, even to the dank air and faded red and black paintings of motorboats and rockets that Kim and he had daubed on the wall one summer. Submerging again, he swam out through the underwater entrance, squelched up to the shore and retrieved the biologicals in their incongruous white bag.

It was harder the second time. His cargo weighed him down, and as he swam through the entrance the bag wedged between two small rocks. Wolfe tugged gently, then let the bag go, resurfaced for another breath of air and dove again. This time he was able to work the bag loose. He surfaced inside the cave, his lungs burning. It was the work of two minutes to store the green metal footballs, vents up, on a wide shelf of red rock at the back of the grotto. Wolfe flashed his torch around to assure himself all was well, then waded into the water.

Fifteen minutes after he had left, he was jogging back up the path, cold and wet but exuberant. Morgan was still sitting where he had left her, but now she was hunched over the display screen, tension in every line of her body. "Finished? Good, because I think we may have visitors."

Wolfe reached the console in two strides, looked at the display and his elation turned to dismay.

A large amber blip was coming in slowly from the north, about three klicks out, apparently on a vector towards the island. He studied the display, his heart pounding. "The Accord?"

Morgan shook her head softly. "Impossible to say. If not, why are they moving so slowly? The only reason I can imagine is to cut engine noise. For an attacker it's a fair trade, stealth for speed."

"Or it could just be a drunken cottager going home late," pointed out Wolfe. "It still happens up here." He stared at the blip inching across the screen and took a deep breath. "Damn. If they hold course much longer we'll have to fire a warning shot."

"I'd rather wait until we're sure, then blow them out of the water."

"Agreed. But how can we be sure?" They watched the blip crawl towards the two-kilometer line and Wolfe restrained a growing desire to switch the system to automatic mode. He shut off the cottage lights, stepped out onto the balcony and stared into the darkness with his binoculars. Nothing but the smell of pine, the rustle of the wind. He went back inside and reported as much.

"Wait a minute." Morgan looked intently at the display. "Now they've stopped."

As they watched the blip, it seemed to give birth. Six smaller amber dots detached themselves from it and began to crawl with infinite slowness towards the island.

"Landing craft. That's the Accord alright." Morgan jumped out of her chair and motioned urgently to him. "You know the system better—set it to ignore the small boats and open fire on the mother ship."

Wolfe sat down, trying to recall the procedure for manual targeting. After a moment's thought he called up a tiny cross of red light, moved it across the screen to intersect the large blip and locked the system onto it. Three seconds passed, five as the lasers came to bear, then the green ready indicator began to flash. Wolfe looked at Morgan, who nodded. His mouth dry, he punched the automatic firing control then ran to the porch in time to see a volley of thin red spears stabbing outward, converging on some point far out in the lake. The spears faded, then stabbed again. A sudden fire sprang into being and the sound of an engine gunning to top speed came clearly across the dark water. He ran back to the console in time to see the large dot disappear at speed off the top of the monitor. Undeterred, the smaller blips crawled relentlessly forward.

"Winged 'em," said Morgan with satisfaction, crossing to the mantel and slinging the Changs over her shoulder. "Badly I hope. Time for a very quick getaway, before they repair the damage and pick up their boats. Can we get out safely with the system on?"

"Sure." Wolfe was bending over the console to reset it when a fresh idea occurred to him. "How about if we also tell it to hold off until they're just half a klick out? At that range the lasers are lethal, and we'll have time to get away."

Morgan nodded. "Good idea—do it." She looked calmly around the interior of the cottage. "Are we forgetting anything? Binoculars? Good, let's move."

Wolfe straightened up from the console, strode to the kitchen, threw some cans of food into a knapsack and followed her out into the darkness, wondering anew at the smoothness with which she had once again taken charge. They glided down the dark path to the boathouse and out onto the dock. A tiny pinpoint of fire marked where the larger boat still burned. "Unfortunate," said Morgan, pointing at it. "It's right between us and Vitality Island and it must have radar. We'd never be able to sneak back without being seen."

Wolfe had no intention of leading the Cleaners to his sister and his best friend. "We'd better head in the other direction then," he said. "Granite Island's about ten klicks down the bay. They may not be able to pick us out against the island, especially if we get close enough."

"And beyond?" asked Morgan as she helped him undo the moorings.

"A few thousand other islands with or without cottages, a couple of native holdings, lots of wilderness." Wolfe threw his knapsack into the cabin and stepped up to join Morgan on the low bridge. She had already started the inboard. He engaged gears, spun the wheel and the catamaran slipped silently away from the dock and out onto the dark water. With the sail down and the small inboard leaving no wake, they must be almost invisible, or so Wolfe hoped. He locked the autopilot on and turned around, straining for a glimpse of the intruders.

Nothing. Even the spark that marked the main Accord boat had vanished—either the fire had been brought under control or the vessel had sunk. Further and further down the bay they slipped and still nothing disturbed the tranquillity of the summer night. He was beginning to wonder if the small craft had turned back when a dazzling line of red light cut across the night. A brilliant purple flash was followed by a hoarse cry, echoing faintly across the water. "One," said Morgan calmly. "Must have hit the motor."

As she spoke another volley of ruby spears danced across the darkness, igniting two small fires which flared suddenly orange like the eyes of a night animal caught in the headlights, then died away abruptly. "Very effective system," commented Morgan. "If the others have any sense they'll turn back now."

A brief pause while the black water gurgled beneath them and then the ruby spears danced through the still night again, unerringly lancing another boat. A sudden plume of white and purple fire rose up from the lake, and a moment later came an ear-shattering explosion. Morgan identified the source laconically: "HT-three. A big packet."

Wolfe stared at where the boat had been, afterimages dancing before his eyes. "What do they need explosive for?"

"Probably planning to blow up the cottage," said

Morgan calmly. "They'd want to deny us sanctuary. Or maybe they're motivated by pure spite."

"How I hate them." Wolfe spat the words into the darkness, as if they carried a bad taste.

"They are rational according to their own world view. That, of course, is the definition of fanaticism," replied Morgan, her attention still fixed on the darkness astern. Several minutes passed in silence. Then she lowered the binoculars and turned to face him. "Bad news I'm afraid—we're not clear. The mother ship must have repaired the damage. It's retrieved the remaining small craft. It's shadowing us about three klicks back."

Wolfe stared into the inky blackness behind, then back at Morgan, wondering if his companion had gone mad. "I see," he said finally. "With respect, how do you come by this information? It's pitch dark—I can barely see our own stern."

"Was I right about the roadblock this afternoon?" asked Morgan quietly.

"Yes," admitted Wolfe, a strange feeling pulling at his stomach. Helen's special agents could be expected to have a few enhancements, but this was beyond his understanding. Some new type of implant—infrared sensors perhaps?

"Then just believe me for now. We're being tailed." Morgan spoke with such absolute authority that Wolfe found he did believe her. "The question is what to do about it," she added softly. "Any ideas?"

Wolfe turned various possibilities over in his mind. If they were being shadowed by a motor launch it was death to venture out into open waters, equally fatal to turn back. If they could reach Granite Island, though, they would have a chance, maybe even a good one. He outlined his idea to Morgan.

"The island's almost impossible to land on. There are submerged rocks all around, and the shoreline is rock shelf covered with pine. For practical purposes you can only come ashore two places, the dock or the beach. But the approach to the dock is murderous—down a narrow channel with rocks on both sides. At least three boats tore their bottoms out there when I was a boy. The beach is easy enough to land on. Once you're on it, the only way off is via the path leading across the island to the cottage."

Morgan's teeth flashed white in the dim light. "So either they sink themselves trying to dock, or they come ashore on the beach and we pick them off as they come up the path. Excellent."

"We'll land at the dock, try to lure them in," said Wolfe with more confidence than he felt. Virtually every night one red-hot summer as a teenager, he had jockeyed his ancient outboard into the harbor to make midnight rendezvous with Mac's sister Jeniva. But that was many years ago. Now he tried to recall the approach in his mind's eye. You came directly in from the north then turned at right angles about twenty meters out and made a dogleg to the dock. Simple.

He stared into the blackness, thinking what a strange way it was to return to Granite Island. The island had been the summer property of Mac's father, a regional vice president with one of the big transnational brokerage firms. He had built himself a rural pleasure palace, and entertained profusely every summer. Then came the Big Bust; on the third day he had retired to the tower room overlooking the bay and shot himself.

Since then, the property had fallen into decay. After graduating from medical school Mac had bought Vitality Island and put the old family property up for sale at a reduced price. There had been no takers. The place had an eerie reputation; lights were reported in the windows of the tumble-down cottage at night—the stockbroker scanning the pages of the newspaper for signs of a returning bull market, it was said—and some even claimed to have seen Mr. MacGregor standing on the decaying dock, looking out over the lake at sundown, a martini in his spectral hand.

Now, looking at the dark loom of land before them, Wolfe wondered again what had driven the collection of cells that was Mr. MacGregor to conspire against themselves, to collaborate in putting the cold metal of a gun to the temple, to pull the trigger. "I think it was the whole concept of the Bust that got him," Mac had said one day, many years after. "He left a note; it just said that he was scared."

"Of what?"

"I don't know. The future maybe."

Wolfe shivered and willed his eyes to see through the darkness. He lined himself up with the granite knob at the top of the island and turned in, expecting any moment to hear the rasp of rock on the metal pontoons of the catamaran. A hundred meters . . . seventy . . . fifty . . . He spun the wheel sharply and the cat turned at right angles. With the engine at dead slow they crept up to an old but solid-looking jetty, making contact with a light bump. Morgan stepped daintily onto the gray planks, a mooring line in hand. When the catamaran was secured, she came back on board and took her Chang from Wolfe. "Thanks. Now let's take a look at where the path leaves the beach."

Motioning her to follow, Wolfe began to climb the narrow path that wound between tall fir trees. At the top it widened abruptly out into an overgrown clearing. In its center, a huge white frame house fell gracefully into decay. The wreck was oddly beautiful, though its white boards were graying and cracked and shutters dangled drunkenly from broken windows. A rusted garden swing still hung on the huge front porch and flowers grew wild around the rim of a grass-choked stone patio. A rusted wire rope tinkled against the leaning flagpole.

Passing the empty house he had known so well as a child, Wolfe felt no horror. If any psychic trace lingered it was more of sadness or resignation.

At the top of the path, two huge granite boulders stood like sentries overlooking the whole island. He could dimly see the catamaran bobbing at its anchorage behind them, and a short beach of white sand at the bottom of the overgrown path that wound down from where they stood.

A huge moon slipped out from behind a rack of clouds, bathing the night in a sudden silver glow and Morgan gently pulled him into the shadow of the massive rocks. "Okay, let's dust off our crystal balls," she said softly, as if afraid of being overheard. "I predict they'll let us sit for a while, see what we do. When the catamaran stays docked and there's no sign of activity, they'll probably guess we're asleep and try to come ashore."

Wolfe leaned back against the boulder, tried to wriggle into a more comfortable position. He looked at his watch: almost midnight. "So I guess we wait."

"That's right," agreed Morgan. "We wait." They sat down on a flat rock and scanned the moonlit night for their pursuers.

An hour crept by, two, and Wolfe's eyes began to grow heavy. The only sound was the wind in the trees, the distant lapping of the lake upon the shore and once, in the distance, the eerie insane laugh of a loon. Then Morgan tapped him on the shoulder and pointed at a darker blot slowly traversing the blackness a few hundred meters from the shore. Straining his ears Wolfe could just hear the deep grumble of a diesel on the threshold of audibility. The hunter—or was it the prey?—had arrived. Fatigue forgotten, he followed the boat until it disappeared into the night to their south.

"They'll come around once more, then try to land a team," predicted Morgan. "With any luck they'll go aground in the process. If they get anyone onto the beach we'll catch them right here and eliminate them once and for all."

The minutes dragged by with Wolfe's senses strained to their maximum pitch; then in the distance he heard the launch. A minute later it reappeared, cruising slowly up the east shore. Past the dock it went, following the curve of the shoreline, staying just outside the mine field of submerged rocks that ringed the island. A few hundred meters out from the beach it slowed and the engine noise died away. Morgan lowered her binoculars and nodded. "It's the beach. Makes sense, they probably think we're still in the catamaran, sound asleep." She looked about her thoughtfully and her manner became brisk. "You stay here, I'll dig in behind the boulder opposite. We'll take them out as they pass; you get the ones at the rear, I'll get the leaders. Open fire just as the lead man reaches that tree." She pointed to a small birch, its white bark gleaming in the moonlight. "A short burst for each and it's over. Don't spray the group, take each target individually."

"Understood." Wolfe nodded, wishing he had taken a refresher in weapons training more recently. "We still have a problem though, in the form of the mother ship."

"We'll deal with them later. Remember, open fire as soon as the leader reaches that birch tree." She laid a hand on his shoulder for a minute then flitted like a shadow across the path and behind the boulders opposite him.

His heart pounding, Wolfe searched for the ideal sniper's vantage, found a shallow depression behind a small pile of boulders and knelt on the moss. Resting the Chang's barrel on a rock he sighted on a point just in front of the birch tree. Full automatic. Safety off, finger tickling the cold metal of the trigger. It occurred to him he had never killed anyone before, although he had been an accessory to violent death many times. Did he have qualms? Wolfe recalled the manner in which Mary had died and decided he did not.

Satisfied with his hiding place, he scanned the dark bay. Even as he looked, two blacker spots appeared upon the black waters and began to slowly grow. Closer and closer crept the boats until they nosed up on the beach. Out of each scrambled three crew members, who drew their craft far up the sand with brisk, alarming professionalism. They were wearing plain black coveralls and carried weapons slung over their shoulders. As Wolfe watched they unslung their rifles and began to search the beach, fanning up and down the sand. A few moments later one gestured to his companions to join him. He had found the path.

Up the hill they came in single file, silent and terrifying as nightmares. Wolfe felt a tickling in his nose, an almost overpowering urge to sneeze, which struck him as ridiculous at the same time as he frantically struggled to repress it. The leading figure reached the crest of the hill, only two or three meters from where he lay, and held up one hand to signal a halt. In the moonlight Wolfe saw with disappointment that it was not Joshua, but a young woman in her early twenties, her blonde hair cropped in the manner of the Temple Guards. She spoke quietly into a throat mike. "We're at the top of the ridge. No sign of our targets so far. Team one will board the boat as planned. Team two will secure the cottage. Out." She listened for a moment as her message was acknowledged, then nodded and made a hand sign to proceed.

The Cleaners began to move forward again. Wolfe desperately wanted to wipe the sweat from his eyes, but dared not take his finger from the trigger. The leader was almost at the birch tree. What did they say in class? Lead the target to allow for motion. Aim a few centimeters below the shoulders. Squeeze the trigger, don't jerk. He took a calming breath, aimed carefully and squeezed.

The night was shattered by the characteristic sawtooth snore of his Chang, echoed a millisecond later from the far side of the path.

It was over absurdly fast. A good holo would have dragged the lethal moment out for at least two or three minutes, thought Wolfe as he slowly stood and brushed the pine needles from his trousers. There would have been slow-mo of the leader, turning in blank-eyed surprise, then lurching forward as if she had been pushed. Or lingering focus on each of the team members, twisting and shuddering and crumpling into a grotesque pile upon the moonlit ground. As it was, you shot them and they died, quickly, quietly and without fuss. And may the Lord have mercy.

Morgan emerged from the shadows and peered at the fallen figures, her expression unreadable. "Just, but regrettable," she pronounced after a moment. "We have about ten minutes until the people on the launch start to wonder why their com link is down. Get two of them into a boat and I'll rig up a little surprise." Wolfe watched her slip away like a cat up the shadowed path.

In a storage shed by the decaying cottage he found an old wheelbarrow and bumped it back up the path. Around the bodies the ground was already soaked in blood, black and flat in the moonlight. The young team leader lay on her side, her arm under her head as if sleeping. As he bent over her, the moon swam out from behind a cloud, lighting the awful scene with a silver glow. With a shock of surprise he noticed a strange and sinister thing, a turquoise level one Institute stud in the young woman's right ear. Gently detaching it he read the ID on the back with the aid of his penlight: M.G. McGee 2023. Wolfe's sense of remorse vanished like a bubble bursting. He picked the body up and dumped it unceremoniously into the wheelbarrow. *Sorry, sister, but you had it coming. If that's uncivilized, so be it.*

Morgan padded back up the path carrying a string of grenades looped together with wire like garlic buds. "Crude but effective," she said, displaying her creation to him. "I'm going to install this now. Quick, we can't have more than a couple of minutes before the rest of the pack gets suspicious." She disappeared down the path towards the beach. Wolfe lifted another body into the wheelbarrow and followed her.

Parking the barrow at the edge of the sand, he manhandled the two corpses into one of the boats while Morgan attached her device to the bow. He stood back on the beach, breathing hard, his hands slippery with blood, and his shoes squelchy and wet. Somewhere out in the blackness the launch must still be circling, waiting. A long minute passed, then Morgan straightened up and nodded. "That should do it. Let's get this thing moving."

They pushed the boat out into the shallow water until it floated free, then Wolfe draped the arm of the dead team leader over the tiller to hold it steady and started the motor. Slowly and silently the boat moved out onto the bay.

They ran back up the path to the dock, unmoored the catamaran, started the engine and waited. Across the bay, a sudden roar of engines. Wolfe squinted into the darkness, saw a smudge of white, the wake of the launch racing to meet the smaller boat. The engine noise abruptly died away and the white wake subsided. "They're alongside," whispered Morgan. "Any second now." Even as she spoke, a ball of flame sprouted low over the water, followed by another and another. A moment later the sound of the detonations reached them. Wolfe blinked and turned away to preserve his night vision. When he looked back he could clearly see the silhouette of a cabin cruiser, a huge fire blazing on its bow, low and motionless in the water. Morgan nodded, with professional satisfaction. "That should slow them down. Let's get out of here."

"Shall we make a dash for Vitality Island?" asked Wolfe as he began to thread the passage out from the dock.

Morgan shook her head. "No, their radar might still be working, though I doubt it. Or they might have backup waiting further down the bay. Better to take to the woods."

"As you say." Wolfe judged they were well clear of the rocks now. He spun the wheel and headed the catamaran north and west.

They sailed all night, taking turns on watch, one steering while the other slept below. Dawn was painting the eastern horizon pink as they dropped sail and anchored in a deserted inlet close under the shadow of the tall, brooding pine trees.

Cyborg

Things are—well, odd—in these overheated post-millennial years. It's as if the world went on a collective binge somewhere in the late 1990s, and woke up in the next era with something more than your ordinary hangover—something, in fact, remarkably like the DTs. Sightings of flying saucers are commonplace, and "reliable witnesses" routinely report seeing the Angel Gabriel flying across the heavens on Christmas or Easter or Mother's Day. Miracles are reported in every quarter, and it is considered mildly gauche to question them. A curious kookiness is in vogue in these overheated upside-down days.

Life in the PM—A Collage
Skellig Michael Press

Thursday, July 15
11:10 hours

When Wolfe awoke it was late morning. Morgan had already gone above; he could hear her light footsteps on the deck overhead. He felt unnaturally tired, drained no doubt by the breakneck pace of events in the last few days.

The cabin was drowsily warm, the old burgundy quilt soft and luxurious against his skin. He lay on his back, watching the shimmering reflections of the

concentration. "For instance, I'm now visualizing this boat from a satellite view in space and focusing down on us talking. The image is a bit hazy because of local interference, but not bad. You're slightly off course by the way; you need to come about eight degrees east." She opened her eyes and grinned proudly, as if she had performed a clever conjuring trick.

Wolfe looked at the compass and discovered she was correct. Mechanically he spun the wheel, wondering what to say.

"Startling, isn't it? I once opened a new textbook on quantum mechanics and found I could solve the equations in my head if I concentrated." For the first time a tone of uncertainty entered her voice: "And the dreams—I can't tell you about the dreams."

Wolfe's mouth was dry and he felt slightly dizzy, as if he had drunk too much. "Let me understand this: Helen sees what you see, and vice versa?"

"It goes beyond seeing." Morgan took a small Swiss Army knife from her pocket, opened it, pricked her index finger with the blade and squeezed out a ruby drop of blood. "If you prick her does she not bleed? Somewhere in orbit, there was an analog to that pain. I just pricked Helen's virtual finger. Or more accurately, Helen and I both cut our fingers at the same time." She sucked the blood off her finger, then folded the blade back into its red handle and tucked it away

Wolfe was unsure whether he was fascinated or repelled. Both, he decided. Another possibility occurred to him, one so outlandish he had to ask: "So if you were to make love, Helen would experience that as well?"

Morgan nodded. "More. She also feels my emotions, or so she assures me. How I don't know. I'm not sure I want to know. The goal is praiseworthy though: she wants to experience being human. She becomes human through me."

"And is that praiseworthy? Should a machine be human?"

Morgan frowned at him. "Helen wields great power, Edward. Better that she cultivates the human attributes of compassion and love."

Wolfe met her steady gaze. "And what if she learns other human attributes—cruelty and fear, for instance?"

"It's a risk the Institute is prepared to take." Morgan stood and stretched herself like a huge, sleek cat. "Don't worry though—Helen isn't cruel, I can vouch for it. Coldly practical sometimes, but not cruel."

"I see," said Wolfe, not entirely reassured. A new thought came to him. "If you're . . . in touch with Helen then you must know how the war is going. Yes?"

"I don't automatically know everything Helen knows, but in this case, yes, I'm being updated since it's relevant to me." Morgan crossed her arms and appeared to consider. "The situation is still fluid. The army has taken the Temple Complex but there's no sign of Mrs. Clements. Government armored units have arrived from the Quebec border and are now being deployed. The Accord has suffered heavy losses, but it's still fighting."

"And our people?" asked Wolfe, dreading the answer. "Did many get away?"

Morgan shook her head slowly. "I'm afraid not. Only three vehicles reached the community hubs, and several passengers were badly wounded. Only nine members of the original staff are still alive. Plus us of course. I'm sorry." Morgan turned away and began to descend the short ladder to the deck. "Needless to say, all this is highly confidential," she added over her shoulder. "Keep it strictly to yourself for the moment." She retrieved her fishing rod and glanced ironically up at him. "It's a bit of a shocker isn't it, my dear Edward? And now I am going to rig a proper line and catch us some dinner."

Wolfe watched her as she constructed a crude but effective deep-rigger from odds and ends around the boat and manufactured a trolling lure. She worked with fantastic dexterity, every so often pausing to shade her eyes and grin up at him. When the rig was finished she baited the hook with cocktail sausage and let the line down into the depths.

Afternoon slipped by, as featureless and relaxing as the rugged shoreline, low cliffs of red rock topped with the jagged steeples of a billion pine trees, marching like a brown-purple legion to the shallow, mosquito-swarmed lakes of the tundra country hundreds of kilometers to the north. It was baking hot.

Wolfe steered a westerly course, drank coffee and tried to arrange his chaotic thoughts. A cyborg! Jesus Antagonist, why did he have to pick a cyborg to fall in love with? From the start he had found her attractive. *Be honest, brother, more than attractive. It was love at first sight; you're prone to that vice.* At the same time, to be fair, he had been nagged by some subliminal doubt. It was as if she was too right. Too perfect. And of course she was, too perfect, more—and less—than human.

Indeed, from one point of view she was little better than a zombie, animated by the unfathomable electronic soul of an orbiting AI. Never to be free of an internal presence: how intrusive, how disturbing. Then again, what power, what intoxication it must be to look down on the turning globe with the piercing electronic vision of a god . . .

Wolfe sighed and scrabbled his toes against the polished wood of the deck. Perhaps these doubts were his subconscious way of not getting involved again, after

Omaha, after his parents? Perhaps he was unable to trust anyone or take them at face value any more. After all, Morgan was no different than someone with a pacemaker, say, or an artificial hip. She merely required mechanical assistance to optimize her existence. That at least was one way of considering the matter.

A large fly flew into his coffee cup and buzzed frantically across the surface of the hot liquid, trying to take off again. Fishing the fly out with a finger, he flicked it into the water. Immediately a fish rose to snap the struggling fly, leaving expanding rings of water on the lake's black surface.

The cyborg—*bipedal interface, lovely woman*—continued to fish placidly off the tiny rear deck. About six o'clock she emitted a whoop of excitement and began to reel in her line. Her rod jerked and bent as the fish fought back gamely. Wolfe shortened sail until the catamaran was almost dead in the water, switched to autonav and went below to assist. Fifteen minutes later, he leaned over the side and scooped a fair-sized lake trout, silver and gleaming into the green-meshed net. "Two kilos, at least. Big enough to eat, not big enough to be toxic. Caught with a cocktail sausage too—I stand in awe."

Morgan laughed in triumph. "I told you I'd catch dinner, didn't I?" Panting slightly from exertion, her hair falling across her face, she seemed infinitely desirable. "And I'll cook it too, my dear sir, to further demonstrate my essential humanity."

As twilight began to fall they finally dropped anchor in a small bay. The quiet chug of the motor died away and the only noise was a loon laughing somewhere in the distance.

Supper was rice from Wolfe's survival pack, canned asparagus and filet of fresh trout. They ate on the map table and watched the green-brown shoreline fade as darkness crept across the face of the evening. Wolfe went below to brew a pot of tea; returning topside he saw a star twinkle out, and another. As he poured the tea he was overwhelmingly conscious of the slim, white figure on the deck, a cyborg staring up at the stars. "They still haven't found Mrs. Clements," she said in a soft voice, as if speaking half to herself. "The Accord has dug in along Steeles Avenue and is making a last-ditch stand there, but they can't hold. South of the border, the Speaker of the House is huffing and puffing about intervention in the name of religious freedom, but there's nothing to it. Global Security is probably going to step in shortly, and that's another dirty little war to add to humanity's extensive collection. End of bulletin." She pointed up at the star-spattered sky. "Look, there's Orbital One."

Wolfe watched the tiny white dot race across the star-speckled night. "Is it? I don't know the schedules anymore. Maybe it's just a hunk of space junk. Or the Angel Gabriel?"

"No, it really is Orbital One." Morgan lowered her gaze to stare out across the darkening water and sighed. Wolfe considered her profile in the moonlight. She was indeed lovely, and she was still Morgan, for all her weird connections. In reality, he thought, it was exactly those connections which made her Morgan. He touched his ear stud for luck. All day he had been playing metaphysics with himself. Enough! "It's getting chilly out here," he said softly. "Let's go below."

She made no objection but quietly rose and preceded him down the short pine ladder into the cabin. Wolfe refastened the hatch above them. The cabin was pleasantly stuffy. In the light of the tiny lantern, long shadows danced and gamboled across the walls. He stroked a light hand across her breasts, then began to unbutton her flimsy cotton shirt. The white fabric fell aside, revealing a central column of skin. He raised his hands to her shoulders, twitched the shirt off, and the soft contours of her upper body were revealed. She put her arms on his shoulders and drew him slowly to her. They swayed together, half dancing, half embracing, then half sat, half fell onto the narrow bed.

Afterwards she lay quietly on his chest. Her hair had fallen across one side of her face and he could see tiny beads of sweat on her neck. He licked them off, tasting the salt. "Love you."

"Love you too." Morgan kissed his nose demurely, slid off him and closed her eyes. "Both of us."

Shaken more than he cared to admit to himself by the comment, Wolfe kissed her closed eyes and lay back, imagining an AI circling the fragile blue and white planet in a cybernetic glow of satisfaction. Was Helen smoking the AI equivalent of a cigarette as she fell endlessly through space? To hell with it, he thought drowsily. If Morgan wasn't a woman he'd take cyborgs every time. Surrendering to the soft swaying of the boat he drifted away to sleep.

On waking, Wolfe recalled a small historical fact. Three years ago this very day, four nuclear suns had boiled up around Teheran. The Samson option, variant five, which had pulled down the temple of his life just in passing. He acknowledged the fact with an internal moment of silence and a quick prayer to whatever deity cared about such things, then put the thought from him and turned to Morgan, as Omaha would surely have wished him to.

It was more than an hour later when they finally went on deck. The sun was sweltering, hot but invisible, behind a white haze of cloud. They dove into the dark, cool water then breakfasted on toast and canned brie. He felt more tired than the previous day; he was irritated with himself. The more rest he had, the more fatigued he became. Ridiculous! And despite the close escape, the sudden passionate affair (with a cyborg, admittedly, whatever that caveat might mean), despite the idyllic surroundings, he was far from lighthearted. The weight of the Institute's loss had begun to oppress him. In absolute terms it was worse than Islamabad, the worst personnel loss in the Institute's history. What would his colleagues, his friends think? "Who was in charge? Edward Wolfe, level three. You mean Long Eddie? I was sure he'd perform better than that. Not his fault entirely, of course. Still . . ."

Still the haze lingered. Morgan wet her finger to feel the wind. "Not a thing. We'd better stay close to shore until this breaks. There's no hurry—Global Security landed its first units in Toronto this morning. With luck we can turn around and head back tomorrow morning. Another bit of good news—two more survivors from Versailles showed up at Hub Three this morning. One was Harper Amadeus."

"Excellent." A sense of weary gratitude lit Wolfe up for a moment then faded. "I'm in no hurry to go back," he admitted as he pulled the dripping anchor aboard.

"Nor me. But duty will call eventually. That's the big drawback of being wired in—you're always available when it does call." Morgan sighed and dabbled an elegant foot in the water. She wore, Wolfe noticed for the first time, a thin gold ankle bracelet.

He fed the anchor chain neatly into its hole and told the autopilot to set sail. Even the small effort drained him; he sat for a few minutes on the bridge while the catamaran skated south a few hundred meters off the pine-covered shore, then clambered down to the afterdeck to join Morgan.

The morning slid by as imperceptibly as the klicks of purple-brown forest; as the sun climbed towards the zenith a huge ship appeared on the horizon—a freighter, black, with dark red rust marks around its bow anchors and a crane on its rear deck. It appeared on the edge of the haze, riding low in the water, a smudge of black smoke drifting in its wake. It was too far to read the ship's name. Wolfe shook his head lazily. "Odd: I would have sworn the last lake freighter was scrapped twenty years ago."

Morgan had been half-dozing beside him; now she came awake with a start. "What did you say?"

Wolfe pointed at the apparition. "That ship right there. A freighter I suppose."

"What on earth are you talking about? There's nothing out there. Are you alright?" Morgan's voice seemed to come from the end of a long tunnel.

No ship? Wolfe was confused. Surely he had seen something? The thought came to him like a fading echo: maybe it was a ship only he could see—the Ship of Death sailing by on its mysterious, endless voyage. Or maybe he was dreaming? Yes, no doubt. He was dimly conscious of Morgan helping him below. From infinitely far away came the low voice of his cyborg lover. "Just rest. I'm sorry, I should have noticed much sooner."

Noticed? Noticed what? Wolfe felt fine, more or less, although it was true his muscles were tight and he was too hot. And sleepy, terribly sleepy, heavy and besotted with fatigue, his arms and legs like sandbags. He tried to sit up; the cabin spun before him like a huge pinwheel, and he lost consciousness.

Driving in a filthy cab in pearl predawn light. He could not see the driver's face, but he knew that Death himself was at the wheel. Then sirens, eerie and far in the cool air. In a small room in the embassy Omaha awakened lazily to a far-off wail. He saw her wake, tousled, warm, suddenly frightened, saw in a dark mirror her fumbling fingers as she dressed . . .

And then the sky broke and fell in a tumble of pure white fire, showering down like violet death, bursting

through walls, floor, ceiling, Omaha melting like a bloody
blonde candle in the unbearable incandescence. In the
cab, the driver started to turn, Wolfe closed his eyes to
shut out the grinning, fleshless face . . .

Awakenings

The Die Back can be considered in different ways. Those of the Gaea persuasion take it as evidence that the planet, the ecosphere itself, is determined to wipe out what has become an intolerable pest. Those of a more calculating bent take the looming possibility of the Die Back as an urgent reminder that diversified portfolios are generally the safest. It is far harder to wipe out a species that has spread itself across the solar system than one confined to the surface of one planet. This obvious truth, they say, has been overlooked too long to the general peril of the race. The solution to the Die Back is to step out to the planets, and then further out again.

> *Breaking Point, A Collection of Essays*
> *on Post Millennial Topics*
> Henrikus Grobius, Jr.

Tuesday, July 20
15:25 hours

He woke screaming. Slowly the horror faded into mere unutterable sorrow. He lay helpless on an antiseptic-smelling pillow. He was alive. But weak, very weak. Arms heavy, slow. He could barely turn his head. And where was he?

Alone in a spacious yellow-walled room with a sharp medical smell. A clear tube snaked from an

IV stand to his arm—some sort of medical facility then. Beside his bed was a pine table. A desk and chair of the same wood stood under the open window across from him. On it was an ancient console. Daylight slanted in through the window, but he couldn't lift his head enough to look outside.

It was very quiet and he hurt terribly all over, his body a mosaic of pains and aches. Mugging? Accident? Illness? He searched for a reliable memory trail and found images: catamaran slipping through dark water, silver satellite falling through stars, Morgan telling a preposterous and frightening tale which he could not exactly recall . . .

A young black woman with droll, alert features bustled into the room and regarded him with a professional smile. "Finally awake, Mr. Wolfe? How are you feeling?"

"Terrible. Where am I?" His voice came out as a hoarse, unrecognizable croak, and he grimaced sadly.

"Vitality Island Clinic." She checked his pulse and looked at his eyes, then stood back, apparently satisfied. "You've had a lovely case of the latest Tokyo Flu. Long incubation period, lassitude and fatigue followed by abrupt onset of fever and delirium. 'Tokyo Nightmare' they're calling it now."

"I believe you." Wolfe struggled to arrange his shattered thoughts. "How did I get here?"

"Your friend brought you in three days ago."

"Which friend?"

The doctor made a face. "You really have been sick if you don't remember her. Long dark hair, face like a holo model. Do I score any hits?"

"Morgan." Wolfe tried to sit up, succeeded in raising himself several millimeters off the pillow before falling back. "Where is she? Where's my sister? What about the war?"

"Easy brother, easy. Everything's just fine, and so are

you—but you're gonna feel a little odd for the next day or two. This'll smooth you out." She held a sprayer to his forearm, pulled the trigger. He tried to draw away but could not. "Now just close your eyes and rest." She left the room on silent feet and he began to sweat again, as drowsiness spread through his limbs like death.

With immense effort he tottered to his feet, threw the sheets off and stood on the thick rose-colored rug that covered the floor. Step by heavy step he staggered towards the desk, reached it and collapsed into the wooden chair. With the last of his strength he keyed his access code, hands like huge blunt objects tied to the end of his wrists. He wondered distantly if the flu had done permanent neurological damage. There was a brief pause while connections tripped into place like tumblers in a lock, then Helen's face filled the small screen. "Good afternoon, Edward. This is a pleasant surprise. How are you feeling?"

Wolfe made a sound like an unoiled door hinge, felt tears of frustration spring to his eyes. He struggled to control his voice, knew he was not succeeding. "I'm a little out of touch. Is the war over? Where's Morgan?" A wave of vertigo washed over him, eddied back. He grasped the desk with the desperation of a drowning man.

"The war is over, my dear Edward. Beaufort remains as Premier. The ultimate fate of Mrs. Clements is still a mystery. And Morgan is back with us at Orbital and quite safe. She acted as a special courier for three objects which we wanted badly to inspect." Helen's icon manufactured a look of concern. "But you still look most unwell. I suggest you return to bed immediately. Everything will be explained in due course."

The table began to rock like a boat at sea. Wolfe felt nauseous, his voice came out a guttural croak. "Yes, perhaps I will. *Au revoir*." He clawed the connection closed with a clumsy hand and tottered back across the room, his ears buzzing as if a swarm of bees had nested deep in his brain. Falling into bed he closed his eyes and sank gratefully into the silky blackness that awaited him.

Mercifully, this time there were no dreams.

When he awoke, the room was light again and a warm summer breeze fluttered the yellow curtains at the window. His body told him considerable time had passed, perhaps a whole day. A young woman sat beside his bed, talking softly into a portable. For a moment he imagined it was Morgan, and a pang of elation shot through him. Then he realized it was his sister, and his euphoria transformed itself into a less intense but still pleasurable emotion. "Good morning," he rasped, and scowled at the sound of his own voice, rough as the grating of a rusty lock in a house where the owner has been too long absent. He cleared his throat irritably, once, twice, and sat up. The owner of the house was back now, and ready to take possession again. Kim smiled at him. She looked revoltingly healthy. "Welcome back from the land of dreams. How do you feel?"

Wolfe considered. His senses seemed remarkably acute; he could smell the lake's dank breath on the warm breeze and see the texture of Kim's fine brown hair. "Good," he pronounced cautiously, and was relieved to hear his voice already sounding more normal. "A bit weak maybe. And very hungry." The fact of his sister's presence finally registered in his dream-sodden brain. "But you look great. Jesus come quick, how are you?"

"Also hungry, but otherwise just fine. Here: hop into this. Mac says you can eat what you want, if you go slow. I have two diet eleven meal cards, we'll go gorge ourselves."

"What in the name of Jesus Financier is 'diet eleven'?"

"You'll see." She helped Wolfe into a wheelchair despite his half-hearted protests and wheeled him down the cheery rose-painted hallways of Mac's clinic to the dining room where a half-dozen ponderous patients were eating.

Parking him at a table by a large window with a view over the lake she went to fetch breakfast from the open kitchen at the far end. Wolfe looked around the sunny dining room and tried to gather his scattered thoughts. At the next table an enormous pink-cheeked man with three chins and incongruously delicate features half-buried in dunes of fat like the ruins of some once-noble city, toyed with an enormous plate of scrambled eggs and ham. Glancing surreptitiously around the room, Wolfe noticed that the other diners were also seated before vast arrays of food. He shook his head, wondering how such voracity squared with the clinic's goal of weight reduction.

Outside it was another perfect summer day. A group of patients were doing gentle calisthenics by the waterside, led by a sleek blonde instructress with a heroic chest. Several more large individuals sported happily in an Olympic-sized wave pool, like hairless walruses, while one submitted to the attentions of an ax-faced masseur at poolside. The war, the Die Back, all the mortal turmoil of the Post Millennium seemed very distant.

Diet eleven proved to be a massive infusion of poached eggs, ham, sausage and hash browns, plus a basket of croissants and a steaming silver pot of coffee. The smell and sight of the banquet sent saliva spurting into his mouth. Schooling himself to moderation, Wolfe ate with deliberate slowness while Kim brought him up to date.

"I came to three days after you brought me in. Very tired, very wasted just like you yesterday. Just about the time I was shaking off the fugue Morgan brought you in. By then I was feeling much better, so I went over to our island with her and helped her retrieve the biologicals. Which is to say, I sat on the shore and tried to remember where the entrance to the grotto was. She did the diving."

"And then?" asked Wolfe, wondering if he dared have another sausage. He decided he could.

"A float plane dropped by and picked her up. I gather she was headed for your Orbital HQ. Gone but not forgotten—she called yesterday to see how you were. Said to give you her love." Kim grinned at him. "I got the impression she half meant it too. More coffee?"

"Thank you." Wolfe held out his cup. The food tasted delicious, better than he could ever remember food tasting, and the thought of Morgan lit a warm glow in some psychic place he could not quite define.

Kim poured herself another cup as well and set down the pot with an emphatic thump. "You're feeling great—am I right?"

"Yes, now that you mention it," admitted Wolfe. "I feel—focused? Clearer in a subtle way. Even colors seem brighter."

"Exactly." Kim leaned across the table and lowered her voice. "Want to know my theory? BioAge has been working on a virus-based neuroaccelerator for a while. Lots of applications from treatment of dementia to sheer commercial sales to would-be geniuses. The problem is, it's rumored to be extremely toxic. I think I was hit with a prototype as a punitive measure by BioAge, and of course I passed it to you."

"Jesus come quick." Wolfe wiped his mouth with a stiff linen napkin as he considered the implications. "You mean we've been accelerated?"

"I shouldn't be surprised to find there was a measurable increase in IQ as well as perceptual indices.

It's just the kind of thing BioAge would do—punish an unruly researcher and make her smarter at the same time in case she returns to the fold."

Wolfe examined the concept from several angles and decided he did not particularly like it. Smart was good in the general nature of things, but he did not appreciate his sensorium being arbitrarily retooled, especially by a virus. "Are there likely to be any side effects?"

"Physically? No, I doubt it, for various reasons which I won't bore you with at the moment. As far as the side effects of being smarter?" Kim shrugged. "Being sadder perhaps? We'll compare notes in a year or so."

His immediate physical and psychic needs fulfilled, Wolfe was about to request an update on current events when a shadow fell over the table. It was the enormously fat man from the next table, carrying a large plate of cakes in both chubby hands. "Ahem," said the newcomer in a beautiful baritone voice. "I was wondering . . . that is, it smelled as if you were perhaps enjoying . . . luxuriating in a diet eleven meal. With respect—and even awe—is that the case?"

"It is," admitted Kim, kicking Wolfe gently under the table.

The fat man seemed to ponder for a moment, looking out the window then down at the plate of cakes, as if performing an elaborate mental calculation. "I wonder if we could arrange a trade, that is a barter, between us." He flourished his platter of confectioneries to draw their attention to it. "I have, as you see, an assortment of ethereal baking here: black forest cake, three-cream gateaux and even an attempt at lemon meringue pie. I would gladly put these items at your disposal, in return for, shall we say, four sausages and a croissant?" He looked at them with the pathetic melting eyes of a spaniel.

Kim adopted a crafty air. "All angel food, of course?"

"Of course." The fat man sighed. "Tasty, but insubstantial."

"Won't the trade interfere with your diet?" asked Kim.

The fat man reflected, then shook his head. "Not in any meaningful way. Between ourselves, I feel the doctors here are a little too strict."

"Very well." Kim nodded briskly. "It's a deal."

"I do thank you." Their trading partner put his plate down on the table, scooped up his sausages and croissant and waddled back to his seat, casting surreptitious glances around. Wolfe raised his eyebrows.

"Diet eleven," explained Kim. "It's real food."

"What's that then?" asked Wolfe, pointing towards the cakes.

"Angel food. From the BioAge Special Products Division. Very tasty, very expensive, absolutely no nutritive value whatsoever. You can eat it all day and not gain an ounce. The patients are mad for real food. Our friend there is typical—a holo executive with endless credit, an insatiable appetite and the propensity to cheat a bit."

Wolfe looked around the room once more, noted the patients gobbling down their non-food. The sight seemed more than a little perverse. He shook his head and turned back to Kim. "How about the war?" he asked after a moment. The whole conflict was very remote, events seen through the wrong end of a telescope.

Kim shrugged. "It's over. The Accord blitzed through the city, took most of the territory down to a line along the Danforth. Then government armor weighed, which of course Zacharian hadn't planned for, and started to push the Accord back. To enliven the proceedings, a few thousand of the more energetic Listers saw fit to go on a general rampage. Ravaged whatever they came across—Accord, civilians, even small concentrations of government forces. Heavy casualties all around. Global Security arranged a cease-fire the day you were brought in, Zacharian evaded an assassination attempt by some Temple Guards and fled to Brazil, and it's been more or less quiet since. What was it you said back in Fat Years? 'We're here to minimize disorder,' or something of the sort."

Wolfe stared moodily out the window, feeling again the oppressive weight of his failure. "That's below the belt right now."

"Sorry, I suppose it is. Just trying to be cheerful." Kim looked contrite.

"Understood." Wolfe blinked several times to clear his vision. The large breakfast had made him very sleepy and his toes tingled as if they were wired to a small battery. "Who were the parties to the cease-fire?"

"The combatants of course. Accord, Lists and government."

Wolfe considered. "Did they ever find Mrs. Clements?"

"What's left of her, you mean? No, Beaufort's in charge."

"I see." Wolfe stored this fact in a containment room somewhere in the back of his mind for later retrieval and inspection. It occurred to him that Kim had omitted one important fact. "So who won?"

His sister made a wry face. "I think that's what they're trying to figure out. And now let's get you back to your room before you start snoring and frighten Mac's clientele."

Later that afternoon, a discreet chiming wakened him from a deep sleep. Rubbing his eyes he crossed to the pine table and told the console to connect, hoping it was Morgan.

It was not. To his intense disappointment the screen cleared to reveal the harsh features of Elvira Peabody, who stared at him with the predatory indifference of a hawk regarding a mouse. "Good afternoon. How are you feeling?"

"Much better, thank you." Wolfe tried to compose his thoughts. Why would Peabody be calling? "To what do I owe the honor?" he asked guardedly. "Have you further information about the issue I raised with you at Orbital?"

"Yes. I mentioned it to the head of AI security, and he assured me all was in order." Peabody surveyed him for a further few moments then spoke in her dryest voice. "I'm calling in an official capacity as it happens. Are you well enough to discuss professional affairs?"

"I believe so," said Wolfe, feeling the hairs on the nape of his neck stir. Suddenly he had a bad feeling in the pit of his stomach.

Peabody nodded. "Good. Stop me if you feel physically ill. First, some background: As you already know, we have suffered unprecedented casualties in Upper Canada in the last several weeks. Of the entire permanent staff, only nine are now alive. Plus yourself, of course. Furthermore, our entire facility was destroyed."

This was news to Wolfe. "Versailles was destroyed?"

"Burned to the ground with all equipment and records. Not an inconsiderable loss, although nothing compared to the human toll." Peabody stroked her upper lip. "The point is this: As on-site director, you are at least nominally responsible for this mayhem. The Board of Governors therefore summons you to answer for your stewardship before a tribunal of your peers. I will be advising you in the case, although you must understand that this is not a legal proceeding."

Wolfe nodded slowly, feeling the magnitude of the disaster seep back up into consciousness again. It had to be faced, better sooner than later before it drove him mad. "Understood. When is my appearance?"

"You're tentatively scheduled to appear before the Board on August First. Please let me know by the end of the week if you require more time to recover or prepare."

"And what shall I prepare for?"

Peabody sniffed. "Prepare to persuade the Board that you are not responsible for our human and material losses, that they resulted from accident or act of God. I suggest you present your arguments to me well in advance of the hearing so I can help you focus them."

Wolfe considered. "To prepare a case I will require access to central files."

"Your access codes have been temporarily deactivated," said Peabody in a grating voice. "Relay your file requests to me and I'll see they are filled. Feel free to communicate with me at any time. However, please do not contact other personnel at Orbital or talk to Helen, as this may be seen as prejudicial to your case."

"I'm somewhat confused," said Wolfe earnestly. "Are you telling me that I'm suspended?"

Peabody twirled her mustache: "Let us say you are in the process of threading the needle. Or not, as the case may be. With full pay naturally. Is this clear?"

"More or less. A final matter," said Wolfe hastily, seeing Peabody's hand straying towards disconnect. "Before I retire to limbo I'd like to speak to Morgan Fahaey. Can you switch me?"

Peabody sat back again and looked thoughtfully at him. "Unfortunately not. Ms. Fahaey was taken to the infirmary here last night, apparently suffering from the same virus that laid you low. If there are any other untoward developments you will be contacted. Keep me informed of how you plan to defend yourself at the tribunal. We will expect you at Orbital in ten days' time." She disconnected and the screen reverted to a pattern of white clouds passing across blue sky.

Wolfe blew out a deep breath and returned to his bed on legs which once again felt unpleasantly shaky and weak, as if he had just passed through some appalling experience. It occurred to him that, in fact, he had. Poor Morgan, now wandering through the land of nightmare. He wondered if Helen was patched in for the ride—or if she could patch out, for that matter. It was an interesting thought.

The tortuous codes for Project Maldon arrived by maxSec link the following morning, two hundred and nineteen pages of finely printed equations supplemented by nearly one thousand pages of terse commentary and notes. Wolfe began to doggedly review them, with the uncertain aid of the clinic's micro AI, a Turing Class One machine of the type known to the research community as artificial imbeciles.

To his intense annoyance, his strength took several days to return. In the mornings he would wake refreshed, but by midafternoon, just when he was becoming tantalized by the pattern that was beginning to emerge from the arrays of elegant equations, exhaustion would force him to stop working. Despite his best resolve, he fell asleep immediately after dinner three nights running. Mac assured him he was doing well. "You had a designer bug, the oomph takes a while to come back."

By Sunday it had begun to. After eight hours of intensive work on the project codes, Wolfe stretched, flexed his body, felt none of the aches and tingles that had plagued him for two days after waking. His sight was keen, his hearing almost preternaturally clear, his appetite ravenous, which was not surprising because lunch time had come and gone again without his noticing. An idea had begun to take form, an idea so outrageous he dismissed it immediately, only to find it scratching its way into his consciousness again a few minutes later, like a persistent mouse trying to gain access to the larder. He dismissed it again, pulled his chair forward and went back to work, conscious of the looming deadline at Orbital.

At eleven o'clock on a bright Wednesday morning, eight days after he had awoken from nightmare, he spoke a final terse command to the little AI, which obliged with a single sheet of paper in the out slot. Wolfe studied the results for a few moments, crammed the paper in his shirt pocket and went in search of his sister.

He found her down by the lake, leading a workout for Mac's fitter patients. She had taken on a few responsibilities around the clinic in the last week, and seemed in no great hurry to leave. So far he had not broached the topic of her plans with her. When the class finished she strolled over to him, wiping her forehead with a white towel. "Phew, it feels good to do something physical for a change. What are you doing here? I thought you were off limits, preparing for your review."

"I'm prepared, mentally at any rate. I need to talk to you."

"Good, as it happens, because I need to talk to you as well. About the Institute."

"What about it?" inquired Wolfe as they scrunched down the gravel path to the lake.

Kim frowned. "The thing is, I had a phone call this morning. From a fairly senior person at your Orbital HQ. After a few polite preliminaries, she asked me if I'd like to join."

Wolfe stopped in his tracks. Here was a new development indeed. "They want you to join the Institute? In what capacity? A Weird?"

"A member of the Special Projects Division was the

job designation mentioned," said Kim frostily. "So what do you think?"

Wolfe took her arm and they began to walk again. "I think we should stroll down to the beach and you can tell me more."

"In essence the Institute will buy out my contract with BioAge and assure my security. Apparently BioAge is agreeable as long as I return all their files. I'll have a free hand in research and a lab in one of the Earth facilities with access to Orbital."

"And the assignment?"

Kim squinted in the blinding sunlight. "Long-term disease control and immunization programs in self-contained small environments."

"Orbital facilities, for example?" suggested Wolfe.

"Slow-haul starships was the example the recruiter used."

Wolfe raised his eyebrows. Clearly he had lost touch with the avant garde thinking at Orbital. "I see. And you said?"

"I said I'd like to think about it for a few days, but that I was favorably disposed towards the offer. What do you say though? Your level of enthusiasm seems lower than expected—afraid I'll disgrace you?"

They had arrived by the side of the lake and Wolfe pondered for a few moments, looking out over the dark waters. "I'd like you to put them off until after my review. In the meantime, I need you to do me several big favors." He began to explain his plan.

Return

The Skellig Michael has a genius for economizing. Like a thrifty housewife, Helen keeps close track of Institute requirements and she drives shrewd bargains. Two examples: the Institute's orbital station was designed and assembled on the cheap by some of the thousands of out-of-work aerospace engineers in the first decade of the century. The Institute has also acquired a small but highly efficient fleet of nuclear submarines, complete with launch devices, at near scrap-yard prices from the penurious navies of the world. The submarine fleet is ostensibly for research purposes. However, it is theoretically capable of launching biological and nuclear weapons. Does the Institute possess such devices? Helen and the Board of Governors are silent on this score.

Monks in the Sky
The Skellig Michael Institute—A brief History

Friday, July 30
13:00 hours

Two days later, Wolfe drove back to the city in the jeepster. Harvey's son had removed the battle armor; the vehicle now looked merely battered rather than grotesque. Approaching the city, reminders of the recent fighting were everywhere: shattered cars, burnt-out buildings, pockmarked walls.

First stop was the Temple Complex. His Eminence Nicholas Mancuso, new Deacon of Upper Canada had agreed immediately to his petition for an interview, and had even come on-screen himself to chat for a moment, his manner effusively cordial. Equally reassuring from Wolfe's point of view, several platoons of Global Security had dug in around the Complex as part of the negotiated cease-fire agreement between government, Lists and Temple.

Nonetheless, as he approached the campus, apprehension began to twist at his intestines. Once again he was going into the very heart of enemy territory, and this time without backup or special arsenal. He had managed to secure an old plastic pistol from a friend of Mac's, but that was all. Quite aside from the chance of a deliberate double-cross, there was strong potential for violence: a war-shocked subscriber seeking revenge, an encounter with a Cleaner who knew him or even with the odious Joshua. He turned his fear down as low as it would go and tried to disregard its whispers as he turned in at what had been the gatehouse. There was a piece of information here he had to have at all costs.

The glass gatehouse had been entirely destroyed; only a few twisted black metal girders now remained of the structure. Beside the ruins stood a sand-bagged checkpoint manned by a half-dozen Temple Guards. They wore camouflage rather than dress purple and their faces were dirty and haggard. A tired wariness had replaced the arrogance so characteristic of the Guards.

The squad leader keyed his credentials into a portable, nodded and turned to him with a deferential air. "This brother will escort you, sir. Just follow him."

Wolfe followed a Guard on a motorcycle, marveling at the destruction around him. The Temple compound had been mangled by the recent battle. The white facade of the medical complex was blackened and pocked by shells; most of the tall maples lining the Avenue of Life were splintered stumps and a hole gaped in the golden dome of the Temple.

As before, he parked in the lot of the Salvation Tower. His escort led him inside, showed him into a private elevator and waited until the door slid shut on him. The display showed only two options: ground floor and penthouse. Whatever rewards he expected in the next life, Wolfe reflected, Mancuso did not stint himself in this one

When the door opened, ten seconds and thirty storys later he found himself facing a very attractive female attendant with long tangles of brown hair, delicate Eurasian features and the high-collared yellow uniform of a second-degree acolyte. She led him through a living room the size of a small park, carpeted with thick gray pile and dotted with live trees, past a ten-meter long chrome and teak bar staffed by another acolyte and out onto a huge semicircular patio with a smoked glass sun roof. By the black wrought-iron railing sat Nicky Mancuso, surveying the Temple compound from a hydraulic massage chair upholstered in orange and red geometrics. The new Deacon of Upper Canada wore a baggy white shirt and trousers and a jaunty scarlet Guards cap, no doubt to conceal his recent head wound. His eyes were invisible behind a pair of silver sunbands. The acolyte called across the patio in a low, melodious voice: "Deacon? I bring you your guest."

Mancuso sprang to his feet, a wide grin on his amiable round face: "Hallelujah, Dr. Wolfe! We come together again in peace and in one piece—more or less." He had lost weight and his pale skin hinted of hospitals and illness. Nevertheless, there was spring in his step and his grip was strong as he shook hands. Wolfe marveled at the man's vitality. Not three weeks ago he had been wired in a life-support crèche; now he looked like an ad for BioAge supplements.

"A pleasure to see you again, Deacon."

Upper Canada's new Temple Elder held both hands out, palms up, in a gesture of good-natured humility. "No need to stand on ceremony with old friends. Anyone who has succored me in my hour of need knows me on a first-name basis—and knows my gratitude too, which is often more immediately useful. Now then, mineral water, or shall it be something stronger?"

"Mineral water, thank you." Wolfe took the proffered chair across from Mancuso. "You seem robust, if I may say so. Are you fully recovered?"

Mancuso grinned, showing large, even teeth. "Thanks to Adonai—and to the fine work of the Institute medical team. I do sometimes have the oddest dreams though." He chuckled richly, as if at some fine private joke, then turned and beckoned to the attractive acolyte: "Mineral water for my friend and the usual for me." He beamed in approval as she curtsied and turned away. "A devout girl, Rebecca, truly eager to tread the paths of righteousness." Lowering himself back into his massage chair he made a large gesture which included the Temple Park and the distant towers of the city, just visible in the haze. "It appears we have managed to preserve something despite the wickedness of our fellows, does it not?"

Wolfe looked out over the railing. All across the compound, work crews swarmed like ants repairing, replacing, replanting.

"In a month it will be immaculate," predicted Mancuso cheerfully. "Adonai rewards industry—a simple enough lesson, though ignored by many in these fallen days." He squinted at Wolfe from under the bill of his cap. "You said you wished to see me. Do you have any particular agenda, or shall we just ramble through the pastures of friendly conversation?"

"No formal agenda. I have to report back to Orbital shortly, and I wanted to include your impressions of recent events."

"Indeed? So Orbital wants my impressions? Have they asked for them?"

"Let us say I would find them useful in preparing my report."

Mancuso merely chuckled. "I am flattered." He watched with approval while Rebecca uncapped a purple bottle of Falklands mineral water, placed it and a chilled crystal goblet beside Wolfe and served him a glass of white wine. Raising his glass he pronounced a toast: "Blessings upon all good folk." He drank and smacked his lips appreciatively. "Say what you will, the greenhouse effect has been a boon to our local wineries. No change is altogether evil, don't you agree? Ebb and flow, fall and rise. So then, where shall we start?"

Wolfe poised the glass of mineral water on his knee. "I would be interested to learn the details of your return to Upper Canada."

"Very well." Mancuso tilted his face up towards the morning sun and clasped his massive hands together as if in prayer. "In fact there's not much to tell. I returned from Orbital via the Diocese of Midwest, where the Elders had already gathered to consider what to do with Zacharian. An edict was issued, expelling him and anyone who supported him from the true Accord. All but the most deluded saw the error of their ways and urged him to leave. By the time I arrived, he had already fled to Sao Paulo. We disciplined some of the more reckless Elders here, replaced them with level-headed brothers and sisters—bottom feeders, you understand—negotiated a cease-fire, and that was more or less that." He spread his hands as if apologizing for the banality of his tale.

"And now?" prompted Wolfe. "What is your view of the current situation?"

"My view is that the world is unfolding exactly according to the plan of Adonai King. How so?" Mancuso smiled benignly and sipped at his wine before continuing. "Upper Canada is delivered from the yoke of mad Zacharian. In the process many subscribers have gone to partake of His glory, but that is their good fortune and it is a sin to envy them."

"Was the war wrong then?" inquired Wolfe.

"Speaking as a bottom feeder, it was unnecessary. The Accord did benefit of course: under the terms of the cease-fire, our delegates will help negotiate the new constitution here. In effect, we have finally become a temporal as well as a spiritual power, as the great Pastor prophesied. But this would have happened anyway, sooner or later."

"The Accord is not the only beneficiary," Wolfe pointed out. "Under the conditions of the cease-fire the Lists are also allowed to send delegates to the constitutional talks."

"And so they should be." Mancuso poured himself more wine with a liberal hand. "Though I have not the gift of prophesy, I will venture to foretell the future for you. The more energetic and motivated will attend. They will negotiate vigorously, they will demand change, and their very energy will estrange them from their more lethargic brothers and sisters. I am personally trying to assist the Exodus Faction to attain their goals. Let them settle in the permafrost reclamation zone or head out to Mars. The Temple of the Accord looks kindly on them—after all, it is built of reclaimed sinners itself."

"What about Zacharian?" asked Wolfe after a short silence. "He's still alive. Might he not strike back?"

Mancuso sighed. "You touch a sore spot. Zacharian, Absolom and their small band of heretics remain a nuisance—although they cannot do much damage as fugitives in the outlands of Brazil. Who knows though?

Perhaps Adonai has preserved them for some greater purpose." He stared out over the compound, as if looking for a sign. "Speaking of heretics, you'll be interested to know that our erstwhile companion Joshua was called to account last Tuesday by the new Elders of the Temple here. I am sad to report he did not show the proper penitential spirit, nor an earnest desire to make amends."

Mancuso removed his sunbands and turned to Wolfe, his eyes suddenly hard and inhuman as two buttons of polished oak. One eye was darker than the other, in fact almost black. Mismatched eyes, just like Morgan's. Despite the warm sun Wolfe felt a sudden chill. He had the information he sought.

"He had much to make amends for," intoned Mancuso, his gaze fixed on Wolfe, his voice the tolling of a deep, sad bell. "My former personal acolyte for instance. And Mary. And others, many others. Had he seen the true error of his ways he might still have been saved. As it was, he proved unrepentant, and was condemned to reap what he had sown. Truly a sad fate—and an example to others." The Deacon of Upper Canada shook his head, as if at the general depravity of humankind.

"In short, he was executed?"

"That was the original intention. However, our medics found he was suffering from advanced prostatic carcinoma. Effectively he was already a dead man. Not wishing to challenge Adonai's judgment of the case, we merely provided him with first-line treatment, and sent him to join Zacharian, as he asked."

Wolfe raised an eyebrow. "And what does first-line treatment consist of? Chemotherapy?"

"Not exactly." Mancuso tutted sadly. "Hormone levels must be reduced, you see. The first line of treatment is orchiectomy—in layman's terms, castration."

To his shame, Wolfe felt a keen, pure delight at the

thought. Revenge was perhaps ignoble, but so too was gross overindulgence in sex. Both were nonetheless sweet.

"Even with treatment he can't last more than a few weeks, I am told." Mancuso nodded to himself. "He will trouble us no more; the Devil will have to recruit a new agent—as I'm sure he already has. There is no shortage of candidates, regrettably." He put his sunbands back on and smiled. "Have you learned what you wanted to know?"

Wolfe had arranged to meet Wu in Little Saigon for an early dinner. With two hours to spare, he drove to Versailles to view the damage for himself.

The building where he had lived and worked for two years was a heap of blackened rubble, a stinking mound of burned brick and charred wood. Beside it, the toiletries factory, oblivious to war and change, was operating at full throttle. Plumes of steam hissed periodically from the roof and fragile bubbles danced in the hot sunshine. The air tasted of toothpaste.

Parking the jeepster he walked slowly around the pile to the back of the building, where the dirty stream ran. In the ruins he caught a sudden flicker of motion. He looked again with disbelief, and the Rooftop Cat looked back at him with wise golden eyes. Wolfe crouched and the aged feline ambled up to him and rubbed against his hand, his rasping purr clearly audible in the quiet. For some inexplicable reason Wolfe found his eyes brimming with tears. For a moment he entertained the mad thought of taking old Rooftop with him, somehow smuggling him up the well, keeping him in his room at HQ until he was reassigned. Or whatever. Tomcats in space. "What about it, Rooftop?" he asked, scratching the old cat behind the ears. "Want to go chase space mice?"

The Rooftop Cat cocked his head as if considering

the offer, then rubbed against him one final time and disappeared back into the rubble. Wolfe looked after him with regret, then nodded reluctantly. For better or worse, the Rooftop Cat was a child of Gaea, rooted in the broken city and the life springing from it.

He dreaded the next stop more than any other, but it had to be made. He parked near the railway bridge and walked up the small incline to the scene of the ambush. The fire-blackened carcass of the Bulldog had been shunted off to one side of Gerrard Street and left for the cleanup crews or scavengers. Strewn along the block were the burnt-out remnants of other vehicles in the convoy. Through the smoke-filmed window of one hulk, Wolfe saw what appeared to be a pair of blackened hands still gripping a half-melted steering wheel. He hastily moved onwards, his eyes averted. At close range the Bulldog smelled of fire and chemicals and something sweet which his mind carefully refused to identify.

With great care he removed a pressed red rose from the book he had brought for the purpose and placed it on the blackened metal. For all he knew it was the first flower ever to be passed across the incomprehensible divide between human and silicon intelligence. Now it was a gift across the equally mysterious gulf between the quick and the dead. He stood for a few moments looking at the wreck, then walked back to the jeepster, feeling numb and alone.

He parked well inside the safe perimeter of Little Saigon and made his way along the crowded sidewalks to a nameless alley, identified only by a huge purple dragon painted on the cracked concrete at its mouth. The streets were alive with bustle; rows of lights over shops turned the warm night into day, illuminating cages of ducks, baskets full of white radishes and tiny purple eggplants, tables of toys, charms, cheap electronics of every description.

Wolfe stopped for a moment to enjoy the lively scene, letting his gaze roam over the stacked and bundled goods, the kaleidoscope of faces. In the middle distance a lone figure caught his eye, oddly still and isolated from the confusion. The woman—he was sure it was a woman—seemed to glance at him for a brief moment before turning away. He pushed through the crowd but by the time he reached the spot where he had glimpsed the apparition, it had vanished. He stared about him in confusion then slowly retraced his steps and turned down the dragon-marked alley.

At its end was a small purple door set into the wall. Wolfe opened it and walked into a low, dark room lit only by tiny orange star-spots on the ceiling and pink and purple squirts of neon Chinese characters glowing on the wall. Booths were built into the walls; in the back booth sat Wu. She stood up when she saw him and, in an unprecedented show of emotion, held out her arms. Grinning, Wolfe wrapped her in a bear hug, reflecting on the odd destiny which had led him to stand warmly embracing a Buddha-faced civil servant in a Chinatown fish bar. After a moment they stood back and grinned at each other, then Wu gestured to the table where two glasses dripped moisture onto the plastic covering. "I took the liberty of ordering you a Flash. I hope that was not impulsive of me."

"Not at all." Wolfe seated himself. "How was your holiday?"

"Peaceful. Safe. Well timed. By strange coincidence we arrived back two days after the cease-fire. At least my husband and I did." Wu met Wolfe's eyes. "Our sons are staying with my brother there until events sort themselves out here. It will be a useful cultural experience for them, don't you agree?"

"Wholeheartedly." Wolfe raised his glass. "Good health."

"Good health to you. You are recovered?"

"I thought so, but I just had a very strange hallucination." Wolfe put his glass carefully back on the table. "I was about to turn down the alley when I saw Mrs. Clements—or someone who looks a hell of a lot like her—standing at a corner, a block away, just looking around."

Wu coughed delicately. "I suggest you change the subject immediately, then let me do the talking. There is an eye up near the ceiling aimed in your direction. Sorry—I should have said something when you arrived."

Wolfe nodded and picked up his glass, glancing casually around the restaurant. Sure enough, high in the shadows on the far side of the restaurant, a small eye looked impassively down at diners below. He turned back to Wu. "A trick of the light no doubt. I gather they never found poor Mrs. Clements. Anyway, tell me your news."

Wu moved her head so that purple-pink ideograms reflected in her glasses, turning her eyes into neon squiggles. "First I will tell you about the Premier. There are many rumors circulating, some patently absurd, others—perhaps less so."

"Indeed?" said Wolfe with an expression of polite interest.

"I will tell you what I know. In the very strictest confidence though."

"Of course." Wolfe nodded earnestly, careful to maintain his bland expression. He hoped he was concealing his sudden dismay. What new deception or treachery was he about to discover?

The Deputy put her chopsticks back on the table and began to thumb through the menu, as if discussing the most inconsequential matters. "We have two witnesses to Mrs. Clements' disappearance: her body-guard and her driver. Initially they were reported killed in the kidnapping. The report was apparently false. In their version, no kidnapping occurred. Mrs. Clements asked to be taken to the Temple compound. She was very close-mouthed, but they gathered she had arranged a secret, high-level meeting with Zacharian Stele to try and defuse the situation."

Wolfe nodded. "I see."

"You begin to, I think. Stele confirms the story. In any event, driver and bodyguard were still waiting for the Premier to emerge from the meeting when the assault began. Mrs. Clements had given strict orders that they were to escape immediately if there was any sign of trouble. They succeeded, but in the confusion they were unable to reach anyone with their version of events until after the cease-fire. When they told their story they were told to stop spreading foolish rumors. They have not been heard from since."

"Fascinating," said Wolfe casually. "Tell me more."

"When the assault began, she was detained in the board room of the health center. There are con-flicting stories about what happened next, but the most credible is that Mrs. Clements was liberated by what appeared to be a government security team about nine o'clock next morning. The Accord has produced a half-dozen witnesses to say so. And that is the last anyone has seen of her—officially. Unof-ficially, there have been dozens of sightings like yours."

Wolfe grunted dubiously and weighed his words, con-scious of the eye in the shadows. "Interesting, certainly. What do you think?"

"Beyond any doubt there is something to the story. The witnesses have been examined carefully. They believe they are telling the truth, which is not a sure guarantee of reliability as you know, but suggestive."

Wu rested her chin on her hand for a moment, then looked across at him. "I have with me a confidential report on the kidnapping which I will pass you once we are outside. Please destroy it once you have read it and under no circumstances name me as your source. And now let us change the subject. Such talk is dangerous." Wu smiled gently and crooked a finger at a passing waiter. "We'd better order while supplies last. The tile fish is available today, the first time since the recent unpleasantness. I can strongly recommend it."

When the order was placed, they fell silent for a few moments, then Wu spoke: "And now you are leaving." It was not a question.

"Yes. I'm commanded up the well for performance review." Wolfe smiled bitterly. "My superiors want me to explain my role in the biggest single disaster in Institute history."

"Surely no one can blame you for the unfortunate turn of events?" asked Wu.

"I fear they may very well blame me. I should have insisted on getting staff out earlier. I should have let everyone scatter rather than convoy out. And I should have ordered an evac immediately when I heard about Mrs. Clements."

"What will they do?" asked Wu.

"What indeed?" echoed Wolfe bitterly. "Make me an associate if I'm lucky."

"My dear Edward, you're being whimsical." Wu put her hand on his for a moment. "Consider the positive aspects of the situation: Upper Canada has survived. We have done the moderate wing of the Accord a huge favor, however inadvertently, and are receiving remarkable cooperation in return. Zacharian is disgraced and banished. We held up surprisingly well, thanks in part to the community hubs. In some ways, the Institute has won at least a small victory on the periphery. Though at a terrible price."

"I suppose. And yet . . ." Wolfe hesitated, toying with his drink.

"And yet?" prompted Wu gently.

"And yet, despite isolated victories, I no longer believe the Institute—or anything else—can hold back the tide. I fear—what do I fear?" Wolfe looked around the dim room, "I fear some terrible thing: a blood-bath like no one has ever seen, a global war, mountains of skulls, a long dark age before the light returns. Worst of all, I'm not sure whether I am working to shut the horror out or to invite it in."

Wu listened soberly. "The Die Back?"

"Call it what you will."

"And will we survive?"

"I don't know."

"Gloomy predictions, my friend." The waiter placed a bowl of steaming noodles on the table and Wu raised her chopsticks with a flourish. "These are called happy noodles. Let us eat. After all, we can only do our best. And we can only participate once in the Die Back, no matter what forms it takes."

Tribunal

How does the Institute afford the massive payments on its orbital station? Where does it find the cash for its multifarious operations? In addition to the bequest of its founder, it funds itself through a diversity of projects many of which bring in large sums. It is even rumored that Helen has turned her chilly intellect to the writing of popular novels, songs and holo plays, and that her literary efforts generate handsome royalties for the Institute.

> *Breaking Point, A Collection of Essays on Post*
> *Millennial Topics*
> Henrikus Grobius, Jr.

Saturday, July 31
23:15 hours

Wolfe journeyed up the well for the second time that month, arriving without incident at Orbital just before midnight local time. For the first time he felt no exhilaration as he passed through the station's airlock, no sense of homecoming. Instead he was forced to entertain the dismal notion that he was again on enemy turf. Morgan was not there to meet him. He was disappointed but hardly surprised. Instead he was greeted with impersonal courtesy by a young male level one with Slavic features, muscular neck and chest and the dreamy black eyes of a poet. "Good evening, sir. My name is Alexei Sergov; I've been asked by Governor Peabody to escort you to her quarters. Would you like to stop by your room first to refresh yourself?"

"I'm quite refreshed as it is, thank you. Let's go directly to see the governor." Wolfe smiled at his escort, concealing the dismay he felt at finding himself met by a well-muscled level one whose manner screamed of security training. Was he in effect a prisoner following his guard, or was Peabody attempting to ensure his personal safety? Either interpretation was disturbing. As he had done since leaving Vitality Island, he forced himself to be keenly aware of his surroundings. It was easy enough to kill even an alert adversary, ridiculously easy to eradicate a careless one.

A quarter hour of brisk walking through the red, green and blue striped corridors brought them to a black plasteel door with Peabody's name on a brass plate the size of a playing card beside it. Sergov knocked and stepped aside as the door slid open. "I'll wait here, sir, to escort you to your quarters after your interview."

"Don't trouble yourself," said Wolfe with an easy manner he was far from feeling. "I may be quite a while. Give me my privacy card and I'll find my own way." He held his hand out as he spoke.

Sergov shook his head and grinned. His muscular hands stayed motionless at his sides. "No trouble at all, sir. It's my job assignment this month."

"As you wish." Wolfe stepped cautiously past him and found himself face-to-face with Elvira Peabody, her mustache sprouting a luxuriant white, as durable and unyielding as ever. Tonight she was wearing a two-piece suit of pink silk decorated with gold dragons and her gray hair frizzled forth from under a square smoking hat of the same pattern. To

Wolfe she looked like the madam of the tawdriest house of ill repute in all Asia. Her manner remained reassuringly familiar. She motioned him inside with an impatient flap of the hand and snapped an irritable command: "Door, some privacy for goodness sake." The black door slid obediently shut and Peabody turned to face him, a glint in her pebble-hard eyes. "So Edward, we meet again in chastening circumstances. Make yourself comfortable, we have a long night ahead of us, thanks to your offhand approach to this case."

"I assure you, my approach is anything but offhand. I've deliberately avoided contacting you for good reason." Wolfe seated himself in one of the black canvas chairs and looked about him with interest. Peabody's quarters were small but luxurious, filled with green hanging plants and statuary arranged on low glass shelves. One small figure caught his eye: a bronze Greek warrior a half-meter high, leaning wearily on his spear. Ulysses by Pasco Indini—a copy unless Peabody was far richer than he had imagined. In one corner stood a group of four chairs surrounding an intricately-carved wooden table on which stood a late-model console showing shifting views of Earth from the station's cameras. A door led through the back wall, presumably into the bedroom and sanitary facilities.

"Well then, we have slightly less than twelve hours until the Board convenes," barked Peabody, seating herself across from him. "Twelve hours, and you still haven't told me what defense you propose to mount. If any. You don't call that offhand?"

Wolfe tried to look contrite. "I believe I have an excellent defense. For reasons which will become clear I was not eager to discuss it long-distance."

Peabody opened her portable and took out her stylus. "You'd better begin at the beginning."

"No, I'd rather begin with my conclusion and work backwards."

Peabody put down her stylus, favored him with a ferocious glare and sat back. "Very well. What is your conclusion?"

"That with a high degree of probability Helen has gone aberrant."

Peabody rolled her eyes. "Don't be melodramatic. I told you, I have already consulted Governor Falmouth and he has assured me Helen is fine."

"Talked to him? Face to face? I'd guess you sent him a message or talked on the phone—am I right?"

"A message actually," admitted Peabody. "He was in Singapore at the time."

"And he responded in the same way?"

"Yes," admitted Peabody.

"Then you have resolved nothing." Wolfe stretched his legs, which were stiff and cramped after the long flight, out in front of him. "You may have been corresponding with Governor Falmouth, or your message may have been intercepted and answered by Helen. I think we should find out immediately."

Peabody made an irritable gesture. "And supposing I were to tell you this whole preoccupation is ridiculous and I have no intention of disturbing Governor Falmouth?"

Wolfe shrugged. "Then I would tell you that unless these allegations are properly investigated I will refer the matter to the AI Security Committee of the United Nations. You should also know that I have arranged for my sister to route certain documents to that committee as well as to the Accord and the Islamic Federation should anything happen to me while at Orbital."

They locked eyes for a long moment, then Peabody sighed and rose to her feet. "I knew this would be a vexing session. As it happens, Joseph—Governor Falmouth—is the other governor hearing your case. His quarters are just down the hall, and he's probably reviewing his notes on Maldon right now. I'll pad down there and ask him—face to face. Meanwhile, make yourself comfortable." She gestured to a low mahogany cabinet in the corner of the room. "There's drinks and whatnot over there. You there, door! Open sesame." The black plasteel door obediently opened, then slid shut again, leaving Wolfe alone with his anxiety. He eyed the console, wondering if he should give Morgan a quick call, then reluctantly decided against it.

When Peabody returned several minutes later, her manner was subdued. "You were right. Falmouth never received my message."

"And did you explore the ramifications of that with him?" asked Wolfe.

"No, I did not." She sat down abruptly, her dark eyes boring into him, and hitched at a crease in her lurid silk dress. "Do you really think Helen has gone rogue?"

"I think something very strange is going on. An aberrant AI is one explanation. There may be others." Wolfe examined Peabody cautiously, trying to gauge her mood. She and the Dean were the only two at Orbital he trusted absolutely; it was vitally important that she believe him. "We should be in a position to get at the truth during my hearing tomorrow."

Peabody picked at a thread on one of her embroidered dragons. "There is another aspect to this which you may have overlooked. If Helen is truly aberrant we will have to get her offline quickly and without warning, before she can take steps to protect herself—if that is the correct phrase." Her features frowned themselves into a knotty devil's mask for a second, then she looked up at Wolfe with a reluctant grin. "Very well, let us review your case point by point. If there is even a chance Helen is malfunctioning I'll notify Governor Falmouth that it may prove necessary to offline her at tomorrow's hearing." Peabody stood and walked to the carved cabinet in the corner. "I believe a tot of Flash might be in order at this point. Will you join me?"

Wolfe arrived outside Helen's garden a few minutes before eleven o'clock the following morning. The corridor was deserted; presumably the governors were already inside. Although he had only had about five hours sleep he felt unnaturally refreshed and alert, as if he was pumped on stims or waiting to take part in a tournament. His heart was beating at a faster-than-normal rhythm and his mouth tasted of adrenaline.

Two emotions warred within him: a keen desire to finish the investigation and a growing concern for Helen. Rogue AI she might be, but she was still his friend. It could be argued that he showed his friendship by pointing out her aberration—the necessary first step towards a cure—but what he was doing felt more like betrayal. And Morgan, mind-linked to Helen—what would become of her if the AI was offlined? She had said nothing about needing a permanent link to Helen; surely there must have been times when she had been cut off, by weather, by local interference or whatever? Surely? He eased his mind past the topic like a man guiding a skittish horse through a maze of razor wire. What must be, must be—there was no way back.

His name was the only one on the board outside Helen's garden. Now it began to flash. Straightening his shoulders and taking a deep breath he pushed through the door, and, despite the urgency of the situation, grinned in admiration at the environment. Today Helen's garden simulated a cliff top somewhere in the Aegean. To his left in the distance rose the white columns of a ruined classical temple with a half-dozen white virtual sheep grazing beside it. To his right and straight ahead of him, flat grassy ground appeared to give way abruptly, falling off in a long, sheer drop down black cliffs to the azure sea below. As before, the illusion was perfect, even to the distant roar of the surf and the light, warm wind caressing his skin.

Directly before him was the empty holo stage, the manipulators dangling from their translucent plasteel pole like some surreal, ultramodern scarecrow. Beside the green disc of the holo stage and at a comfortable distance from the illusory cliff top stood a long white wicker table. Seated at it were Governor Falmouth, massive and formidable as a tank, and the silver-haired aristocratic Dean, who was patting Helen's black Scottie. Facing the table were two matching wicker chairs. One was occupied by Peabody; the other, presumably his, was empty.

Wolfe bowed to the Dean and Falmouth, reflecting that he was about to match wits with several of the brightest and best-educated people ever thrown up by the random churnings of the gene ocean, as well as the world's most powerful AI. The thought did nothing to calm his jangled nerves.

The two Institute executives returned the greeting. He had met them both at one time or another: middle-aged Falmouth, burly and bearded as an old-time pirate, his aura of animal vitality contrasting with the Dean's fragility. Age was eating away at the Dean's physical fabric despite the elixirs of BioAge and a low-gravity environment. His hair was white, his face crisscrossed with a thousand fine lines, his long frail arms and legs as thin as a spider's, but his blue eyes were alert, his manner brisk, and when he spoke his voice still had the warm Scandinavian lilt Wolfe remembered so well from his first interview. "Welcome home, my friend. You have been through great travails, expected and otherwise. Please sit down. Let me first ask you, are you well enough to appear before us today?"

"I'm quite well, thank you, sir," said Wolfe, taking a seat by Peabody, who nodded crisply to him, two quick bobs of the head. Wolfe relaxed somewhat. Two nods was the signal that Peabody had alerted Falmouth to the possibility of malfunction.

The Dean sat back. "Then as soon as Helen joins us we will proceed." Moments later a greenish glimmer showed on the holo stage, and Helen coalesced, bestowing a dazzling smile on the assemblage as she stabilized, and bent over to pat Toto, who scurried up to her icon. The AI seemed positively rakish today, projecting a stylish, wide-shouldered suit of pale green linen, her grave yet youthful face framed by stylishly bobbed dark hair.

Wolfe inspected the icon closely and was amazed at himself for not perceiving what he now so plainly saw: Helen had morphed herself into something bearing a strong family resemblance to Morgan. He looked again. Another correspondence was implicit, tantalizingly familiar but just beyond his conscious grasp. He turned away, trying to ignore the churning mass of butterflies in his stomach.

The Dean held up a frail blue-veined hand to signal the meeting was commencing. "As you are aware, the SoCy intervention known as Project Maldon went tragically awry in the last several weeks. We lost one hundred and nineteen men and women and nearly two hundred million deutsche marks in equipment and data. This constitutes the Institute's worst setback ever, worse even than the Islamabad debacle." He bowed his silver head for a moment as if to conceal the expression of sudden grief that shadowed his weathered face, then addressed Wolfe: "We have convened today to determine what responsibility, if any, accrues to you as on-site director. Please understand this is not a formal trial. We are searching for the truth, but we may approach it from unconventional angles or sneak up on it so to speak. As far as structure, I will act as moderator, Governor Peabody as your advisor and Governor Falmouth has kindly agreed to serve as devil's advocate. Helen, of course, is here as observer." He swept his gaze around the virtual cliff top. "Let us proceed."

Governor Falmouth leaned forward. "Very well. Dr. Wolfe, presumably you agree that Project Maldon went wrong?"

Wolfe blinked to try and dislodge the image that had suddenly and forcibly come to mind—a Bulldog armored vehicle spouting orange fire from its hatches. *Time to make amends, Long Eddie.* "It would be hard to disagree. The people lost were more than just statistics, they were friends, good friends. The outcome of Maldon was a disaster, professionally and personally." He blinked hard to clear his vision.

Falmouth nodded, a bleak expression on his buccaneer features. "Just so. And did you anticipate a disaster?"

"Yes, though not of this magnitude."

"Please explain," requested Falmouth.

"I was concerned that directives issued by Helen would tend to destabilize the situation—as indeed they did. For this reason I twice recommended a partial evacuation. The recommendations were refused."

"Why was that?" asked the Dean, turning to Helen.

The icon shook its head in apparent bewilderment. "I have no recollection of any such requests."

"There appears to be some confusion here," said Governor Falmouth, returning his attention to Wolfe. "Perhaps the problem was in communication. One person's recommendation is another's casual comment. You have a subtle manner, Dr. Wolfe, if I may say so. Did you make your feelings quite clear to Helen?"

"Quite clear," declared Wolfe, conscious of Helen's reproachful eyes on him. The sharp sense of loss he had felt when standing before the burnt-out Bulldog tugged at him again. He was betraying an old friend. And yet, what was his alternative? A smell of sea air wafted to him and somewhere a seagull cried plaintively, detailed enhancements to the environment so characteristic of the AI.

"If you felt that your staff was in danger, why did you not make stronger representations to Helen?" persisted Falmouth. "Or better yet, contact your supervisor to review the situation?"

Wolfe glanced at Peabody, who continued to toy with her silver stylus. "I mentioned my concerns to Governor Peabody almost three weeks ago and she agreed to look into them. I heard nothing further."

Falmouth blinked in well-simulated surprise. "Governor Peabody? Can you corroborate this?"

Peabody looked up with a feral expression, reminding Wolfe of a cat disturbed while watching a particularly promising mousehole. "On his last visit to Orbital, Dr. Wolfe expressed concern that Helen was deliberately racheting up the level of violence for reasons that he could not understand. He speculated that she was malfunctioning or had developed, as he put it, free will."

"I see." Falmouth pulled his heavy red lip thoughtfully. "And what did you do?"

Peabody sniffed indignantly. "You must know. I linked a query to you in your capacity as Chair of the AI Security Board. In due course I received your reply assuring me all was well."

Falmouth shook his heavy head. "This becomes stranger by the moment. I never received such a message, much less sent a reply."

Helen raised a slim hand. "If I may interject, there have been a number of glitches in Earth-Orbital messaging recently due to sunspot activity. I have had several reports of cross-transmissions and suchlike. This is not an isolated case."

"Did I say this was an Earth-Orbital message?" barked Peabody.

Helen seemed unruffled. "It must have been, my dear Elvira. Your correspondent was on Earth during the time frame you mentioned, and you were here."

The Dean intervened, a troubled expression on his face. "We seem to be straying far afield. Let us leave this item aside for a moment and continue the examination."

Falmouth glanced at the postcard-sized screen of his portable for a moment then back at Wolfe. "To recommend partial evacuation you must have felt that Maldon was going poorly. Why was the intervention so ineffective?"

"I asked myself exactly that on many occasions," agreed Wolfe. "My intuition was that there were flaws in the program code, but Helen assured me otherwise, and I did not have facilities to run an independent check."

"So you weren't able to verify the code?" Falmouth tapped out an impatient rhythm on the table with his stylus.

"Not until after the massacre. However, about ten days ago I requested the complete code for Project Maldon so I could review it for this hearing. What I received was incomplete." A flicker of movement caught his eye. In the distance, the virtual sheep had stopped grazing and were looking over at him.

"You mean it contained an error?" asked Falmouth.

"No. It was not wrong, merely incomplete." Wolfe ticked off his points on his fingers. "For example, there was no allowance for the so-called Hitler Factor as represented by Zacharian Stele, no recognition of Mrs.

Clements' known biases, no factoring in of the schism within the Lists. These are serious omissions, and they are not the only ones. Either what I reviewed was hopelessly botched or it was not the real code. The first alternative seems unlikely."

"What are you suggesting?" asked Falmouth, resting his chin on a hand like a hairy soccer ball.

"I am suggesting that what I saw was not the actual code for Project Maldon," said Wolfe, aware that he had reached the point of no return. "I am further suggesting the true code was designed to bring about exactly the result that has been achieved." He turned politely to Helen. "Perhaps you would care to comment?"

Helen's holo had been scratching Toto behind the ears. Now it straightened up, its perfect features molded into an expression of kindly concern, shook its head sadly. "We all know that Dr. Wolfe has been under a great deal of strain recently. In particular he has just suffered an illness which might well have neurological sequelae. His statements are largely delusionary; plainly he is not well. I suggest we postpone this hearing until he has had a complete physical and mental checkup."

"I assure you I am perfectly well," said Wolfe, concealing his consternation. Surely this attempt to discredit him was a further sign of aberration?

"The witness seems lucid enough," grunted Falmouth. "I would like to continue."

"You have heard Dr. Wolfe." The Dean sat back and looked at Helen. "I think we must allow him his day in court?"

"As you wish," agreed Helen. "I am only concerned for Edward's welfare." She looked down at her emerald ring. Wolfe was startled to see that her alignment with the manipulators was not perfect: the upper part of a plastic claw emerged several centimeters from her perfect wrist like some alien growth.

Falmouth turned back to Wolfe. "Are there other anomalies you wish to bring to our attention?"

Wolfe cleared his throat, which felt unaccountably dry and raspy. "Yes. I would like to draw your attention to the circumstances surrounding the alleged kidnapping of Mrs. Clements."

"Proceed," instructed Governor Falmouth, now grimly attentive.

"These reports triggered the assault on the Temple, and thus the war. They came from three separate sources: a call for help from the Premier's driver, a police report on the incident and a taped call from some Listers who supposedly witnessed the kidnapping." Wolfe spoke slowly, looking from face to face to make sure his audience was following the complex tale. "But the Premier's driver insists he never called for help. Furthermore, the officer who supposedly filed the police report had been admitted to hospital that evening with a mild case of Tokyo G, and the booth from which the Listers called was out-of-order at the time in question. In other words, the crisis was triggered by three source-less lies floating across the Net at just the right time."

The Dean frowned in puzzlement. "How could anyone know that the Premier would try to meet with Deacon Stele?"

"The Premier's homing device was a digital repeater," explained Wolfe, his eyes on Helen. "Her location could have been monitored continuously by anyone who knew the correct wavelength and had access to sufficient nodes. It was Helen who suggested the homing device. And she knew the wavelength. In fact, as far as can be ascertained, she is the only entity that could have provoked the crisis."

Falmouth raised heavy black eyebrows as the impli-

Falmouth raised heavy black eyebrows as the implications of Wolfe's comments fuzzed into focus. "Odd," he said mildly, turning to Helen. "Your comment?"

The icon shrugged its shapely shoulders. "I was aware of the Premier's homing device and its wavelength, this is true."

The Dean thought for a few moments then turned to Wolfe. "You have presented us with several curious facts. Taken together, what do they suggest to you?"

Wolfe sighed. "They suggest Helen has been manipulating the outcome of Project Maldon for purposes unknown."

Helen shook her head sorrowfully. "As I said before, Dr. Wolfe is clearly not well. I must insist we adjourn immediately and escort him to the infirmary."

Wolfe addressed the Dean urgently. "Sir, I suggest that Helen needs attention, not me. The evidence I have presented strongly suggests the possibility of an AI malfunction."

There was long silence during which the sound of the surf below became louder. Wolfe glanced around and saw that the virtual waves were indeed rising higher, to dash against the illusory cliff. In the far distance he glimpsed what looked like a trireme with ragged sails running before the wind. Helen made an indignant face. "I am amazed you can suggest such a thing."

"Then how do you explain the facts I have put before you?" asked Wolfe softly.

Helen did not answer. She seemed rapt in thought. As he watched, Wolfe saw something he had never witnessed before. Helen's icon was losing definition. The left side of her face was wavering in and out of focus and cycling through different shades of pink as a significant fraction of her processing power was directed to some unknown task.

The others noticed it too. "Helen?" called the Dean softly. "Are you with us?"

The icon turned to them, half its face now a pulsing pink mass, the other trim and correct as ever. "This is the way the world ends," she intoned. "Not with a bang but a glitch. Do you agree?"

The Dean turned his troubled gaze on Governor Falmouth. "We appear to have a crisis on our hands. You are the expert here: how shall we proceed?"

Falmouth shook his head. "I agree with Dr. Wolfe— we are dealing with an AI malfunction." He turned to Helen. "I think, old friend, you should prepare to go offline for a few minutes while maintenance does a few routine checks."

"Certainly not. I protest with all the vigor at my command," said Helen in an outraged tone, her icon striding to the edge of the holo stage nearest the executives' table, the manipulators trailing just outside her holo. "Going offline will crash at least a dozen major projects, not to mention doing irreparable damage to my psyche. I positively refuse." Her voice, Wolfe noticed with odd detachment, was high and quavering.

Falmouth addressed the Dean directly. "This reaction by itself is very significant. A healthy AI is prepared to consider any and all suggestions in a logical manner. I suggest we go to manual override, and immediately." He took a silver cylinder the size of a thumb from his breast pocket and flicked back a plastic cover on the top. The Dean turned to Peabody. "To offline Helen requires the assent of the Dean and at least two governors. I concur with him. What is your vote?"

Peabody stroked her lip for a moment. "I must reluctantly agree." She reached under her collar and pulled up a chain, on which hung a metal cylinder like the one Falmouth was holding. Flipping open the plastic top she placed her thumb on a small red button below.

"You forget one thing," said Helen softly.

"What is that?" asked the Dean.

"I have three-dimensional extensions," cackled the icon, and two extensible claws reach out of her body and seized the arms of the Dean and Governor Falcon in a vice-like grip.

Falmouth dropped his cut-off device and with a convulsive movement knocked it onto the grrass in front of the table. Wolfe bent down and scooped up the small cylinder. It was very heavy.

"I think that settles the matter," said Peabody dryly. "Signals must be entered within thirty seconds of each other in order to activate the offline sequence. Are you ready?"

"Wait!" Helen stretched her arms out to Wolfe in a desperate appeal. With her two human arms and two plastic extensions she reminded Wolfe of some post-millennial Hindu goddess of destruction conjuring chaos from apparent order. "Think of Morgan. Taking me offline will kill her, sure as if you fired a bullet into her brain. Do you want to lose this?"

She began to morph, shifting form so rapidly that Wolfe's eye was bewildered. Suddenly, Morgan stood before him on the holo stage as he had seen her on the deck of the catamara, pure as Eve.

From beside him came Peabody's voice: "On my count: one, two . . ."

Wolfe's finger hovered on the red button. He stared in fascination as the shape before him shifted to become something he had never hoped to see again: Omaha standing before him, dressed in her green and black Italian dress, her arms outstretched. The display was the final sign of madness, but for all that it shook him to his core. "Don't do it," said the icon in Omaha's low voice. "I can be anything you want, do anything you want. Join me now—we'll eliminate these three— who will ever know? It can seem an accident—they happen all the time in space." As if to underline her words, the manipulator holding Falmouth's arm moved with lightning speed to his throat and the governor began to struggle and choke. "We can do it. All I need is your help now."

Wolfe looked into Omaha's eyes and saw something there that was alive, but not Omaha. With a shudder he pressed down on the button and his wife died for the second time, spattering out in a sizzle of violet light. The holo stage was suddenly empty and Toto was whining and scratching at the manipulators which hung limp and swaying from the plasteel pole. Wolfe bowed his head and let the tears run down his cheeks.

Slowly he became aware of a hand on his shoulder. He looked up into the wise old face of the Dean. "It's alright," he said softly. "It's alright. It's over and you have done well."

A strange and incongruous sound came to Wolfe's ear. The three Institute executives has risen from their seats and were applauding him. Had they gone mad? He looked in wonder from the Dean to Governor Falmouth to his old patron. An emerald flicker lit the holo stage, and Helen spasrked into being again, and joined the applause, a triumphant smile on her face. Wolfe wondered if his reason was crumbling, or if perhaps his brain was still in the grip of Tokyo Nightmare, his consciousness adrift on the neon billows of delirium.

The Dean held up a hand. "I think we'd better explain ourselves before Edward calls the infirmary to report a psychiatric emergency." He motioned the others to sit and addressed Wolfe.

"You are no doubt wondering what this is all about. Let me explain: this hearing was in the nature of a test, and I'm happy to say you passed. You have just, as the expression goes, threaded the needle."

Wolfe's legs felt weak and rubbery. He tried to speak, found he could not. Relief mingled with a growing fury as he realized he had been duped. He cleared his throat and tried again. "But why?" he asked weakly.

"According to the Bible, a rich man can no more enter the Kingdom of Heaven than a camel pass through the eye of a needle," rasped Peabody. "In the same way, an inferior person cannot be allowed to enter into the upper levels of the Institute. There is too much at stake. Somehow or other we must weed out the candidates who do not quite pass muster, intellectually or morally. This little drama was one such weeding-out device."

Wolfe stared at her blankly, still scrambling for some sure footing in this sudden avalanche of unreason. "And why have I not been weeded?"

It was Helen who answered: "You have proved that you can act with decision, even put your most profound personal interests aside if needs must."

"Surely you already knew that?" snarled Wolfe.

"Only real-time testing can ultimately establish a person's reactions in these circumstances." The icon made an apologetic gesture. "One of your traits is a sort of audacious caution, my dear Edward. You wait until the last moment to decide how to act in a given situation. In most cases this is just prudence. But prudence, like any other virtue, can be carried too far. We had to ensure we did not advance a post-millennial Hamlet to the upper levels, if you see what I mean." She twinkled her eyes at him, her private joke. "We are genuinely sorry to put you through this. Let me here and now apologize for the deception, and beg you to put resentment aside." She stood with her hands folded in front of her, a meek expression on her perfect face. "Are we forgiven?"

Wolfe stared at her, admitting to himself that he vastly preferred Helen, rational and polite, to the menacing travesty he had seen a few minutes ago. That did not mean he forgave her, or any of them for that matter.

"What about Project Maldon?" he asked. "Was I right? Did you interfere with the codes?"

Helen beamed around the room, as if inviting praise for the performance of a particularly gifted child. "You are quite correct, Edward, as the governors are well aware. When Zacharian Stele unexpectedly came to power in Upper Canada we saw an opportunity to squelch the radical faction of the Accord. That goal was factored into the codes, resulting in some of the directives that aroused your suspicion."

The Dean took up the tale in his pleasant Scandinavian accent: "About a month ago it became clear that only a miracle could save the government in Upper Canada. Our key goal became to develop some alternate form of government to replace the worn-out tatters of twentieth-century democracy. To do this we needed the Accord." He studied the backs of his blue-veined hands, as if amazed at the decrepitude age had worked on him, then resumed his story: "The Accord is in many ways an archaic nuisance, but it does promulgate some useful values: hard work, thrift, strict adherence to a moral code which by and large is relevant to the real world. We hoped to graft these ideas onto a trunk of an old-fashioned liberal democracy, thus creating a workable form of government, to put some very subtle mathematics rather crudely. In essence, we were hedging our bets, playing red, black and zero. Your version of the project was black; the ball came up red."

"The Accord is bound to come to power sooner or later in North America," added Peabody. "By intervening we nudged the inevitable Accord nation towards a moderate rather than a radical format." She preened her mustache in satisfaction.

Wolfe considered. The explanation made sense on one level—which still left him far from satisfied. "All very well, but why expose Institute fellows to the dangers and difficulties of trying to make another plan succeed? Why not let us into the secret?"

"It was vital for the Accord and the government to believe you were working on the only significant arm of the project," said the Dean gently. "If you were captured or interrogated, it was crucial you knew nothing of the broad scheme."

"But why approach it in such an ambiguous fashion?" growled Wolfe.

Helen leaned forward with a winning, white-toothed smile. "Because we are all limited. Your peers are human. I am, when all is said, a machine—although a complex and powerful one. We are not gods, yet the scope of the problem we face is inconceivable. And so we feel our way. We hedge bets. We make mistakes."

"And what hideous toll have we paid for the Institute's little errors?" shouted Wolfe, his fury flaring like a fire doused with gasoline. "The incineration of Rickki Harrow, the deaths of one hundred and nineteen of my staff, of my wife—were these mistakes?"

"Yes, they were. Tragic mistakes." Helen fixed him with a piercing stare. "We do not desire anyone's death, Edward, you know that. And we cherish our fellows in the Institute. But bad things sometimes happen. We accept that and continue in our mission. The question before us is, will you be a part of that process?" Her eyes were glowing green and there was the trace of an echo in her speech. Now he knew who else the icon reminded him of. It was his mother. Helen was trying, Wolfe knew, to overawe and baffle him, and she was succeeding.

"Surely the choice is yours?" he asked.

"No, you have threaded the needle," said the Dean mildly. "Now the choice is entirely yours. This is the fundamental tenet of the Institute, that we choose and are chosen by each member."

"What inducements can you offer me to stay?" asked

Wolfe bitterly. "After you've duped me, sent my wife and best friends to their deaths?"

"We offer you the chance to come home," said the Dean simply.

"Home?" Wolfe stared around at the governors. "And what or where, do you suppose, is my home?"

"Your home is the future," said the Dean. "And wherever it may lead." He waved his arm to include the globe, the starry spaces beyond. "To Mars, or Ganymede or further, on board a slow-haul star ship if it be decided so."

"And the alternative?"

"Your home is the past, and you are not of our company. So then, will you continue with us? Or perhaps you need time to think?"

Wolfe bit back an immoderate answer. "I do," he said coldly, looking around the magnificent artificial environment for inspiration. Would he feel so betrayed, so humiliated a day from now? Two days? Always? Difficult to say. In the distance the virtual surf boomed, and a bird sang. He was tingling with fury at the deception practiced on him, and eager to hit back, yet his usual caution was already reasserting itself, his breathing, he was pleased to note, was slow and deliberate. He might be overmatched in this tournament of wits but he would not surrender. Beyond anything, he needed more answers. "Before making any decision I would like to ask some further questions," he said finally.

The Dean nodded his silver head in placid agreement. "Certainly. This is perfectly natural." He turned to Helen's icon. "This exercise does not require the whole review board. Can you enlighten Edward on our behalf?"

"With pleasure," agreed Helen.

Wolfe turned back to the Dean. "One thing I would like to hear from you personally. You say you wish me to continue with the Institute. In what capacity exactly?"

"As fellow, level four." The Dean made a gesture of appeal with his long white hand. "I understand that at the moment your impulse may be to refuse. Please think very seriously before you do so. We need you."

Wolfe nodded. "I will certainly give the matter great thought."

"That is all we can ask." The members of the board of inquiry stood and filed past him on their way out. Wolfe shook hands with the Dean, Falmouth, and finally Peabody, who winked at him with an eye as cold and blank as that of a fish. "When they did this to me I spent four months as an associate before I changed my mind," she said, squeezing his hand in a leathery grip. "It's damned irritating, that I know. But it is necessary."

When they were gone the holo of Helen settled back into her chair of green laser light, patted Toto and looked at him expectantly. "Now then, my dear Edward, where shall we start?"

That was easy, thought Wolfe. "How about with a solemn assurance that the Institute doesn't plan to dupe me again?"

Helen shook her head in reproof. "We do not dupe our members, as you put it, except in exceptional circumstances such as threading the needle."

Wolfe crossed his arms, not willing to compromise. "Very well. Can you guarantee that I will henceforth be given all significant information on assigned projects?"

"In all honesty, no." Helen made an apologetic gesture. "We cannot always tell our members all that we know or do. For one thing, the scope of our work is too vast. We attempt to plan centuries ahead, using a science which requires us to crunch billions of variables to predict next week."

"I'm not sure I can accept that."

"Then you must decline our offer." The long silence was interrupted by Toto's shrill bark. The animal had tried to lick the icon's face and tongued nothing but air. Helen put the puzzled terrier back on the ground and turned back to Wolfe. "One assurance I can give you—we are completely committed to you in ways you may never understand or guess at. We always care for our own and we always bring them home— or avenge them. Consider Joshua." Her green eyes narrowed for a moment to blazing emerald slits.

Wolfe considered. "In other words, I must have faith? Difficult—I'm a scientist, not a priest."

Helen shrugged. "Browse through the archives and judge us on our actions. As I freely admitted before, we do make mistakes. But we are not venal, greedy or small-minded. We are true to our ideals. I don't know what more to tell you."

"Very well." Making a mental vow to verify this claim, Wolfe passed on to the next topic. "If I were to accept a posting as level four, what would my next assignment be?"

"Aha!" Helen's icon winked at him and sat back. "Now that is an interesting question. First some background."

Wolfe looked about him in fascination as the environment began to flicker and change. The light grew dimmer, the sea faded, stars winked out all around him, pure white against the absolute black of space. Off to his right and above him coalesced the huge blue, green and white globe of Earth, so near it seemed he could reach out and touch it with the fingers of a god. Across from him, Helen's icon glowed in an eerie light.

The AI projection turned to him, a sober expression on her lovely, familiar features. "You see, Edward, confidential projections show that global pressures may soon become intolerable. A major virus may soon break out of Africa or Asia and march across the globe.

Outcome—a protracted Dark Age." As she spoke, a dark cloud seemed to boil up and spread pestilential green fingers across the blue face of the Earth.

Helen looked at the globe then back at him. "Or the Greenhouse Effect may accelerate, raising ocean levels, searing the land and leading to a century or more of violent storms. Outcome—possible anarchy." As she spoke the blue zones of the planet seemed to spread and merge, land masses turned from green to arid brown and vanished behind swirling whirlpools of storm cloud.

Abruptly the clouds cleared away to show the whole face of Earth again. "Worst of all," said Helen softly, "it may come to war. The Islamic Federation may come head to head with the Accord or the Pacific Alliance, and the clash may go nuclear." Red flashes marched across Europe, the Middle East, the Americas, festering into purple nodes, like some hideous skin disease.

After a few moments the holo globe cleared again and spun serenely though space. "The Die Back is uncomfortably near," said Helen softly. "It could start with the Balkan Breakout, or the fiscal collapse of Argentina, or the Fourth Jihad or a dozen other ways. Or not at all, if we are very lucky. But if any of these tragic scenarios is played out, we have contingency plans. The Dean has mentioned the possibility of a voyage to Ganymede or even to the stars. These were more than figures of speech."

It was a day for wonders, thought Wolfe, drawing a deep breath and expelling it through his teeth. "Do we really have the technology to get to the stars?"

Helen did not answer for a moment. Then she leaned towards him to the limit of the stage, so that the edge of her image blurred and rippled in the field like a ghost. "We don't know, but we may have an opportunity to find out. Recall that this station recently had a large extension placed on its south pole."

As she spoke, the globe seemed to recede and a holo of Orbital appeared in the foreground "Can you guess the purpose of that extension?" asked Helen. "Then watch."

A red line appeared across the silver cylinder of Orbital; the bottom third appeared to detach itself and move slowly away.

Wolfe's eyes widened. "A spaceship?"

"Let it be our little secret for the moment." Helen's icon grinned mischievously, looking suddenly very like Morgan. "It can support several hundred people indefinitely without refueling or reprovisioning. It also mounts a new drive system, although I am not at liberty to discuss it. I will send an archive number to your console and you can review the data for yourself over the next few days. You'll have access to everything except details of the propulsion mechanism."

Wolfe goggled at her, his anger temporarily forgotten. "And the mission?"

"To proceed to Mars or perhaps Ganymede and establish a base there. Depending on functioning drive efficiency, mass conservation and other performance factors, possibly to attempt an interstellar crossing. It would be a long voyage. Multigenerational most likely. We are talking, in fact, about a space colony." Helen grinned, suddenly looking very young. "Personally, I'm very excited."

So, despite himself, was Wolfe. He felt a surge of exhilaration, as if the key had been turned in some psychic prison, the door flung open. It was possible, after all, to escape from the growing desperation of Earth, to shelter from the coming storm. "I'm astounded," he said with total honesty. "What would my involvement be?"

"You would have two roles." Helen peered benignly across the stage at him. "First, you would spearhead the campaign to let us depart unmolested. You would be a latter-day Moses, saying to the various self-appointed pharaohs of Earth, 'let my people go.'"

Wolfe suddenly felt very cold, as if he were truly hovering out in space, with his suit's temperature control on the blink. "Why would anyone want to hinder us?"

Helen sighed. "Several reasons, my dear Edward. For one thing our departure could be taken as a sign that the final days are at hand. It could trigger panic— or worse. Also, our enemies will be reluctant to see an Institute colony flourishing in the outer planets or bound for the stars."

"I see," Wolfe digested the idea for a moment. He felt most distinctly unpatriarchal, but then again, from what he could recall of the Old Testament, so had Moses. There would be time later to argue the point. "And after that?"

"To be part of the expedition of course."

It was, he realized with surprise, the answer he had desperately desired, but it made no sense. "Why me?" he demanded. "I'm no space expert."

Helen seemed to hesitate for a moment, then shrugged. "It will be an elite crew. At least half its members will be senior Institute staff, levels four and above. However, senior usually means older, and we need the youngest possible crew. Therefore your age is also in your favor. Last but not least, you are lucky."

"I'm what?" Wolf stared at the icon in fresh amazement, wondering if he was the butt of some arcane AI joke.

Helen, however, appeared to be serious. "You and your sister are lucky. Just plain lucky. When trouble strikes you're not there. Consider Teheran, or your recent escapes in Upper Canada. When the man beside you takes a bullet in the brain you escape with a scratch. When a civil war rages in the city, you and your sister are sidelined in the country with the flu. Your parents were also lucky: they escaped the Bust, they kept their home, they died, as you once pointed out, in bed. Luck exists, and you have apparently inherited it. We need your luck on our side, perhaps ultimately as part of our collective being. So much so that we may actually try to breed your characteristics into future Institute candidates."

"I see." Wolfe stared at the holo of the space ship before him, wondering what such a breeding program would entail. First he was to be Moses, now a luck stud . . . what next? Better perhaps not to ask. "So if I choose to go, I have a ticket?" he asked instead.

"Yes. But first you must answer one question finally and forever," said Helen. "Will you be able to leave this behind?" The environment shifted again, the Earth appeared in the foreground, serene and lovely. "Think well, Edward," whispered the holo. "Once you go, you can never come back. You will be going further, far further than early explorers dreamed. It will be dangerous, demanding—and the ultimate adventure."

Wolfe could feel excitement surge through him like an electric current. "Will Morgan be coming?" he asked.

"Yes. And myself, of course, though a clone will stay behind. We are currently working on her." Helen smiled. "It will be interesting to have a twin, I think."

"And my sister?" pressed Wolfe. "Could she be part of the crew?"

"If she wishes. She also shares the luck gene, which is reason enough to include her, even if she was not a genius in her field."

Wolfe looked at the Earth, and back at Helen, feeling exalted, yet strangely humbled. Here was a task, a challenge to crown and occupy any life. "I'm overcome," he admitted finally. "I don't know what to say. No, actually I do. You can have my answer now if you like."

Helen held up a hand to stop him. "No. Take a day or two first to be sure." A thin path of yellow light appeared on the floor beside him. "We will talk again," said the AI softly. "For now, just follow the yellow brick road."

Wolfe stood to go. He was experiencing an odd emotion, sheer delight at the prospect ahead mingled with a sensation of inevitability, of destiny. He followed the line to the door then swung to face Helen, who was still sitting, a glowing figure in space. "A final question: was Morgan told to make love to me?"

"No. She was acting entirely of her own will. Admittedly I did not discourage her. And now, you have a rendezvous—the art gallery at noon sharp. *Adieu*, Edward, and well done." She flickered away, was gone. Wolfe looked a last time at the image of the troubled Earth beneath, rolling slowly across a sparkling black carpet of stars then turned away. It was good-bye to all that, to Omaha, to the black waters and red rocks of the bay, to Earth itself. It was time for the stars, how not to rejoice? He left the garden that was more than a garden, hoping he had interpreted the AI's parting remark correctly.

As Our Force Faileth

I am sometimes asked what artifact, what idea, what aphorism best sums up humanity for me. That is, of course, an impossible question because the answer changes as I contemplate different aspects of my creators. However I will tentatively cite one fragment from an old Saxon poem called "The Battle of Maldon" as evoking an aspect of the human spirit that I profoundly admire—perhaps because I do not yet understand it. Spoken by one of the few survivors of a fierce battle as he makes his last stand, it is a refusal to flee or surrender in the face of hopeless odds—a refusal both supremely foolish and supremely human:

> Heart shall be stronger,
> Keener the will.
> Mood the more
> As our force faileth

Conversations with Helen
Turing Category: Artificial Intelligence level 7 @
Skellig Michael Orbital
Skellig Michael Press, 2026 CE

Sunday, August 1
12:00 hours

He had.
Morgan waited outside the entrance to the art gallery.

She looked pale and her face was thinner. Careless of the scandalized expression of the young level one curator's assistant, Wolfe took her in his arms. If Orbitals were not used to such scenes they should be. And cyborg or not, she felt, smelled and tasted remarkably like a female human as he remembered the species.

Several minutes later they drew back, a little breathless. "I would have called, but I wasn't allowed," explained Wolfe.

She waved the thought away. "I know. I was sick anyway for most of the time."

Wolfe examined her with renewed concern. "And now?"

"Very much better. Sharper too, in a funny way." Morgan cocked her head as if considering the matter. "Still, I wouldn't care for a second helping. Helen has the experience stored somewhere but she hasn't run it yet. I'm curious to hear her impressions when she does."

"Me too." Wolfe took her hand. "Come—we have some serious catching up to do."

"So we do. But first I want you to see something." Morgan grinned at him. "Remember I mentioned that Helen was planning an exhibition? Well, here it is." She pointed at the sign beside the closed steel doors of the gallery.

AS OUR FORCE FAILETH
IMPRESSIONS OF PROJECT MALDON
A NEUROSTIM-ENHANCED MULTI-MEDIA EVENT
BY
MORGAN FAHAEY, WITH ASSISTANCE FROM "HELEN"

Wolfe stared at her, then read the sign again. "You mean you really came to Upper Canada to put together an art exhibition?"

"Only in passing, so to speak." Morgan waved him

towards an alcove beside the entrance. "Let's get fitted and you can judge for yourself."

Wolfe submitted once again to the placement of electrodes—seven of them this time—around his cranium by the eager curator's assistant while Morgan watched. Finally the level one stood back, checked the placement of the 'trodes with professional approval and gestured grandly to the closed doors. "Enter and revel." The doors swung open, revealing the dimly lit interior and they passed through.

Inside it was late twilight in a ruined city. They stood in a lane defined by two graffiti-daubed walls of red brick. Morgan took his hand. "Come."

The first exhibit was at the end of the holographic lane: an image of a recree—half-humans dancing in the lurid red light of fire barrels. Wolfe heard the confused carnival chanting, smelled the diesel smoke. His emotions writhed and twisted like a knot of snakes: fear, dismay, an underlying feral ecstasy, a savage desire to mingle with the mad dancers. Was this where he had come from, where his life had been spent, among the ruins of a dead civilization? He shook his head to clear it and whispered to Morgan. "Let's move on."

They moved through a succession of city images, and then the holo pathway began to morph. Wolfe found himself on a trail leading through dark evergreens to a tumble-down cottage with broken windows, black and gutted in the moonlight. The smell of pine carried in the air, and he felt a pang of profound sadness, a sense of loss so sharp that tears came to his eyes. It was as if all the times he had ever left home, turned his back on the familiar had been distilled together and pressed into an anguish so pure it was almost unbearable. Hastily he walked along the path until the sensation faded. A few moments later Morgan joined him, apparently lost in contemplation of the exhibition.

They moved on up the path and turned the corner. The life-size image at the end of the path drew him inexorably: a study in black, gray and white with a single crimson highlight—a tall black figure, back turned, rifle slung over the shoulder, legs planted as if in defiance, staring down at a tumble of red-washed bodies in the white moonlight. Himself. Once again he was almost swept away by a current of violent, vexing emotion: love, desire, a sense of approaching doom which could be faced but not overcome. Was this how Morgan had experienced him that night? Were these the emotions she had been transmitting back to Helen? It was too much. He reached up and disconnected two electrodes and the psychic pressure eased. He let his breath out with a hiss and realized Morgan was speaking to him. "Sorry, what?"

"I was asking what you thought of the exhibition."

"Overwhelming. But I think I've had enough for one day."

Outside they surrendered their headsets to the smiling assistant and walked a few steps down the hall for privacy. Morgan turned to face him, hands on hips. "So now you must decide whether to stay with us." It was not a question.

"I already have," said Wolfe. "Helen wanted me to think for a day or two, but there's no need." He assumed a thoughtful expression. "You know of course that Helen briefed me on some of Orbital's contingency plans. She mentioned a slow-haul starship. There would be a great deal of time on such a craft." Wolfe touched his ruby ear stud thoughtfully, realized with a start that he would soon have to replace it with a level four emerald. "Do you have any idea how passengers might occupy their time in interstellar space?"

"As a matter of fact, I do." Morgan's eyes held his steadily and he felt a wave of sudden lust boiling up.

Author's Note

The Battle of Maldon: A Parable for Our Times

The Battle of Maldon was fought in 991, during the reign of Aethelred the Unready, between the English and an invading Viking army which arrived in almost a hundred ships.

The result was a stunning and unnecessary defeat for the English, one which cost the lives of the English Earl Bryhtnoth and his closest companions and left the countryside defenseless. The battle had little or no strategic significance. It is remembered for the tragic ineptitude of the English leader and for the heroism of the members of his guard (who paid with their lives for his incompetence). *The Battle of Maldon*, one of the first English poems ever written, records and immortalizes the event.

The Vikings shouldn't have had a chance. They had been raiding the English coast all summer, striking at coastal villages, looting and vanishing. In late summer of 991 they camped on Northey Island, near the Blackwater River in southern England. The island was connected to the mainland by an eight-foot-wide

wide causeway, visible only at low tide. The English deployed at the far end of the causeway and waited. To attack, the Vikings had to advance across the narrow finger of land in single file, a military impossibility. Had the English held their position the Vikings would have had no choice but to sail away.

However, the English leader was impatient to fight a decisive battle. In his "arrogant pride" he invited the Viking army to cross over to the mainland unopposed, form up on the shore and engage his own troops. The Vikings were quick to take advantage of Bryhtnoth's misplaced sense of fair play. The result was a disaster for the English.

After some indecisive fighting, the English earl was wounded. Falling to the ground he drew his sword, but the Vikings rushed in upon him and one struck a blow that severed the tendons of the old earl's arm. Moments later, the Vikings beat down his personal bodyguard and killed the earl as he lay.

The tide of battle now began to turn decisively against the English. Seeing their leader dead on the field, some of the English began to slink away. Then a spectacular and calamitous act of cowardice: one of the dead earl's closest companions, thinking the battle lost, mounted the earl's own horse and rode off. Many of the remaining English soldiers, believing the earl himself was fleeing, left the battlefield to save their own lives.

To leave the body of their leader on the battlefield, to leave his death unavenged, was unthinkable for the earl's closest associates, his "Hearth and Shoulder Companions" or personal guard. Their only honorable options were to avenge Bryhtnoth by defeating the invaders or to die trying. In the event, die is exactly what they did.

As defender after defender fell beneath the Viking onslaught, it became clear that the battle was hopeless.

With the end near, one of the earl's oldest companions, a white-haired old warrior named Bryhtwold, raising his shield and shaking his spear at the enemy, shouted his defiance. His words are perhaps the ultimate expression of the unconquerable human spirit—the spirit that has moved brave people everywhere and in every age to keep fighting in the face of impossible odds:

> "Heart shall be stronger
> Keener the will.
> Mood the more
> As our force faileth."

To be braver, more resolute in the face of onrushing barbarism, even as our strength fails: the concept is perhaps as valid just before the second millenium as it was nine years before the first.

Nor is the portrait of a leader who in his "heart's arrogance, grants ground too much to the hateful enemy" entirely without resonance more than one thousand years after night fell over the hacked and bloody victims of the Battle of Maldon.